SANDSTORM

SANDSTORM

a novel by

Laurence Gough

Each soul is the hostage of its own deeds
— *The Koran*

VIKING

This one is for Jan

VIKING
Published by the Penguin Group
Viking Penguin, a division of Penguin Books USA Inc.,
375 Hudson Street, New York, New York 10014, U.S.A.
Penguin Books Ltd, 27 Wrights Lane,
London W8 5TZ, England
Penguin Books Australia Ltd, Ringwood,
Victoria, Australia
Penguin Books Canada Ltd, 10 Alcorn Avenue, Suite 300,
Toronto, Ontario, Canada M4V 3B2
Penguin Books (N.Z.) Ltd, 182–190 Wairau Road,
Auckland 10, New Zealand

Penguin Books Ltd, Registered Offices:
Harmondsworth, Middlesex, England

First American Edition
Published in 1992 by Viking Penguin,
a division of Penguin Books USA Inc.

1   3   5   7   9   10   8   6   4   2

PUBLISHER'S NOTE
This is a work of fiction. Names, characters, places, and incidents
either are the product of the author's imagination or are used ficti-
tiously, and any resemblance to actual persons, living or dead, events,
or locales is entirely coincidental.

LIBRARY OF CONGRESS CATALOGING IN PUBLICATION DATA
Gough, Laurence.
Sandstorm: a novel/by Laurence Gough.
p.   cm.
ISBN 0-670-83466-1
I. Title.
PR9199.3.G652S26   1992
813'.54—dc20   91–32440

Printed in the United States of America

Prologue

Sandstorm was wearing a snappy black Homburg, an ankle-length topcoat of black lambswool, the sort of sturdy black shoes favoured by policemen on the beat. His outward appearance was dark, solemn, even funereal. But behind the drab clothes, placid brown eyes and pale, smooth convexes of his face he was one happy fella – virtually all aglow.

Fritz Hauser was a senior director of the Banque Centrale de Zurich. Hauser was everything Sandstorm had hoped he would be – with his close-cropped grey hair and dark blue pinstripes, he seemed perfectly suited to the bank's massive conference room, its piped-in dirges and oppressive, triple-filtered atmosphere.

Clinging tenaciously to the gritty skinful of bones that was Hauser's outstretched hand, Sandstorm made a point of memorizing the details of the moment: the soft hum of the air-conditioning system, exact shading of the grey and gold-flecked wallpaper, even the texture and density of the expensive wool carpet beneath his feet. He held on to Hauser's hand for a few more seconds, gave it a final squeeze and then let go.

Hauser responded by exhaling through his open mouth, a soft explosion of distress. He said, "Please make yourself comfortable."

Sandstorm slouched into an oversized chair with a heavy bronze metal frame and padded seat and backrest of gleaming black leather. He tore the foil wrapper off a half-pound block of Swiss chocolate, offered the chocolate to Hauser. The banker declined with a polite wave of his hand. Sandstorm popped a chunk into his mouth, licked his fingers.

They were sitting opposite each other at a conference table fashioned from a massive slab of cold-rolled bronze that was six feet wide and easily twenty feet long. The surface of the table was smooth as glass and cold as ice, a vast, featureless expanse marred only by Sandstorm's mirror-lensed aviator-style sunglasses and the tent made of Hauser's small white hands.

Sandstorm cleared his throat. He resisted a strong urge to fiddle with the knot of his tie. In truth, he was a little nervous. Okay, more than a little. Call it a lot. But didn't he have a right? After all, it wasn't every day he opened an account worth five million American dollars in untraceable twenties and fifties.

Not that the money was all his. Expenses were invariably heavy, in a caper like this. He said, "I realize this must be a fairly routine procedure for you, about as exciting as flossing your teeth." *Or dropping them in a glass of water.* "But I hope you understand that for someone like me, this is a highly unusual and even somewhat harrowing experience."

"Yes, of course." Hauser was nodding his head but Sandstorm had the distinct impression that the slow movement of the banker's narrow skull had more to do with a level of exhaustion than a meeting of minds. Hauser was excessively thin, with a physique that was verging on cadaverous. If he was eighty years old, he looked every minute of it. What saved him were his eyes. Hauser's eyes were the eyes of a much younger man, alert and opportunistic – the exact same shade of green as freshly printed money.

"First of all and most important," Sandstorm said, "I've got to have immediate access to every penny in the account at all times, without notice."

"During regular banking hours," Hauser amended.

Sandstorm blinked. "Yeah, right. Naturally." He hunched forward in his chair, shifting his weight. "Also, I have to be able to find out by telephone or fax or whatever, exactly how much cash is in the account at any given moment. Plus be able to get an up-to-the-minute verbal of all deposits and withdrawals."

"This is possible only because you have signed a waiver. But I emphasize that you *must* use your codeword at all times. Without the codeword, you will not be able to access the information."

Hauser's interlocked fingers played a little game. This is the church. This is the steeple. Open the doors . . .

"And all deposits will automatically be converted into American dollars no matter how goddamn unfavourable the exchange rate might be?"

"Exactly as you instructed."

Sandstorm leaned across the table. "Maybe you think I'm trying to pull a fast one on the IRS. Nothing could be further from the truth, my friend. I'm so patriotic, even my shit is red white and blue."

Hauser smiled, showing teeth that were long and yellow, but still plenty sharp. "In any case, I'm sure you'll find that the Banque Centrale de Zurich is no less discreet than it is efficient."

"Perfect."

Sandstorm put on his sunglasses, signalling an end to the meeting.

In the bank's small but functional lobby, the pretty blonde woman who had disappeared with his overcoat now reappeared as if by magic to hand it back to him. With a little bow, she offered him a blood-red velveteen box the approximate size and weight of a fragmentation grenade.

"With my compliments, Mr Sandstorm," Hauser said, using the ridiculous codename for the first and last time.

Sandstorm hefted the box in his hand. "Let me guess, is it Brie?"

Hauser chuckled politely as he pushed open the bevelled glass door leading to the street. Sandstorm paused at the threshold. There was a faint smear of white powder on the narrow lapel of Hauser's otherwise immaculate three-piece suit. Nose candy? Was the dude into coke? Sandstorm stepped outside, into a brisk wind and the thin, shellacked light of early October.

He'd spent nearly half an hour in the bank, but his taxi was right where he'd left it, nailed in place by a running meter and the promise of a hefty tip. He turned his face to the wind and took several deep breaths, letting the fresh air from the lake wash the pompous atmosphere of the bank from his lungs.

The driver, deeply engrossed in a copy of *Playboy*, did not look up as Sandstorm opened the back door of the cab and climbed inside. Sandstorm punched him lightly on the shoulder to get his attention. The man flinched, reflexively trying to avoid the blow that had already struck him.

"The airport," said Sandstorm. "Quickly, please." He settled back in his seat, opened the furry red box and was not much surprised to discover that Hauser had given him a solid gold Rolex Oyster Perpetual.

A fucking gold watch. What was the guy trying to do, lay some kind of obscure Swiss curse on him, pension him off in a crazy attempt to stop him from ever coming back for his money? Sandstorm checked the Rolex against his Seiko. The Seiko was three seconds slow. Or maybe the Rolex was three seconds fast. He turned the watch in his hand, taking pleasure in the sheer bulk of it, the heft and density of the gold.

What was it worth, maybe four grand, wholesale? His five million wasn't drawing a cent in interest. He wound down his window and chucked the Rolex into the traffic.

A girl on a bicycle, a student by the look of her, swerved to avoid running over the glitter. She gave him a quick, incredulous look as she skidded to an abrupt stop and jumped off her bike. A horn blared. There was a shriek of brakes, what might have been a scream. Sandstorm rolled his window back up. The driver was peering into his rearview mirror but there was nothing for him to see: the swiftly-moving traffic had already filled the gap behind them.

Sandstorm opened his briefcase and began to take notes. Now that the cash was in place, he could start putting together the hit team that – on paper at least – was capable of assassinating the Libyan dictator Mu'ammar al-Gadaffi.

He was thirty thousand feet above the North Atlantic and still a long way from Washington when he finally realized what the white stuff on Hauser's collar was, and why the banker's palm had felt so gritty.

Talcum powder.

He grinned at a passing stewardess. Old man Hauser wasn't nearly so cool as he'd pretended to be.

But then, who was?

I

CAIRO

Trapped in a cobweb grip of hashish-induced optimism that flickered bright as sheet lightning and as quickly vanished, Charlie stumbled through layers of shadow to his cheap wind-up clock, set the alarm for nine sharp. Then slept, mouth wide open and his left hand trailing limply on the drab and threadbare carpet, all through the rest of the night and the following morning, undisturbed by the jangle and wheeze of his fetid breathing.

At a few minutes past one o'clock in the afternoon, the soft, increasingly hesitant ticking of the clock faded completely away. Charlie grunted and rolled over on his back. The frame of the old bed creaked under his shifting weight, springs hummed and twanged discordantly. Motes of dust rose from the sheets and waltzed in the light. Charlie coughed, opened his bleary eyes. It was the silence that had finally awakened him, the absence of the clock's reassuring heartbeat. He idly scratched his groin, and found he was still wearing his tuxedo.

He rolled over on his side, squinted into the thick, warm yellow light sifting in through the *mashrabiyah* – the large bay window with a delicate wooden latticework and topping of stained glass. The light was chopped and diced by the lattice, and then flowed together as it crossed his room to form a dazzling yellow rectangle that hung like a minimalist painting on the opposite wall, directly above a rusty cast-iron sink full of dirty dishes and pools of fetid water. The window dated from the fifteenth century. It had been designed to allow the room's occupants to look out and not be noticed from the street; to see without being seen. Charlie spent a lot of time at the window – he was a man who had come to value his privacy, who preferred to mingle at a distance.

He coughed again, a long, dry, racking spasm that went on and on. Too much hashish. Far too much sugary Spanish brandy. Not enough this, not enough that. With an effort, he struggled to a sitting position and swung his legs over the side of the bed. His head throbbed. His mouth felt full of sand. He patted himself down and found a crumpled but nearly full pack of Cleopatras in the tux's breast pocket, fished a cigarette from the pack and struck a wooden match. Typically, it hissed and fizzled mightily, but produced no fire. He tossed it in the sink and tried another. The second match threw off great plumes of acrid smoke and then burst spectacularly into flame. Charlie, concentrating hard, managed to get the Cleopatra going without setting himself alight. He filled his lungs, exhaled with a sigh of relief.

Out in the street, a donkey brayed cataclysmically and a man screamed with rage.

He staggered over to the sink, turned on the tap and ran the water until most of the rust had cleared. He bent from the waist and began to drink greedily from the flow, but was unnerved by the sight of the water swirling down the drain. His stomach rose and fell. His shadow trembled on the wall. He picked up his battered aluminum kettle and tilted it to the light to search the inside for drowned insects. Satisfied that the kettle was unoccupied, he added a careful measure of fresh water, then pumped up his portable two-burner Butagaz stove. It was one of the many curiosities of Cairo that, although electricity had been available since before the turn of the century, many parts of the city still continued to do without piped-in gas.

Charlie lit the burner with the tip of his cigarette. The donkey brayed again. There was a dull and meaty thud. He went over to the window and peered outside. The dirty, narrow street was filled with shop-keepers, sidewalk vendors, pedestrians. A crowd had gathered around the unfortunate donkey and its owner, a tall, morose-looking Arab wearing a pale-blue double-breasted suit jacket over a filthy brown *galaba*.

The Arab was apparently in the scrap-metal business. His wheeled cart was filled to overflowing with rusty chunks of automobiles, an assortment of small appliances, what looked like part of an antique printing-press, a thousand unidentifiable bits and fragments of metal. He was a spare parts depot on wheels but he wasn't going anywhere at the moment. And the crowd, as usual, was on the side of the beast.

The donkey was armed with an intransigent nature, the Arab with a sawn-off broom handle. He used the stick to play a tune on the animal's protruding ribs, and was snapped at by teeth yellow as old ivory. Charlie blew a stream of smoke at the ceiling. The kettle reached full boil, and the room was filled with a manic, cheery whistling.

Charlie went over to the stove and turned off the gas, poured half the water into a wooden bowl and added a pinch of Ceylon tea to what was left in the kettle. He removed his rented jacket and pants and unbuttoned his shirt. The French cuffs and frayed collar were black with grime. He took off the shirt and gingerly sniffed it, filled his nostrils with the perfume of fear and despair that poured out of him in buckets when he worked, so that by the time he walked off stage at the end of the evening he was as wet as if he'd been dunked in the Nile.

He rolled the shirt into a tight ball and tucked it under his arm, poured strong black tea into a chipped cup decorated with bright pink roses. He sipped at the tea, blew on it, lit his second Cleopatra of the day.

He could still hear the drumbeat of the stick, but the donkey had fallen silent. Curious, he went over to the window. The animal was sitting passively on its bony haunches. Its ears lay flat and its tongue hung listlessly from its open mouth. The Arab whacked it between the eyes, a vicious two-handed blow. The donkey staggered up on all fours, bellowing madly, and then fell over on its side, taking the cart with it. A screeching avalanche of iron and steel spilled across the road. The crowd scattered, shouting and laughing.

The donkey's hooves thundered against the cart, struck blindly at spilled chunks of metal and sent them skittering across the road. It licked at the pavement with its fat mauve tongue.

Then it shuddered, and it died.

Steam from Charlie's cup drifted up through the red and green and blue shafts of light cast by the stained glass panels at the top of the window. He finished his tea and went back to the kettle and poured himself a refill, then carried the cup and wooden bowl full of hot water into his tiny bathroom. He plugged the bath with a stopper carved from the limb of an acacia tree, turned the hot water tap on full. There was a subterranean burping and gurgling and then a hesitant trickle of lukewarm water the approximate colour of diluted orange soda pop flowed from the tap.

While the bath was slowly filling, Charlie worked up a lather with a bar of local soap and hot water from the bowl. When he was satisfied that his beard was as soft as it was going to get, he reached for his mirror and razor.

Shaving took a long time. Charlie's hand was a little unsteady, the blade was dull. As he studied himself in the mirror, he saw a face that was blurred, somehow out of focus. He finished shaving and turned off the tap. There were three or four inches of lukewarm water in the tub.

He lit his third Cleopatra of the day and climbed into the water. A thin scum of yellow dust immediately formed on the surface. He lay back, using his dirty shirt as a pillow.

He closed his eyes . . .

Charlie had been living in Cairo a little less than two years. His crumbling, badly neglected Old City apartment was well off the beaten track, and very cheap even by the standards of Cairo. Tourists seldom risked the neighbourhood, and the white-coated Tourist Police rarely made an appearance either. He wasn't too fond of the police. He had been a tourist once, but it was a phase that hadn't lasted. His visa had become invalid thirty days after he'd entered Egypt. His passport had expired two months later. Now he was a man of several dubious occupations and, until recently, of no particular destination.

Down in the street, the local butcher was chopping the donkey into marketable-size chunks, using a machete on the flesh and an axe on the bones.

Charlie found the bar of soap. It was dirty grey in colour and had the texture of a lump of sandstone. He began to wash his shirt. His gold wedding band glinted in the light. Seventeen lost years. He took a last drag from his cigarette, doused it in the bath and threw it on the floor.

He was forty-three years old, a little over six foot tall, comfortable at about one-eighty but now at least twenty pounds underweight and showing all his bones. His black hair was flecked with grey. He had an intelligent forehead, dark-blue eyes, a perfectly straight nose and a firm, good-humoured mouth, a strong chin. He had been handsome, once upon a time, but lately his features had subtly but drastically changed. Now he looked like someone who slept too much, drank too much, smoked too much.

The axe rang on metal. There was a brittle cry of pain.

Charlie grinned for the first time in weeks. Maybe it wasn't going to be such a bad day after all.

2

MAGDALENA VALLEY, COLOMBIA

Hubie Sweets had spent the past half-hour watching Mungo Martin stare at a bug crawling slowly up the barrel of Mungo's M16 rifle. There was a thin sheen of oil on the metal, beads of water on the oil. The bug had charted himself a treacherous, slippery course.

Kind of like life itself.

The bug was fluorescent green sprinkled with bright orange freckles. It had a pointy black head and a nasty set of saw-toothed mandibles. The thing was pretty much the overall shape of a beetle, but bigger, about three inches long. It looked capable of high speeds but at the moment it was taking it slow, moving one skinny leg at a time, careful not to make a mistake.

Sweets twisted his head to read Mungo's watch. It was twenty-two minutes past nine. For a little under four hours, ever since first light, they'd been hunkered down in the wet and dripping sauna of the jungle. Time had crawled by like a wounded insect. He was so bored he wanted to scream. Not a good idea. He nudged Mungo in the ribs and whispered, "Want to make a little bet?"

"About what?" Mungo had lost interest in the bug and was staring intently through the thin scrim of jungle which separated them from the two or three acres of open coca field, the coca leaves that shone silver in the sunlight.

"I got five thousand pesos says that bug makes it to the end of your barrel by nine-thirty."

"What time is it now?"

"Twenty-three minutes past."

"How much is five thou in real money?"

"About twenty bucks."

"You're on, sucker." Mungo flexed his leg muscles. He was starting to cramp up again. A sure sign of old age.

A few minutes later, Sweets made a hissing sound. Diagonally across the field there had been a movement, a tiny flash of white that had come and gone in the blink of an eye. Sweets flicked the safety off his weapon. He moved the selector to automatic fire.

"Where?" said Mungo Martin.

"Far right corner."

There were five of them, four heavily-armed Indians and a tall, thin white man wearing a white suit and pale pink shirt, a floppy white hat, dark glasses. They came out of the bush fifty yards to the left of where Sweets had expected them, not that it made a whole lot of difference. The Colombians fanned across the field. They were short, with pale brown skin and broad, flat faces, and could have come from any of the country's more than four hundred tribes. Sweets kept waiting for them to spread out a little, but they never did. For all the attention they paid to staying alive, they might've been on a day trip to Disneyland.

The man in the suit was a little more cautious. He waited for the space of five minutes before leaving the cover of the trees and following his point men into the glare of sunlight.

"You think that's it," said Sweets. "Just the five of them?"

"Looks like it to me." Mungo was in a kneeling position, sighting along the barrel of his rifle. The bug lay on its back on the cluttered floor of the jungle. Its six legs were kicking in unison, as if it was trying out for the Rockettes, and it was spinning slowly in a clockwise direction.

"Five of them and two of us," said Sweets. "How we going to divvy them up so it comes out equal?"

"First come, first served. Let's just do it, okay? Waste the suckers. Blow 'em away."

Sweets laughed softly. "Man, I love it when you talk dirty."

The four Colombians and the man in the suit were now about twenty yards into the coca field. The suit fumbled in the pocket of his jacket and produced a knife. The chrome-plated blade threw skittery shafts of light as the man sliced at the vegetation, checking the ripeness of the crop. The Colombians scanned the sheer walls of jungle that boxed them in.

Sweets knew from past experience that when the shooting started, the survivors would hit the dirt and crawl as fast as they could in whatever direction they happened to be facing. On hands and knees, tearing through the thick stems of the coca plants, it would not be a quick or easy journey. "You better go first," he said. "Anybody you miss, I'll see what I can do."

Mungo pressed his cheek firmly against the plastic stock of his rifle. He sighted in on the pink shirt, aiming at the second button from the top. The man had cut a length of foliage from one of the plants. He was examining it carefully, holding it in both hands, his head slightly bowed. Mungo took a deep breath, held it for a moment and then exhaled softly, letting half out and keeping the rest. He fired a three-round burst.

The man in the pink shirt spun around so that his back was to them. He flung his arms high above his head, as if in surrender. The knife cartwheeled through the air. The white jacket turned bright red.

Mungo flicked the selector on full automatic and ripped through the rest of the magazine, aiming low. The man he had killed fell crashing into the plants. The four Colombians vanished. He inserted a fresh magazine.

There was a loud bang as Sweets fired a round from his M203 grenade launcher. Mungo saw the vegetation tremble where the grenade struck the ground. One of the Colombians stood up and screamed and began to run towards them. Mungo got a bead on him but before he could pull the trigger the grenade went off.

Whump!

The Colombian went straight up, almost as if he'd launched himself from a trampoline. Bits and pieces of plant and chunks and clods of earth rose into the air and then fell back, pattering like heavy rain on the coca leaves.

Sweets fired another grenade. No joy.

"Shit," said Mungo.

Sweets glanced at him, grinned. Waited.

Mungo stood up.

Immediately, there was a burst of fire from the field. An Uzi, by the sound of it. The bullets shredded the foliage several feet above Mungo's head. He threw himself to the ground. Twigs and bits of leaf spiralled down on top of him.

"Got him," said Sweets. "Nice work." He fired another grenade.

Whump!

A Colombian hobbled through the field, dragging a leg. Wounded. Panicked. Mungo cracked his thumbnail flipping the selector switch to semi-auto. He led the man by the thickness of his body and chopped him down.

The M203 went bang again. Another fountain of earth and shredded plant material erupted.

"Cut that out," said Mungo.

"Way I figure it, there's at least one of them we didn't get yet."

"Good. He can tell his friends and neighbours what terrific shots we are."

"I got five grenades left."

"So what? I got a headache would kill an elephant, and the nearest aspirin must be about a hundred miles away." Mungo fumbled in the breast pocket of his field jacket, came up with a packet of Winstons. "Smoke?"

"Yeah, sure." Sweets continued to watch the field of coca plants. The jungle was quiet, absolutely silent in the wake of the gunfire and blast of the explosions, the screams of the wounded. Who said animals were dumb?

Mungo handed Sweets a lit cigarette. They squatted under the shiny fat leaves, smoking and saying nothing, letting time pass. Eventually Mungo squashed the remains of his Winston under the heel of his boot.

The beetle lay on its back, legs clawing uselessly at the air. Sweets tweaked it with a stick and it made an angry clicking sound, like a broken pay telephone. "That bug definitely got a design flaw," he said.

"Don't we all?" said Mungo.

"Speak for yourself, babe." Sweets used the stick to flip the beetle right side up, and then he and Mungo went out into the coca field to see what damage they had done.

The man in the suit which had been white was carrying a French passport in his breast pocket, but the passport had taken several hits from Mungo's M16 and was soaked in blood. Sweets took a peek at it anyway, wiping the gore away from the shredded gluey pages with the tail of the man's shirt.

"Jean something. I don't know what. Can't make it out. Should we take it anyhow?"

"That's what they told us to do, Hubie."

"Right," said Sweets. Blood seeped from the pages and dripped down on to the toe of his boot. He flipped the passport into the bushes.

The dead Frenchman was in his early fifties. He had bright blue eyes and a long thin nose, hardly any chin at all. There were gold fillings in his teeth. Sweets shut the mouth and closed the eyes. He found the man's knife lying in the soft, crumbly red earth a few feet from the body. It was a double-bladed penknife with an ivory handle. Sweets tested the blade against the ball of his thumb. It was sharp enough. He folded the knife and dropped it in the pocket of his fatigues. Mungo gave him an odd look but didn't say anything. Sweets knew what he was thinking, though. Stealing from the dead was too much like grave-robbing and was considered to be tempting bad luck. Well, fuck it. It was a nice knife. If he didn't take it, some other asshole would.

Sweets stood up and pushed through the close-spaced plants, looking for more bodies. He found two of the Colombians lying side by side, almost touching. Both men had taken several hits and Sweets judged that they'd died instantly. The best way to go, if you had to make the trip. He stepped carefully over the corpses and moved through the coca field in ever-widening circles until he found the third body, almost two hundred feet away. The fragmentation grenade had cut the man up pretty bad, but he was alive, eyes wide open, doing his best to take it all in. He was lying on his side, curled up in a tight brown and red ball, clutching his stomach. Sweets crouched down next to him, wary of a knife or handgun. He started to pry the man's hands away from his stomach and saw that it would be best to leave things as they were.

Mungo pushed towards Sweets through the bushes. He said, "How bad is he?"

"Grenade slashed him wide open. He stands up, he's gonna spill all over the place like one of those plastic garbage bag ads you see on TV." Mungo looked puzzled, and Sweets felt it necessary to add, "Feature that weird albino-type guy with white hair."

"What're we going to do with him?" said Mungo.

"Be kind," said Sweets. He moved around behind the Colombian and crouched down, drew his Colt.

Mungo Martin took the packet of Winstons out of the pocket of his fatigue jacket, shook out a cigarette and offered it to the wounded Colombian. The man nodded his head weakly. Mungo tore off the filter. He lit the cigarette and stuck it between the man's dry, puffy lips. The man sucked and coughed, exhaled smoke through his nostrils and mouth. He mumbled a few words of Castilian Spanish, looking Mungo right in the eye. Sweets shot him in the back of the head, killing him instantly.

"Think we fooled him?" Sweets said as he holstered his pistol.

"I doubt it, but let's hope so."

Sweets took the Winston from the dead man's mouth and ground it out in the dirt, then stood up and slouched away, towards the far corner of the field. Time to plant the anti-personnel mines and his leftover grenades and get the hell out of there.

Back to civilization. Cold baths and hot women, or was it the other way around?

"What's so funny?" said Mungo Martin.

"Nothing," said Sweets. "It's just I'm going crazy a little quicker than I expected, is all."

3

CAIRO

Charlie had spent a couple of years at Stanford and then astounded his family and friends by enlisting in the army. Afterwards, it seemed to him that he'd spent most of his time *underneath* Vietnam, worming his way through those dark and twisty tunnels, defusing tripmines and setting his own little traps. To Charlie, memories of the war were mainly the death-smell of wet earth, filmy cobwebs of exposed roots, a lingering claustrophobia. Afterwards, he'd returned to Stanford. He met Janet at a frat party, married her and made her pregnant. The war was something that was never, ever talked about. He graduated in the early Seventies, taking a degree in engineering. His grades were in the top ten per cent of his class, and he was recruited by a company called Trueforge, which designed and manufactured locks – from simple padlocks all the way to bank vaults. He'd sweated his ass off for five years, getting nowhere. And then, in his own time, working at the kitchen table, had come up with the idea for a simpler, more effective deadbolt.

He'd quit work, raised money for a prototype, lined up a distribution and profit-sharing deal with a national chain of hardware stores. Three years later, he bought a place in Beverly Hills. Their daughter, Heather, grew up in a house with seven bedrooms, six bathrooms and servant's quarters over a four-car garage. The years slipped past. Charlie, fighting middle age, built a tennis court and sixty feet of aquamarine pool.

There was also a one bedroom ocean-view condo in Marina del Rey. The condo was occupied, rent free, by a nineteen-year-old redhead named Leslie. Leslie was always home on Monday and Wednesday afternoons and hardly ever forgot to smile and say thank you when he dropped a couple of hundred dollars on the hall table to help out with the groceries.

Charlie had it all, or so he thought.

Towards the end of June, he used his platinum Amex card to buy three first-class Air Egypt tickets to Cairo.

The next night, a Saturday, he took Janet out to dinner at her favourite Italian restaurant, a tiny little hole-in-the-wall in Venice. Over the last of the wine, he said, "Guess what, honey?"

Janet peered at him over the top of her glass, not blinking.

"We're going away on a holiday," said Charlie. He smiled. "A vacation, our first vacation in years."

Janet lifted her napkin from her lap and patted her lips. Afterwards, replaying the scene in his mind, he realized that the gesture had been a delaying tactic; she'd been so surprised by the tack the conversation had taken that she'd needed a moment to compose herself.

"We're going to Cairo," said Charlie.

"*Cairo*? In Maine?"

"Jesus, of course not. Egypt."

"Have you mentioned this to Heather?"

"It's a surprise. Her graduation present." Charlie had a lot more to say, but there was a look in Janet's eyes, a sudden darkness. He said, "What is it, what's the matter?"

"Heather's got a summer job, Charlie. At the Chevron station down on Melrose."

"You're kidding. Since when?"

"You drove in there last week, the Wednesday before last."

"I did?"

"You were driving the Saab. She sold you a tankful of premium. You never even looked at her."

"Wednesday," said Charlie thoughtfully, swirling the dregs of his wine.

"About quarter past four. If your memory still needs refreshing, you were with that cute little redhead you've got tucked away in Marina del Rey."

"Hey," said Charlie, "wait a minute . . ."

"No, Charlie. Not one more minute. Not a single minute more." Janet threw her napkin down on the table. It knocked her glass over and a mouthful of red wine spilled across the white tablecloth. She said, "I'm leaving you, Charlie."

Charlie just sat there, staring at her, in shock.

"My lawyers will be in touch. The terms are quite straightforward. I want half of everything, including your cosy little hundred-and-eighty-thousand-dollar love nest with the waterbed and nice view of the marina. So you better tell Leslie to pack her bags and get her cute little ass out of there, understand?"

Charlie's mouth had fallen open, but other than that, he hadn't moved an inch. He watched Janet chart a course through the tightly-packed tables, outrace the major-domo to the door. Finally he came to his senses. Groping in his wallet, he dug out his plastic and flung it on the table, yelled for the waiter.

By the time he reached the sidewalk, Janet was wheeling his Seville out of the parking lot. The big white car was parked haphazardly in the driveway when he got home, but there was no sign of his wife.

As it happened, he'd never seen her again. Or his daughter. When he'd driven down to the Chevron station on Melrose he was told that Heather had quit work – no one knew where she was or how to get in touch with her.

He got on the telephone and called everyone he could think of who might have some idea where Janet had gone. Nobody knew anything. A conspiracy of silence. Five days later, Charlie's travel agent called and asked him about the tickets to Cairo. Was the trip still on? Did he want the tickets courier'd over?

"Why not?" said Charlie.

The plane was scheduled to depart the next day, at seven in the morning. He stayed up all night, drinking Wild Turkey, and then drove the Seville out to LAX.

His flight left right on schedule. The plane was full but he had plenty of elbow room – a row of first-class seats all to himself.

In Cairo, he handed himself over to his tour guide, a chubby Arab named Abu. Abu showed Charlie the Citadel and several mosques; the tombs of long-dead Sultans whose names would have been totally incomprehensible even if Charlie hadn't been half-drunk. He was given a fleeting glimpse of the Khan el Khalili, the Turkish Bazaar. He wandered in an alcoholic haze through the Museum of Islamic Art, the Coptic Museum and the numbingly vast Egyptian Museum. On the second day, a bus with a broken air-conditioner trundled him out to the pyramids at Gezira, where he stumbled through intense heat, Abu's incessant, toneless droning.

A boat ride up the Nile was scheduled for the third through the fifth days. Charlie pleaded sea-sickness and hunkered down at the Hilton's bar, managed to stay just this side of what the waiters were willing to tolerate in the way of loutish behaviour from a rich American drunk.

On the day his return flight left for Los Angeles, Charlie was politely told by the hotel management that he would have to vacate his suite; a prior reservation had to be honoured.

Charlie tossed his clothes and bottle into his suitcase and let a taxi driver find him the kind of hotel not to be found in the colourful pages of the tourist brochures.

He didn't know when it had happened, but somehow he had decided not to go home. Not just yet, anyway . . .

He'd spent the next two years as a kind of citizen-at-large, on the run from the boys in pin-stripes and the men in the white uniforms – the Tourist Police. More or less constantly broke but picking up a few bucks now and then, thanks to his background in lock design. He was even a ventriloquist, when things got really tough . . .

His last job had been at a dump called the Snapper Club. The stage was four feet long by four feet wide: a half sheet of rough plywood painted matt-black and given stature and elevation by a quartet of concrete building blocks stolen from a nearby construction site. The rear of the stage was hidden by frayed purple curtains, the front thrust out into a mass of twenty or so small round tables. A few candles flickered in the darkness, but because the low-ceilinged, windowless basement room was stuffy and overheated and the average patron not inclined to romance, most of the flames had been snuffed out.

Standing motionless in the gloom behind the sagging curtains, Charlie stared bleakly out at the audience. In the uncertain light of the candles he saw brief Cheshire grins, the glint of reflected light on the curved surface of a glass, the spark of a diamond or some other precious stone.

Charlie cleared his throat, turned his head very slowly and very carefully, and spat into the darkness behind him. He stood with his hands thrust deeply into his pockets, right hand on the small power box with its two rows of buttons. Marilyn was nestled in his right arm, Jimmy in his left. Marilyn's bright red skirt had ridden far up on her impossibly long legs. So much the better. Titillation was the name of the game. Charlie stepped slowly from behind the curtain. He took three small steps out on to the stage, sat down on a matt-black wooden stool and crossed his legs at the ankles.

His clothing was dark, his movements slow and cautious. He thought at first that no one had noticed him move into position, but then he saw the three men staring unblinkingly up at him from a ringside table, their eyes dark and lustrous, full of secrets.

Charlie switched on his floods, all five hundred watts, and the room abruptly fell silent.

Somebody coughed.

The men blinked like owls, eased away from the glare.

Charlie punched a button and the pink and green and blue spots faded, pinning him in a circle of brilliant white light. He hit another button, killing all the lights but one. Now he was in total darkness except for his face, which had been transformed into a crumpled jigsaw puzzle of shadow and light. He arranged Marilyn in a seductive pose, his thumb caressed the buttons, pressed down. A light flashed on and off, a burst as quick and dazzling as a camera flash. In the blackness that followed, the audience saw a dazzling after-image of Marilyn and Jimmy kissing passionately, bodies outlined in a halo of neon green.

"Now cut that out," Charlie said, adopting the tone of a stern parent. "After all, you two haven't even been introduced yet!"

There was a sprinkling of laughter. Most of his audience didn't understand more than a word or two of English, although you'd never get them to admit it.

Charlie resumed his monologue. As he spoke, he shifted constantly on his stool. Nerves. He didn't have much faith in his talents as a comedian. He believed that it was the lights that got him what little work he managed. Probably his judgement was correct.

The lights were unique, fantastic. He'd designed the rig himself – a foam and leather padded ring of plate aluminium as wide as a hatband which fitted snugly on his head and supported a dozen yard-long hollow metal stalks that thrust up and out in an evenly-spaced circle. The stalks were wired to his hand-held control board, each one terminating in a miniature spotlight that was trained on Charlie or one of the sex-crazed dummies in his lap. When he moved, the lights moved with him, in perfect unison. He could turn the lights on individually or in combination, achieving a variety of theatrical effects that rarely failed to please.

A man near the back called for a waiter, his voice strident and piercing, shattering the mood. Charlie cut his monologue short, letting Jimmy interrupt.

"Like a peanut, Marilyn?"

"Actually, Jimmy, I'd like something a little bigger than a peanut." She gave the trio of Saudis a broad wink and the Saudis glared angrily at Charlie, as if he was responsible for her conduct. Marilyn reached out and stroked Jimmy's thigh, bright red fingernails trailing lightly across his pinstripes.

"Cut that out!" Charlie yelled at her.

"Speak for yourself," said Jimmy, clearly annoyed. His hand came up to his collar. He tugged at his tie, loosening the knot.

"Make yourself comfortable," said Charlie. "I'll keep *my* clothes on though, if you don't mind."

"Shy?"

"No," said Charlie. "It's just that I happen to be working."

"For a change," said Jimmy. He mugged the audience, displaying a mouthful of teeth the colour of niblets. He winked lasciviously at Marilyn and said, "Hot in here, isn't it?"

Charlie's left hand cupped Jimmy Carter's wooden buttocks. His middle finger slid up through a gap in the back of Jimmy's suit and wriggled between his skinny wooden legs. Charlie pushed upward. His finger made a lengthening bulge in Jimmy's trousers.

Jimmy seemed to be unaware of his tumescence, but Marilyn was all aflutter, impossibly blue eyes sparkling in the lights. She said, "Is that a pickle in your pocket, or are you glad to see me?"

Waiters were moving back and forth across Charlie's line of sight, indistinct shapes cutting swirling paths through the funk, dispensing drink, lubricating the hilarity of the roomful of temporarily lapsed Muslims. Marilyn kept making moves on Jimmy. Charlie stayed busy manipulating the two dummies and his ring of lights. Five minutes into the monologue he switched off everything except a single hot pink spotlight. Despite his loud protestations. Marilyn crawled across Charlie's legs and plopped herself down on Jimmy's lap. Charlie's rigid finger quivered beneath the thin material of Jimmy's pants.

"Don't just stand there," shouted Marilyn. "Come on out and play!"

A shocked silence.

Charlie fiddled with the lights, turning himself blue and green and pink and then back to blue again. Someone threw a piece of fruit. A couple of months ago, he'd started to pull himself together, cut down on the booze and hash. Work harder and more often, stick a few bucks under the mattress. He didn't know why it had happened, but he'd finally decided it was time to go home, face the music. It was time, finally, to start all over again. But there was a problem. Every so often, probably more out of habit than anything else, he'd screw up, go too far. Piss off his audience and lose his job, start to slide back down into that deep black hole.

The hallucination passed.

Charlie found himself back in the tub, stewing in his own juices. He trailed a finger across the thin scum of yellow dust that had gathered on the surface of the water. The Nile, river of clichés. His laughter echoed off the tile walls of the room, disintegrated into a fit of coughing, harsh and dry.

He lay still for a moment, recovering, and then lit another cigarette.

In the other room, the cheap tin clock squatted darkly on the bureau, measuring off the slow irretrievable seconds and ticking them softly into silence.

4

ALEXANDRIA

For lunch on the final day of his life, Aziz Mehanna ordered a small salad made of diced green peppers and paper-thin slices of grossly misshapen tomatoes from the Nile delta. His taste buds aroused, he followed the salad with a dozen raw oysters and a loaf of *baladi*, a soft round bread. He washed the food down with mouthfuls of ice-cold Roederer's Cristal Brut drunk from a brandy glass embellished by his waiter with a delicate lacework of greasy fingerprints.

Aziz finished his meal with a handful of dates, two cups of coffee and a Rothman's cigarette, then wandered gently burping out of the hotel's air-conditioned dining room and through the lobby towards the front entrance.

He pushed open the hotel's revolving door. Polished mahogany panels and sheets of dusty bevelled glass flashed a monochromatic kaleidoscope of light as he manoeuvred his way outside. The temperature was in the low thirties, about ninety degrees Fahrenheit. The urchin he'd paid ten piastres to watch his Mercedes 650SL convertible was still at his post, crouched on the crumbling sidewalk in the scant shade of the car. Aziz gave him a cigarette to keep up his morale, and then went back inside.

The desk clerk wished him good afternoon. Aziz ignored him. The hotel's ancient chain-driven elevator carried him to the third floor, stopped with a fitful jerk.

His suite of rooms was located at the far end of the corridor, on the left, facing the sea. He stepped inside and kicked shut the door. The window was open, and the lazily rotating ceiling fan combined with a breeze coming in off the Mediterranean had kept the room reasonably cool. He could hear the sound of the shower, hiss of water and rumbling of pipes. Early that morning he had picked up two young French tourists, Monique and Lisa, in a straight-forward and mutually profitable exchange of sex for accommodation. So far, he felt he'd had by far the better part of the bargain.

He went over to the window, lit a cigarette and tossed the match down into the street. Lisa came out of the other bedroom. She said, "Did you finish your business?"

Aziz nodded. He had avoided buying the girls lunch by telling them he had to go to a meeting. He turned and stared out the window. The gentle curve of the horizon was a thin, shimmering band of gold that separated the soft greens of the ocean from the pale blues of the sky.

Lisa came to stand beside him. He put his arm around her and flipped the butt of his cigarette out the window and kissed her gently on the nape of her neck. She returned his kisses and he began to unbutton her blouse.

"Why don't we join Monique in the shower?" she said. She stuck her tongue out at him. "You look as if you could use a good scrub."

Water pummelled his face, blinding him. He turned his head from the blast of the nozzle and discovered that a large black bird was perched on his shoulder. The bird had small yellow eyes and a sharply pointed yellow beak. He tried to push the bird off his shoulder. It fluttered its wings and dug its claws into him. Blood bubbled out of the wounds. The bird uttered a soft cry of triumph. It scooped at the scarlet rivulets with its beak, tilted its head to swallow. Aziz heard the fluttering of many wings. The sky grew dark.

He snapped awake. He was lying in the middle of the sagging hotel bed, sandwiched between Lisa and Monique, his naked body gleaming with sweat. A dream, only a dream. He sat up and looked around, orienting himself.

It was late evening. The sun was settling into the Mediterranean. The room was filled with a fragile mauve light, and the shrieking of black birds had become the eerie, plaintive cries of the muezzin of Alexandria calling the faithful to prayer. Aziz lay quietly, listening to the familiar music of the voices and to the gradually slowing drumbeat of his heart. Lisa muttered something in her sleep, a name Aziz couldn't quite make out but was certainly not his own. He trailed his hand lightly over the rising swell of her hip, taking an intense pleasure in the sight of her pale flesh beneath his long dark fingers. After a little while the muezzin retreated like mechanical clockwork figures back into their mosques, and there was nothing to listen to but the sound of a vehicle passing in the street below, tires rumbling over the cobblestones.

Aziz began to drift off. The bedsprings creaked, bringing him fully awake again. The mauve light had given way to a rich purple. The room was filled with shadows.

"Are you all right?" whispered Monique.

Aziz nodded, although he wasn't sure she could see him in the rapidly gathering dark.

Monique turned towards him, offering him the last of the two bottles of Roederer's he had ordered from room service. He took the bottle and shook it gently. It was about a quarter full. He raised his head from the pillow and drank, pressed the cool glass against his forehead.

"You had a bad dream. A nightmare."

"A bird was eating me."

"Lucky bird!" She moved on top of him, straddled him. He offered her the champagne. She took the heavy bottle from him and tilted it to her mouth, holding it in both hands. Aziz watched her throat as she swallowed. She dropped the bottle on the bed. He was reaching out to fondle her breasts when she said, "Why do you have a gun?"

"What gun?" he said reflexively.

"This one."

Purple had turned to black. In the darkness it was impossible for Aziz to tell if she was pointing the gun at him or simply holding it up for his inspection.

"I sell diamonds," he said. "I'm a wholesaler. In my line of work, naturally there are times when I must be able to protect myself."

"Diamonds? Can I see them?"

"They're in the hotel safe, Monique."

"Oh yes, of course."

"Be careful," he said. "We don't want an accident."

Monique wriggled her hips. "A premature discharge, you mean?"

Aziz's stomach muscles contracted involuntarily as the cold barrel of the .44 touched him, moved slowly down his groin. He felt the blade front sight drag through his matted pubic hair. The muzzle of the weapon prodded and poked at him, nudged his testicles. Monique began to stroke him.

"Is something wrong?" she said after a moment.

"I'm a little distracted, it seems."

"Don't you like me?"

"It isn't that at all."

The empty champagne bottle was just out of reach. He tugged at the sheets, hoping to drag the bottle closer to him.

"Don't move, please!"

Aziz froze. The barrel of the revolver nuzzled his anus. Monique backed away and then lowered herself over him. He felt the weight of her breasts on his thighs, and then her tongue and the hot moisture of her mouth as she took him inside her. When he was fully erect she rolled away from him, on to her back. She held out her arms and Aziz moved on top of her. He pushed deeply inside her and then reached out and retrieved his gun.

"Were you frightened?" she said.

"Of course not."

"Not even a little?"

"Of you, no. Of the gun, yes."

"Do you really sell diamonds?"

"I don't usually give them away, if that's what you think." He kissed her on the mouth, putting an end to her questions.

At midnight, he took a much-needed shower and then went into the bedroom and turned on the overhead light and began to dress. Sleepy-eyed, the women watched him from the bed.

"What are you doing?" said Lisa, her voice thick with sleep.

"I'm leaving."

"What do you mean, leaving Alexandria?"

"Yes, exactly." Aziz stooped to tie his shoelace. "Don't worry about the room. It's paid for through the end of the week." This was a lie, but they wouldn't find out until check-out time the next morning. By then he would be too far away to hear their curses.

"Where are you going?"

"Cairo."

The girls exchanged a look. "Can we come with you?" said Monique.

Aziz shrugged. "I suppose so. But once we arrive, you'll have to go your own way, do you understand?"

"Of course," said Lisa.

"Well then, see if you can put your clothes on as quickly as you took them off. I'm already several hours behind schedule, thanks to you."

Aziz zipped his trousers and went over to the window. The Mercedes was parked in the rancid orange glow of a streetlight. The urchin had vanished. Half a dozen large bats circled rapidly around the light, hunting insects. As the bats moved swiftly in and out of the darkness, they seemed as large as pheasants.

"Merde!" He thumped the windowsill with the palm of his hand, went into the bathroom and came out with the largest of the towels.

"A souvenir?"

"No, something to wipe clean the upholstery."

They left Alexandria by the Sharia Canal, where in Ptolemaic times the local grapes had been crushed to make the world's first cask of wine. Aziz drove at a pace well under the speed limit past the shallows of Lake Maryut and then the salt-fields, over ground that gently rose and fell. Monique sat next to him; Lisa was curled up in the back with the luggage. Soon they had left the city far behind, and the darkness that was all around them was broken only by the firefly clusters of tiny green and red lights that marked the routes of the oil pipelines.

The road was straight, almost perfectly flat. Aziz made an effort to concentrate on his driving. In the glare of the headlights, the mica in the sand licking at the edge of the road shimmered like an endless string of costume jewels. In Cairo, if there were jewels to be had, they would not be fake. He imagined he heard the click of tumblers falling into place, saw himself open a small round door, cup his hands to receive a flood of precious stones.

They were travelling at a steady one hundred and twenty kilometres an hour. The dividing lines in the middle of the highway seemed to reach out to one another, blur into a single endless white streak that faded into the distance.

Monique unfastened her safety belt.

"What are you doing?" he shouted. Giggling, Monique kicked out of her shoes, grasped the chrome-plated frame of the windshield and stood up.

"Stop that, are you crazy!"

Monique ignored him. She leaned forward to brace herself against the windshield. Her hands were busy at her blouse. The flimsy material billowed in the wind, streaming out behind her as she unfastened the last of the buttons.

"Faster!" she cried.

Aziz pressed down on the gas pedal and the car leapt forward. Monique gasped and then laughed out loud. The blouse vanished into the night.

"Faster, Aziz!"

The wind tore at her hair. Her pale breasts gleamed in the light of the stars and the fingernail moon that hung low in the eastern sky.

Aziz pressed the gas pedal to the floor. The orange needle of the speedometer swung wildly to the right.

"Faster, faster!"

One hundred and seventy kilometres an hour. Then one hundred and eighty. Aziz had never pushed the Mercedes to its limit. Perhaps now was the time.

Monique's skirt was up around her waist, the material dancing wildly in the wind. He took his left hand off the steering wheel, caressed her thigh, tugged playfully at her bikini panties. The wind shredded her laughter. He hooked his fingers under the thin silk and tugged a little harder.

She screamed.

Aziz stabbed reflexively at the brakes. The Mercedes hit a patch of sand and drifted sideways. The camels strung out across the road doubled and redoubled in size, suddenly loomed large than life. Aziz had a blurred impression of hooded eyes, flaring nostrils. The windshield exploded. The Mercedes careered off the road and flipped upside down. His two French tourists and their cheap fibreglass suitcases were thrown free, but Aziz was trapped behind the wheel. The car ploughed a ragged furrow across the rocky floor of the desert. His neck was broken. His eyes and nose and gaping mouth were filled with impacted sand.

A patrol found the wreckage in the pale grey light of early dawn. The accident was handled routinely, that is to say without undue haste, until an officer opened the trunk and found Aziz's little bag of stolen diamonds, his prized collection of spring-steel picks, tension wrenches and key extractors, the aluminum suitcase with the foam lining in which he kept his sophisticated, highly illegal electronics equipment.

News of Aziz Mehanna's untimely death reached his business associates in Cairo later that same afternoon. A copy of the police report was obtained at no little cost, and all the details of the accident were thoroughly explored.

Particular attention was paid to the backgrounds of the two French women.

Finally it was decided that the accident had truly been nothing more than an accident. The will of Allah, Allah be praised.

The green light was still burning brightly. The operation could proceed exactly as planned. The only problem was, the team was short of one safecracker.

Charlie's name was one of the first to come up. He seemed an ideal choice for the operation, since he was both experienced and expendable.

5

CAIRO

The fellahin call the city *Misr, umm al-duunyan*. Cairo, mother of the world. Richard Foster's vision was somewhat less romantic. To Foster the city was nothing more than one hundred and twenty square miles of drab, dun-coloured buildings, oppressive heat, noise, dirt, and maddeningly frequent and unpredictable power cuts.

Foster was CIA chief-of-station, Cairo. He'd been transferred from Washington six months earlier, in the spring. His attitude had been negative right from the opening whistle. He would always remember circling the city, overflying the vast roof-top villages of the abysmally poor as the Air Egypt 747 set up for its final approach to the airport. He'd stared down at a level of poverty he'd never even dreamed of. Subdivisions of tiny shacks, mobs of naked children playing on the very edge of disaster, running around in the sunlight and exhaust fumes three or four stories above narrow crooked streets eternally choked and overflowing with humanity. Christ, herds of scrawny goats tethered to fields of TV antennas.

Even from a thousand feet up, he'd been able to see that accepting the post had been a horrible, a terrible mistake.

Then he'd stepped out of the air-conditioned comfort of the plane into the incredible heat, blown sand as fine as dust, a wind so dry it seemed to suck the moisture right out of his eyes.

Welcome to Cairo, mother of the world.

Foster stared out through the bulletproof glass of his office window, his small pale hands clasped loosely behind his back. The American embassy was located on Shari Latin America, directly opposite Shepheard's and only a few minutes walk from the Nile. Foster liked to eat his lunch at Shepheard's – he'd discovered that the bartender mixed the most drinkable Tom Collins in the whole damn country.

He turned away from the window and sat down at his desk. Jack Downey frowned grimly up at him, his broad, high-gloss forehead creased by a jumbo paperclip. Foster picked up a pencil and tapped Downey on the tip of his nose. The red light on the intercom flashed brightly. He glanced at his antique Marlin pocket watch and saw that it was exactly three o'clock. He shut Downey's file and turned it face down on his desk, decided that wasn't quite good enough and put the file away in the bottom drawer. He shut the drawer and reached out to flip the intercom switch. The light stopped flashing. He said, "Send him in, Dorothy."

The door opened and Jack Downey swaggered into the office. According to his file, Downey was five foot ten inches tall and weighed one hundred and seventy pounds. His hair was a lustreless brown and was thinning at the crown. His cheeks were plump and he had the complexion of a Santa Claus. But he dressed well, and people seemed to think he had a certain charm, although Foster couldn't see it.

Downey also, as he came into the office, had the air of a salesman who specialized in the indispensable. It had been several weeks since the two men had last met. Foster rose and shook hands, pointed at a Queen Anne reproduction. Downey had a small gift-wrapped package tucked under his arm. Foster wondered what it was, but didn't ask.

Downey grabbed the back of the chair and dragged it a foot closer to the desk. He sat down, crossed his legs English-style, fished a packet of Camels and a battered Zippo lighter from his jacket pocket. He flicked the wheel of the lighter, grinned at Foster and said, "Mind if I smoke?"

Foster made an elaborate gesture with his hand that clearly said – I'd rather you didn't, but if you can't stop yourself, go ahead.

Downey lit up, exhaled a cloud of smoke, a sigh of pleasure.

"What can I do for you, Jack?" When he was dealing with people like Downey, Foster believed very strongly in getting straight to the point.

"I'd like a cup of coffee and a lemon tart," said Downey. "The trolley's just down the hall. Mind if I ask Dorothy to grab us a bite?"

"Dorothy types and takes shorthand, Jack. She isn't a goddamned fast-food franchise and she gets real pissed off if you ask her to act like one."

Downey blinked: the equivalent of a small shrug. He said, "Got an ashtray?"

"Sorry."

Downey slumped in his chair, a cupped hand ready to catch the lengthening ash from his Camel.

Foster studied his pocket watch.

34

"Two things," said Downey. "Numero uno. There's some guys I want to put on the payroll."

"Names?"

"Hubie Sweets. Mungo Martin. Liam O'Brady."

"Refresh my memory. Have they worked for the agency before?"

Downey nodded. "In Central America, most recently. Some stuff in Colombia."

"Like what?"

"Defoliating coca fields."

"Have they ever worked for you, personally?"

"Yeah, sure."

"Where?"

"In Nam."

"Shit," said Foster. "You were their case officer?"

"No, their lieutenant."

"What's the project?"

"It's early days," said Downey. He smiled. "I'm just trying to set something up, that's all."

"Tell me about it."

"Well, at this point, all I can say is that I've heard some pretty loud rumours. Plenty of shadow, not much light. You know how it is."

"These Colombian friends of yours, they do any wet work?"

"In Colombia? C'mon, Richard. You know what it's like down there. Life is cheap and there's no shortage of ammo." Downey paused. "The Colombians use kerosene in the process of turning the coca leaves into cocaine. The usual scenario, what Sweets, Martin and O'Brady would do is use the fuel to set the coca fields on fire. Then sit in the weeds and wait for Farmer Brown to show up."

"And splash him," said Foster.

"The kind of people we're talking about, Richard, they beat their ploughshares into Uzis a long, long time ago."

Foster nodded his understanding. Jack Downey had been stationed in the Middle East off and on for almost a dozen years. Cairo was his city and he knew it well. But Foster took his job seriously, and so he was making Downey jump a little rope before granting his approval to what was really nothing more than a routine request.

Downey, watching Foster carefully, had no idea what the man was thinking. He stood up and walked over to Foster's gleaming rosewood desk. This close, he could smell the furniture wax. Resting his hip on the edge of the desk, he smiled down at Foster and said in a voice so low it was hardly more than a whisper, "The word is out an Intelligence

Corps colonel attached to the Libyan embassy in Syria wants to defect to the good old USA. The Colonel will be in Cairo on a covert mission sometime in the next two months, and that's when he intends to jump ship. I've got a safe house lined up. What I need is somebody to hang around and answer the door."

Foster waited.

Downey took a folded slip of paper from his shirt pocket. "I've worked out a brief preliminary budget. I'm going to need about fifteen thousand dollars." He was staring intently down at Foster's face as he spoke. Later, Foster wondered if there was something Downey saw in his eyes that made him casually add, "For starters."

Foster nodded. "I'll have Dorothy take care of it," he said. He was also going to have Dorothy arrange a photo session for Downey. The man had gained at least twenty pounds since his file picture had been taken. He said, "Keep me up to date, Jack. Daily reports, rain or shine."

"No problem." Downey loitered indecisively for a moment, then pushed away from the desk and started across the carpet towards the big double doors leading to the reception area. His hand gripped the brass knob. Foster saw the tendons on his wrist stand out as he squeezed hard. Then the hand fell away.

Here it comes, thought Foster.

Downey said, "When this Libyan thing gets cleared up, I'd like some time off."

"Sounds good."

"I'm talking about a real holiday, Richard. A couple of weeks, maybe more."

"Whatever. Got any plans?"

"There's a lady in London I want to spend some time with."

"Anybody I know?"

"Let's hope not," Downey said, and winked to take the sting out of the words. He walked back to the desk, handed Foster the gift-wrapped package.

"What is it?"

"Swiss chocolate."

"I've got an allergy, Jack."

"Jesus, you do?" Downey didn't look particularly surprised. He said, "Sorry, Richard. Next time, I'll bring flowers." Then scooped up the box of chocolates and turned his back on Foster and walked out of the office.

You cheeky bastard, Foster thought. Not for the first time, he considered that if Downey wasn't so good at his job, he'd have been out on his ass a long time ago.

And not for the first time, he took solace in the thought that nobody stayed sharp for ever, that sooner or later Downey would make a mistake. When it happened, Foster would pounce. Shred him. Or better yet, stick him in the burn bag.

In the outer office, Downey made small talk with Dorothy, sniffed her perfume as he leaned over her desk. Dorothy was from Alabama, some dinky little town he'd never heard of. He thought her southern accent was just peachy – had told her once he loved it so much he was willing to take dictation. He said, "You happen to know where the tea trolley would be at this time of day?"

"It went right by this desk no more than two minutes ago. Why, was there something you wanted?"

Downey sucked in his stomach. "A cup of coffee and a couple of those real gooey lemon tarts would have gone down pretty good," he wistfully admitted.

"Well why in the world didn't you give me a shout on the intercom," she said in her wonderfully mellifluous cracker accent. "I'd have got you whatever you liked."

"Really?"

"Would I lie to you?"

Probably not, thought Downey, but your boss sure as hell did. It was something to think about, something to bear in mind. Jesus, if you couldn't trust your goddamn chief-of-station, who could you trust?

Nobody.

6

The door swung open and banged against the corner of the bureau. The mirror shattered. Shards and splinters of silvered glass cascaded across the bare wooden floor.

Charlie sat up, struggling to free himself from the tangle of sheets. He heard the crunch of measured footsteps on broken glass. A blow to the face knocked him flat.

"Look at me."

There were two of them – small, dark, muscular men in rumpled white suits. The one who had spoken was wearing orange-tinted glasses with gold-wire frames. He loomed over Charlie; his companion had taken up a position at the foot of the bed.

"You are Charlie McPhee?" The man with the glasses was doing the talking. He lit a cigarette, tossed the smoking match on the bedsheets.

Charlie managed to nod his head. Guilty as charged. He heard a sharp metallic click, peered down the length of the bed and saw that the second man had produced a submachine-gun. The ugly snout of the gun was pointed in the general direction of Charlie's heart. His mind raced. These people could be anybody, but he doubted very much that they were from Immigration.

The man with the gun stared right through him, unblinking.

"What is it you want, is there something I can do for you?"

"You take hashish, Charlie?"

"Is that what this is all about? Drugs?"

Glasses made an expansive gesture.

"Get out of bed."

"What?"

Gunner lunged at him. The barrel of the weapon hit him in the ribs. His body went numb. A second blow left him boneless and disoriented, dizzy. There was a moment when he felt nothing, and then the pain filled him to overflowing. He sensed movement behind him. The collar of his T-shirt tightened around his throat, cutting off his wind and choking him.

Jimmy and Marilyn sat side by side on the room's single wooden chair, staring up at him.

"Sit up, Charlie. Good. Now sit on your hands with your legs spread wide. Excellent."

The pressure on his throat eased. Glasses smiled down at him. "A cheap night club comic. Is that your life's ambition, is that what you always wanted to be?"

"If you hit me again," said Charlie, "I'm going to scream."

"Scream and we'll kill you." Still smiling, Glasses lashed out, his fist catching Charlie square in the chest, just beneath his heart. Charlie grunted. The back of his head hit the wall. Jimmy grinned at him with teeth stained yellow and then varnished to give them a nice gloss.

Charlie struggled back into an upright position. It wasn't easy, without the use of his hands. His ribcage ached. He wondered if they'd cracked something.

"Don't speak until you're spoken to, understand?"

Charlie considered his options, nodded.

"Good." The man bent stiffly from the waist, picked up a black canvas bag. He dropped the bag in Charlie's lap. "Open it."

Charlie unzipped the bag.

"Go ahead, take a look inside."

He spread the mouth of the bag, tilted it to the light.

"Do you know how to use those tools?"

"Yes," said Charlie wearily.

"Are they adequate to open a Barouh wall safe?"

"I don't know the name. Is the safe Egyptian, made in Egypt?"

"Yes."

"It shouldn't be too much trouble, then."

As he talked, Charlie had been rummaging through the bag. His fingers stumbled across a revolver with a snub barrel and rounded wooden grips. The light was bright enough for him to see the copper casings of the bullets in the cylinder. He touched the metal. It felt cold and heavy, dense.

The man with the submachine-gun flicked a switch on the side of the weapon.

Charlie saw that there was ingrained dirt in the ball of the man's thumb and that the nail was bitten to the quick.

The man pointed the gun at Charlie and then slightly away from him. He squeezed the trigger. The muzzle spat flame and there was a blunt, thudding sound. Jimmy was flung from the chair and collapsed in a shredded heap against the wall. Marilyn's eyes bulged. She thrust out her tongue. The back of her head exploded in a shower of pine splinters.

Charlie took his hand out of the bag, slowly zipped it shut.

"Put your clothes on." A twisted smile. "It's a very informal occasion. No need to wear a tie."

Charlie swung his legs over the side of the bed. He managed to stand up. His clothes were on the floor, all in a heap. He reached for his pants.

They waited impatiently while he stuffed in his shirttails, zipped up. Glasses placed the palm of his hand against Charlie's chest and pushed hard, shoving him backwards towards the door. "On the way out, stay between us. Don't look or even think of speaking to anyone. If someone speaks to you, ignore him. Unless you do exactly as you are told . . ."

Outside, the night air was full of noise and light, and the streets, as always, were crowded with humanity. Charlie smelled onions, lamb. There was a vendor on the corner selling shish-kebabs. Drops of fat hissed on the coals of his portable grill. The man caught Charlie's eye, invitingly waved a skewer. His mouth watered. He had never been hungrier.

The car was a yellow Fiat, a two-door model with chalky paint and a conchoidal fracture on the driver's side of the windshield. Charlie was pushed into the back seat. Glasses settled behind the wheel. Gunner climbed in beside Charlie. His breath smelled like a spice rack. His hip pressed up against Charlie's, and Charlie moved away. The Fiat's engine started with a cough, and the car bulled into the thick, slow-moving traffic. Glasses smiled into the rearview mirror and said, "Don't worry, it'll all be over before you know it."

"Very reassuring."

Gunner had walked to the car with his weapon hidden beneath his jacket. Now it was nestled in the crook of his arm. The smell of light machine oil mingled with the scent of spices. The snout of the gun was pressed against Charlie's belly. He thought about the gassy sound it had made when it was fired, the way Marilyn's bright blue eyes had bulged comically a tiny fraction of an instant before her head exploded.

Glasses lit a cigarette. He didn't offer them around, and Charlie didn't want to ask. He had a crazy idea that if he kept quiet, they might forget all about him. He wedged himself against the side of the car, moving as far as possible from the gun, trying to make himself as small as he felt.

They drove over El Tahrir bridge, under the sickly orange glow of the arc lights and across to the island of Gezira, shaped like the blade of a knife. At the Cotton Museum they slowed and turned right, cruised sedately down Shari Hasan Pasha, along the embankment. Here the Nile looked more like a canal than a river. They passed the Sporting Club, the race track and the perfectly flat expanse of close-cropped green that was the Polo Grounds. Glasses flicked the stub of his cigarette out the window. Orange sparks skittered across the pavement. They made a left up Shagaret El Durr, into the prosperous Zamalek district.

Charlie knew nothing about this part of Cairo. The streets were clean and brightly lit, and there was vegetation everywhere – jacaranda, bougainvillaea and poinsettia, towering clusters of plane trees. In a city where water was a luxury, greenery was an obvious sign of wealth.

They turned sharply into a side street, a cul-de-sac terminating in a cramped roundabout. Charlie studied the houses as they drove to the end of the block and turned to face the way they'd come, parked in deep shadow.

Glasses twisted in his seat. He reached back and gripped Charlie's arm. "It's the second house along, the one with the light over the door."

Charlie nodded.

"The light will go out in a moment or two. If it doesn't, we'll give you a ride home and that will be that. So be calm and don't worry, all right?"

"What about Jimmy and Marilyn?"

"Who?"

"My dummies."

Gunner laughed, a hoarse, braying sound that reminded Charlie of the donkey that had been beaten to death in the street outside his apartment.

"They cost me twenty pounds each," he said, doubling the figure.

"There must always be victims, Charlie. It's the way of the world. Better them than you, yes?"

Charlie stared past the man's shoulder and the back of his head, out of the cracked windshield of the Fiat. The landscape had somehow changed significantly. It was as if a large tree had suddenly shifted position, or the sidewalk had vanished. Like one of those two-panel cartoons. What's missing from this picture? Charlie concentrated hard. After a moment he realized the porch light had gone out.

The car door swung open and the passenger seat was folded forward. Charlie took a poke in the ribs. He climbed out of the little car and waited obediently on the sidewalk while Glasses whispered a few words to Gunner. During the conversation he glanced without warning at Charlie. Charlie quickly looked away. He could smell the flowers on the jacaranda trees. The black canvas bag was handed to him. He hefted the weight of it, wondered if the revolver was still inside. Gunner took him firmly by the elbow and led him down the sidewalk, treating him as if he were a recalcitrant child. Glasses stayed behind, at the wheel of the car. Charlie could feel the man's eyes on his back. Their shadows lengthened and then split in two and shrank and fell behind them as they passed beneath the acid glare of a streetlamp.

The house was three storeys high. It was made of concrete and had a flat roof. The windows were protected by iron bars. Practical, not fancy. The building was surrounded by a waist-high boxwood hedge. There was an iron gate. Glasses pushed it open. They walked down a flagstone pathway flanked by bushes with large black leaves, climbed the steps to the porch. No need to ring the bell – the door was off the latch.

"Open it." Gunner's speech was thick, guttural. Charlie thought he might be a Turk, but wouldn't have bet money on it. He pushed the door with the tips of his fingers. It swung open on well-oiled hinges, making no sound. Gunner put a finger to his lips. They stepped inside and he softly pushed shut the door.

Directly in front of them a narrow hallway ran the length of the house. To the right there was a wide, curving stairway with a highly polished banister, the wood glowing softly in the semi-darkness.

Another push, and Charlie began to climb. The stairs creaked loudly. He tried to keep most of his weight on the banister. He moved to the left side and then to the right. Nothing seemed to help. The wood was old and dry. With every step he took the stairs popped and cracked, little explosions of sound. They continued their ascent, Charlie in the lead, Gunner right behind him.

A faint yellow glow at the top of the landing came from an ornate ceiling fixture. Charlie paused beneath the light, waiting for further instructions. At the far end of the landing the stairs turned sharply and climbed to the top floor of the house. Gunner dug the barrel of his weapon into the small of Charlie's back, herding him towards the rear of the building.

The hallway was thickly carpeted, the walls on both sides covered with ornately framed black and white photographs, formal portraits of ancient men with solemn, time-worn faces.

They stopped in front of a polished mahogany door. Charlie received another presumptive poke in the ribs. He turned the knob and the door opened with a sharp click. He stepped inside.

Gunner shut the door behind them with the toe of his boot.

The room was small, high-ceilinged. There were windows on two sides. From where Charlie was standing he could see down into the street, a glint of chrome from the parked Fiat. Gunner snapped on the lights. The room was apparently used as a study, or office. There was a small desk, a wingback chair on castors, painted wooden bookshelves enclosed in glass. Three large watercolours hung on the wall opposite the desk, pastoral scenes of the Nile Delta. A Libyan flag dangled limply from a pole in one corner of the room.

The safe was behind the picture on the left. It was an Egyptian one all right, a Barouh.

He tried the handle but it was locked. He turned the watercolours over, looking for pencilled numbers on the frame or canvas. No joy.

He knelt and unzipped the canvas bag. Gunner stood by the door, his finger on the trigger of his weapon. Charlie rooted around in the bag. It contained a large selection of house-breaking tools, including a number of steel picks. The revolver had vanished. His fingers closed around the only piece of equipment in the bag that could possibly be of any use to him. The box was made of metal, painted dove-grey. It was about the size of a carton of cigarettes and weighed perhaps half a pound. There was a flip-up liquid crystal screen, a suction device and a pair of miniature earphones. A red plastic rocker switch projected from the side of the unit.

Charlie flicked the switch with his thumbnail. A septet of bright green zeros flashed on the screen. He used the suction cup to clamp the device on the smooth metal face of the safe, adjusted the headphones. A faint humming filled his ears, like the sound of a distant refrigerator. He turned the safe dial counterclockwise, working very slowly, taking it one digit at a time. He made three complete circuits before he managed to catch the first number.

48.

He cleared the screen and started turning the dial back the opposite way, again taking it very slowly. The second number was 5.

Gunner moved up behind him. The muzzle of the gun caressed the base of his neck. "Hurry."

The third number was 22. Charlie spun the dial and tried the handle. The thing didn't budge. A five-digit combination. He'd been given a short reprieve.

In less than ten minutes he was sure he had the last two numbers, 17 and 53. He dialled the combination and grasped the handle but didn't twist it. He could still hear the sound of the refrigerator in the headphones, but there was something else there as well.

Something in the background, but moving closer. He closed his eyes, listening intently. The sound he heard was like short, regularly spaced bursts of static, as if someone was walking through a field of slush.

Or along the hallway, on the carpet.

The way Charlie remembered it afterwards, everything happened at once. He opened the door of the safe partway and pretended it had jammed, turned to Gunner to ask for help. The door to the room swung open. The submachine-gun burped.

Shell casings tumbled through the air in a graceful arc, like the links of a golden chain. The air stank of cordite and plaster dust. Spent brass tinkled merrily on the floor and a lurid orange light staggered across the walls.

Silence.

Charlie found the courage to turn and look behind him. A tall, thin man wearing yellow pyjamas splotched with red was leaning against the splintered door. He looked right at Charlie, opened his mouth as if to ask for help, and then fell face down on the floor, half in the room and half out of it, as if he couldn't make up his mind whether to leave or stay.

There was another burst of fire from the gun. The man twitched and lay still.

Gunner ejected his empty magazine, caught it neatly and reversed it. He'd taped two magazines together, head to tail. He inserted the fresh magazine and raised his right hand to draw back the bolt.

Charlie pushed away from the wall, tripped over the painting, canvas screaming as his foot went through the material. The barrel of the gun swung towards him. He reached out, thrusting hard.

It was a lucky hit. He'd aimed wrong but the sprung steel pick deflected off the jawbone and went in just below the ear, slid easily into the flesh right up to the knuckles of Charlie's fist.

Gunner clawed at his throat. He crashed against the desk and lost his balance and fell on his back on the floor, gagged as his throat filled with blood.

There had been time in that moment before everything had happened at once to glimpse the fact that there was a lot of money in the safe, crisp bundles of Egyptian ten-pound notes packaged just as they came from the bank. Charlie grabbed a handful of money and started across the room. The only way out was over the body of the man in the yellow pyjamas. He took a deep breath and jumped awkwardly over the bloody, ragged corpse.

In the hallway, a woman crouched in a corner in the barred shadows cast by the banister. She was wearing a cream-coloured negligée and her hair was in curlers. Charlie took the stairs two and three at a time, tore open the front door and then had a moment of sanity and slammed it shut. He heard the roar of the Fiat's engine, the shriek of tires. He raced down the hallway towards the rear of the house, found himself in a stark white, brilliantly lit kitchen. He fumbled with the bolts of a windowless door. Something rubbed up against his legs. A cat. He heard heavy footsteps on the stairs, a wet, choking sound. He tore a fingernail on the safety chain, yanked the door open and threw himself down a short flight of concrete steps, stumbled into blackness.

He heard voices, shouting. A woman screaming. The sound of a gunshot.

He stuffed the wad of money into his jacket pocket and ran for his life.

7

Panic-stricken, Charlie ran blindly through the night until he tripped over a wooden lawn chair and pinwheeled headlong into a fishpond.

Somewhere nearby, a dog barked repeatedly.

Charlie crawled backwards out of the water. A porch light snapped on. He crouched behind the overturned chair. A door opened and a man peered into the darkness. A bright cone of light swept across the width of the yard. Shadows jumped at him. Beads of dew glittered. Charlie crouched low.

He heard a woman's voice, the words indistinct, a meaningless blur.

"Bloody cats after the fish again," said the man. He had an English accent. The light traversed back and forth, flicking across the overturned lawn chair, the black water of the pond. Then the door slammed shut and the porch light was extinguished.

Charlie cautiously stood up. His shirt was soaked through, stank of decaying vegetation. He looked around, trying to get his bearings. He wasn't sure how far he had run since the shooting. Two blocks, maybe three. The sudden dousing had cleared his mind. He had to get back to the street.

He made his way diagonally across the yard towards the side of the house. A high wooden gate separated the house from the neighbouring building. He drew the bolt, swung the gate open and slipped through to the other side. The space between the two houses was covered with crushed gravel, and the sharp-edged stones grated noisily with every step he took, the sounds magnified by the enclosed space and his imagination.

There was another high wooden gate at the front of the house, but it, too, was secured by a simple iron bolt. He opened the gate and slipped through, shutting it quietly behind him.

The house was set back only a few feet from the sidewalk. Charlie loitered in the shadows, studying the street, and then stepped boldly out of the yard and on to the sidewalk. He was trying to look as if he had every right to be there, but he was all nerves, ready to bolt at the slightest sign of trouble.

The street was empty, deserted. A faint breeze rattled the leaves of the hibiscus bushes.

Charlie started walking – slowly at first, and then as quickly as he thought he could manage without arousing suspicion. He was fairly sure that the murder site was behind him and to his left, and he stayed well away from that area of the neighbourhood. He walked for the better part of an hour and then found himself on a street he recognized, Shari 26 July. The bridge was less than a block away. It would carry him back to the heart of the city, his apartment.

He was not quite halfway across the bridge when he heard the roar of an automobile engine, the screech of tires. He glanced over his shoulder, into the rapidly approaching glare of headlights. Too late, he realized that he'd made a very stupid mistake. There were three bridges on each side of the island, six altogether. He'd chosen to make his way back to the city by the most direct and obvious route. He peered over the side of the bridge. In the sickly orange glow of the lights, the slow-moving river looked smooth and gelatinous, thick as jelly. He thought about jumping, imagined his throat and lungs filling with Nile silt, saw himself disappear beneath the surface of the water, his grave marked by a few bubbles, and then nothing.

The car was very close now.

Charlie's only hope was to cut across to the far side of the bridge and run back the way he had come. He tried to break into a sprint and found his legs would not obey him.

The car was only a few feet behind him now, keeping pace but making no move to overtake him. Charlie veered towards the rail.

"Excuse me, do you want a ride?"

A New York accent, the voice harsh and abrasive but not unkind. Charlie risked a quick look over his shoulder. The car was a bright red BMW with a sunroof that was wide open despite the night chill. The driver was in his late twenties. He had curly blond hair tinted orange by the lights, a round, cheerful face and a snaggle-toothed smile. There was a woman in the front passenger seat. In the back of the car sat a second couple. The man was staring straight out the window and the woman seemed to be sleeping. All four were dressed for a night out on the town.

"Been at the Sporting Club?" said the driver.

Charlie tucked in his shirt. "I went out for some fresh air," he improvised. "Someone hit me. Stole my wallet. Cash, credit cards, everything." He paused and then added, "They even took my watch, the bastards."

No response.

"It was a Rolex," said Charlie. "My wife gave it to me."

The driver revved the BMW's engine. "American, aren't you?"

"Los Angeles," said Charlie. During his time in Cairo he'd worked hard at burying his accent; now he struggled to revive it.

"Which way you going?"

It was a remarkably stupid question. Charlie finally realized that the driver and all three passengers had spent the night doing some serious drinking. He gestured vaguely across the bridge.

"Well, hop in. We might as well give you a ride."

Charlie opened the car's rear door. The woman was wide awake; hadn't been sleeping after all. She moved over, making room. She was probably no more than twenty years old, and she was very beautiful, with short blonde hair and creamy white skin, a clinging, low-cut dress of sequins and gauze. Charlie squeezed in. She smiled. Her companion blinked rapidly, trying hard to keep Charlie in focus. Slurring his words, he said, "How the hell you doing?"

"He's just been beaten and robbed," said the woman. "How do you think he's doing?"

The man shrugged, leaned back against the seat and closed his eyes.

The driver had managed to get the BMW in gear. The man sitting next to Charlie began to snore loudly. The concrete railings of the bridge merged into a blur as they picked up speed.

"My husband," said the woman. She pinched the man's nose. He stopped snoring and she let go of his nose and he started snoring again. "Quite the conversationalist, isn't he?"

"Very musical," said Charlie.

She smiled. "Would you like a drink?"

Charlie nodded. The woman frisked her sleeping husband and came up with a pint-sized silver flask. She unscrewed the cap and passed the flask to Charlie.

"Vodka?"

"Perfect."

He tilted the flask to his lips, allowed a little of the liquid to trickle into his mouth. The alcohol lay thick on his tongue, seeped into the spaces between his teeth. He could feel his gums shrinking. He swallowed. His throat burned. He helped himself to another shot and handed the flask back to his benefactor.

They were approaching the end of the bridge now, moving along at forty or fifty kilometres an hour, the tires humming on the paved road. There was a small black car parked in the shadows on Shari el Khadra. A man on foot walking across the bridge wouldn't see the car until he was right on top of it. The woman was drinking. She lowered the flask and Charlie grabbed it, startling her. He lifted the metal container to his mouth, using it and his raised arm to conceal his face. The parked car was a Volkswagen. There were two men inside, both of them sitting up front.

The Volk's engine was running. The car was burning oil.

"Thirsty, aren't you?"

"Sorry." Charlie handed the flask back without drinking. His voice was a little unsteady, his hands shaking with tension. The BMW sped down Shari 26 July, going much too fast. Charlie glanced behind him. No pursuit.

"What's your name?"

"Charlie." She was still staring at him. "Charlie McPhee," he said.

"I'm Sally."

"Pleased to meet you."

"Why do you smell like a swamp, Charlie?"

"I fell in a fishpond."

Charlie felt the weight of her hand on his thigh. She sipped from the flask, and he covertly studied her profile. She was a honey-coloured blonde, a starlet. In California the beaches and supermarkets were full of healthy young girls who looked exactly like her. But this wasn't California, it was Cairo. He forced himself to look away. It had been a long time since he'd been homesick.

"Where are you staying, Charlie?"

That was a good question, wasn't it. Now that he'd had time to think about it, he was sure that they'd be waiting for him back at his room.

"We're at the Continental-Savoy. Do you know where that is?"

Charlie nodded.

"I wanted to stay at the Hilton, or the Meridien. Or even the fucking Sheraton. In fact anywhere on the river would have been great with me." She abruptly turned towards Charlie. Their knees bumped. He inched away, but she followed him, maintaining the contact. "Rivers are romantic, don't you think?"

"Yes, of course."

"We couldn't get reservations. Donald had left it too late. Slept in again." She slipped her arm through Charlie's. The weight of her breast pressed against him. "We took a suite. Two bedrooms." Her lips brushed the lobe of his ear. He felt her teeth, small and sharp.

She whispered, "Do you think you'd like to make love to me, Charlie McPhee?"

"Yes," Charlie whispered back. Even the Savoy would be preferable to a night spent wandering the streets.

"Did you hear that?" said Sally loudly. "First we give him a ride, then he propositions me!"

"Lucky Donald's here to protect your honour," said the driver, laughing.

"Yes, isn't it."

At the hotel, Charlie mumbled his goodbyes and thankyous and got out of the car. The driver seemed to have forgotten all about him. His wife managed a tired smile. He wondered what they'd think if he told them they'd just saved his life. Or what they'd say if they knew he'd slipped Sally's packet of Cools and her silver flask of vodka into his trouser pocket.

It was twenty minutes past one by the clock on the console when the BMW pulled up in front of the hotel. For the next few hours, Charlie wandered aimlessly through the south-east quarter of the city. Now and then he sipped at his dwindling supply of vodka, drinking more for companionship than anything else, since the liquor seemed to have no effect on him.

At four o'clock in the morning he was still wandering through the city. The bright lights of the buildings on the Muqattam Hills had drawn him steadily to the east, towards the first greyish pink blush of false dawn. Turning a corner, he found his progress abruptly blocked by a high barrier of buff-coloured stone: the windowless walls of a row of miniature houses that crowded shoulder to shoulder and formed one of the four outer walls of a necropolis – one of Cairo's many Cities of the Dead.

Charlie shuffled slowly along the wall, trying each door until he found one that opened. He stood on the threshold for a moment, while his eyes adjusted to the deeper gloom of this low-slung, geometric neighbourhood. He was facing a narrow courtyard, an open space between the tombs. It was, as they say, as quiet as a grave. But the necropolis was not populated only by the dead.

In Cairo, where in some areas the population density is as high as two hundred and sixty thousand souls per square mile, it was inevitable that the most desperate and resourceful of the city's poor would eventually seek shelter in the tombs – especially since they are often in better condition than any other housing they might hope to find.

Charlie walked slowly down the middle of a narrow street lined both sides by low, dark, windowless tombs. The light had a greenish tinge, and was so faint he could hardly see where he was going. He wondered how many of the tombs had been abandoned by the families who owned them, and were now occupied by squatters.

The light suddenly became a little brighter. False dawn was giving way to the real thing. He continued down the street until he found a door that had a dusty, unused look. He tried the door and it grudgingly swung open. The air that rushed past him was warm and dry and smelled faintly of animal droppings.

Charlie called out, softly. There was no reply. Certain that the tomb was empty, he slipped inside and groped around in the darkness, lay down on a slab of stone.

Exhausted, he fell asleep almost immediately, and helplessly tumbled backwards in time to the very heart of the nightmare he'd been running from.

In his dream, he climbed a long, steeply-pitched flight of stairs into a small room filled with pulsing red light. He was terrified. His fingers were slippery with sweat. He kept wiping his hands on the wall and pieces of the wall kept shearing away.

Behind the wall, there was nothing.

Finally the small round door of the safe popped open. Gunner laughed – his wide open mouth another round black hole with nothing behind it.

Charlie reached into the safe. Something grabbed him by the wrist. He screamed. Gunner turned towards him, smiling brightly. He pointed his gun. Red light splashed across the walls. Somehow Charlie managed to shake free of whatever had him by the wrist. He clutched at Gunner but the man easily shook him off. A body fell gracelessly to the floor. A woman in yellow pyjamas. Charlie ran out of the room, past the corpse of his wife. On the landing at the top of the stairs his daughter Heather crouched against the banister. The red light pulsed. She reached out to him but he ignored her, hurried down the stairs and out of the house, into a small yellow car. The car drove swiftly down the street. It stopped in front of a house that was somehow vaguely familiar.

Charlie got out of the car and went into the house, walked up a flight of stairs into a pulsing red light.

He dreamt the same dream over and over again, a mobius strip of horror. Each time he relived the dream, the pulsing red light glowed a little brighter. Finally the light was so bright that Charlie had to shield his eyes to stop himself from being blinded.

A man was speaking to him in Arabic. His voice was soft and deep, calm. Charlie sat up. In his sleep he had kicked off one of his shoes. In the glare of the Arab's flashlight he watched the man put the shoe back on his foot and carefully tie the lace.

In a halting mix of Arabic and fractured English the man explained that he was a *bawab* – the resident caretaker. It was unfortunate, but Charlie would have to leave.

Charlie sat up, and the dust made him sneeze. The old man smiled. He led Charlie out of the tomb and into the hot, still air of mid-afternoon. The bawab was a very old man. He was wearing a black galaba and sandals made out of pieces cut from an old tire. His face was a mass of wrinkles, but his eyes were clear and steady. He held Charlie's arm as they walked, tendering sympathy as well as support. At the threshold to the necropolis, Charlie, humiliated, broke away from him and hurried down the street.

At a mosque he used the public fountain to wash his hands and face. He slapped the dust from his clothes, combed his hair with his fingers. Not long afterwards, he came across a coffee-house. Inside, the air was warm and sweet, redolent with the smells of fresh pastry and hot milk. Charlie sat at a tiny table with a green and white tile top. There was a black and white TV over the bar, tuned to a dubbed episode of an American soap that had probably made even less sense in the original English language version.

The waiter was busy inhaling the last of a waterpipe left by a previous customer. He expelled a huge cloud of smoke and wandered over to Charlie's table, enquired as to his needs. Charlie ordered a glass of tea and a plate of sweet rolls, matches for his cigarettes. He took the packet out of his pocket. He shook one free and tore off the filter, smoked and watched television while he waited for his food.

It had been a long time since he had seen America, and he was not seeing the country now. Only cardboard backdrops, and misplaced actors, like himself, who hardly comprehended the lines they spoke.

Outside, the street was jammed with people. Viewed through the window of the café, they seemed no more real to him than the tiny, wildly gesticulating figures up on the screen. The waiter arrived.

Charlie sipped his tea, chewed and bravely swallowed sticky-sweet fragments of roll. Sugar stuck to his lower lip and dribbled down his chin. Lost in thought, he tasted nothing.

Everything he owned was back in his room. He had assumed at first that going back for his possessions would be too dangerous to risk. But now he wondered if that might work in his favour. Would his pursuers reason that since there was no chance he'd return, there was no point in waiting for him?

No, that was dangerous thinking. They'd have someone waiting for him at his apartment, no doubt about it.

Well, let them wait.

There were copies of *El Ahram* and *El Aknar* fixed to wooden poles on a rack near the bar. The thin sheets rustled softly as he carried the newspapers back to his table. The waiter was watching him. He ordered another glass of the strong, sweet tea favoured by Cairenes, and then went carefully through the two dailies, scanning the headlines from the top to the bottom of each page, avidly reading any article that even hinted at the possibility of a robbery or crime of violence. There was no mention of a break-in and shooting on Gezira. Nothing. Not a word.

Charlie glanced around the bar. There were three other customers – two older men at a table near the window, and a boy in his teens dawdling over a glass of lemonade. The couple near the window were deeply involved in their conversation; the boy was staring fixedly at the television.

Using the newspaper as a shield, Charlie began to count the money he had snatched from the safe. There were two thick bundles of used Egyptian ten-pound notes. Halfway through the first bundle Charlie found a buff envelope sealed with a blob of red wax. There was no name or address on the envelope. He put it to one side and resumed counting the money.

There were fifty bills in each packet. Altogether, a thousand pounds. He felt a momentary sense of elation that quickly fizzled, went flat. The police would find his fingerprints all over the house in Gezira, on the safecracking tools and long sliver of steel protruding from Gunner's neck.

He could plead self-defence. But if he'd been forced to break into the safe, if he was truly acting under duress, then why hadn't he made any effort to help the woman in the nightgown at the top of the stairs?

Because they were after me and I thought they were going to kill me.

But what happened afterwards, Charlie McPhee? The people in the BMW who picked you up on the bridge. Why didn't you follow them into the lobby of their hotel and phone the police?

Because I was afraid.

He didn't imagine his coward's answer would elicit a very sympathetic response from the jury, even if they did happen to believe him. He'd be looking at what, ten to fifteen years in maximum security? And then, assuming he survived prison, prompt deportation to the States.

But what options did he have, other than to hand himself over? None.

Cairo was a huge city. Twelve million people. But very few of them were Californians, and even fewer were a shade over six feet tall, with bright blue eyes.

The thousand pounds in ten-pound notes would keep him out of trouble for a little while, but it wouldn't stop Glasses from hunting him down. They'd have his passport by now, and his photograph. It was only a matter of time until he was found.

His cigarette was nearly gone. He lit another from the stub, sucked the smoke down into his lungs and held it, exhaled slowly.

He'd almost forgotten the buff envelope. He picked it up, hefted the weight of it in his hand, held it up to the light streaming in from the window. Finally he broke the wax seal with his thumbnail. The envelope contained a single flimsy sheet of onionskin. He unfolded it. A list of eight names had been written in a cramped hand in the middle of the sheet, in Arabic. At the bottom of the list there was a completely illegible signature.

Charlie crumpled the sheet of paper into a ball. To his amazement it burst violently into a smokeless, hot white flame. He cried out in surprise. The newspapers caught fire. The waiter started towards him, face twisted with anger.

Charlie's reaction was automatic. When there was trouble, get away from it. He knocked over the waiter, ran towards the door. One of the old men stood up and clutched at his sleeve. Charlie swore at him and tore free. He pushed through the crowd that was already gathering in the doorway. A policeman shouted at him. He broke into a run.

Behind him on the tiled table lay a more than generous tip – exactly one thousand pounds in used ten-pound notes.

8

BOGOTA

Hubie Sweets lay in the old cast-iron tub in a sort of half-assed reclining lotus position, his head cradled between the girl's breasts and his bony knees sticking out of the hot, steaming water. The girl was maybe sixteen or seventeen years old. Sweets had taken one look at her and decided he was in love, proved it to both of them by paying her the truly outrageous sum of one hundred and fifty American dollars to spend the week with him. When he'd asked her what her name was, she wouldn't tell him, had only smiled shyly and looked away.

So Sweets had called her Lolita.

He'd let Lolita run the bath, because she got such a kick out of it, the novelty. As usual, she'd filled the tub too full, so that whenever either one of them moved, soapy water slopped over the brim and puddled on the linoleum. They'd moved around quite a bit at first, but now they were still; Sweets' head nestled between the cutest little set of pillows this side of heaven.

It was his third bath of the day. He was starting to feel clean again, as if he'd finally shucked the last clinging layers of jungle sweat and jungle grime. When he wasn't in the bath, he was either at the kitchen table, fuelling up, or in the sack with Lolita. The girl was earning every peseta of her wages, no doubt about it. A chrome-plated Colt .45 automatic with pearl grips and a ruby mounted on the front sight lay on a wooden stool within easy reach. In Colombia, there were an average of fifteen thousand murders a year. The leading cause of death for men between the ages of fifteen and forty-four was homicide. The price for a hit was as low as twenty-five dollars, barely enough to cover the cost of ammunition. Bogota was the worst city in the whole country. The place was crawling with dope dealers and thieves. Step outside and somebody'd take a shot at you just to stay in practice. Stay home, chances were they'd come to visit.

Sweets' calf muscles were starting to knot up. He sighed, and straightened his legs. Water sloshed over the side of the bath, slapped the floor.

In the other room, Mungo had turned on the old console radio. There was a burst of static. Mungo tried singing along and then gave up, his Spanish failing him.

Sweets twisted his head sideways and licked at a nipple the size and shape and colour and taste of a ripe raspberry. Lolita squirmed beneath him. More water hit the floor.

On the radio, the music faded, gave way to a weather report. The temperature was eighty-four degrees. Ninety per cent humidity. Afternoon thundershowers a certainty. Under the soft, liquid gargling of the announcer's voice Sweets heard a metallic clicking, guessed that Mungo was field-stripping his weapon. In this climate, rust never slept.

Sweets reached for the soap.

There was a knock on the apartment door. The knock was loud and authoritative. Full of bullshit. Sweets made a grab for his Colt. The slippery smooth grips squirted out of his hand and the gun hit the floor. He cursed and floundered out of the tub. His feet went out from under him and he landed on his ass. Cursing, he wiped his hands on a towel, then snatched up the gun and used both thumbs to pull back the hammer.

The door rattled against the frame. Sweets motioned Lolita to stay low but she was way ahead of him; only the tip of her nose showed above the surface of the water.

In the other room the radio clicked off and Mungo Martin called out, "Quién es?"

No reply. Sweets hurried out of the bathroom, down a short hallway and into the living room. Mungo was kneeling on the floor, bits and pieces of his Uzi spread out on pages of oil-stained newspaper. Sweets watched him work feverishly to reassemble the gun. He shook his head, and sighed loudly, disgusted.

"Fuck you," said Mungo, "at least I got my clothes on." He knocked over a tin of gun oil but Sweets didn't notice because his eyes were on the door.

"Quién es?" Mungo called out again. "Cómo se llama, por favor!"

Something white and rectangular slithered under the door. An envelope. Sweets almost shot it. He glanced at Mungo, who shrugged and continued putting the Uzi back together.

Leaving a trail of bathwater behind him, Sweets got down on his hands and knees. His cheek pressed against the scuzzy carpet as he

56

peeked through the crack between the bottom of the door and the floor.

"If your mother could see you now," said Mungo.

Sweets crouched a little lower, conscious of his ass sticking up in the air, goosebumps. It was a bitch, trying to stay dignified every goddamn minute of your life. All around him, the room suddenly darkened. A ripple of electricity skimmed down the length of his spine. The short hairs all over his body stood on end. There was a brilliant white flash of light. All the colour seemed to drain out of the room, and in the same instant, a tremendous thunderclap rattled the windows and made the very air in his lungs vibrate and shimmer with energy.

"Seems the weatherman got lucky," said Mungo. There was a muted drumroll, distant and percussive. He laughed, and wiped his oily fingers on a scrap of rag.

Sweets studied the envelope. It lay face up on the carpet and had both their names typed on it in capital letters. In the upper right-hand corner was the logo of a well-known Bogota travel agency. Well, that didn't mean shit. He inched a little closer. He could feel a chill coming on. He crouched and gave the envelope a sniff.

"What the hell you doing, Hubie?"

"Know what a letter bomb smells like?"

"No idea. Want me to open it?"

Sweets waved Mungo away. "No, that's okay. I'll do it. After all, somebody has to be a hero."

"Right," said Mungo. "If you need me, I'll be hiding under the bed."

Sweets snatched up the envelope and ripped it open. Inside, there were three Avianca Airlines first-class tickets, Bogota to Miami.

"What you got, Hubie?"

Sweets eased the hammer down on his Colt and showed Mungo the package.

"Ticket to ride. Avianca Flight 171 out of Eldorado International."

"Return?"

"One way."

"Praise the Lord," said Mungo. "When we supposed to leave?"

"Wednesday."

"What time?"

"Two o'clock sharp." Sweets had to think about it a minute. Brow furrowed, he said, "What the hell day is it, Mungo?"

"Wednesday, Hubie."

Sweets tilted his head to look at Mungo's watch. He took another quick look at the tickets.

Mungo said, "That's right, you best get some clothes on, or you just might get your ass left behind."

"Promises, promises," said Sweets. But he was already working out what to wear on the plane, the yellow three-piece suit or the pink shirt and canary-yellow jacket with the lime-green trousers. Also, there was the fact he'd paid Lolita for a week and that had only been three days ago. He was entitled, the way he saw it, to a rebate.

At Miami Beach, arrangements had been made. They were spared a customs check and ushered by an elderly black agent disguised as a maintenance man into a small, windowless office.

"Don't it piss you off getting typecast like that?" said Sweets to the man, indicating his overalls and cap.

"Wait here, please."

"Why?" said Sweets.

The black agent wordlessly shut the door in Sweets' face.

"Because he said so," Mungo explained.

"And also, I got to admit it, I was intimidated by his snappy uniform."

The office was furnished with a double pedestal grey metal desk, a naugahyde couch and a plain wooden chair. On the desk there was a plastic console with two rows of red buttons and one row of green buttons. High on the wall opposite the desk were mounted five nine-inch black and white television sets, each with a wide-angle view of a different area of the airport.

"Big Brother," said Mungo.

"I grew up with six of 'em," said Sweets. "A few more don't make no difference." He watched the girl at the Hertz counter fill out a form for a man in baggy shorts and a sleeveless T-shirt. She looked like she was probably a blonde, but it was hard to say. Sweets sat down on the edge of the desk and punched a bright red button. If something happened, he didn't see it. He hit another button and then a whole row of them.

"You just started World War Three," said Mungo.

"Somebody had to do it." Sweets hit a green button. It flashed on and off and the blonde at the Hertz counter was replaced by an overhead shot of the airport bar.

"Look what I see," said Sweets.

A skinny bald man wearing a dazzling white shirt and a black bow tie was standing behind a cash register, industriously polishing a glass.

"Real fascinating," said Mungo. "Jesus Christ, talk about the stuff of life." He lay down on the naugahyde couch and tried to get comfortable. The couch was hard and lumpy. It was like trying to get cosy in a municipal bus.

Sweets pointed up at the screen. "That's him, that's the one."

"Who?"

"Guy we're waiting for. Crewcut at the bar, drinking the Moosehead beer."

"You think so?"

"Gotta be. Look at the way he's sitting there. As if he's got a feather pillow for an ass, and all the time in the world, nothing to do but keep us waiting."

"People are *supposed* to take it easy at bars. That's what bars are for."

"I'm saying the guy is a Company man. Check that suit. Did that suit come off a rack, or what? And look at that haircut. Is that a Company haircut, yes or no?"

"He could be a cop. Airport security, maybe."

"You'll never see a cop with a haircut that bad. Not in Miami. Fifty bucks says that's our man."

"You're covered." Mungo watched as the man pushed his empty glass away from him and waved at the bartender, indicating he wanted a refill.

"Why don't *we* go wait at the bar?" said Mungo. "I'm so fucking dry I can hardly blink."

Sweets flicked open the blade of the pearl-handled knife he'd picked up in Colombia. He went to work on the bottom right-hand drawer of the desk.

"Think there's a bottle in there?"

"I can smell it."

"You gonna get us in trouble, Hubie."

"Trouble's my middle name."

Up on the TV screen, the blonde from Hertz sat down next to the six-dollar haircut. A day-time rendezvous, by God.

"Jealous?" said Mungo.

"I had her twin sister, and she was nothing."

Mungo laughed. The bartender brought the blonde what looked like a martini, plunked a telephone down in front of the haircut. The man dialled a three-digit number, and the telephone at Sweets' elbow rang shrilly. Mungo stared at the instrument as if it had come alive.

Sweets picked up, said hello.

"Is this Sweets or Martin?" said the voice on the phone.

"Yes," said Sweets.

"Look, I'm sorry to keep you waiting, but something came up at the last minute. Can you guys hang in there for another half hour or so?"

"No problem," said Sweets cheerfully. "Tell me, what time is it, down here in Miami?"

On the screen, haircut shot his cuff and took a peek at his watch.

"Quarter past two."

"Thanks," said Sweets, and hung up.

Mungo pulled a fifty out of his wallet, crumpled the bill in his fist and threw it at Sweets.

"A graceful loser. My favourite kind."

"Something came up, the man said. His dick, I bet."

"Better wait for him here," said Sweets. "We thump him in the bar, somebody might call the cops."

Mungo nodded. "Yeah, okay."

Sweets went back to work on the desk.

"She just gave him one of her olives," said Mungo. "Stuck it in his mouth with her fingers and then licked them clean."

The drawer popped open. There was a cardboard box in there, Adidas running shoes, size eleven. Sweets lifted the lid and saw that the box was crammed full of the kind of tiny liquor bottles they served in tourist class.

"Name your poison."

"Johnny Walker red."

Sweets started to root through the tightly-packed bottles and then gave up and turned the shoe box over, dumping the contents on the desk.

"Could we have died and gone to heaven?" said Mungo.

"You, maybe. I'm too young."

Mungo laughed harshly. "Wake up, Hubie. The world we live in, a man's warranty lasts about as long as it takes to cut his umbilical cord."

Sweets tossed a bottle of Scotch to Mungo, cracked open a London Dry Gin. "Too bad these bottles are so small, otherwise we could piss in 'em and screw the tops back on."

Mungo drained his bottle. Helped himself to a refill and drank that down and had another. He glanced at the TV screen. The bartender was using the edge of his hand to bulldoze a few coins off the counter. Hertz and the Haircut had vanished.

"Heavy tipper," said Sweets.

"Impress the lady. Must have dropped seventy-five, maybe eighty cents." Mungo picked up an empty bottle, held it between his thumb and index finger. "Know what these'd be good for?"

"What?"

"Molotov cocktails for blowing up Dinky Toys."

"Or putting rescue notes in, you a midget shipwrecked on a desert island."

The door opened and Haircut came into the room. He was smiling broadly but the smile faltered and died when he saw the bottles spilled across the desk, the two very serious-looking black guys, both of them pretty goddamn huge, the bigger one with a nasty-looking scar that gave him all sorts of character he didn't need, his buddy wearing funky wraparound sunglasses, his hair too shiny and worked up in tight braids, plastic buttons and bits of shiny metal hanging at the ends.

"Hey, fellas. What's going on?"

"Who wants to know?" said Sweets.

"I'm Agent Nolan."

Sweets stood up. He took off his canary-yellow jacket. The silk lining rustled as he hung the jacket carefully on the back of the chair.

"What are you doing?" said Agent Nolan.

"You got something for us?" said Mungo. He held out his hand, palm up.

"Air France tickets. Fresh passports, visas. You're on flight 317 to Orly." He reached inside his jacket. "First-class all the way, guys. Eat as much filet mignon as you want." Nolan hesitated, the blue and white Air France folder half-extended towards Sweets. "I thought there were supposed to be three of you."

"There was."

"Excuse me?" said the agent.

Mungo pointed at the bank of television screens, and Nolan twisted his head to look behind him. Sweets hit him with a left hook to the jaw, knocking him across the desk. The telephone and most of the bottles crashed to the floor. Nolan lay still. His eyes were shut but his mouth was wide open. A trickle of blood seeped from a split lower lip.

"We could count to ten," said Sweets, "but I sense it'd be a mere formality."

"Didn't leave much for me, did you?"

"How was I to know he'd go down so easy?" Sweets unscrewed the cap from a bottle of Canadian rye. He pried Nolan's mouth open and emptied the bottle down his throat, spilled the contents of another bottle across the agent's face and chest.

"Tricky," said Mungo.

Sweets scooped up several more bottles and stuffed them into Nolan's pockets. Nolan groaned. He lifted his right hand an inch off the desk and mumbled something incomprehensible. Mungo grabbed his tie and hauled him upright. Nolan's eyes popped open.

"Fair game?" said Mungo.

Sweets nodded. "Technically, I'd have to say the man is conscious."

Mungo hit Nolan with a straight right, using the tie to snap his head forward, into the path of his fist. The back of Nolan's head hit the desk and the metal rang hollowly.

"Nice tone."

"Yeah. White folks can't dance worth shit, but some of 'em sure are musical."

The Air France flight departed exactly on schedule. Sweets called the coin toss and won. As always, he chose the window seat.

Their stewardess was the kind of woman Sweets liked to think of as a 'sitcom nigger'. She was tall and thin, with coffee-with-cream skin, a straight nose and hardly any lips. Black, but barely. She was an actress, she'd probably work the Cosby Show. Mungo was six-three and weighed two hundred and thirty pounds, all bone and muscle. It was obvious from the way the stew came on to him that she liked the way he looked. Finally she said she had an overnighter in Paris, was he interested in dinner?

"Maybe some other time, honey," said Mungo. He didn't trust stews, thought they were too easy. Sweets had no such prejudices, but was too proud to chase leftovers.

As it happened, there wouldn't have been time for the stew even if Mungo had been interested, because when they touched down at Orly there was an Agent Nolan clone waiting for them with three first-class Air Egypt tickets to Cairo.

"Wait a minute," said the clone, "aren't there supposed to be three of you?"

Sweets studied his ticket and then glanced at the clock on the wall behind the agent. They had ninety minutes. Egypt was Muslim country, and Muslims belonged to the AA crowd. "Want to hit the bar?" he asked Mungo.

"We got time to see the Eiffel Tower?"

"Never heard of it."

"The bar, then." Mungo turned to the agent. "You supposed to stick around until we're outta here?"

The agent nodded.

"Okay," said Mungo. "But you have to pay for the drinks, and you aren't allowed to say anything back no matter how much we make fun of you."

The man hesitated, not sure if Mungo was kidding or not.

"He isn't," said Sweets. "If you don't believe me, ask Agent Nolan."

9

CAIRO

Downey came quietly into the room, not making a fuss. The firebug was sitting at a square wooden table, smoking a cigarette. As Downey shut the door, Charlie flicked a length of ash at the jam jar lid that served as an ashtray. The ash hit the table and lay there in a little grey heap. Charlie glanced covertly over at Downey, saw that Downey was watching him and looked quickly away. Downey continued to lean against the wall with his hands in his pockets. The cigarette had burned down almost to the filter. Charlie took a last desperate pull and then deliberately dropped the butt on the marble floor and squashed it under his heel.

Downey liked that, but didn't let it show. He pushed away from the wall and said, "I'm Jack Downey. You're Charlie McPhee?"

Charlie nodded.

Downey walked briskly over to the table, his heels clicking on the marble. He perched on the edge of the table with his hip a fraction of an inch from Charlie's right arm.

"How long have you been in Egypt?"

"Two years. A little over two years."

"How much of that time was spent in Cairo?"

"Nearly all of it."

"Be more specific, please."

Charlie shifted in the chair. A CIA carpenter had sawn a quarter of an inch off one of the legs – just one more way of keeping the occupant off balance. He braced himself against the table. "Look, I've already been over all this with . . . your colleague."

"Jimmy Abrams. Let me tell you a little secret, Charlie. Jimmy's new at his job and he isn't very good at it. That's why they sent him down here to talk to you, because he needed the practice. See, Jimmy's big problem is that although he's been trained to ask all the right questions, he has no idea at all how to interpret the answers. How old are you, by the way?"

Charlie had to think about it for a moment. "Forty-three."

"You look older, pal. When's your birthday?"

"March."

"Be more specific."

"Sixteenth."

"No kidding," said Downey. "I'm exactly eleven years and three days older than you. We're both Pisces. Know anything about astrology?"

"No."

"There are two kinds of Pisceans. They're sweet as a bowl of sugar, or real bastards, deceptive as hell. No middle ground." Downey rested his hand on Charlie's shoulder. He squeezed a little too hard. "Bet you've already figured out which slot I fit into, right?"

Charlie lit another cigarette.

"Careful now," said Downey. "Don't torch the place."

Charlie blew out the match and dropped it in the jam lid.

"What part of the States did you say you were from?"

"Los Angeles."

"You claim to be an American citizen?"

"That's right."

"How many career home runs did Babe Ruth hit?"

"What?"

Downey slammed his fist down on the table. Charlie jumped. Downey pointed a finger at him and said, "That's another thing about that wimp Abrams. Pain can be a wonderful cathartic but he doesn't like to hurt people. Guy's soft as the inside of a goddamn oyster."

"But you do like to hurt people, is that what you're telling me?"

Downey shrugged. "Don't get me wrong, it doesn't come naturally. I'm no sadist, have to get myself in the mood, work up a lather. But, you ask any really good interrogator, he'll tell you the same thing. You got to have the potential to get real nasty, slice deep." He fumbled in his jacket pocket. "You like chocolate?"

Charlie blinked.

"Swiss dark. You'll love it."

"I've got a bad tooth."

Downey gave up the search for his candy bar. "We're all bastards at heart. It's part of the human condition. What'd you do before you came to Cairo?"

"I was in business."

"No shit. What kind of business were you in?"

"I owned a company that manufactured a wide range of locks and security devices."

"Including safes?"

"Yes."

"Aha! So that's why these guys snatched you and took you out to Gezira. They figured, the guy knows how to make a safe, he must know how to break a safe. Question is, how did they know who you were?"

"I don't have any idea."

"Maybe you kept yourself solvent by doing a little breaking and entering, is that possible? Had to fence the goodies, mix in with the criminal element?"

Charlie studied the burning tip of his cigarette, the way the smoke curled towards the ceiling.

Downey smiled. He'd just had an interesting thought. "Forty-three years old. Do any time in Nam?"

Charlie nodded.

"An educated guy like you. Rank?"

"Lieutenant."

"Where?"

"Khe Sanh, at the end."

"No shit, you were a marine? You enlisted?"

Charlie nodded.

"Tell me more."

"I specialized in Tunnel Warfare."

"Explosives?"

"Yeah."

"Don't like to talk about it, huh. But you know all about locks, security devices. And how to blow stuff up." Downey chewed his lower lip, thinking. "The house on Gezira. What kind of safe was it?"

"I don't remember."

"Should I threaten to pull out your fingernails?"

"It was Egyptian."

"The three guys who snatched you. What nationality were they?"

"There were two of them."

"Yeah, right."

"I don't know."

"Could they have been Israelis?"

"Possibly."

"Other than English, what language did they speak?"

"I don't know."

"Would you be able to identify them if you saw them again?"

"I think so, yes."

"Describe the one who went into the house with you."

"He was about five foot ten. Heavy, probably close to two hundred pounds."

"Fat?"

"No, not fat. Just big."

"What colour was his hair?"

"Black. His eyes were dark brown. He had a dark complexion, big hands."

"Scars?"

"No."

"Was he wearing any jewellery?"

"I don't think so."

"A watch?"

"I didn't notice."

"Did they use names?"

"No."

"The one who did the driving, who waited in the car when you were in the house. Tell me all about him. The way he combed his hair, the size of his earlobes, if he used a deodorant, every little goddamn thing."

With Downey's coaching, Charlie described the man in detail. When Downey was sure he'd drained him dry, he went on to the second man, the Gunner. Downey paid strict attention to Charlie's recital. Every so often he interrupted to ask a question or confirm a particular point. He didn't take notes, and Charlie wondered if he was carrying a concealed tape recorder. Maybe the room was wired. Not that it mattered. It didn't take Charlie long to realize that it was Glasses and the Gunner that Downey was interested in, not him.

"After you left your apartment, then what?"

Charlie told Downey about the yellow Fiat with the chalky paint and cracked windshield, the missing hubcaps and leaky stuffing in the back seat. What he couldn't remember was the number of the licence plate. Nor could he recall any of the streets they'd driven past, although he was sure the route they had taken to the island of Gezira was fairly direct. There had been no side-trips, no contact with other vehicles.

"Try to remember what street the house was on. It's important."

"We went over El Tahrir bridge, past the Sporting Club and up Shagaret El Durr. Do you know the city?"

Downey nodded.

"I couldn't tell you where we turned off. It was dark."

"And you were too scared to see straight. Describe the house."

"It was three storeys high. Stucco. Off-white or maybe pale yellow. There was a hedge around the front, and an iron gate. Iron bars on the windows."

"How many windows were there?"

Charlie closed his eyes. At first all he could see was the porch light, burning brightly one moment and vanishing the next, extinguished. Then a picture of the building formed in his mind. "There were two windows on each floor, one on each side."

"Jimmy tells me you claim the front door was open."

"It was."

Downey didn't know whether to believe him or not. He let it go. Enough stick, time for some carrot.

"Want something to eat? They've got these terrific bran muffins, you'll love them." Downey went over to the door and opened it, spoke softly to an unseen presence.

Charlie hadn't realized there was a guard. Why would they take him so seriously? Or was it only a routine precaution?

Downey shut the door and came back to the table. He stood directly in front of Charlie, looking down at him. "How much you weigh, any idea?"

Charlie shook his head.

"You ingest drugs?" Charlie hesitated. Downey read the look in his eye. "Hashish?"

"Yes, but not for the past couple of months."

"Anything else?"

"No, never."

"Roll up your sleeves." Downey examined Charlie's arms, looking for tracks. "Ever indulge in illegal or non-prescription drugs when you were living in Los Angeles?"

Charlie shook his head, no.

"You're one in a million, pal." Downey walked around behind Charlie and started to massage the back of his neck. "You need a shave and a haircut, some new clothes. That stuff you're wearing is real scummy." His hands kneaded, prodded. "Tell me what happened after you went into the house."

Charlie remembered the door swinging shut, the soft click of the latch and then the barrel of the gun in his ribs, pushing him towards the stairs.

He'd started climbing. The wooden stairs had popped and cracked under his weight, and at the first sharp explosion of sound he'd thought for a dreadful fraction of a second that he'd been shot.

He described the second floor, the dimly-lit corridor lined with the ornately framed photographs of his jurors, mouths tight with disapproval and dark eyes stuffed with accusations. Mute witnesses to his cowardice on the landing, when he had abandoned the woman in the nightgown to her fate.

"Where'd you get the stuff you used to break into the safe? Was it yours or theirs?"

"Theirs."

"Sure about that, are you?" A sardonic grin. "So you popped the safe and then the shooting started. Pow! Pow!" Downey clapped his hands. "Pretty exciting stuff, huh?" He grinned, his eyes alight with laughter.

Charlie didn't notice the look in Downey's eyes. He was crouched at the open door of the safe. Orange light staggered across the walls. Shell casings tinkled on the floor. The man in pyjamas fell into the room, his chest a mass of blood.

The air was bruised, still.

"And then you knifed the guy who went into the house with you, grabbed the cash and ran like hell. Okay, so where's the money now?"

"At the coffee house."

"Yeah, right. Jimmy said you couldn't remember the name of the place or even where it was."

"Somewhere in the Abdin district."

"Could you find it, if we went looking?"

"Unless it burned to the ground."

Downey laughed. "What else did you take from the safe?"

"Nothing."

"No Ali Baba stuff? Jewellery?"

"Nothing like that, no."

Downey held up his right hand, like a traffic cop at a busy intersection. "The reason I ask is because about a week ago a guy named Aziz Mehanna was killed in an accident on the road from Alexandria. We think you were snatched because his team needed a replacement. Aziz was a safecracker. He was also somewhat political. Ever hear of a dude named Mu'ammar al-Gadaffi?"

"The Libyan dictator."

"The 'mad dog of the Middle East', Reagan called him. Well, Ronnie's come and gone, but Mu'ammar's still dancing up a storm. Aziz was a prime suspect in several bombings we believe were funded by Libya. What I'd like to know is, were your pals working for Gadaffi, or were they just plain garden-variety crooks?"

"There was nothing in the safe but money."

"Okay, fine. You grab the cash and run like hell. Then what?"

As if to atone for his failure to mention the buff envelope and flimsy sheet of onionskin, Charlie recounted the rest of his tale in minute detail. Downey clucked sympathetically when Charlie mentioned falling headlong into the fishpond, but by now Charlie was wise to all his tricks, unaffected by his sympathy or concern. Downey may have sensed this, because at this point his questions became scattered, perfunctory.

Charlie struggled on. When he told Downey about the BMW full of drunks and Sally's whispered invitation to share her bed, Downey actually laughed out loud, making no attempt to hide his disbelief.

There was a discreet knock on the door. A marine stepped into the room carrying a bright red plastic tray laden with a large thermos and a paper plate piled high with steaming hot bran muffins.

"Enjoy," said Downey. He paused. "Oh yeah, the tooth. It bothering you? I'll get somebody on it, no problem. Stay tuned." He snatched a muffin from the plate and followed the marine out of the room. The door thudded shut.

Charlie sat quietly for a moment and then unscrewed the lid of the thermos and poured some black coffee into the mug. He thought about the way Downey had mixed and shuffled his attitudes – chummy one moment, hostile the next. It was a way of keeping Charlie off-balance. When Downey resumed the interrogation, Charlie was going to have to be very careful what he said.

Richard Foster had his feet up on his desk and a day-old copy of the *Washington Post* spread out on his lap. The paper had arrived in the morning's diplomatic pouch. Foster was reading the sports section. The 'Skins had taken gas again, blown a fifteen-point third quarter lead to the Patriots, who'd aced a field goal in the dying seconds and won by a single point. His buzzer sounded. He leaned across his desk and pushed a button on the intercom.

"What is it, Dorothy?"

"Mr Downey would like to see you, Mr Foster."

"I'll be with him in a few minutes." Foster rattled the *Post*'s pages. The Redskins weren't scheduled to play again until the following Monday night, when they had an away game at Jack Murphy stadium against America's team, the Dallas Cowboys.

Foster put the paper back together and folded it up the way he'd done it when he was a delivery boy, far too long ago. He dropped the paper in his solid brass wastebasket. Tidy desk, tidy mind. He hit the intercom and said, "Okay, Dorothy. Send him in."

The first thing Foster noticed about Downey was that there was a sprinkling of dark brown crumbs across the lapels of his suit. Judging from the look on Downey's cherubic face, however, it might've been a canary he'd been chewing on, rather than a chocolate chip cookie.

"What's up, Jack?"

"Charlie McPhee." Hands in pockets, Downey strolled over to the window and looked out. At the far end of the block the Union Jack in front of the British embassy hung limply, and the sentries at the gate were so still they might have been made of painted tin. He studied Foster's reflection in the polished glass. The double-glazing gave him an out-of-focus look that was definitely an improvement.

"I thought Abrams was handling him."

Downey turned and rested his hip on the windowsill. "Jimmy filled you in, did he?"

"I got a quick rundown," said Foster cautiously. "No details, just an overall picture."

"Charlie told me all he got out of the safe was a fistful of cash, but I think he was lying."

"Why?"

"He got real antsy when I pressed him about how the fire started in the restaurant. Indicated the B and E was an inside job, even though there wasn't much in the safe. Then he gives me this weird bullshit about being propositioned by a woman who picked him up in a red BMW, turning her down and spending the night in a tomb in one of the necropolises." Downey paused. "There are rumours of a Libyan safehouse on Gezira . . ."

Foster frowned. "That's news to me, Jack."

"Jimmy got Charlie's address, wandered around the neighbourhood. Nobody remembered seeing any heavies, a yellow Fiat. Jimmy's no quitter. He drove over to the Continental–Savoy, the hotel where McPhee claims the girl in the BMW was staying. The desk remembered them. She and her husband and another couple were on a package tour. Flew back to the States this morning."

Downey finally noticed his lapel. He idly brushed the crumbs on to Foster's immaculate carpet.

"So, what have we got?"

"There's a Vietnamese expression. In every paddy of lies, there is a single grain of truth."

"We need a confirmation of a break-in and shooting on Gezira," said Foster.

"Hold him for a few days, wait and see what happens. Somebody finds a body floating face down in the river with a steel pick in his neck, call the cops. It turns out this whole thing is something he sucked out of the bowl of his waterpipe, ship him home. Assuming, of course, that he's an American citizen."

"His wife's lawyers have been climbing all over us for the past eighteen months. The guy's worth millions. The estate's been twisting in the wind."

"You wire them yet?"

"Not quite. I mean, what if this bozo isn't who he says he is? The lawyers sent me a snapshot, but I wouldn't call it conclusive. Be a bitch to send home an impostor."

"Why not give him a few days to regain some strength after his terrible ordeal," said Downey, grinning. "Put him on a diet of red meat and scopolamine."

"No drugs, Jack. I'm holding him to make sure he's the genuine article, and that Cairo homicide doesn't want him. Not so you can inject a magic potion and play twenty questions."

"But we can *talk*, can't we?"

"Quietly. No shouting."

"Word of honour," said Downey, licking his lips.

A hand gripped Charlie's shoulder, shook him gently. He opened his eyes. Jimmy Abrams was staring down at him, his narrow face pinched with concern.

"You okay, Charlie?"

Charlie nodded. He was still getting his bearings, remembering where he was. Abrams had a high forehead and sparse, arched eyebrows. His eyes were a pale, watery blue. He had a long nose and flaring nostrils. The nose and small round mouth gave him an inquisitive, grasping look. Charlie didn't like Abrams, but was careful not to let it show.

"They told me you'd been sick."

"I ate too fast. It's my own fault."

"Fucking muffins. What kind of meal is that for a grown man. Didn't you get any dinner?"

Charlie shook his head.

"Jesus Christ! I told them to send you a complete meal. Nice thick slice of ham, a baked potato and some vegetables, glass of milk." Abrams patted Charlie on the shoulder. It was a gesture of apology and friendship, awkward and masculine. He said, "Let's get the hell out of this goddamned dungeon."

Charlie kept pace with Abrams as they walked briskly down a long, narrow corridor, into a waiting elevator. Abrams pushed a button. The doors whispered shut. They accelerated and decelerated. The doors popped open. He was led down a dimly lit hallway and into a small, dark room. Abrams flicked on the overhead light, crossed to the room's single window and pushed aside the curtains. "Nice, huh?"

"It's fine," said Charlie. What was Abrams going to do next, hold his hand out for a tip?

He went over to the window, tried to open it and found it wouldn't budge. He saw that it had been nailed and painted shut. The glass was dusty, and very thick, with a faint greenish tinge. Bulletproof. He tapped it with his fingertips and then hit it hard with the side of his fist. Abrams gave him an odd look.

Outside, dusk had fallen. In the embassy courtyard, almost directly below him, three foreshortened men were climbing into a long black car, a limousine. Chrome glittered under the lights as the car swung in a wide circle towards the gates. The small flags on the limo's front bumpers stiffened as the car picked up speed. It passed through the gates and they automatically swung shut. There must have been a loud clang as iron struck iron, but the distance and thick glass of the window cut off all sound.

Abrams had disappeared. Charlie heard the sound of running water coming from an open doorway. He examined his new quarters.

The room was rectangular, with off-white walls. The floor was pale, varnished wood. There was a woven rug of red and blue and green, a small desk, a chest of drawers and a narrow bed covered by a dark-blue quilt decorated with pale-blue stars.

The curtains had a cowboy motif.

On the wall above the bed there was a poster-size photograph, a huge blow-up of a young boy in a baseball uniform. There was a diamond pattern of out-of-focus wire mesh behind him – he was standing at home plate with a bat slung negligently over his shoulder. The boy had a face that belonged on a cereal box. His dark brown eyes were wide-spaced and his snub nose was a mass of freckles. His head was tilted slightly upwards so he could look out from under the stiff brim of his cap. He was grinning. His front teeth were too large for his mouth. Charlie realized the room must once have belonged to the boy. He sat down on the bed.

It was obviously a child's room, now that he'd had time to think about it. Everything was a little smaller than it should have been, as if scaled to youth. He leaned forward and opened the top drawer of the desk. Inside were several yellowing sheets of paper, a box of crayons and a picture book of dinosaurs. He shut the drawer and opened the middle and bottom drawers in turn. Both were empty except for a lining of brittle newspaper. *The Chicago Tribune*, dated 11th August 1979.

On the bed, there was a cardboard box that Charlie hadn't noticed before, had somehow overlooked. The box was full of clothes. Charlie turned it upside down and dumped everything out.

There were two pale-blue Oxford Cloth shirts with button-down collars, two pairs of dark-blue socks, one pair of black and one pair of fire-engine red bikini underpants, two pairs of lightweight beige cotton slacks. Everything was brand-new, with price tags and labels still attached. The clothes had been bought at Sears. Charlie stared at the code numbers on the tags, at the dollars signs and numbers. He ran his thumb along the smooth edge of one of the tags, tested the strength of the thin umbilical cord of clear plastic that moored the price tag to the item of clothing.

He picked up one of the shirts, held it in his lap. The fabric was wonderfully, almost miraculously soft to the touch. He unfastened and refastened one of the buttons. The shirt was an Arrow. Made in America. Size 16 neck 34 sleeve. Abrams might as well have stitched his initials on the pocket.

Charlie put the clothes back in the box. He went over to the desk and sat down in the undersized chair, began to leaf through the book of dinosaurs. His shirt itched. His trousers chafed at the crotch. He stank of fishpond and dust, sweat, hashish, gunpowder and sudden death.

He heard the sound of the toilet being flushed. Abrams appeared in the doorway, zipping up. He jerked a thumb over his shoulder. "Bathroom's in there, you want to freshen up."

"Are the clothes for me?"

"Hope I got the size right."

Charlie went into the bathroom. There was a gleaming enamel sink, a toilet, a shower stall made of sheets of white plastic. The shower curtain was yellow with age, stiff with disuse. Charlie twisted the taps. There were pockets of air trapped in the lines. The nozzle spat at him.

He undressed, tested the temperature of the water, made an adjustment and stepped into the little cubicle. The shower curtain was decorated with orange and yellow seahorses. There was a folded washcloth and bar of Ivory Soap on the lip of the tub. The soap was still in its wrapper.

Charlie stood under the spray so the water hit him at the base of his neck and across his shoulders. The water was much hotter than it had been in his room in the Old City. He tore the wrapper off the bar of soap and began to rub the soap into his hair, working up a lather.

He spent a long time in the shower. When he finally came out, Abrams was plugging a pale-grey telephone into a wall jack next to the bed.

Abrams glanced over his shoulder. "Jesus, you're skinny. Top priority, gotta put some meat on those bones." He lifted the receiver to his ear, nodded and replaced the instrument, stood up and pointed at a thermos and plate of cheese and crackers on the desk. "Ordered a little something from room service, thought you might be hungry."

Outside, darkness had fallen, and the lights in the courtyard seemed much brighter. Charlie tried a wedge of cheddar. It was well aged, sharp and slightly bitter. The cheese made him think of a deli on South Robertson, back in Los Angeles. A crowded little place, all shiny glass cabinets and wonderful smells. The owner was Austrian. He kept a twice life-size poster of Arnold Schwarzenegger pinned to the wall behind the cash register, claimed to be distantly related.

Abrams loitered in the doorway, still playing the role of bellboy. He said, "You need anything, dial three twenty-seven. That's my office. If I'm out, leave a message and I'll get right back to you." He hesitated, as if there was something he wanted to say but felt he shouldn't. Finally he added, "Those guys who took you out to Gezira. We'll find them sooner or later, clear this whole thing up. So don't worry about it, okay?"

Charlie nodded.

Abrams stepped into the hallway, shut the door. Charlie heard the deadbolt slide home.

Omar Jalloud leaned against the rear fender of the yellow Fiat, watching the light bleed from the sky, the rectangle of the warehouse doorway turn dark grey, fade to black. He glanced at his watch. It was time. He moved away from the car, signalled to his driver, Abdel al-Hony.

Abdel sorted through his keys, unlocked the Fiat's trunk.

The man Charlie thought of as Glasses was in a pre-natal position, bound hand and foot with tight loops of electrical wire. He squinted into the harsh glare from the Butagaz lantern.

In Arabic, Jalloud told Glasses that the word had come down from Tripoli. He had been found guilty of gross incompetence, and was to be executed. Jalloud signalled to Abdel to remove Glasses' gag. He asked him if he had anything to say.

Glasses tried to spit at him, but fear had sucked all the moisture from his mouth.

Jalloud slammed down the trunk lid.

Abdel unscrewed the 2-litre Butagaz cartridge from the lantern.

The hiss of escaping butane gas filled his ears. He flicked the wheel on a disposable lighter, touched it to the cartridge. A jet of pale-blue flame lanced upward. He crouched, slid the cartridge across the concrete floor of the warehouse until it was directly beneath the Fiat's gas tank, the blue flame spreading wide where it hit the metal.

Jalloud settled into the plush back seat of the rented Mercedes as Abdel slid behind the wheel. They drove out of the warehouse and a hundred yards down the street, pulled over to the curb.

Seventeen minutes after Abdel had struck his lighter, the Fiat erupted in a ball of fire that lit up the whole block. A split second later, the sound of the explosion hammered them, the shock wave making the Mercedes rock on its springs.

Jalloud twisted in his seat to look behind him. Every window in the warehouse had been blown out. There was glass all over the street, and the building had already begun to burn.

Jalloud leaned forward, tapped Abdel on the shoulder. The Mercedes slipped smoothly away from the curb. It was time to check on the squad of men waiting for Charlie at his apartment. Jalloud smiled, remembering an English expression he had heard during one of his trips to London.

No rest for the wicked.

Downey had an early breakfast of fried eggs, hash browns and sausages, and then went for a walk along the esplanade, towards the Egyptian Museum. The distance from the embassy to the museum was only just over half a mile, and the pathway for the most part was flat or even slightly downhill. It was an easy journey, scenic as hell. Downey made a point of taking his time. He had a few things to think about. The murders on Gezira had taken place at a Libyan safe house. The way the whole caper had gone down, combined with Charlie's description of the two hit men, made Downey pretty sure they'd been Libyan. Why would the goddamn fucking Libyans take out one of their own houses? He could think of only one reason. Of more pressing concern was the encoded fax he'd received late the previous night, from Miami. Liam O'Brady hadn't been on the flight out of Bogota. Very bad news indeed.

Downey dawdled along the riverbank, admiring the feluccas, glints of sunlight on the slow-moving surface of the Nile, the magpie clusters of sun-burnt tourists in their gaudy new holiday clothes.

It took him almost forty-five minutes to reach the tended-to-death grounds of the museum, and by then he was absolutely certain that he wasn't being followed. Still, he took the routine precaution of waiting until the two lead taxis in the waiting rank had been taken before he chose a cab himself.

The driver smelled of onions and garlic. His meter was broken, or more likely he'd deliberately disconnected it. Downey negotiated a rate to the airport and return. He was careful not to be too generous or too cheap. He didn't want the driver remembering him. Another routine precaution. He was a very cautious man. Liked to kid himself that it was why he'd managed to survive so long, but didn't really believe it. Toiling for the CIA had its moments, but firemen and bus drivers led far more dangerous lives.

The cabbie clashed gears, cursed noisily and bulled into traffic. A horn blared. He spat contemptuously out his window and turned to grin at Downey, flashed a mouthful of pearly-whites that might have been made in the crockery factories in the North of England.

Downey nodded politely, acknowledging the man's verve and skill. They were drifting into oncoming traffic. A huge semi-trailer carrying a load of chickens deigned to use its air-horn but did not give way. Downey's face registered horror, imminent death. The cabbie turned unhurriedly to see what all the fuss was about. His eyes widened. He yanked at the wheel and the taxi swerved sharply. The semi roared past, taking the taxi's side mirror with it. Just another near miss, but the cabbie hunched his shoulders dejectedly – he'd been the first to blink.

At the turn-off to the airport progress was slowed by a construction site, a flagman and a waiting line of huge articulated trucks. The air was thick with concrete dust and the buzz and roar of heavy machinery. Downey rolled up his window. The driver considered trying to negotiate a higher fare based on his unexpected delay, took a quick look at Downey's pinched face and decided not to bother.

Anticipated headwinds off the coast had failed to materialize; the flight in from Paris had arrived a full twenty minutes ahead of schedule. Downey didn't bother to check the carousel. By now, his crew would be in the bar.

He found Sweets and Mungo sitting at a window table, drinking sweating bottles of Fürstenburg at three dollars a pop. Sweets was fingering his beaded hair and chatting up a couple of German girls at an adjoining table. Mungo was stroking his scar and staring morosely out of the big picture window at an Air Italia 747 which was just sitting there doing nothing. Sweets blew the fräuleins a kiss as Downey approached the table. Mungo continued to stare out of the window.

Downey pulled out a chair, made himself comfortable. He said, "Where the hell is Liam?"

Sweets gulped some Fürstenburg, eyed Downey warily over the rim of the bottle. Finally he said, "Want a beer?"

"A fucking beer is the last fucking thing I want. Jesus, you look like that movie star, Bo something. How in hell did you get past the metal detectors, with all that shit in your hair?" Downey turned to Mungo, who was still staring at the 747. "Is Liam here, or what?"

"Only in spirit," said Mungo. "And we can't even be sure about that."

Downey sighed heavily. He'd had a premonition. He noticed that the two German girls were listening in, being obvious about it. Maybe they were hustling Sweets and Mungo and maybe they were just fine-tuning their English, getting a free lesson. Or maybe it wasn't that simple. Downey was aware that he had tendencies towards paranoia. In his occupation it was nothing to be ashamed of. "Got any luggage?" he said. Sweets pointed at the black leather shoulder bag on the carpet between his feet. "There's a cab outside," said Downey. "You can tell me all about it on the way into the city."

Sweets waved his hand at the empties. "Your party, your tab."

Downey was too depressed to argue. He threw some money on the table and got up and started to make his way through the lounge. He was no fan of airports. Where else in the world could you drink overpriced beer, have a surly waiter serve you inedible food, and suck vaporized kerosene into your lungs while you suffered through your meal?

Outside, Sweets slipped in next to the driver, so Mungo had no choice but to sit in the back with Downey. The driver glanced quickly at Sweets, taking in the pink shirt and bright yellow jacket, the popsicle-coloured pants.

"What the fuck you lookin' at?" said Sweets.

The driver immediately launched into a bitter tirade, complaining about how long he'd been kept waiting, the boredom he'd suffered and income he'd lost.

"Shut up and drive," said Downey. He turned to Mungo Martin. "For Christ's sake, where in hell is O'Brady?"

"We sent you a telegram."

"I didn't get it."

Mungo twisted in his seat. He was a big man, and there wasn't much room to spare. "We figured as much, when you sent us three tickets, instead of two."

Downey yanked a Baby Ruth out of his pocket, stripped away the wrapper and began gnawing at his frustration. Foster liked to ride him about his eating habits. Fine. Downey had decided long ago that he'd rather be a little on the chunky side than riddled with bleeding ulcers.

"It happened about a month ago," said Mungo. "We heard about a freshly planted coca field, a good-sized one, maybe three acres. It was on the side of a hill, tiered. Real pretty." Mungo shook his head. "Colombia can be a beautiful country, you know? The sun way up in the sky, plants throwing a web of shadows on the ground. The earth is a reddish colour, Jack. The coca leaves dance in the breeze and they shine like silver. Every once in a while a big flock of parrots rattles through the air, screaming like crazy."

Mungo smiled faintly, not showing his teeth. "I asked Liam once, what the hell you think they're yelling at each other. Know what he said?"

Downey bit a big chunk off his Baby Ruth.

"Have a nice day," said Mungo.

Downey chewed slowly on the candy. Making it last, not saying anything. His cheeks bulged.

After a few minutes Mungo said, "Up at the high end of the field there was a little wooden building about the size of a toolshed. I went over and checked it out. Nothing in there but some bales of empty sacks. For collecting the coca leaves, understand?" Mungo looked down at his hands. "It was a beautiful day. Clear sky, bit of a breeze crawling up the side of the hill. We weren't sure what to do with the field. Burn it, natch, but that wouldn't be easy 'cause the plants were young and kind of spread out, so they'd have room to grow."

Downey watched Mungo's hands twist and pull at each other. The way Mungo'd started his tale of woe told him everything he needed to know about how it was going to end.

"It'd been a long hike in," Mungo continued. "We were tired, worn out. The three of us talked it over for a while and then decided to do it the easy way. Plant a couple dozen anti-personnel mines and get the hell out."

The mines were eight inches across and three inches deep. The standard pattern was to bury most of them around the perimeter of the coca field and then scatter the remainder randomly through the heart of the field, among the plants. Except for the detonator elements, the devices were all plastic and high explosives – virtually impossible to find with a metal detector. There was very little shrapnel, but if you happened to step on one, it was time to kiss your leg goodbye. Out there in the jungle, a bad wound meant a slow and agonizing death if you happened to be alone, a bullet in the head if you were among friends.

The first blast usually resulted in a work-to-rule situation, and the promise of large cash bonuses. A second or at most third explosion almost always resulted in the abandonment of the crop. Downey pictured Liam O'Brady victimized by a careless moment. The mine going off with a heavy percussive blast, like a great big firecracker. Liam's body catapulting through the smoke. Splashes of blood and a red pulp where his foot used to be. Parrots screaming in the trees. *Have a nice day! Have a nice day!*

"It took us about an hour to bury the mines," said Mungo. "Liam worked the high end of the field. When we were finished, me and Hubie started up the hill towards him, keeping off to the side. We were maybe a hundred feet away when Liam went inside the shed."

They were stopped at an intersection, first in line, waiting for a traffic cop to wave them through. Mungo watched a bus grind past. There were people clinging to the doors and open windows, up on the roof. Some of them didn't appear to have any contact with the vehicle, but were simply hanging on to other passengers. How in hell could you collect fares in a situation like that? Jesus, he'd thought New York was crowded.

"Then what?" said Downey.

"He was only inside the shack for maybe ten seconds, walked out backwards, bent over double. Holding on to his stomach. Staggering. We ran up the hill. He had a machete in him, the handle pushed right up against his belly, two feet of blade sticking out his back. He turned around and looked at us and fell over on his side. I remember the dust puffing up when he hit the ground. Red, you know? By the time we got there, well . . ."

Mungo gave Downey a sidelong, apologetic look, like a dog that's chewed up the morning paper. It was as if he was pleading with him, asking for forgiveness. Downey shook off the notion. Mungo Martin wasn't the kind of guy who needed a pat on the back.

"There was a little kid squeezed into a corner near a bale of sacks. Sitting on the floor, curled up like a ball. Trying to make himself look even smaller than he already was. I grabbed a handful of hair and dragged him outside. Pot belly and big brown eyes. Raggedy pants, no shirt or shoes. Nice white teeth because he was only about eight years old, still too young to chew coca leaves.

"Kid took a peek at Liam with the machete in him and his blood turning the dust to mud, started crying. Little bugger probably panicked when Liam walked in on him, hardly knew what he was doing when he knifed him. But so what, right?" Mungo paused, thinking about it. "What he'd done, was done forever."

The traffic cop blew a whistle and waved them through the intersection.

"We made him help dig Liam's grave," Mungo continued. "A good hole, Jack. Nice and deep. We laid him in there and covered him up and tamped him down."

Mungo was rubbing his scar, rubbing it hard.

"Me'n Hubie flipped a coin. I lost. Put a three-round burst right through the kid's heart. Little fucker died so fast his shadow still don't know what to do with itself."

Downey popped the rest of the Baby Ruth into his mouth. There was melted chocolate on his fingers. He licked them clean, making a big production out of it, minimizing the horror in his own sweet way. There had been an accident somewhere ahead and traffic had slowed to a crawl, the taxi moving in spasmodic jerks, like a mechanized cripple. The temperature was in the high eighties. There was no wind. The air was so hot and dry that each breath Downey took seemed to scorch the back of his throat.

Mungo put on a pair of mirror sunglasses and sat quietly with his hands in his lap. In the front seat, Sweets seemed to have fallen asleep.

The coca leaves rippled silver in the wind. A flight of parrots drifted like fragments of a shattered rainbow across the cobalt blue sky. Liam O'Brady strolled into a shack the size of an outhouse, staggered out clutching his guts, punctured by an eight-year-old kid wielding a yard of rusty steel.

Downey shook his head. He couldn't picture it, not really. Liam hadn't been some fuzzy-cheeked asshole fresh out of Langley. Liam was no dummy. Liam knew the ropes. Downey sighed wearily. Nobody was perfect. What it all boiled down to was how badly someone wanted to take you out, how lucky you happened to be as you danced on the needle-sharp point of that particular sliver of time. Liam was gone. Snuffed by a fucking toddler. And that was that.

Hubie Sweets twisted in his seat and shook Downey's shoulder, rousing him from his dreams of death. The cab was parked in front of the museum.

"Real nice place," said Sweets. "You own it, or just renting?"

"The hotel's a couple of blocks away. We'll walk."

"In this heat?"

"Got to acclimatize sooner or later, Hubie."

There was a gap in the traffic streaming along Shari Qasr el Nil. The three men hurried across the wide street towards the hotel.

"The Hilton," said Sweets. "Oh well, I guess it's better than camping out in the woods."

"I put you in a nice suite on the third floor, view of the river."

"What river?"

"The Nile, Hubie."

"Oh yeah. Right. So what's the schedule? We got a little time to relax, see the pyramids, all that shit?"

Downey didn't answer. His mind was elsewhere. The kid with the machete had left him with a major problem, a legacy of disaster.

They walked in silence to the hotel, entered the lobby. Downey felt the shock of the air-conditioning, his skin reacting to the abrupt change of temperature. He waved off a bellboy as they moved towards the bank of elevators.

There was a clot of tourists in the lobby, festooned with guide books and Instamatics, sunglasses. Red faces, red necks. They looked as if they were waiting for something, but Downey wouldn't have bet a used Kleenex any of them knew what it was. He punched the UP button.

A fat man in a safari outfit stared at Downey and his two huge black companions. Downey gave him a look. The man swallowed, and turned away.

Downey concentrated on the indicator needle. The elevator was on the third floor, and falling. The clot of tourists moved towards him, anticipating touchdown.

The elevator doors slid open. Everybody pressed inside. Downey hit the third floor button with the heel of his hand. He smelled suntan lotion, expensive perfume, sweat. He caught the safari outfit staring at him again and snarled at the guy, actually showed his teeth. The man put his arm around a woman so ugly she had to be his wife. The doors slid open. Sweets and Mungo followed Downey out of the elevator. They walked down the thickly carpeted hall to the third-floor suite. Downey unlocked the door and pushed it open on a roomful of pale-green light. He went over to the balcony and looked down at the river, almost directly below. There was an island off to the right. Gezira. You wouldn't be able to hit it with a stone, but it was close.

Mungo said, "What we doing here, Jack?"

Downey shrugged. Without Liam, he had nothing. He said, "Enjoy the pool, have some fun. There's a casino up on the top floor. What you lose at the tables comes out of your own pocket."

"I wanna see the pyramids," said Sweets.

"I'll call you tomorrow. Sometime before lunch."

Downey let himself out. The automatic lock clicked softly.

"Pretty good bullshit," said Sweets. "The kid had a machete, did he?"

"What was I supposed to tell him, the truth?"

Mungo was staring out the window at the Nile, but what he was seeing was Liam O'Brady taking a snap shot at a young boy leading a mule down a switchback mountain path. Some kid they'd never seen before, just happened upon by accident. Faceless at a range of three hundred yards, his face mostly blown away when they got to him, lying motionless on the stony ground.

Too much for Mungo. He'd taken Liam's rifle away from him and then killed him with a single blow to the neck. Sweets had been a little surprised, but not much. The mule was loaded with five gallon tins of kerosene, used to soften the coca leaves. They walked the animal a little ways down the path and shot it between the eyes.

Sweets kept watch while Mungo dug a hole for Liam, rolled him in.

The boy was left where he'd fallen. It wasn't that they didn't care about him enough to bury him. The thinking was that he'd been somebody's baby. Whoever loved him had a right to find him, know what happened to him, mourn his death and give him a proper funeral.

They walked down the trail past the dead mule. The animal burped, venting gas.

The jungle was silent, the parrots speechless. It had not been a very nice day.

"How's it going?" Downey said.

Charlie blinked, trying to bring his small piece of the world into focus. He was lying on his back on the narrow bed, hands clasped behind his head. He'd been dreaming, in an unfocused, fragmented way, about his life in Los Angeles, the life he thought he'd left behind. His hair was rumpled. He needed a shave.

Downey waited.

"It's hot," said Charlie at last.

Downey nodded his agreement. The room was stuffy, temperature in the high seventies. Copies of the *International Herald Tribune* and several Cairo papers lay on the bed. *El Akhbar, El Ahram* . . . there was even a copy of the *Egyptian Gazette*, a tiny English language paper with a circulation of only five or ten thousand.

A fitful breeze ruffled the topmost pages of the *Tribune*, but had no discernible effect upon the temperature of the room. Downey had enlisted the aid of the marine stationed in the corridor to help him pry the window open six inches, but it hadn't seemed to help.

Downey indicated the papers. "Find anything in there about the break-in?"

"No, nothing."

Downey said, "There was something other than money in the safe, wasn't there?"

Charlie, caught off-guard, found himself nodding.

"What was it?" Downey's rotund, seamless face was very quiet. His eyes were dark and solemn, but with no hint of recrimination.

"A list of names."

"Tell me about it." Downey wanted to know if his name was mentioned. He told himself he was too shy to ask.

Charlie hesitated. "There isn't much to tell. An envelope was stuck in between the two bundles of money. I took it by accident, didn't even know it was there."

"You remember any of the names on the list?"

"No."

"Was the list written or typed?"

"Written."

"In what language?"

"I don't know, nothing I recognized. It could have been some kind of code."

Downey gave him a sceptical look. "You're sure it wasn't English?"

Charlie found himself telling Downey everything he could remember about the buff envelope and the single flimsy sheet of paper it had contained. There wasn't much Charlie recalled that seemed important or useful to Downey, but he was a practised and a skilful listener. He rarely interrupted but frequently murmured small sounds of encouragement. When Charlie finished all he said was, "You've got a good memory, Charlie. A sharp mind, despite all the rust. What the hell were you doing wasting your time in Cairo?"

"Call it a middle-age crisis. I was saving money to go back home. Another couple of months, I'd have been on my way."

"You're supposed to be a wealthy businessman. Why didn't you pick up a phone and tell your accountant you wanted a walletful of cash?"

Charlie shrugged. "I screwed up all by myself. I figured I'd at least find my own way back." He lit a cigarette, offered the pack.

"No thanks. I don't smoke."

Charlie remembered Jimmy Abrams' reaction when he'd offered him a cigarette. Abrams had taken the cigarette but held it in the awkward, uncertain way of someone who didn't smoke. It was a clumsy deception, and it had not endeared Charlie to him. Abrams was a confidence man, a trickster. With Jack Downey it was just the opposite. Downey almost made it a point of honour not to be too congenial.

"Oh yeah," said Downey, "how's the tooth?"

"Just fine, thanks."

"Jensen said it was nothing, a filling that had to be replaced. I told him to do a quality job, that you were a quality kind of guy."

"I appreciate it," said Charlie.

"Hey, no problem."

Downey let Charlie smoke his cigarette, giving him a chance to cool down, relax. After a few minutes he started asking him questions about his apartment in the Old City. Once again, the abrupt change of pace took Charlie by surprise. He described the place in general terms. Downey let him ramble on about the low water pressure and the sagging bed, the stained-glass window and view of the street. Gently, he led Charlie into specifics. The apartment was on the second floor. How many steps to the landing? How large was the landing? Was there a light? How sturdy was the door? What sort of lock did it have? The questions went on and on, but the pace was so leisurely that Charlie never felt the slightest sense of urgency, pressure.

By the time Downey had finished, they'd gone over every square inch of the apartment in detail, and he felt confident he knew the exact placement of virtually every mote of dust. Standing, he looked down at Charlie and said, "I wouldn't mention our little chat to Jimmy, if I were you."

"Why not?"

"I don't think the list of names you torched in the coffee-house is probably of any real importance to us. So I'm going to forget about it. But Jimmy isn't like me, and neither is Foster. See, Dick and Jimmy are the kind of guys who believe *all* information is potentially valuable. They could go after you, know what I mean?"

"No," Charlie said, "I don't think I do."

"There's a whole fucking pharmacy down there in the basement, Charlie. Drugs you've never even heard of, and believe me, you don't want to know about. Kind of stuff you can't get at your local drugstore, catch my drift?" Downey grinned mirthlessly. "There are people here who call Jimmy 'Mr Mosquito'. Know why? Because he likes to use the needle. Gets a kick out of it. I've watched him. He'd poke you full of holes, enjoy every minute of it. Drain you dry, kiddo. By the time he finished with you there'd be nothing left but skin and bones."

Downey moved towards the door.

"When am I getting out of here?" said Charlie.

"If it were up to me, you'd be gone," said Downey as the door closed behind him.

Charlie lit a fresh cigarette. He decided to take Downey's advice, and keep his mouth shut about the list of names he'd stolen from the safe. He wouldn't mention Downey's interest in his apartment, either. He trusted Downey. He considered himself a good judge of men, and he knew, instinctively, that Downey was telling the truth about Abrams.

But it was Downey, not Abrams, who was the expert in the art of deception. It was Downey who had a face for every face he met, could put a chameleon to shame. And it was Downey they called 'Mosquito', who took pleasure in using his needles to make a meal of a man, bleed him dry, and then, without a moment's remorse, discard the husk.

13

When Downey had finished scaring Charlie McPhee's pants off, he took the elevator down to the embassy's staff restaurant. All that talking had left him with an overpowering thirst. He bought two large glasses of pink lemonade, found a table and sat down. He had some serious thinking to do. Only problem was, there wasn't anything much to think about.

He drank a mouthful of lemonade, gulping it down. The juice was so cold the back of his throat went numb. He thumped the glass down on the table. He was running out of time and there he was sitting on his ass like a dummy, letting the minutes tick away while he waited for his goddamn lemonade to warm up. What a dope.

Angrily, he pushed away from the table and made his way out of the room.

At the Hilton, he found Sweets and Mungo enjoying the pool. Mungo was working out, swimming slow and ponderous laps. Sweets was taking it easy at the deep end, his muscular forearms resting on the lip of the pool as he spoke softly to a blonde girl in a yellow string bikini.

Sweets saw Downey a fraction of a second before Downey saw him. Even while he was hustling the blonde, he was constantly monitoring the situation. It was a reflex action, like breathing. He gave Downey a terse little nod. Downey kept moving. He strolled past Sweets and the overfilled bikini, sat down at a vacant patio table in the shade at the shallow end of the pool.

There were four chairs at the table. Downey sat with his back to the sun, facing the water. The blonde was squatting on her haunches, leaning down towards Sweets, the weight of her breasts straining against the yellow material of her bathing suit. She said something and Sweets laughed, throwing back his head. He reached up and stroked the inside of the girl's thigh, his fingers moving like long black shadows across her golden skin. He said something to her and she nodded. He blew her a kiss and sank beneath the surface. Downey saw his distorted form rotate into a compacted ball and then straighten as he kicked out, propelling himself like a human torpedo on an interception course with Mungo, who was still churning heavily up and down the pool.

A waiter drifted towards Downey through the rippling heatwaves rising up from the pool's concrete apron. The waiter was thin and dark, no more than sixteen years old. He was wearing a spotless white shirt, baggy trousers and a cheap gold-coloured watch that was far too large for his narrow wrist.

Downey ordered three bottles of Löwenbräu. The local beer, Stella, was perfectly adequate, but he figured that since the Company was paying, he might as well order whatever was most expensive. The Company had endless sums of money and Downey was fond of spending it. It was a weakness, he supposed.

Sweets and Martin were at the near end of the pool now, both of them striding effortlessly through the knee-deep water, kicking up a froth. Mungo was a couple of inches taller and fifty pounds heavier than Sweets, who was six foot two and weighed in at one-eighty. Not an ounce of fat on either of them. Mungo had the bone structure of a mastodon. But, in a fight, Downey would give Sweets the edge, because his temperament was a shade more ruthless. Downey squinted across the sparkling rectangle of water, at the blonde. He wondered if she liked it as much as she thought she did. If not, she was in for a big surprise.

Mungo padded across the concrete, sat beside him on his left. Sweets took the chair on Downey's right, moving the chair around to face the pool more directly, aluminium scraping on concrete. He waved at the girl and she waved back.

"This gonna take long?" Sweets said.

"Doesn't matter how long it takes, Hubie. When we're finished she'll still be too young for you."

"Jealous, huh."

"Bet your ass." Downey tilted his chair back to give the waiter easier access to the table. The kid's fancy gold watch was a dimestore copy of a Rolex. It was ten minutes fast.

Mungo leaned away from the table, tilted his head sideways and briskly ran his fingers through his modified afro. A mist of chlorinated water droplets hung in the air, evaporated into nothingness.

Downey poured some beer into his glass, ran his thumb across the condensation on the side of the bottle.

"So what's up?" said Sweets.

"Bored, are we?"

"Any minute now." Sweets was concentrating on the bikini, eating her up. She was talking to a guy in his early fifties, heavy tan, shock of white hair. Probably the dude was her father, but you never could tell.

"Better watch your step, Hubie."

"Hey, all I want to do is fuck her."

Downey nodded, letting it go. "You see the pyramids yet?"

"Went to the casino instead," said Mungo. "Man, I thought *I* was a fool with money. You should see some of those guys from Kuwait and Saudi Arabia go at it. Win or lose, they just don't care."

"Oil money," said Sweets. "Now I've seen where it goes, I won't feel so bad next time I pump a twenty-dollar bill into my Chevvy."

"Pretty soon," said Downey, "you can throw away the Chev and buy yourself a Rolls. Get the chauffeur to fill it up while you fool around in the backseat with someone looks just like her." Downey jerked his thumb at the blonde.

Sweets and Mungo sat quietly, waiting. Mungo was using his glass, but Sweets drank his beer straight from the bottle.

There were two bulky black leather valises under the table, sitting side by side between Downey's feet. He used the toe of his right foot to push one of the bags gently towards Sweets. The bag bumped against Sweets' ankle. He glanced at it, raised an enquiring eyebrow.

"A present? For little old me?"

"Just don't try to check it through customs." Downey shoved the other bag across to Mungo.

Sweets picked up the bag, zipped it open. Inside was a brand-new Uzi submachine-gun and three fully-loaded spare magazines. A noise suppressor. A knife with a teflon-coated six-inch carbon steel blade. Assorted concussion and fragmentation grenades. A fourteen-shot Browning 9mm automatic and a pair of shiny stainless steel handcuffs. A basic kit. Sweets drained his beer and helped himself to the dregs of Downey's bottle. He said, "When's the party, Jack?"

Downey glanced around the patio. Tourists. The men drinking American beer, their women sipping from frosted glasses topped off with sprigs of greenery and small chunks of pastel fruit run through with plastic swords. Downey wondered just how different this Hilton pool could possibly be from a Hilton pool in, say, Topeka, Kansas. He scanned the crowd again, trying to turn the homogenous mass into a series of individuals. There could be a dozen shotgun mikes pointed at him, he wouldn't have the faintest idea. He said, "Let's go upstairs, where it's more private," pushed his chair away from the table, and stood up.

"Gimme a couple of minutes," said Sweets. He'd lost his bikini but now he'd found her again, over by the diving board, perched on the lip of the pool with those long legs dangling in the water.

"Right now," said Downey. He walked briskly away from the table, towards the hotel. Mungo grabbed his bag and headed after him.

Sweets thought it over for a moment or two, squinting as he stared from under the shade of the striped umbrella into the spark and ripple of the pool. He waited five or maybe six seconds, just long enough to make his point, and then blew his girl a kiss, and fell in behind.

In the suite, Downey made himself comfortable on the sofa, sitting on the middle cushion with his arms spread wide along the backrest. He ran his fingers across the nubbly, sand-coloured fabric, picked at a loose thread and held it up to the light to examine it with a critical eye.

Mungo sprawled out in an armchair, waited. Sweets snuck over to the window, discreetly eyed the pool.

"There's an apartment I need sanitized," said Downey. He took out his notebook. There was a loose sheet of paper inside. He unfolded it and flattened it out on his knee. On one side there was a line drawing in black ink of Charlie's street. On the flip side was a detailed sketch of Charlie's two-room apartment, including the location of the furniture.

"Come on over here and take a look at this," Downey said to Sweets.

Sweets ambled over with his hands in his pockets, a picture of studied disinterest.

"I cruised the place a couple of hours ago," Downey said. "There's one man in the street and another at the door. Could be a third guy at the top of the landing, but I doubt it. Charlie tells me there's no place to hide."

"How many inside?" said Mungo.

"I'd guess no less than two and no more than three. Outside guys didn't look all that alert. Probably don't think Charlie's stupid enough to go home. Or expect any trouble if he does."

"You coming along, Jack?"

"Love to, but I have to stay home and wash my hair."

"So who the fuck is Charlie?" said Sweets.

"Charlie drives you to the apartment. Waits while you tidy up. Drives you back to the hotel."

"A specialist."

"If I gave him a gun, he'd probably shoot you in your great big foot. And then you wouldn't have anything to stick in your great big mouth, would you?"

"He *can* drive though, can't he?"

"He'll drive you crazy," said Downey. "Grab all the paper you can find. Any drugs or related paraphernalia you can lay your hands on. Anything incriminating."

"We'll rip the joint apart," said Sweets.

Downey gave him a sour look. To Mungo he said, "The people watching the place. If you can, bring one back."

"Yeah, okay."

"Don't kill anybody unless you have to."

"Do my best."

"Be nice to make a dry run," said Sweets. "Not have to go in cold."

"There'll be a black Citroën outside the hotel at ten o'clock sharp," said Downey. He stood up, moved towards the door. "You need me in the meantime, leave a message with the front desk."

Mungo showed Downey out, locked the door. When he came back into the living room, Sweets was at the window, peering down at the pool through a pair of Zeiss 7x50s. He scanned the pool and adjacent area and then threw the binoculars down on the sofa, his face slack with disappointment.

"Gone?"

"Her name was Sarah. She's from Idaho. I was gonna give her a swimming lesson."

"The breaststroke, right?"

"You know how often I get a chance to jump a blonde from Idaho?"

"My guess is never." Mungo chuckled, pleased with his wit.

At five minutes past ten, Sweets finally got his hair just right. They took the elevator down to the lobby. Through the glass doors they could see a black Citroën parked at the curb, a man sitting bolt upright behind the wheel.

"He looks tense."

"White, too," said Sweets. "Let's ride in the back, talk real loud about how his ears stick out."

"And how there's dirt on his collar."

"Oh my, you are wicked!"

They crossed the sidewalk to the car. Mungo yanked open the door. Charlie had been staring anxiously at the hotel, looking for them so hard he'd looked right through them. Mungo slid across to the far side of the seat and Sweets got in beside him, slammed shut the door.

Charlie put the car in gear and released the clutch. The Citroën shuddered and jerked forward. The engine died. Mungo looked at Sweets and rolled his eyes in mock dismay. Charlie restarted the engine. He released the emergency brake and put the car in gear. They pulled smoothly away from the curb.

Sweets leaned forward, patted Charlie gently on the shoulder. "Can you sing?"

Charlie shook his head, no.

"Then turn the fucking radio on, man. Let's grab some music."

"No rap," said Mungo. "We can't stand that shit."

Charlie took a peek in the rearview mirror. The big one looked like he'd once played linebacker for the Los Angeles Raiders, but got kicked out of the league for excessive use of steroids and violence. His pal looked like he'd never have been allowed to play in the first place. They both looked mean as hell and twice as mad. Sweets caught his eye. He leaned forward to switch on the radio. The dial was between stations and the volume was turned up high. The Citroën filled with the scratchy sound of static.

"*Oh yeah,*" said Sweets. "*That's just perfect!*"

14

Abdel picked up Marilyn. The back of her head had been entirely blown away, but she was still dangerous because there were plenty of splinters and they were sharp. He sat her in the palm of his hand, arranged her legs on either side of his wrist. "How are you feeling," he said. "Do you have a headache?" Her chin fell on her chest. Both her bright-blue eyes fell out. Abdel caught one but the other rolled under the bed. He got down on his hands and knees. Omar Jalloud kicked him in the slats. Abdel shrieked, scuttled out from under the bed.

Omar's face was like the dark side of the moon. He stared at the bright-blue eye lying in the cupped palm of Abdel's hand. Finally, he said, "I'm hungry. Let's get something to eat."

15

The larger of the two blacks leaned forward and patted Charlie on the shoulder. His fingers were long and slightly spatulate, the flesh beneath the nails almost the same shade of pink as the dancing elephants on his pale-yellow shirt. He said, "I'm Mungo Martin. My buddy's name is Hubie Sweets. You must be Charlie, right?"

Charlie nodded, keeping his eyes on the traffic. He was nervous. His last time behind the wheel had been the ride out to LAX in the white Seville. A long time ago. He swerved to avoid running down a fat man in a dusty red fez riding an oil-spewing moped. Traffic in Los Angeles was nothing compared to Cairo. Back home, people drove too fast but not necessarily recklessly. In Cairo it was just the opposite: a dent or scratch was something to be proud of – a mark of courage.

"How long you been working for Jack?" said Sweets.

Charlie glanced at the Citroën's clock. "About five minutes."

Sweets laughed like a hyena, slapped his thigh.

"I don't think that was supposed to be funny," said Mungo.

Sweets stopped laughing.

Charlie parked the Citroën a hundred yards from his apartment, straddling the curb so he wouldn't block the narrow road. Sweets and Mungo had spent much of the ride arming themselves, dipping into Downey's black bags with mock cries of delight.

The street was dark now, empty except for the odd hurrying pedestrian. In a few minutes the muezzin – live or on cassette tape – would call the faithful to prayer for the fifth and final time that day. Sweets and Mungo had timed their arrival to coincide with that moment, but the men guarding Charlie's apartment had not abandoned their positions. If they were Muslims, they were lapsed Muslims. Charlie turned off the engine. The whisper of the air-conditioner faded.

"Stay down low so nobody can see you," Sweets said to Charlie. "You hear shots, start the car and cruise real slow down the street towards the apartment." He squeezed Charlie's arm. "Take off without us, we'll catch up with you sooner or later. Drag you into your kitchen in the middle of the night. Lay you down on the stove and turn on all four burners. Fry you in your jammies."

Sweets and Mungo got out of the car. Charlie watched over the rim of the steering wheel as they strolled down the street.

As they drew near Charlie's apartment, Sweets' stride faltered. He stopped walking, a bewildered expression on his face.

"Something wrong?" Mungo's voice was loud and abrasive, bitter.

Sweets slipped a business card out of his wallet. He stared at the card, frowned. "We must've taken a wrong turn somewhere. I think we're lost."

Mungo shot his cuff. He peered angrily at his watch. "You're always running late, Hubie. What you think you are, a fucking train?"

"Hey, I'm doing my best."

"Maybe that's the problem!"

Sweets produced a map of the city. He turned it sideways and then upside down.

Mungo lunged at the map. "Gimme that!"

The argument had carried them to the bottom of the enclosed wooden stairway leading to Charlie's second-floor apartment. Sweets gave every indication of being pleasantly surprised when he finally noticed the two Arabs loitering in the shadows. He stuck his hand in his jacket pocket. The men stiffened, but before they could react Sweets hauled out his phrase book and began to thumb through the pages.

"I'mil ma'ruf," he said, "Do me a favour."

Mungo smiled at the men, his expression hopeful but also a little worried. Sweets grabbed him by the elbow and dragged him towards the stairs. Mungo held back. He glanced along the length of the deserted street, and then quickly up towards the top of the stairs.

The landing was deserted.

One of the men said something in Arabic. His partner laughed, flashing teeth that were badly neglected except for the two incisors, which were made of stainless steel, and were unusually long and pointed.

Sweets thrust the map of Cairo towards the man with the steel teeth. He instinctively glanced down, and Sweets kicked him in the groin. The man gasped in pain and sank to his knees. His left hand went to his crotch but his right hand fumbled under his jacket. At the same time, he tried to bite Sweets in the leg. Sweets chopped him in the side of the neck, just below the ear. The Arab's eyes rolled up, twin moons of dirty yellow. He fell over on his side, shivered and lay still.

"You kill him?" Mungo had the other one up against the wall of the building, his knife at the man's throat.

"Unless he died of old age." Sweets picked up the corpse in a fireman's lift.

Mungo moved the blade of the knife. "Speak English, pal?" The man licked his lips, swallowed noisily. Mungo spun him around, pushed him towards the stairway leading up to the apartment.

"Ever been a tour guide?" said Sweets.

"No, why?"

"You got the right attitude, is all."

At the top of the stairs Sweets slipped the body off his shoulders and leaned it up against the door. Mungo gestured that he wanted the second man to support his dead companion. The man looked panic-stricken, ready to bolt. Mungo pointed his silenced Uzi at him. Sweets pounded on the door with the butt of his gun. There was a soft query from within. The man holding up his dead partner screamed a warning and at the same time twisted sideways and tried to jump over the railing. Mungo killed him with a three-round burst.

Sweets emptied his magazine into the flimsy wooden door. There was a burst of answering fire. He inserted a fresh magazine. Mungo shot the hinges off the door and kicked hard. Both men swept the room with their weapons. There was a moment of silence and then the darkness was split by a sequence of red flashes.

"Fuck this," said Sweets, "let's nuke the bastards." He pulled the pin and tossed a fragmentation grenade into the apartment. Someone inside shouted a warning. The grenade exploded. In the bluish-white magnesium glare, Sweets caught a quick glimpse of a man cartwheeling through the air. Then a hot gust of wind staggered him, and he heard the cheerful sound of glass shattering.

There were three men in the apartment. Two of them were dead and the third was dying. Sweets slapped out a small fire that had started on the bed. The air was thick with smoke and the stink of cordite. Grey light filtered in through the shattered remains of a huge stained-glass window. There was blood on Mungo's arm. Sweets said, "You hit?"

"Flesh wound."

"Aren't they all."

One of the dead men was lying on the floor at the foot of the bed. Sweets went through his pockets, found a pack of cigarettes and disposable lighter, a quantity of lint. The second dead man was, inexplicably, sitting in the sink on a pile of dirty dishes. Sweets rolled him over and patted him down while Mungo rifled the wounded man's pockets.

"Bingo."

"What you got?"

Mungo flipped quickly through a thick wad of papers. "Our chauffeur's passport, tourist visa. Snapshots of the wife and kid." Mungo stuffed his pockets with the scraps and fragments of the life Charlie had left behind.

"Figure that's enough to keep Jack happy?"

"It'll have to do," Mungo had already lost a lot of blood. He felt weak, dizzy. There were sirens in the distance.

"What're we going to tell him, he asks we rousted the joint?"

"Lies," said Mungo. But he went over to the bureau and started pulling out drawers, the bottom drawer first so he wouldn't have to push a drawer back to get at the next one. The bottom three drawers were empty. The top drawer contained an unwashed pair of socks and an empty water glass. Mungo unrolled the socks and turned them inside out. The sirens were very close. He went over to the bed and squeezed the pillow. Nothing in there but feathers. He flipped the mattress upside down. The springs creaked. His arm hurt like hell. The wounded man made a wet, bubbling sound.

Peering through the tinted windshield of the Citroën, Charlie saw Hubie Sweets and Mungo Martin amble down the street, stop to consult the map. He saw two men come out of a doorway, emerge suddenly from the shadows. Sweets showed one of the men the map, abruptly kicked him in the crotch. The man went down and Sweets hit him again. The second man stood motionless. Charlie saw Sweets pick up the man he'd hit. He watched the four men disappear from view as they started up the stairs to his apartment.

With the air-conditioner turned off it soon became hot and stuffy inside the car. Charlie began to sweat. From the apartment came a series of muffled explosions, like corn popping. He craned his neck to look down the dark, empty street. More popping sounds, a brief silence and then a luminous white flash, a tremendous roar.

The stained-glass window bulged outward, exploded in a thousand pieces and fell into the street.

Charlie lit a Cleopatra. He started the car. Even through the closed window, he could hear sirens.

He revved the Citroën's engine, checked to make sure the emergency brake was off, then checked it a second and third time. A crowd began to gather on the street. It was exactly five minutes past eleven, according to the Citroën's digital clock. Charlie rubbed his wrist. He hadn't owned a watch since he'd hawked his Rolex. He remembered the pawnbroker, a big, balding man wearing a permanent frown of suspicion wrapped around a jeweller's eyepiece that seemed to have been screwed into his flesh. There was movement in the crowd, a sense of jostling, compression.

The sirens were very close now, shrill and ecstatic.

He saw Mungo and Sweets reach the crumbling sidewalk and start towards him. Then the crowd swung around in front of the Citroën and blocked his view. He put the car in gear, leaned on the horn. The sound was strident, demanding, vulgar. Very French.

Someone shouted at him, cursing him with a great deal of vigour but not much imagination. A gob of spit landed on the windshield, slithered down the glass. Charlie hit the gas pedal. The car shot forward. He slammed on the brakes, hit the gas again. The crowd evaporated except for one man.

He was in his early twenties, wearing baggy grey pants and a black T-shirt. He had a bandit moustache and small, dark eyes, and he was standing directly in front of the car. His legs were spread wide. He was holding a big chrome-plated pistol in a two-handed grip, the gun pointed at Charlie's face.

In the background, Charlie saw Mungo stumble and fall to one knee, Sweets kneel and help him to his feet. The man with the pistol jerked it sideways, motioning Charlie out of the car.

Charlie took his hands off the steering wheel. He laced his fingers together and put his hands on his head. The sirens seemed to be everywhere now, all around him. He stared at the muzzle of the gun, forced himself to wait, do nothing, stay calm. Sweat poured down his face, into his eyes. His scalp itched. His stomach muscles twitched and jumped. Sweat trickled down his ribs. He willed himself not to blink.

At last, the pistol jerked sideways again, a gesture that was presumptuous and abrupt. In the split second that the gun was pointed away from him, Charlie slammed the gas pedal to the floor. The Citroën lurched forward. There was the dull thud of metal on flesh, and the man with the gun leapt high into the air and came down on the hood. His head smashed into the windshield. The glass frosted over at the epicentre of a series of concentric circles.

Charlie kept his foot down. The man rolled off the hood, vanished into the darkness.

He drove fifty yards down the street, shrieked to a stop next to Mungo and Sweets. Sweets yanked the back door open, bundled Mungo inside and climbed in after him. Charlie hit the gas, acceleration slamming the door shut. The Citroën shot down the narrow street. At the end of the block Charlie braked hard and turned left. A police car rounded the corner and raced towards them, its blue roof light flashing, siren wailing.

"Go right at the bastard," yelled Sweets, "Stomp on it!"

Charlie hesitated. He thought about Jack Downey's description of Egyptian prisons, the fate that awaited him if he were caught. He pressed the gas pedal to the floor.

The police car and the Citroën hurtled towards each other. A collision seemed inevitable. In a moment of inspiration, Charlie switched on his lights, flicked the high beams and leaned on the horn. The squad car veered sharply, hit the curb, flipped on its side. The blue light exploded. The siren howled.

"Turn at the next corner!" yelled Sweets.

Charlie glanced in the rearview mirror. Sweets was making a tourniquet out of Mungo's shirtsleeve.

"How is he?"

Sweets said, "He'll live, if your driving don't kill him."

Charlie turned left and drove two blocks and then made a right. Mungo groaned. A police car came after them from a side street, lights flashing. Charlie made a sharp right turn and slammed on the brakes.

"What the fuck you doing!" Sweets screamed.

There was the shriek of tortured rubber as the driver of the pursuing car realized, too late, that the Citroën had stopped.

Charlie braced himself. The police car skidded to a stop no more than a foot behind the Citroën. All four doors flew open. Charlie put the Citroën in reverse and gunned it. The Citroën's rear bumper hit the police car high, smashed the headlights and drove jagged chunks of grillwork through the radiator. Glass tinkled on the asphalt. Steam hissed in the air. Charlie changed gears and hit the gas. Behind them, there was a ragged volley of pistol shots.

"Nice stunt," said Sweets. "Just don't ever do it again."

"Where to now?"

"We got to get hold of Jack, lose this fucking car."

Charlie found a pay telephone that worked. Following Downey's instructions, they abandoned the bullet-pocked Citroën in an alley behind the Midran Opera House. Mungo had lost consciousness during the ride. Sweets slung him over his shoulder and carried him across Ezbekiya Park to the Puppet Theatre, now empty and dark. Downey was waiting in a black Ford with diplomatic plates. He'd brought an emergency medical kit. "Gimme a hand," said Sweets. Charlie caught a quick glimpse of the exit hole, ruptured flesh and oozing blood.

They sped west through the city, towards the Nile. Sweets squeezed Mungo into Downey's suit jacket. The jacket was several sizes too small, but it covered the wound, bandages, spill of blood.

Mungo's teeth were chattering. His face ran with sweat. Charlie tried not to think about him. He stared out of his window at the lights of the city, the ghastly orange of mercury vapour lamps, thin white of fluorescent tubes, soft blue glow of televisions flickering in the café windows. He wondered if he'd killed the man he'd hit.

By the time they reached the Hilton, Mungo was wide awake, grinding his teeth to stop himself from screaming in pain. Sweets pulled him out of the Ford and dragged him towards the hotel's brightly-lit entrance.

Charlie waited in the car. Downey pointed at him and said, "Beat it." Charlie got out of the car and Downey drove swiftly away.

In the lobby, the desk clerk stared at them but said nothing. Probably thought Mungo was drunk. The elevator carried them up to the third floor. Charlie unlocked the door to their suite, and in they went.

A man sitting on the sofa stood up as they entered the room. He was old and paunchy with Albert Einstein hair, and carried a black leather Gladstone bag. He clucked softly to himself as he cut away the pressure bandage and removed the bloody wad of gauze. Mungo's head lolled on his chest. The doctor removed a hypodermic from his kit, filled it with sixty cc's of a clear fluid, found a vein and injected the drug into Mungo's arm. The effect was immediate. Mungo fell back against the sofa and began to snore.

The doctor cleaned and trimmed the wound. He bit his lower lip as he squinted into the glare of a table lamp, threaded a needle. He stitched the wound shut and applied a dressing, then tossed a plastic vial of pills to Charlie. "Your friend is going to have a hell of a headache when he wakes up. Give him two of those right away, the rest as needed. Don't let him have more than three in any six-hour period."

Charlie nodded.

"When you coming back?" said Sweets.

"In a day or so, to change the bandages." The doctor snapped his bag shut. "I'll find my own way out."

Charlie and Sweets carried Mungo into the bedroom, stretched him out on the bed and pulled the covers over him. Mungo's eyelids fluttered. Sweets rested a hand on his forehead.

"How is he?" said Charlie.

"Too soon to say." Sweets turned off the bedside light. "Want a beer?"

"Yes, please."

Sweets chuckled. "He's deadly, but polite."

Charlie followed Sweets into the kitchenette. Sweets pulled two bottles of Stella beer out of the fridge. He found a bottle-opener, popped the caps and handed a beer to Charlie.

"Here's lookin' at us, kid."

The bottles clinked together. Sweets drank deeply. He wiped his mouth with the back of his hand. "They put up a pretty good fight, whoever they were. One we picked up on the street warned his buddies even though he knew Mungo was gonna punch his ticket."

They were on their second beer when there was a soft knock on the door. Sweets answered it. Downey came in on tiptoe, holding his shoes in his hands, making a joke of it.

"Relax," said Sweets. "You could play the bagpipes, it wouldn't bother him."

Downey helped himself to a beer. "How's the rest of the crew?"

"We're just glad that God was watching over us, is all."

"What happened to the man I hit?" said Charlie.

"Dead and buried. Windshield broke his stupid neck." Downey drank some beer. "Don't feel too bad about it, he'd have shot you if he had the chance." Downey drank some more beer. "What've you got for me, Hubie?"

Sweets waved at the bundle of papers on the coffee table. Downey went over to the couch and sat down. He flipped open Charlie's passport.

The black and white photograph was of a man who seemed much younger than Charlie, and whose easy smile exuded self-confidence. Downey found the Egyptian entry stamp on page three. The remaining pages were blank.

He examined the passport's paper and binding, rubbed the cover between his index finger and his thumb. He'd have the experts at the embassy examine the passport, but he was willing to bet his left lung it was the genuine article. He glanced at the snapshots of the child and said, "Nice kid," then turned his attention to the expired visa. It looked clean. He said, "I want to talk to Hubie for a few minutes. Go take a shower."

Charlie hesitated, then put down his beer and walked out of the room.

Sweets went into the kitchen and grabbed another cold Stella. Killing people was thirsty work.

"How'd Mungo get it?" said Downey.

"When we kicked in the door."

"They had automatic weapons?"

Sweets nodded. "It got real noisy, Jack."

"How many were there?"

"Five."

"Any of them speak English?"

"Nope."

"What language *did* they speak?"

"Nine millimetre."

Downey's temper flared, but he didn't let it show. Now wasn't the time. Questioning Sweets was like pulling teeth. Best to take it slowly, one at a time. "You get along with Charlie?"

"He scraped by."

"Could you work with him?"

"For a while, maybe. Up to a point."

"That's about what I had in mind," said Downey. "I got this guy needs to get wiped out – that's no surprise to you – and then I have to access a safe. It's the part of the deal that ain't on the agenda, but it's important. The safe's why I needed Liam, got to keep Charlie in my pocket. But once he's done his job . . ." Downey's shrug was eloquent, dismissive. "I'm leaving town for a few days. Think you can handle things while I'm gone?"

Sweets snapped his fingers. "Money."

Downey took a fat white envelope out of his pants pocket. The envelope was stuffed with American ten and twenty-dollar bills. Downey made Sweets sign a voucher. He called Charlie back and had him sign the voucher as well.

"Spend it any way you want, but stay at the hotel until I get back, understand? Don't wander around the countryside pinching the antiquities. And I want you both to get a haircut."

"Where are you going?" said Charlie.

Downey ignored him. He folded the signed voucher and put it away in his wallet.

When he got back to the embassy, first thing on the agenda was a couple of those gooey-sweet lemon tarts and a glass of milk. Then he'd add the voucher and Charlie's passport and other papers to the rapidly-thickening file that only he knew about, the file code-named *Sandstorm*.

16

LONDON

The first time he'd visited the city, Downey had been a child of eight. He still remembered meeting the Queen as vividly as if it were yesterday. Her Royal Highness had been standing on a street corner in Soho. She was wearing a dark-blue see-through blouse, red feather boa, black leather mini-skirt and orange mesh stockings, and she'd been more than happy to give him her autograph – in exchange for one of his father's pound notes.

Downey loved London. The class structure, accents, marvellous architecture, unnaturally courteous clerks, sudden firecracker bursts of tasteless neon, all those stone churches, the cumbersome double-decker buses and the plaintive thunder of Big Ben, the West End, jostling crowds, the expensive hotels and even more expensive hookers, the unexpected opportunities for solitude, all that history – everything.

The flight in from Cairo arrived at Heathrow at seven twenty-two a.m., fifteen minutes ahead of schedule. Because he'd come direct from the Middle East, customs made a thorough search of his nylon carry-all, the only piece of baggage he'd brought with him. He watched the pale, manicured fingers of the agent trundle mole-like through his spare shirts and dirty socks, the polka-dot boxer shorts he saved for days that promised to be unusually bleak and gloomy. The customs agent's hands seemed to have a life of their own – they roved like two small, mute, anaemic animals through Downey's clothes and toilet articles; all the various necessities of a civilized man on a forced march. His Braun razor clicked on and off. Finally, the bag was chalked. He received a terse but courteous nod of the head. His passport was vigorously thumped. And that was that.

He took the bus into the city. Had breakfast, bought a pack of mints and took another bus to the Regent's Park Zoo. In the Insect House, he was approached by a fat bald man wearing a gold pinky ring, who licked his lips with a lizard's tongue, and smiled a lizard's toothless smile. "Fuck right off," said Downey, and gave him a punch to get him started. The hours slipped past. He gradually became confident that he was not being followed.

He travelled to Sloane Square and, still in a feisty mood, got into an argument with a clerk in a men's clothing store while buying an umbrella. A nice, tightly-rolled black one with a varnished wooden handle and brass tip. By the most circuitous of routes, he ended up in a small square off King's Road. The square was furnished with a trio of varnished wooden benches, a cluster of plane trees, the corroded marble bust of a man with curly locks and an inquisitive nose, the usual bulging, sightless eyes. Directly across the street there was an antique shop, gilt lettering on the plate glass.

He walked across the street and browsed the span of the shop's window, his head down. There was a very nice collection of *Netsuke* – the ornate carved ivory buttons used by ancient Japanese as ornaments on their ceremonial robes. The robust little figures were made of ivory, but age had given them the colour of old gold.

Downey stepped a little closer to the glass, peered inside. Jennifer was near the back of the shop. She was wearing a skirt and matching jacket of dark green velvet. Her hair sprang wildly across her shoulders, a waterfall of liquid fire.

Once upon a time, Downey and Jennifer had spent a disastrous, weepy weekend together at a gaudy beachfront hotel in Brighton. Of all places. Crumbling piers. Chunky families with bad teeth gambling for pennies in the arcades. The pebbly beach littered with dog shit. Jennifer stepping out of the shower, her pale skin sleek and gleaming, the thick mass of her hair falling to the cleft between her buttocks. He suddenly had a vivid image of the beauty mark high up on her left cheek, just below the line of her panties. In the shape, it was, of a tiny fish.

Now, at last, he was in exactly the right mood to face her. He left the cover of the plane trees, crossed the busy street and pushed open the door. A bell jangled discreetly. Jennifer turned towards him, into the light, seeing him in profile. He used the tip of his new umbrella to push shut the door, made his way slowly down the central aisle through ranks of gleaming inlaid furniture, the smells of wax and metal polishes, spark and wink of silver and brass.

Her smile faltered. She'd finally recognized him.

He stopped, picked up a glass paperweight, murmured a few words of admiration. Giving her a moment to adjust to the shock of his sudden, unexpected visit.

Finally he looked up at her, smiled and said, "You look surprised. I'd have thought that after all this time, you'd be expecting me."

The words were still tumbling out of his mouth when he realized they were not alone. Sunk into an oversized wingback chair, a chair upholstered in a tufted, plum-coloured fabric that shone like silk, reclined a young girl of thirteen or perhaps fourteen years of age. The girl was sitting with her arms in her lap and her long, thin legs tucked beneath her. She was wearing a school blazer with an embroidered badge, a plain white blouse, grey pleated skirt, white knee socks and sturdy black shoes. Her eyes were mauve. She had her mother's hair, abundant and wilful, copper shot through with strands of gold. Downey said, "Such a lovely child. Cynthia, isn't it?"

He smiled at the girl and said, "You don't remember me, but I remember you very well." No response. Downey smiled again and added, "I've brought you a present."

The girl's chin came up, betraying interest. Downey took a small, badly tarnished silver box from his pocket. The box was in the shape of a pyramid and had a hinged lid. He handed it across.

The cobra lay coiled on a bed of Egyptian sand, its hood flared, golden scales glittering, ruby eyes flashing like dots of blood. Cynthia's eyes widened, the mauve irises darkened to purple.

Downey heard the sibilant hiss of a sharply drawn breath. He was certain that neither Cynthia nor Jennifer knew that the snake represented the Egyptian goddess Mertsager – the goddess of silence.

Cynthia took the ring from the box and slipped it on the little finger of her left hand. A few grains of sand spilled from the hollow pyramid to her lap. She held up her hand and turned it in the light. The Cobra's eyes were on fire.

"Do you like it?"

"It's beautiful." She smiled at him. She had skin like milk, teeth white as a puppy's. She was blessed with wonderful cheekbones, a faint sprinkling of freckles across the bridge of her nose. Give her a few more years and the boys would be howling after her. If they weren't already.

Downey said, "Renewing old acquaintances never fails to sharpen my appetite. I wonder, are the two of you free for lunch?"

"I have to meet a friend," said Cynthia quickly. She was staring at the ring, and Downey was pleased, because he knew she wanted to show it off.

"Just the two of us then," he said to Jennifer.

Cynthia wriggled off the plum-coloured chair. She pecked Jennifer on the cheek, hesitated, gave Downey a quick, shy smile of thanks and hurried towards the front of the shop.

"Lovely child," said Downey, watching her go. The bell jangled. The latch clicked. He turned to Jennifer, found her standing with her arms folded protectively across her breasts. She was wearing a man's watch; a thin gold disc with a black leather strap. The second hand shuddered around the dial.

Downey insisted that Jennifer choose the restaurant. He knew the length and breadth of the King's Road as well as he knew the back of his father's hand, but wanted to make it clear that, in this small matter at least, he was at her mercy. A way of ingratiating himself. Crude but effective. Just another trick of his sleazy trade.

Jennifer led him to a tiny little place, subterranean and French. Seven mismatched tables squeezed into the basement below a laundromat. There were no windows. The walls were covered with crude watercolours, landscapes of blue skies and impossibly verdant fields. Downey sniffed the air – a saliva-gushing mix of bleach and steam. He ordered half a fried chicken, believing that it took a certain amount of cunning to ruin such simple fare deliberately. Jennifer ordered a seafood salad, tea. The food, when it came, was about what he'd expected. They ate quickly, as if they both wished they were somewhere else.

When the bill arrived, Downey said, "Would you mind initialling that, Jennifer, so I can claim expenses?"

Jennifer accepted the pen and scribbled her initials on the receipt. JF, Downey noted. Her husband's name had been Scott, but when the divorce had come through she'd reverted to her maiden name, Forsyth. He capped the pen. The receipt went into his wallet.

Outside, under the lowering clouds, Downey took the lead as they started back in the direction of the antique shop. The sidewalk was crowded. He paused several times to stare at window displays, using the glass as a mirror, studying the flow of traffic. By the time they reached the square across the street from Jennifer's shop, he was fairly confident that they weren't being followed.

They found an unoccupied bench beneath the plane trees. He sat with his umbrella between his knees. She sat with her hands resting primly in her lap. The ground in front of them was hard as concrete, littered with candy wrappers and cigarette ends. Downey prodded at the mess with the tip of his umbrella. On the far side of the street, a one-legged man was peering into Jennifer's window. Downey saw him steady his crutch and then raise his left hand in a kind of salute as he tried to cut the glare.

"Does Cynthia ever help mind the store?" Downey asked.

Jennifer brushed a loose strand of hair from her cheek. "She'll grow up soon enough. I don't see any point in rushing her."

She was staring across the road at her window, and this was what Downey had intended. He wanted her where she could see, actually look at, the life he was asking her to leave behind. Then, if she said yes, he could be all the more confident that she meant it.

"How's business?"

"Why, are you thinking of buying me out?"

"Name your price, if that's what you want." Downey was serious, and he let it show.

"Within reason, of course."

"Be as unreasonable as you like. There are all sorts of things I can do for you. Arrange to have Cynthia educated in Switzerland, for example. Does she have a second language? Does she like to ski?"

"That's hardly the point, is it. You don't see her as a person at all, but simply as an emotional handicap, something that might stop me from doing what you want."

"You misunderstand me."

"Do I? She still misses her father. I don't know how she'd take it if I told her I had to go away." She turned to look directly at him. "How long would it take, how long would I be gone?"

"Two months, at the most."

"Or for ever."

Downey jabbed with the tip of his umbrella at a candy wrapper, pierced it through. "I shouldn't have to remind you, Jennifer, that you came to me. If memory serves, you said Gadaffi had tortured and murdered your father but you couldn't prove it, and no one cared, and could I help you, pretty please. You actually cried on my bloody shoulder. I remember the shirt I was wearing, white with blue pin-stripes. It was soaked through. And how did I respond? Did I deceive you? Certainly not. I said there was nothing I could do. Not now, and maybe never. But I also told you that if the time ever came when I could help, I'd let you know."

"And here you are."

"Yes, here I am."

"It was a long time ago."

"Your father's still dead, isn't he?"

"That isn't fair. It isn't fair at all. Cynthia needs me. William doesn't pay a penny in child support and I have no idea where he is. Things have changed, everything's changed. I'm not even sure my father was murdered, to tell you the truth. Looking back on it, it all seems so . . . unlikely."

Downey nodded his understanding. Shortly after her father had died, he'd sent her a letter. If you were in the mood for conspiracies and threats, it was all there, squeezed in between the lines. At worst, the letter was stuffed with ambiguity. Downey knew that youth was full of certainties, that growing old could come to mean not being sure of anything.

Jennifer had grown up a lot during the interval. He believed he knew exactly what she was thinking.

He became aware of the soft patter of raindrops high above him in the leaves of the plane trees. It had begun, at last, to rain. He glanced up as the first fat drops trickled down through the imperfect canopy, struck the hard-packed earth and made the close-cropped blades of grass twitch and jump.

With a tiny sigh of pleasure, he unfurled his new umbrella. The rain came down with more force. He stood up and moved away from the bench, from beneath the shelter of the tree.

He had known it would come to this. Known it from the very beginning. Many times during the past few months he'd caught himself looking forward to the moment, almost shivering with anticipation. His capacity for cruelty filled him with self-loathing, and with fear. Well, bastard time healed all wounds. In time it would heal this one. Quietly, speaking just loudly enough to be heard above the muffled drumbeat of the rain, he said, "I have a short film I think you should see."

He had arranged the use of a Company safe house in Chalk Farm. A cab sped by as they reached the edge of the square. Downey waved at it and to his surprise it screeched to a halt. The trip took less than half an hour. He and Jennifer sat in silence at opposite sides of the back seat, watching London drift past. The driver wanted to know about Boston. His sister had married an American serviceman and moved there several years ago. What was the city like? Was it safe? How high was the crime rate? Downey made up his answers as he went along.

The Housekeeper had been waiting for them, peeking out through a gap in the curtains. She left the house as they started up the front steps, not bothering to shut the door behind her. The rain had stopped. A cold and fitful wind tugged at her coat as she hurried down the street. Downey couldn't help wondering where she was going. To have something done to her hair, hopefully.

They climbed up the steps and he ushered Jennifer inside, closed the door and locked it. The house was far too warm. Hot air gushed at him from a floor vent, making his trouser leg balloon. He walked down the hall and into the living room. A projector had been set up on a coffee table in front of the sofa. The roll-down screen was suspended from the opposite wall. Downey turned out the light. He took a small metal canister from his coat pocket, opened it, tipped out the main feature and threaded it on the projector. The film was less than three minutes long. A short short, although it had taken him a long time to put it together, splicing bits and pieces of this and that. Downey as *artiste*. There wasn't much dialogue but there was plenty of action. He checked to make sure the heavy curtains were tightly closed, no gap for the milkman to peer through. Light filtered weakly in from the hallway. The room wasn't completely dark, but it would do.

Jennifer was standing by the door with her hands in her pockets. He asked her if she would like to sit down.

She shook her head, no.

It was all systems go, but Downey hesitated. He felt an almost overpowering urge to utter warnings, fashion excuses, offer explanations, apologies. But what was the point? The film was bad, but people being what they were, probably she had imagined worse.

He flicked a toggle switch. The reels began to spin. Numbers flashed across the screen. He adjusted the focus and unceremoniously left the room.

No shoulder for her to cry on this time around.

In the tidy little cubbyhole of a kitchen he found an unopened bottle of Teacher's and clean glasses on the counter by the fridge. He broke the seal and poured two doubles. The film had a soundtrack, of sorts. He could hear Edward Forsyth screaming, and in his mind's eye saw the man's naked body leap against the leather restraining bands as the voltage was increased, saw his eyes bulge in his head and his pubic hair smoke and then burst into flame, the skin of his testicles bubble and turn black. Blood pouring from a toothless mouth. The corpse lying limp and shrunken on a stainless steel table awash in a swamp of blood and urine and faeces.

Then a quick cut to Gadaffi, his dark, heavy face dominated by his glittering eyes, his thin, cruel mouth.

The loose tail of film clattered on the reel. Downey drained his glass and poured himself a refill. The clattering stopped, and all that was left was the steady drone of the projector's fan. He poured himself another stiff one, drank it down and went back into the room.

Jennifer was slouched on the sofa, her hands in her lap. Her eyes were shut. She might have been sleeping. He thumped the whisky down on the table in front of her, rewound the film and put it back in the canister.

She still hadn't moved.

Downey leaned forward and, ever so lightly, touched her shoulder. She was pale, trembling. He found that he enjoyed seeing her like that – vulnerable, hurt. It was terrible, but he couldn't help himself. She opened her eyes. He offered her the drink.

She said, "It's ridiculous, isn't it?"

Downey tilted his head solicitously.

"When you first came into the shop, I thought for an instant that he wasn't dead after all, that you'd come to tell me it had all been a stupid mistake."

"Gadaffi's built a fucking poison-gas plant at Rabta, in the desert south of Tripoli. Recently, the Ruskies have supplied him with a number of long-range supersonic bombers, Su-24-Ds. There are factions in the Pentagon . . . five-star generals who'd like to nuke the son of a bitch, turn the whole damn Libyan sandbox into a sheet of glass. Fortunately, wiser heads prevailed. Instead of blowing away the whole goddamn country, we're going to send a hit team into Libya to assassinate Gadaffi. Strike him down."

Downey paused. She seemed to be taking it all in, bless her. The idea was to make an effect without giving her an opportunity to remember specifics. He continued with a rush.

"It's a joint operation; the Egyptians are minority shareholders. For reasons of security, I can't go into detail, but we need to get a security and explosives expert into Libya."

"I don't know anything about security or explosives," Jennifer pointed out.

"No, but your date does." Downey grinned. "Feelers have been put out. The Libyans have agreed to exhume your father's body and allow you to take him home, back to England. A public relations gesture, presumably."

She was crying, the tears streaming down her cheeks. Watching your daddy fry, probably it wasn't all that much fun. He gestured towards the projector. "Would you like to see it again?"

"God, no!"

Downey used the tip of his umbrella to play a simple, careless little tune as he followed her down the hallway and out of the door. He shot the bolt and dropped the key through the mail slot. It had started raining again, and the rain had swept the pedestrians from the streets. As they reached the gate a rusty red Cortina raced past, its windshield wipers throwing sheets of water across the glass. No chance of a taxi, but the Underground was less than two blocks away. He linked his arm through Jennifer's, gathering her in beneath the flimsy shelter afforded by his umbrella.

He could smell her perfume, feel the swell of her hip against him. He held her a little closer. She made no attempt to move away.

"How soon can you be ready?"

"I haven't made up my mind. I need a few days to think about it."

"Fine," said Downey. She was still crying, but he thought it best not to make a fuss. He sidestepped a puddle, gave her arm a proprietary squeeze.

Vengeance. Guilt. Whatever the reasons, he had her. She was part of the team.

Whether she knew it or not, she belonged to him.

17

Abdel al-Hony was in a foul mood. Omar Jalloud, furious because he had missed the firefight at Charlie's apartment, had sent him to England to liquidate Jack Downey. Abdel had asked Jalloud why he wanted the fat American wiped out. Jalloud had replied that Downey was the mastermind of a CIA plot to assassinate The Leader. The list stolen from the safe house in Gezira had been replaced by a copy flown in from Tripoli. Downey's name was right at the top. Jalloud had also broadly hinted that he believed a dissident faction of the Libyan Army was involved in the plot. He had no solid evidence, but there were meetings he had been excluded from, secrets he felt he should have been privy to . . Abdel had been so shocked that he'd laughed out loud.

A major error.

While he sweated and groaned through his punishment of one hundred sit-ups, Jalloud, in a tone of voice that was painfully loud and strident, lectured him non-stop on the pitfalls of humour. Jalloud was a deadly serious fellow. He truly believed that the snorting, wheezing, braying expulsion of sound disarmingly called 'laughter' was nothing short of low-level germ warfare – kind of like sneezing. Laughter was decadent! Symptomatic of a capitalist plot! Abdel's stomach muscles were on fire. Although he wasn't at all sure he got the point, he was quick to nod his agreement enthusiastically.

There had been a scramble at the airport. In order to make Downey's flight to London, Abdel had been forced to accept a seat in the smoking section.

The air in London was not much cleaner than it had been in the cramped confines of the 747.

On the bright side, tailing Downey through the city streets had not been the least bit difficult. Abdel hoped Downey would lead him to the other American, the tall one called Charlie. It was clear to him that Downey'd taken an interest in Charlie because he, too, was somehow involved in the assassination plot. Jalloud wanted them both knocked off, and that was fine with Abdel.

The zoo was a bit trickier than the crowded streets of the city. It was a cold and cloudy day and there weren't very many people around. Cover was often sparse. It was, for reasons Abdel had no time to analyse, always remarkably difficult to loiter in a place where loitering was the norm. He had nightmares about public toilets, for example.

When Downey went into the Insect House, Abdel fell back, uncertain as to what course of action he should follow. The building was not large. He decided to wait outside.

Downey was only in the building a few minutes. He left in a hurry. Abdel stayed close behind as Downey made his way along a path that ran parallel to the canal. Downey walked halfway across an arched footbridge that led to the Snowdon Aviary, then paused to lean against the railing and peer down at the water.

Abdel crouched, waited.

A short, fat man wearing black leather trousers and a tie-dyed T-shirt came out of the Insect House holding his nose and shouting indiscriminately. Downey glanced up at him, turned and hurried across the bridge and turned towards the aviary, acres of netting held in place by soaring triangles of metal pipe. Abdel was halfway across the bridge when Downey suddenly spun on his heel.

Abdel back-pedalled.

He turned and ran straight at the man in the leather trousers, the homosexual who'd accosted Downey in the Insect House. The man lunged at him, punched him in the face. The force of the blow snapped Abdel's head sideways. He grabbed the man by the crotch and throat and picked him up and threw him head first into the canal.

The man struck the water and vanished in a welter of greenish foam. A black leather glove decorated with rows of macho chrome studs floated briefly on the surface and then sank without a trace. In the aviary, an unseen bird made a sound like someone shaking a sackful of walnuts. After a moment the ripples dispersed and the canal became flat and calm. The man did not reappear. It was as if he had never existed.

Shortly afterwards, Abdel realized that Downey, too, had managed to slip away.

18

Jennifer Forsyth had always been a woman who liked to travel at her own pace. Downey knew it would be futile to try to rush her, hurry her along. He'd made his case with all the cunning and brutality at his command, and now there was nothing he could do but wait. During the return trip from Chalk Farm his mouth was crammed with arguments but he kept his discipline and uttered not a single word. At the door to her shop, he gave her the name and room number of his Mayfair Hotel, and quietly withdrew.

He spent the next three days slouched in a fat overstuffed chair by his window, reading Sun Tzu and Clausewitz, watching television game shows, sports, the news.

The tension of waiting for the telephone to ring gave him an enormous appetite. Room service was kept hopping. He soon knew the names of all the staff.

Long blocks of time were spent lying motionless on his bed. He stared up at the ceiling, listened intently to muted footsteps in the hallway, the soft hum and click of the elevators, distant laughter.

Twice he used his telephone to summon expensive and overly imaginative prostitutes to his suite of rooms. Both times he stipulated that the women must have long, coppery red hair. He made no demands with regard to intelligence, eye colour, accent. He was above all a pragmatist. In his life he had always enjoyed himself as best he could, taking his pleasures as they came.

Afterwards, when he'd had all the sex he wanted, he took the women into the shower with him and stood quietly under the spray while they lathered his penis and testicles, washed him clean. They didn't like getting their hair wet but Downey paid them extra, his habit being to leave a tidy pile of crisp new five-pound notes on the bedside table. He was always careful not to see the money being taken, went so far as to press his face into the pillows to avoid hearing the quick, soft shuffle of counting. He was a man with needs, but also fancied himself a bit of a romantic.

It was sleep that he dreaded. That was when the corpse made its appearance.

The scenario never changed. He was in a dentist's office, and the body lay under the lights, mouth gaping wide, head lolling from side to side as the dentist drilled and prodded, gouging out a cavity in an upper molar. The corpse had been dead for several days. As the dentist laboured, he never stopped complaining about how difficult it was to work on a dead man, especially a dead man with a broken neck. Downey was recruited to hold the head in position. He had never thought of himself as squeamish, but the corpse's skull was soft and rubbery, the hair fell out in clumps, and the eyes, glazed and sunken, never stopped staring up at him as his nostrils filled with the stench of scorched bone, putrefied flesh, his own sweat . . .

On the afternoon of the third day, just as he was finishing his lunch, the telephone rang. He was caught with a forkful of cheesecake in his right hand, the television's remote control in the left. He turned down the volume, reached for the phone. Jennifer's voice was calm, distant. Downey kept to a neutral tone. He arranged to meet her in exactly one hour at the sports department of Harrod's, and gently disconnected.

He'd been watching a soccer game, telecast live from Munich. On screen, the ball leapt back and forth and the players danced across the grass. There was a quick cut to a scuffle in the crowd. On the field the players stood quietly. The referee posed with one foot resting on the ball and his hands on his hips. Another cut to the crowd. A Rottweiler stared at Downey through a chain-link fence, watching him as if it was sure it had seen him somewhere before and didn't like what it remembered. It barked, showing sharp white teeth, and then looked haughtily away. Downey turned the television off. He scratched his stomach and walked across the carpet to his bedroom cupboard in search of something dark with pinstripes, the uniform of a banker, solid and reassuring.

He was admiring the dense diamond-pattern chequering on the pistol grip of a double-barrelled Purdy when he saw Jennifer coming towards him. He put the shotgun to his shoulder and sighted on the gleaming plaster skull of a mannequin wearing a fishing vest and chest waders. A colourful plastic trout dangled from a length of string attached to a stick slung across the creature's shoulder. Downey adjusted his aim, taking a bead on the mannequin's slender white throat. The clerk coughed nervously, a light, fluttering sound. Downey took his finger off the trigger and laid the weapon on the counter. The clerk stood the Purdy in a polished mahogany rack, carefully ran a carbon-steel chain through the trigger guard.

Downey had arrived early and scouted the terrain. He led Jennifer to a camp in the jungle, sat her down next to a bright-blue tent, on a tiny folding stool made of gaily striped canvas and hollow aluminum tubing. There was a fire, but no one had thought to plug it in. He sat next to Jennifer, leaned towards her, attempted through sheer proximity to create an atmosphere of intimacy and trust.

"Have you talked to Cynthia?"

Jennifer nodded. Her hair fell across her cheek. She brushed it back with a quick, impatient gesture.

"What was her reaction?"

"About what you'd expect. She doesn't want to go to Switzerland or anywhere else."

Downey was surprised, but was careful not to let it show. He said, "No, of course not. Why would she?"

"My sister-in-law has agreed to take care of her. I told her what you'd suggested; that I'd heard my father was alive, and I was going to the Middle East to look for him."

There was a pot suspended above the fire on a steel tripod. Downey lifted the lid on a glazed papier-mâché chicken.

"That's all you told her? Nothing more specific?"

"She offered to help with the shop."

"Don't worry about it. Money isn't going to be a problem."

"I'm not doing this for money."

"No, but there's plenty of it lying around. So why not take some?"

Jennifer stared into the grill of the dead electric fire.

"When will you be ready to leave?" Downey said.

"Now. Right this minute."

Downey took a sheaf of papers from his pocket. He unfolded the papers and fumbled for his pen. "What we have here are the standard Company recruitment forms. Waiver of liability, all that crap . . . Life insurance . . . I've put Cynthia down as your sole beneficiary, if that's okay with you." He uncapped the pen. Jennifer scrawled her signature across the bottom of a dozen pages. The ink was jet black. He took his pen back and offered her a heavy brass key.

"What's this?"

"Locker one twenty-nine, Heathrow. You'll find everything you need in there, including a matched set of pigskin luggage that put me back almost four hundred pounds."

Jennifer's hand closed on the piece of stamped metal. The sharp ridges dug into her palm.

"Have you got your passport with you?"

"Yes, of course."

"Hand it over. You won't need it. There's a new one in your new attaché case. Is Cynthia going to be all right, or do you want someone watching her?"

"She'll be fine." The sister-in-law lived in a small town called Alnwick, on the Scottish border. Her daughter would be bored, but safe.

"Your ticket's with the passport. Air Egypt flight 318. If you leave now, you should just make it."

Jennifer looked at him. "What made you think I'd be ready to go today?"

Downey stood up. His knees creaked. He'd bought a seat on at least one flight a day for the next two weeks, but he wasn't about to tell her that.

"See you in Cairo." He gave her a wave of his hand, and walked briskly away. He moved fast, not quite believing his luck, still afraid she might change her mind.

Jennifer rubbed the ball of her thumb. Downey's expensive pen had leaked, the jet-black ink staining her flesh. She suddenly had the feeling that she was being watched. She stood up. The ridiculous little camp stool fell over and collapsed with a clatter. A clerk stared at her from behind his polished glass counter.

She took the elevator down to the main floor, found the nearest exit. A cab idled by the curb, the driver crouched behind the wheel. Jennifer started towards the cab and then saw Downey sitting in the back, his mouth wide open. Their eyes met. A chocolate the size of a quail's egg perched on a tripod of thick blunt fingers. He gave her a droll wink, popped the chocolate into his mouth and then pushed open the door and stepped out on the crowded sidewalk, waved her into the cab.

"He knows where you're going. The fare's been taken care of."

Jennifer slipped into the cab and the driver cut sharply into traffic. She turned to look out of the rear window. Downey had vanished. She settled back in her seat for the long ride out to the airport.

The locker was at the end of a row. Jennifer tried to insert the key into the lock.

It didn't fit.

She peered at the number on the locker, and then at the number imprinted on the key. The numbers matched. She tried the key again, and this time it slid easily into the lock.

The locker contained two pigskin suitcases and a matching attaché case. She removed the attaché case, shut the locker door, inserted a coin. Dropped the key in her purse and walked quickly towards the nearest public washroom.

In the washroom, she found an unoccupied cubicle, shut and bolted the door. The initials 'JM' were inscribed in ornate script on a rectangular brass plate on the case's handle. She flipped the case open. It contained a wad of crisp new Egyptian ten-pound notes totalling one thousand pounds, and an envelope in which she found an Air Egypt folder containing a first-class ticket, London to Cairo return.

There was also a much-travelled British passport, a driver's licence, medical and AA cards, a Barclaycard and several other pieces of identification. The items were familiar, but the name wasn't. Jennifer Forsyth had become Jennifer McPhee. She flipped open the passport. The data listed above the photograph, date of birth and so on, had not been changed except for the notation regarding next of kin. The name printed in the space provided was of someone Jennifer had never heard of. She leafed through the passport, noting previous trips to Barcelona, Paris and Hamburg, several recent flights to Washington, DC.

There was an urgent tapping at the door. Jennifer looked up, startled.

"You going to be in there for ever, love?"

Jennifer flushed the toilet, shut and locked the attaché case, stood up and unbolted the door. A young woman wearing too much makeup and a fake fur coat smiled her thanks and brushed quickly past her.

She collected the two pigskin suitcases and checked in at the Air Egypt desk. She accepted her baggage tags and boarding pass from a small, dark man in a crisp white shirt and maroon bowtie. Her flight was scheduled to depart in three-quarters of an hour. She bought several magazines at a stand and then went into a bar, found a table and ordered a drink.

Downey watched her from a distance. She was too attractive and had too commanding a presence simply to blend into the background. But there was something about her, a calmness, a certain depth of spirit, that somehow deflected suspicion. He tried to analyse what he felt, compartmentalize his feelings and break them down and make sense of them. But you couldn't pin a label on what Jennifer had. Either you were born with it or you did without.

Not good enough. He tried again. She had a knack for settling in, looking as if she belonged. Wherever she happened to be, she gave you the impression she might have been born there. He watched her toy with her drink. Half the men in the bar were staring at her – the others were probably either gay or too frightened of their wives to risk a peek. He knew she must be very nervous, and noted with approval that she didn't pay any attention at all to the clock over the bar.

Everything was going to work out just fine. He bit into his Mars Bar, turned his back on her and confidently walked away.

Next stop, Cairo.

Abdel al-Hony had paid an American serviceman three thousand dollars for the Claymore. His attempt to bribe the maid at the Mayfair was summarily rejected. He garrotted the stupid woman and, after he'd used her pass key to gain entrance to Downey's suite, stuffed her in under the bed.

It took him only a few minutes to position and arm the Claymore. The antipersonnel mine went off at a few minutes past one o'clock that afternoon.

The Mayfair's chief of security, investigating a complaint that several known prostitutes had frequently visited Downey in his rooms and that he might therefore be a pimp, inadvertently triggered the mine as a pair of honeymooning lawyers from Orlando, Florida happened to stroll by on their way to the elevator. The happy Floridians had managed to secure tickets to the revival of the popular musical *Me And My Girl*, and they were looking forward to a night on the town. The security chief nodded to them and slipped his passkey into the lock and opened Downey's door. All three victims were turned to jelly by the force of the blast, their lifeless bodies riddled through and through by the Claymore's seven hundred steel balls.

Downey, cruising along in the Air Egypt 747 at a speed of four hundred fifty knots and altitude of thirty thousand feet, didn't hear a thing.

The security man was ex-Scotland Yard. *The Times* ran the full text of an IRA phone call claiming responsibility for the explosion.

By the time Abdel al-Hony finished lip-reading the piece, he was running on an extremely short fuse.

19

CAIRO

The file on Richard Foster's desk was almost an inch thick, but it didn't weigh much because the contents were nothing but fluff. He'd read it from cover to cover and found virtually nothing to justify the horrendous expense of the three agents he'd assigned to keep tabs on Downey in London.

Foster was royally pissed off. He was one hundred and ten per cent positive that the expatriate Californian Charlie McPhee had not walked out of the embassy under his own head of steam.

Someone had pumped McPhee up, showed him the way out the door. Downey had denied any involvement, but Foster was certain he'd arranged McPhee's vanishing act. Jack had something cooking; Foster could smell the burnt meat. Was Downey planning to somehow use McPhee to reel in the defecting Libyan Intelligence colonel? Or did he have something else in mind? Downey always had so many goddamn irons in the fire that it was impossible to keep track of them all.

There was another file on Foster's desk. The file contained a sheaf of faxes from McPhee's wife's legal firm. Several hundred words, but what it all boiled down to was a demand to know what in hell had happened to their client's errant husband. A fair question. Foster wished he had an answer.

He turned a page in the file from London. The file was less than twenty-four hours old, but the folder was already starting to look dog-eared, a little worn around the edges. He stared glumly at a 500mm shot of Downey in the bar at Heathrow. Downey had a pint of beer and packet of crisps in front of him, a decidedly cold expression on his usually jovial face.

Foster turned the photograph belly up and shuffled rapidly through several similar shots, including a rather sombre picture of Downey standing in the small square off King's Road, his plump face unnaturally pale against the black backdrop of his fancy new umbrella.

There were also half a dozen snapshots head-on and in profile of the spectacularly gorgeous woman with whom Downey had spent the afternoon. Her name was Jennifer Forsyth. Foster studied a low-light candid of Downey slouched in a King's Road restaurant, pouring her a glass of wine from a thirty-dollar bottle.

He picked through the photographs for a little while, and then turned his attention back to the text. His field agent believed that the relationship between Downey and the woman was not sexual. Foster found the judgement credible – Jennifer Forsyth was obviously out of Downey's league.

But what other motives for entanglement could a man like Jack Downey have? There were only two that Foster could think of. The first was money and the second was power. Foster had put a team to work digging up Jennifer Forsyth's past and present lives. He wanted to know all about her, every detail.

He scrutinized the three shots of the child who had walked out of the antique shop precisely eleven minutes after Downey'd entered the building. The girl was perhaps twelve or thirteen years old, and she was very beautiful – the resemblance between her and her mother was nothing short of remarkable. Foster put the three photographs to one side and returned to the text.

From Heathrow, Foster's trio of agents had discreetly chased Downey into London. There had been an altercation in a cheap self-service restaurant. Something about a cup of tea and a cinnamon bun. Jesus. Later, Downey bought a pack of mints from a tobacconist's. It was diligently noted that he'd eaten the mints very quickly and stuffed the cellophane wrapper into his pocket – rather than littering the sidewalk, as any ordinary citizen would do.

Foster wondered about that. No one who knew Downey ever thought of him as a particularly tidy fellow. But Foster knew that, although Downey had travelled all over the world, London was his favourite city. So perhaps that explained his uncharacteristically fastidious behaviour.

Or maybe it didn't.

Foster massaged his temples. He turned to the next page.

At the zoo, Downey had come into contact with half a dozen people, most of them zoo employees. There was the man at the gate who'd sold him his ticket, a woman from whom he'd purchased a bag of popcorn and cardboard cup of coffee. Both cup and bag had been discarded in refuse containers. The agent consumed a fifteen-line paragraph pointing out that it would have been especially easy for Downey to palm a message mixed in with the popcorn.

Right, right.

Foster turned to the next page. At the popcorn stand, Downey had received his change and walked away, then spun on his heel and snatched a thick wad of paper napkins from a dispenser on the counter. Another chance to exchange information. Or maybe his nose needed a wipe.

Foster followed Downey at third hand as he wandered with apparent aimlessness around the thirty-six acres of grounds for the better part of an hour, then cut under the East Tunnel and went into the Insect House. The tail had been caught unawares, but was fairly sure the tunnel was empty when Downey entered it. Foster sighed, and scratched his nose.

The agent, anxious to maintain visual contact, had followed Downey inside the Insect House. The building was apparently a popular meeting place for homosexuals. Downey had thought he was being propositioned, punched the agent in the nose. Then he'd gone outside, crossed the canal towards the Snowdon Aviary.

The wounded agent, trailing blood, had hurried after him and then vanished. Simply fucking disappeared. His last coherent remark was that there was blood all over his lapel mike. His partner remembered hearing something that might have been a splash. But, at the time, he was in the men's room, taking a whizz, and he was somewhat distracted.

Downey had caught a bus and then the Underground to Sloane Square. There had been a heated exchange at a men's clothing store, where he had lost patience with a clerk who'd tried to sell him the wrong model umbrella. He'd made his indirect way to Jennifer Forsyth's antique shop in King's Road.

Eleven minutes had passed and then Cynthia, the woman's daughter, had come out. Ten more minutes ticked slowly by. Downey and the woman had hurried out of the shop. He looked tense. She looked harried. They walked three blocks to a French restaurant strategically located in the basement of a dry-cleaner's. In deference to the fire bylaws, the restaurant had a front and a rear entrance. What it didn't have was windows. Assuming that Downey and the woman would talk during their meal and that what they said might be worth hearing, one of the surviving agents – a woman – followed them inside.

She was seated at the opposite end of the restaurant from Downey, but during one of her frequent trips to the washroom, had heard him say, "I guess by now you've figured out why I'm here, huh?"

Intriguing, yes. Illuminating, no.

And now, of his three original agents, one was blown and one had vanished, and the end-result was a big dent in his budget.

His eye moved down the neatly typed page, jumped back to the third paragraph.

When Downey was given the bill, he'd had Jennifer initial it. Why bother with her autograph? Why keep the receipt in the first place? What did it mean? That Company business had been discussed? Or was it simply that Jack had the bad habit of padding his expenses?

Foster flipped back to the sheaf of photographs at the beginning of the file. He studied the pictures of Jennifer that had been taken in the restaurant, and then the telephoto shots of her sitting on a wooden bench beneath the dripping plane trees in the little square across the street from her shop. He was notoriously bad at estimating ages, but he thought she was probably in her early thirties, certainly no older than thirty-five. A very attractive woman. Beautiful. Even ravishing. Her bone structure was strong but delicate, her hair simply incredible. He reminded himself that it would be unwise to rule out the possibility of a romantic interest, even though for the life of him he couldn't understand how a woman like that could be interested in a man like Downey.

Unless . . . she was working for the damn Brits.

Foster pushed away from his desk. He went over to his Mr Coffee machine and poured himself a fresh cup, added half a cube of sugar and a dollop of cream.

In the square, sitting on the wooden bench beneath the trees, Downey had talked and talked, and the woman had listened and listened and never said a word.

It had begun to rain.

Downey had immediately jumped to his feet, unfurled his new umbrella and walked several steps away from the shelter of the tree. Deliberately exposing himself to the elements, inadvertently exposing himself to the risk of being overheard.

Foster's last clean agent, all ears, hurried down the path.

Downey raised his voice – presumably so that Jennifer could hear him despite the distance between them and the sound of the rain beating on the canopy of leaves splattered with starling droppings.

The agent heard him say, "I have a short film I think you should see."

Downey'd offered no explanation as to what he meant, and she hadn't asked.

The rain was sluicing down, by then. Estimate of dry-cleaning bill attached. Downey walked Jennifer out of the square to the side of the road. A taxi pulled up as if on cue.

The agent had noted the taxi's licence number. London was tracing it, would let him know as soon as they came up with something.

The cabbie. Cashier in the self-serve restaurant. Clerks who'd sold him the mints and the umbrella. The people at the zoo; all of them were squeezed together under the lens of the Company microscope and would be examined minutely, at length and in great detail.

But Foster was convinced it was Jennifer Forsyth who held the key to all Downey's secrets.

He shuffled slowly through her pictures, searching for some small detail he might have missed. He wondered what kind of body she had hidden under her severely-cut jacket and loose, pleated skirt. Hot, but repressed, you betcha. He could see it in her eyes, the taut way she held herself. He tapped the bottom edges of the pictures on the polished rosewood surface of his desk, getting them nicely aligned. When everything was just so, he fastened the pictures together with a jumbo paperclip and slipped them back in the file, stuck everything in the wall safe hidden behind the portrait of President Bush.

Standing by the safe, he hooked his thumb and index finger in his jacket pocket and pulled out his grandad's pocket watch, an old Marlin with a white enamel face and heavily engraved 18-carat gold case. It was ten minutes past one. Foster turned the bezel a full rotation. The watch was almost one hundred years old. To maintain accuracy, it had to be wound frequently and regularly. Foster gave the bezel two more turns and put the watch back in his pocket, straightened his vest and flicked a speck of lint from his lapel.

In twenty minutes he had a lunch date with one of the junior secretaries in the typing pool, a sweet young thing called Sheila, who'd flown in from Washington only two days earlier.

Relationships between embassy staff and the natives were, of course, not allowed. Therefore secure sexual outlets had to be made available. Foster was convinced this was the reason behind the rapid turnover in the typing pool.

Twenty minutes. Time for a shower and a quick pass with a razor. He pressed the intercom and told Dorothy he'd be gone for the rest of the day. Her reply was garbled, bordered on terse. Foster believed she snacked from her desk. He hadn't been able to catch her at it, but he was

was confident he'd nab her sooner or later – that it was only a matter of time.

Richard Foster was an extraordinarily patient man, and he was very good at catching the sort of people who did things they really shouldn't have been doing.

Or so he thought.

20

Charlie unwound the dressing from Mungo Martin's arm. Six days had passed since the firefight in his apartment. Mungo's flesh from elbow to shoulder was a murky yellow streaked with bands of mauve. But the swelling was down and the wound was healing cleanly. There was no sign of infection. Charlie glanced at his watch. Just over two minutes. He pulled the thermometer from between Mungo's pursed lips and carried it over to the window.

Ninety-eight point six.

A baby-blue speedboat raced down the Nile, trailing a wake of muddy-brown froth. A seagull rose splashing from the water, screeched its annoyance and flew laboriously upstream. The Egyptians called the gulls 'Iraqi Eagles'.

The dreadlocks and brightly-coloured beads were gone, cut away by the hotel barber. Sweets ran his hands over his close-cropped head. "He going to make it, or do I get to be executor?"

Mungo laughed, making the bed shake. His eyes were clear, his teeth whiter than the sheets that covered him. Charlie slipped the thermometer back into its plastic case. He applied a fresh dressing to the wound. Mungo sat up, moving very slowly. He swept aside the blankets and swung his legs over the side of the bed.

"What are you doing?" said Charlie. The doctor had told Mungo to stay in bed for at least a week, and Downey in turn had told Charlie he'd hold him responsible if Mungo didn't do what he was told.

"It's a nice day. Thought it might be a good idea to take a walk. Maybe stroll over to the museum, soak up a little culture."

"Jack said you were supposed to stay in bed until he got back from London."

Mungo went over to the built-in closet, swung open the louvred door, selected a pair of bright-red trousers and a lime-green shirt with red buttons. "You think he expects me to do what I'm told?"

"Aren't those mine?" said Sweets.

"Not unless I suffer a major fuckin' relapse."

"I'm going with you," said Charlie.

"Suit yourself." Mungo turned to Sweets. "What about you, Hubie?"

"Have fun, kids."

It was less than a block from the Hilton to the doors of the Egyptian Museum, but the air was hot and dry and by the time they got there Charlie felt dehydrated, limp, ready to return to the air-conditioned comfort of the hotel. Mungo took a quick look at the crowd of tourists milling around the museum entrance. "Screw this. Let's go get something to eat."

Charlie pointed to a restaurant half a block down the street.

Mungo chose a corner table near the back of the restaurant. He sat in a chair facing the door, rested his wounded arm carefully in his lap, as if it was a valuable and fragile package that he would not risk leaving behind. A waiter drifted past. Mungo pinched the man's shirt cuff between his thumb and index finger, holding him in place. "A couple of steaks, hot and raw. You got Heineken lager?" The waiter nodded. "Four lagers, nice and cold."

"I'm not hungry," said Charlie.

Mungo waved the waiter away. "Red meat's the best thing you can eat. Helps you stay mad."

"At what?"

Mungo looked at him as if he was from another planet, had just fallen through the ceiling of the restaurant and landed in his chair.

"What part of California you from?"

"Los Angeles."

"Jack tell you anything about me and Hubie?"

Charlie shook his head, no.

"Don't take it personal. He's a real secretive guy."

The waiter arrived with their drinks. Mungo's hand shook as he emptied the can into his glass. "Look at that, man. I'm a fucking cripple, can't even pour myself a beer."

Charlie took a small plastic vial from his shirt pocket. He put the vial down on the table and flicked it with his index finger, rolled it across the table.

"Drugs?"

"Codeine."

Mungo used his thumb to lever the child-proof cap off the vial. He brought the vial to his lips, tilted his head and gave it a shake, then put it down on the table.

Charlie said, "How many did you take?"

Mungo stuck out his tongue, spotted with several small white pills – too many to count. He gave Charlie a daffy, conspiratorial wink, and lifted the glass of Heineken to his mouth, drained it dry.

"Einstein said you weren't supposed to drink while you were taking medication."

"Who the fuck is Einstein?"

"Guy from the embassy. Frizzy hair. Wears argyle sweaters, carries a little black bag. Jack said he was a doctor."

Mungo gave Charlie a suspicious look. "Don't think I remember him."

"You were out cold."

"And you were busy wiping my fevered brow, right?"

Charlie didn't say anything.

"Just so long as you weren't busy wiping my fevered ass, is all. Where was Hubie while all this was going on?"

"I don't know. Around."

"Bullshit. He was out having a good time, enjoying the nightlife. And I'd have done exactly the same thing, it was him that'd been shot, 'stead of me." Mungo gave Charlie a long, slow look. "Hubie saw you were primed to play Doctor, decided to take advantage of the situation. Be a mistake to think he took off because he don't care about me."

Outside, there was a sudden festive tinkling of glass, crunch of metal. A horn blared. The restaurant was quiet for a moment.

"I remember that used to happen in school sometimes," Mungo said. "Everybody'd be talking away and then stop for no reason. A hush, know what I mean? My mom told me it was 'cause an angel had just flown over us but, even in grade three, I never fell for shit like that."

"Where'd you go to school?" said Charlie. He had been reminded that he knew nothing of Mungo Martin's past, and he was curious. But there was more to it than that. Mungo had been injured, and Charlie had helped heal him. For almost a week, Mungo had been the focal point of Charlie's life. He had made an emotional investment in Mungo, and now he wanted a payoff. "What part of the States are you from?"

"City of Angels, same as you."

"Did you and Sweets grow up together?"

"Met him in the army."

"You were drafted?"

"Only way they'd get me."

"You were in Nam?"

"What'd a guy like you know about it? What you read in the papers,

I guess." Mungo smiled a distant smile, remembering. "Looking back, it was a fun time, kind of."

"I know," said Charlie. "I was there."

Out in the sun-washed glare of the street, five or six white-uniformed tourist police were jumping up and down on a small blue car that had locked bumpers with an ancient pickup truck. Somebody in the crowd of onlookers started clapping his hands, trying to get the policemen to jump in unison.

The door to the kitchen swung open and the waiter came towards them carrying their plates and two more cans of Heineken. He put the food and beer down on the table and left without a word.

Mungo's steak had been cut into bite-size diamonds. He stuck his fork into a piece and sniffed at it, chewed slowly.

Charlie wasn't hungry, but he began to eat anyway, just to give himself something to do.

Mungo drank some more beer. "What'd you do in LA?"

Charlie told him about his business. Mungo thought it was a funny coincidence that while Charlie was busy manufacturing home security devices, he was working his way through his teens by robbing apartments. He asked Charlie where in Los Angeles he had lived, about his wife and daughter, the marriage.

"Beverly Hills? No shit. What kind of car you drive? No, don't tell me. You're too fucking old for a Porsche. So what was it, a Mercedes, maybe a Rolls?"

Charlie smiled, shook his head.

"Caddy?"

"That's right, a Cadillac."

"Fucking amazing. What colour?"

"White."

"Rag top?"

Charlie nodded, feeling like a fool.

"Jesus Christ, I don't believe it. You got your own fucking company, a whole bunch of people working for you that you can push around, a big house in Beverly Hills. You can do whatever you want, go wherever you like. And here you are in Cairo, working for Jack. What in hell happened, you don't mind me asking."

Charlie told Mungo about the break-in and three murders on Gezira, his flight to the American embassy. He explained how Jimmy Abrams and Richard Foster had kept him under a kind of informal house arrest while they tried to decide what to do with him. The way Charlie saw it, they had two choices: either hand him over to the Cairo

Murder Squad or mail him back to LA, where his wife's lawyers were waiting to cut him up into small pieces.

Then Downey had wandered into the picture, set him free.

Mungo listened carefully to Charlie's story. He sat very still, only his eyes moving. They finished the steaks and the waiter brought tiny cups of strong black coffee, a selection of sweet cakes. Mungo nibbled at the cakes, discarding them one after another. When it was clear he had no intention of asking any more questions, Charlie said, "What about you, what are you and Hubie doing in Cairo?"

"Beats me. Something illegal, probably." Mungo used his napkin to wipe fragments of red and yellow and blue icing from his fingers. "Jack hasn't told us what he's got in mind this time out, but he'll get around to it in good time." Mungo told Charlie about life in the jungle, how they'd been making it hard for the cocaine growers.

"You were working for the Colombian government?"

"Not exactly." Mungo balled up his napkin, stuffed it into his water glass. "One thing about working for the fuckin' CIA, people aren't too quick to mess around with you."

"This is a CIA operation you're involved in, here in Cairo?"

"Got to be, if Jack's running it." The waiter was lounging against the wall near the door to the kitchen. Mungo caught his eye and waved, made a scribbling motion to indicate he wanted the bill.

Outside, there was a wind from the east, and the air was thick and muggy. They made their way slowly along the crowded sidewalk towards the rectangular bulk of the Hilton. In the lobby, Mungo stopped at a revolving carousel of postcards.

"Take a look at this."

Charlie pondered a photograph of the Aswan Dam that seemed in no way remarkable or interesting.

Very quietly, Mungo said, "The guy you ran over with the Citroën was on the payroll."

Charlie stared at the card. White concrete, blue water.

"He was one of Jack's boys. A local. Freelance. Type gets paid by the hour, know what I mean?"

Mungo returned the postcard to the rack, selected a shot of the statue of Rameses II at Rameses Square. On the elevated walkway behind the enormous golden statue, a group of Japanese tourists posed for a photograph within the photograph. He flipped the card over. To anyone who might have been watching them, it would seem as if he was reading the few words of information on the back of the card out loud to Charlie.

"Jack wanted to see how you'd react under pressure, so he hired the guy to stand in front of the car and wave his gun."

"Would he have shot me?"

"The way I see it, Jack figured if you panicked, all the guy had to do was toss you out of the car and take the wheel."

"But what he hoped would happen is that I'd run over him, is that it?"

"From what I saw, when you put your hands up, the freelance figured that was it, game over. You faked him out. He moved in too close to the car, started playing to the crowd. His last mistake."

Mungo jammed the postcard upside down in a slot and took another one at random.

"It was a test. You passed and he failed. That's the way Jack is. Efficient. Always looking for a way to get two jobs done for the price of one." Mungo glanced around the hotel lobby. No one was paying any attention to them. The postcard was a replica; an old sepia-toned shot of a belly dancer. Mungo stuffed the card in his pocket and started towards the bank of elevators, Charlie tagging along behind.

Charlie said, "He isn't going to let me go back to Los Angeles, is he?"

"Ask him."

"I want to go home, but whatever he's got planned for you and Sweets, he wants me to be part of it."

They heard the faint hum of a distant electric motor. The indicator light over the door of the nearest elevator winked on, and a moment later the doors slid open. They stepped inside. Mungo slapped the button and the doors glided shut.

"There was a third guy supposed to come to Cairo with us. Liam O'Brady. He died maybe a week before the plane tickets arrived. Liam was real good at neutralizing security devices. And he was an explosives expert. You ever work with explosives, Charlie?"

"In the war."

"Yeah, where else?" Mungo grinned. "Look on the bright side. Me and Hubie didn't come cheap. Neither should you."

"I don't want to get involved."

"You're singing the national anthem, baby."

The elevator stopped. Down the corridor, the door to their suite was wide open. A shaft of sunlight lay across the hall carpet. Mungo clutched at Charlie's arm. "What I told you, it's just between the two of us."

Charlie nodded. They entered the suite, stepped into the full force of Jack Downey's baleful glare.

"Where the hell have you been?" Downey screamed. His face was the colour of an eggplant. The veins in his neck bulged. "I told you not to leave the goddamn hotel!"

Mungo said, "You want mindless obedience, why don't you go buy yourself a fucking poodle." Sweets laughed. Downey glared at him. Mungo pushed his way past Downey and went into the bathroom. The three men stood quietly, listening to the splash of urine in the bowl.

"Where the fuck were you?" Downey yelled at Charlie.

"At a fucking restaurant!" Charlie yelled back.

Downey eased off. "Whose idea was that, yours or Mungo's?"

"It's slipped my mind."

Unexpectedly, Downey grinned.

They heard the flush of the toilet. Mungo walked back into the living room, a puzzled look on his face.

"Somebody steal my toothbrush?"

"It's in the car."

"Why?"

"We're outta here," said Downey. "I didn't think you'd want to leave it behind."

21

They had reached that point of the operation where Downey felt a certain degree of privacy was required, and so he'd rented a house in the suburb of Maadi, to the west of the city and Old Cairo.

The house was rectangular, low and sturdy, with an exterior of rough-textured tan concrete and roof of faded red tiles. The various rooms were arranged around an open central courtyard.

The grounds were well-lit, surrounded by an eight-foot-high cinder-block wall topped with shards of broken glass. At the front there was a gravelled forecourt, to the rear a small patch of coarse yellow grass and trio of neglected fig trees, their spindly branches heavily laden with overripe fruit and many drowsy flies.

Downey had passed himself off as a senior employee of Reuter's who was in desperate need of a romantic weekend retreat. The rental agent had confided that the house was owned by a distant cousin of the late Abdel Nasser, that the man was out of the country and had not used the house for several years. Downey scrawled his signature on a six-month lease, paid in cash. He had the locks changed the following day.

The lease had been signed two months ago. Downey stocked the house with liquor and all the tinned and frozen food he'd thought necessary. Until a few days ago, he hadn't been back since.

Now he parked his rented Ford so it was straddling the sidewalk in front of the house. He got out of the car and unlocked the ornate iron gate and pushed it open, climbed back into the car and drove into the forecourt, parked next to a matched pair of brand-new dun-coloured Land-Rovers. "Everybody out," he said jovially. "Hubie, get the gate."

Above them, the sky was a flawless expanse of pale blue. Waves of heat radiated off the cinderblock walls and coarse, sharp-edged gravel. Downey unlocked the front door and waved his crew inside, Sweets in the lead and Mungo a close second, Charlie tagging along behind.

There was an entrance hall and then, to their left, a living room with a floor of maroon tiles and the sort of furniture that looked as if it had been picked from a mail-order catalogue by someone in a hurry. Leaded glass doors gave access to the courtyard.

To the right an open door led to a small, windowless room with whitewashed walls. Several large wooden crates were stacked on the floor. Two of the crates were long and narrow; coffin-shaped. Sweets stared speculatively at the crates. Downey offered no explanation.

Access to the bedrooms was provided by a U-shaped hallway that followed the courtyard. Downey led them along the hall towards the rear of the house. He pushed open a door.

"Hubie, this is where you hang your hat."

The room was furnished with a narrow bed, a bureau, plain wooden desk and a bright red folding metal chair.

"Take me back to the Hilton," said Sweets.

Downey led them further along the hallway, showing the place off, enjoying himself. The next bedroom was Mungo's. The adjoining room belonged to Downey and the one after that was Charlie's. The two remaining bedrooms were empty. Downey showed them the bathroom, led them back up the far side of the house through the kitchen and into the living room. Charlie noticed that the dining room table had been set for five.

Downey went over to the leaded glass doors, unlocked them and swung them open. There was a bronze statue of a small boy in the middle of the courtyard. The boy stood on a bronze lily pad in a dry pool. Downey crouched and turned on a tap hidden in a recess at the boy's feet. The pool slowly filled. Rusty brown water spurted from the boy's penis. After a few moments, the water cleared.

One end of the courtyard was shaded by a pair of twenty-foot palm trees in huge clay pots. Downey walked around to the shady end of the pool. He ran his hand through the deepening water and then flicked a few drops on to the tiles. The water vanished almost immediately, swallowed by the hot, dry air.

Five wicker chairs had been placed in a semi-circle in the shade. Downey sat in the chair nearest the fountain. It creaked beneath his weight. He gestured to Sweets and Mungo to join him. He pointed at Charlie and said, "Beer in the fridge. You mind?"

Charlie went into the kitchen. The refrigerator was a very old Moffat. It was crammed with food, everything in unopened packages. On the bottom shelf lay a dozen bottles of Stella beer. Charlie took four. He found an opener, went back out on to the patio.

And then stood there like an idiot, squinting in the sunlight at the woman sitting in the chair next to Downey.

"Charlie," said Downey, "I think it's about time we introduced you to your new wife."

Charlie put the beer down on the tiles, dropped the bottle-opener in Downey's lap, turned and walked away.

"Don't leave the house," said Downey loudly. He glanced at Jennifer. She was sitting in the wicker chair with her hands clasped in her lap, staring up at the sky through the loosely interlaced leaves of the palms.

"It was supposed to be a surprise," said Downey. "But then, some people don't like surprises, do they?"

Jennifer ignored him. A tiny green lizard clung upside-down to the scaly trunk of one of the palm trees. The animal seemed to sense that it was being watched. It rotated its bulging eyes and then dropped to the tiles, raced across the floor and vanished into a crack at the base of the pool.

"You folks just take it easy and enjoy yourselves," said Downey. "I'll be back in a few minutes."

Charlie was in his room, sprawled out on his back on the bed. Thin slices of dazzling white light lay in a distorted chevron pattern on the floor. Downey opened the window wide enough to reach out and push aside the shutters. Outside, the patch of lawn had withered under the heat of the sun, and the leaves of the fig trees were like beaten silver.

Downey went over to the bed and sat down. He took a sheet of onionskin from his shirt pocket, waved it in Charlie's face.

"That's your death warrant, kiddo. You left your prints all over that house in Gezira. On the door going in. On the newel post and banister as you climbed the stairs. On the wall safe, inside and out. On the black bag and tools you left behind, including the pick you used to kill your partner. Who had several of your hairs clutched in his fist when the cops found him. *Plus* the cops have a number of cotton threads that'll match up with that nifty tuxedo you were wearing when you arrived on our doorstep."

Downey rolled the piece of paper into a ball and bounced it off Charlie's head. "The Cairo Murder Squad knows who you are, and they're after your ass. First degree, Charlie. Three counts."

"I'll take my chances."

"They'll give you a high-profile trial," said Downey, "and then they'll give you twenty years with no hope of parole". He gazed out the window at the fig trees, home now to a flock of tiny, bright yellow birds. He'd always been interested in birds, in a haphazard kind of way. When he was older, and had more time, maybe he'd dust off his field guides, join a club . . .

In the courtyard, Hubie Sweets and Jennifer Forsyth were talking, their voices a low, indecipherable murmur. Downey jotted a mental note to make Jennifer's situation perfectly clear to Sweets. If she wanted to jump in the sack with Charlie, fine and dandy. Everybody else was off limits.

Downey unfolded a second piece of paper and let it flutter to the bed.

"That's an internal memo from Richard Foster. You remember Dick?"

Charlie nodded.

"And he remembers you, Charlie. Vividly." Downey twisted his face into something that might have been a smile. "Tell the truth, he'd like nothing better than to hand you over to the cops, score a few brownie points.

"See, what makes Dick get the runs is the thought of an early posting out of Cairo. He's made threats. Told me to bring you back alive or kiss my big fat government pension goodbye."

"Why does he think you know where I am?"

"Could you have made it out of the embassy all by yourself? Come on, Charlie, be reasonable. Christ, you needed a fucking guide dog to find the toilet."

The birds were busy with the fruit, silent except for the soft fluttering of wings. Downey went over to the window for a closer look. There was a chorus of alarmed chirping. They were easy to look at, but they sure weren't musical. He thumped his fist against the wooden shutter. The flock tumbled out of the trees in an explosion of feathers, gained altitude and disappeared over the top of the wall.

Downey fumbled in his jacket pocket, came up with a packet of individually wrapped multicoloured candies. The cellophane crackled like electricity. "You've got two choices, pal. Uncle Jack, or the cops. Easy Street or the Crowbar Hotel." Downey popped the candy into his mouth, bit down hard. "Mungo tell you how much he and Hubie are making on this little caper?"

"Why would he bother, when he knew you'd do it for him?"

"Two hundred and fifty thousand dollars. Each. No taxes, not a dime." There was a fragment of candy caught between Downey's front teeth. His upper lip bulged as he tried to lever it out with the tip of his tongue. "No reason at all why a man of your talents shouldn't make at least that much, maybe even a little more."

"What talents?" said Charlie.

"You're everything a friend of mine named Liam O'Brady was supposed to be. You did well in the war. You know how to handle explosives. You're a fucking expert when it comes to security devices and how to get around them. Also, Jennifer needs a husband, and your skin's the right colour." Downey popped another candy in his mouth. "Not that Hubie wouldn't volunteer, if I asked him."

"Why does Jennifer need a husband?"

"You know too much about the plot, you won't enjoy the movie." Downey scooped up the papers he'd used to threaten Charlie, stuffed them back in his pocket. The flimsy was a copy of the Hertz rental agreement on the Ford. The second piece of paper had the phone number and address of a Cairo whorehouse written on it.

He unwrapped another candy and stuffed it into his mouth. He had a problem with his eating habits, no doubt about it. It wasn't so much a question of hunger as a need to relieve his nervous tension. The past month or so, he'd really been feeling the pressure, and he was never more aware of it than when he was trying to button up his trousers.

"Something else. You turned a citizen into a hood ornament, played chicken with a car full of Egyptian cops. Two of those cops were badly injured, Charlie. Forensics lifted your prints off the steering wheel of the getaway car, the Citroën."

"If you turn me in, what's to stop me from telling them about you?"

Downey stared at him, his eyes bright. He was going to have to step carefully, Charlie's night on the town with Mungo and Sweets had got him breathing again. He said, "Nothing, now that you mention it. And although they probably wouldn't push too hard, it's a chance I can't afford to take."

Charlie tried to sit up. Downey straight-armed him. His forearm pressed down on Charlie's chest, pinning him to the bed.

"Cuts your choices down pretty considerably, doesn't it?"

"Are you telling me that if I don't cooperate, you'll kill me?"

"Well, no. Not exactly. Probably I'd get Hubie to do it. But yeah, you're right. It'd be my decision, my responsibility."

Charlie was convinced that despite Downey's casual attitude, he meant every word he'd said.

"What would I have to do?"

"Hubie and Mungo are going to waste a joker called Mu'ammar al-Gadaffi, runs a little one-camel country named Libya. You and Jennifer are going to set the guy up, arrange it so Gadaffi's at a specific place at a specific time. Make it easy for Hubie and Mungo to pull his plug."

"Is she a professional assassin, too?"

"She's a lady with a grievance. You're curious about it, ask her."

"Why do you want Gadaffi killed?"

"He's a fucking terrorist. What's the matter, you don't read the papers? We've got all the documentation we need. A big fat bundle of colour shots of airport massacres you can look at, think it'll help you sleep better."

The bed creaked as Downey stood up. He went over to the door, paused with his hand on the knob. "You're an expatriate, Charlie. I haven't tried to appeal to your sense of patriotism. But your country has been good to you, and now she needs you. Maybe that's something you ought to think about, before it's too late."

Downey opened the door and stepped out of the room. Charlie could hear Jennifer Forsyth's voice over the low, cheerful babbling of the fountain. Then Downey slammed shut the door and all he could hear was the sound of his own breathing, rapid and shallow, and the hollow thumping of his heart.

After a little, when he was sure that Downey wasn't coming back, Charlie rolled out of bed and went over to the window. The three half-inch thick iron bars had been painted matt black, and from the bed had been invisible against the backdrop of the trees. He grasped one of the bars with both hands and gave it a sharp tug. There was no movement. He tried the other two bars and found them equally secure.

Afternoon passed slowly into early evening. Charlie stood at the window, watching as the gathering darkness tarnished the motionless leaves of the fig trees, stained silver to black.

Downey spent most of the afternoon with Jennifer, filling her in on as much of Charlie's background as he thought wise.

Later on, in the kitchen, he tried without much success to whistle accompaniment to the bouncy Arab music coming from his portable short-wave Sony. He was making dinner, putting together a *salata beladi*, a green salad, to go with the pot of rice on the back burner and quartet of pigeons roasting in the oven. For dessert there was *baklawa*, a layered pastry made with nuts, honey, syrup and oil that was very popular with the Egyptians, but was claimed by the Greeks to be a confection of their own design. He didn't doubt that the Greeks had the prior claim. In his mind there were no characteristically Egyptian dishes. Native Egyptian food was for the most part Mediterranean recipes made with too many spices and far too much fat.

He found himself whistling out of tune again as he diced a green pepper. A fly circled lazily and then made a perfect landing on the cutting board. He hacked at it with the knife, missed, slashed wildly as it flew upwards towards the ceiling fixture.

From the small and windowless room at the front of the house, there came a sharp, short scream – the sound of a nail being pulled. Downey smiled. Hubie and Mungo had finally decided to go to work.

He scraped the creamy-white pepper seeds into the palm of his hand, tossed them into the garbage, rinsed himself off under the tap. As always in Cairo, the water was lukewarm and the pressure annoyingly low. He crossed to the stove, yanked open the oven door, tugged at a pigeon leg. Another twenty minutes. The rice was going to be a near thing.

He went over to the fridge and took out a bottle of Castel Nestor, a local dry white wine, that he'd had cooling in the freezer. He stripped the foil wrapper from the neck and pulled the cork, poured himself a full eight-ounce glass. Held up to the light, the wine had a faint greenish tinge. He drank half the glass at a gulp, opened a packet of chickpeas and emptied three handfuls into the liquidizer, added lemon juice and a sprinkling of sesame seed oil. He punched buttons and the spinning blades churned the chickpeas and liquids into a glutinous mass.

He drank some wine, checked the pigeon again and found the leg joint sufficiently relaxed. The rice was perfect. He ladled it into a serving bowl and arranged the four birds on a large platter which he carried into the dining room. He lit the candles and shouted for Sweets and Mungo, took off his apron and went down to the far end of the house to tell Charlie and Jennifer dinner was served.

They were halfway through the meal and just getting into the third bottle of wine when Sweets finally said, "I guess Charlie can't make it, huh?"

Downey lowered his fork. "Charlie feels he's being manipulated." He smiled at Jennifer and said, "Nothing we can't work out. What did you think of him?"

"I think I'd like to spend a bit more time with him, before passing judgement. If that's what I'm supposed to do."

"That's what you're supposed to do, all right."

Sweets waved the bottle at Jennifer, tilted the neck towards her. "A little more wine, honey?"

Downey stared coldly at Sweets, but Sweets pretended not to notice.

It was a last supper, of sorts. Downey had hoped it would be a success. But Mungo had withdrawn into himself, Sweets was being petulant and Jennifer wasn't particularly hungry. Too soon, Downey found himself alone at the table. He kept eating long after he'd lost his appetite. The thought of the baklawa congealing in the fridge made him salivate. He wiped his chin with a napkin, drank some more wine.

Sweets and Mungo had gone back to work. In the windowless room at the front of the house, Sweets slid the forked head of his crowbar beneath a nail, pried upwards.

"Where'd all this stuff come from?" said Mungo.

"A warehouse in a village out in the Delta."

"Where'd he get the Land-Rovers?"

"Where'd he get Jennifer, that's what I'd like to know."

"Yeah," said Mungo. "Charlie's a goddamn amateur. She an amateur too?"

Sweets said, "About time Jack told us what the hell's going on. It don't happen soon, I'm on my way back to Colombia." He twisted the crowbar back and forth, inched another nail out of the wood. "Can't help wondering why he'd hook up with a couple civilians."

"Depends what he's got in mind, I guess."

"The night you got shot, Jack asked me how Charlie handled the situation, wanted to know if we could work with him. Know what I said? For a while, maybe. Up to a point." Sweets levered another nail out of the crate. "Know what Jack said?"

"What?"

"Said that's exactly what he had in mind. Using him for a little while. Up to a point." Sweets reversed the crowbar and levered the lid off the crate. He grabbed a handful of shredded paper and threw it on the floor.

"I'm a pro," said Mungo. "That's the kind of people I like to work with. A chain is only as strong as its weakest link, know what I mean?"

"Yeah, sure." Sweets grinned slyly. "On the other hand, somebody pointed a gun at you, and you got shot. And somebody pointed a gun at Charlie, and Charlie wiped him out. So who'm I better off working with, a pro like you or an amateur like Charlie?" Sweets grabbed another handful of paper and then froze, his grin fading, a look on his face like the paper spilled on the floor had just leaked out of his ears.

Mungo became aware of an odour, a sour, ripe stench.

Inside the crate there was something long and bulky wrapped in a layer of thick, milky-white plastic.

Sweets yanked the sheet aside.

"*Jesus Christ!*"

Ahmed Mah – the hired help Charlie'd run over with the Citroën – stared blankly up at them through foggy eyes. There were purple and black contusions all down the left side of his face where it had impacted with the hood of the car. His jaw had been broken, the ligaments and muscles ripped and torn. His mouth hung wide open, and among the pools and encrustations of dried blood that filled his throat and the gaps between his teeth glittered a brand-new filling of polished gold. At the back of his jaw there was a gaping, bloody hole where a lower molar had been torn out. His lips were puffy and swollen. Flakes of dried blood were splattered across his face and in his close-cropped hair. Rivulets of blood had run down his chin. There were broad splashes of blood on his shirt and jacket, the crotch of his trousers.

"Don't get me wrong," said Mungo, "but I think I'd sleep a whole lot better if we drove a great big goddamn wooden stake through the guy's heart before we go to bed tonight."

"Yeah, me too."

"Wonder what Jack wants him for."

"Keep Charlie in line, maybe."

Mungo let go of the plastic sheet. Ahmed Mah's eyes were glazed like donuts, seemed to stare right through him. He gingerly pulled the sheet a few inches higher, so it covered the corpse's bloated face. Sweets replaced the lid and then used the crowbar to pound home the nails.

"Could've been worse," Mungo said when the last nail was in place and the lid sealed tight.

"How's that?"

"Well, at least he didn't get invited to dinner."

22

At the moment of impact, there was a flash of white light. Charlie sat bolt upright. He was tangled in a froth of water, the sheets . . . Jennifer Forsyth stood beside the bed, her coppery hair backlit by the sunlight that poured in through the glass wall separating the hallway from the central courtyard.

"Are you all right, Charlie? It sounded as if . . ." Her voice trailed off. Her eyes were calm, clear. She waited patiently.

"A dream, I was dreaming." He'd been in an airplane, the Mustang his father had wilfully flown into the sea a few days after his war had ended, more than forty years ago. Was that what it had been like, those last few moments? He struggled to sit up. Under the blankets, he was fully dressed.

"There's some tea. Would you like a cup?"

Charlie blinked against the light, the fading images of his dead father, the confident, smiling face that he knew so well but was not really his father's face at all, simply a clever paste job – bits and pieces of half a dozen dimly remembered photographs he hadn't seen in more than thirty years.

Jennifer was gone. He threw aside the blankets and swung his legs over the side of the bed. He was fully dressed – hadn't even taken his shoes off. He stood up, scrubbed his face with his hands. From the kitchen he could hear the familiar, comforting sounds of cabinet doors being opened and shut, the rattle of cutlery and hiss and pop of frying bacon.

He went down the hallway to the bathroom. There was a flush toilet with the water tank mounted high up on the wall, a pedestal sink, rust-streaked bath. He fiddled with the taps and levers until he got the shower working, adjusted the temperature of the water and then stripped naked and stepped under the spray. The plastic shower curtain was brand-new, still showed the fold marks. Pudgy yellow ducks wearing red gumboots tilted bright red umbrellas against angled blue lines of rain.

There was a bar of soap in a chromed wire cage that hung over the side of the tub. He washed his hair first, and then his body, stood motionless under the shower for several minutes, letting the water pound down on his shoulders, the back of his neck.

As he stepped out of the shower, he saw that the clothes given to him at the embassy had been replaced with new underpants and socks, a pale blue shirt, beige cotton trousers, a pair of lightweight leather hiking boots. He towelled himself dry and got dressed. A battery-powered razor, toothbrush and toothpaste lay on the shelf above the sink. He scrubbed his teeth, shaved, ran his fingers through his hair. When he had finished, he turned off the bathroom light and walked slowly down the hall towards the dining room.

Jennifer was sitting at the far end of the table, drinking tea. She smiled at him and said, "I've made some eggs and toast. The plate's warming in the oven."

"Thank you." He took his breakfast out of the oven. The plate was piled high with slices of buttered toast and scrambled eggs. He carried the food into the dining room.

Jennifer sipped her tea. He sat down opposite her. The glass doors leading to the courtyard were open, but the fountain had been turned off. In the absence of the chuckling and burbling of the water, the silence that surrounded them seemed very loud indeed.

Charlie picked up his fork. The tines rang against the plate. He speared a mouthful of egg, chewed and swallowed. The food was delicious. The eggs had been done just the way he liked them, with a dash of white wine and sprinkling of paprika.

Jennifer, hiding behind her teacup, covertly watched him eat. She had scrambled five large eggs and he ate them all without lowering his fork. When he'd finished the eggs he went to work on the toast.

Why was she so attracted to him? She wanted to know all about him. It was obvious she would have to go slowly, even though there wasn't much time.

"Would you like some tea?"

Charlie started. He had completely forgotten that he was not alone. It was a habit – assuming he was all by himself – that he'd had two years to perfect. He gave Jennifer a lopsided, apologetic smile.

She sipped her tea and said, "Jack didn't do a very good job of introducing us, did he?" The tea was cold, but gave her something to do with her hands. "He told me you've spent the past two years in Cairo."

Charlie concentrated on his toast.

Jennifer said, "What did you do in Cairo?"

"Nothing very interesting."

"How and when did you meet Jack?"

"At the embassy, a little over a week ago. I had a problem. He took advantage of it."

"What do you mean, that he's blackmailing you?"

"I doubt if that's what he'd call it."

Unexpectedly, Jennifer laughed.

"What's so funny?"

"I thought you were a mercenary, like the other two."

Charlie shook his head. "All I want is a ticket out of Egypt."

"Back to the States?"

"I haven't thought about it." He stared out at the courtyard, wondering about the lizard, what would happen to it now that the water had been shut off. "Do you know what Jack wants with me, what he's planning?"

"I'm not supposed to talk about it."

"Why not?"

Jennifer shook her head, refusing to answer. Her hair flashed pale sparks in the light.

"I killed two people," Charlie said. "They were the qualifying rounds. I wonder what the main event's going to be like."

Outside, at the front of the house, there was the sudden clatter of a diesel engine.

"What's Downey got on you?" said Charlie.

"Nothing. I volunteered."

"He's paying Sweets and Mungo two hundred and fifty thousand dollars each."

"I'm not in this for the money."

"It isn't fear, and it isn't money. What else is left?"

"Revenge, Charlie. What's left is revenge."

A second diesel engine started up, and a few moments later, Downey stuck his head inside the door. "Let's go, kids."

"Where?" said Charlie.

Downey frowned. "You know Beni Suef?"

Charlie had heard of it. A sizeable town about fifty miles up the Nile from Cairo.

"Just past Beni Suef there's a scenic little village called Gabal el-Nur, then twenty-five miles of dirt track that dead-ends in the middle of the desert, at one of the major wadis."

"A wadi?" said Jennifer.

"It's a dry riverbed," Charlie explained.

"Except during the rainy season," added Downey. He was wearing freshly-pressed khaki trousers, a matching shirt with flap pockets and epaulets, black knee-length boots. The outfit gave him a military air. He shot the cuffs of his shirt and made a show of checking his watch. "Our schedule's tighter than a banker's asshole, you tell him shit's worth money. Let's move out."

Jennifer made a point of finishing the dregs of her tea, a gesture Charlie didn't miss. Downey screwed up his face, gave her a gaudy wink. "You remember to turn off the stove?"

"Excuse me?"

"It's a joke, forget it."

Outside, the air was heavy and still, ripe with the perfume of rotting figs. Charlie walked slowly across the crushed gravel forecourt. The sun beat down on him. Sweets and Mungo waited in the Land-Rovers.

Downey clapped Charlie on the shoulder. "You ride with Mungo," he said. "Jennifer, you're with me and Hubie."

"Shouldn't Charlie and I travel together?" Jennifer said.

"Not just yet. Loose lips sink ships." Downey led Jennifer to the nearest Land-Rover. She shook herself free of his grip and climbed into the back of the vehicle. Most of the available space was filled with boxes of equipment. She made herself as comfortable as possible. Sweets spun the Land-Rover in a tight circle and drove through the open gate and out on to the street.

Jennifer twisted in her seat. The second Land-Rover was close behind. Charlie was slumped in the passenger seat, his head tilted back.

"He'll be okay," said Downey.

"You think so, do you?"

"Trust me."

"If you'd seen the way he wiped Ahmed Mah," Sweets said, "you wouldn't have any doubt about it".

"How did that happen?" said Jennifer.

Sweets started to tell her, but Downey cut him off. "Ask Charlie," he said. "It's his story, let him tell it, if he wants to."

In the other Land-Rover, Charlie sat up front with Mungo Martin as they followed the lead vehicle in an apparently aimless pattern through the outskirts of the city, down a series of narrow, crumbling streets. As they moved gradually towards the outer reaches of Cairo, the district became increasingly rural. They drove past endless blocks of low dark houses with flat roofs upon which ungainly stacks of firewood competed for space with children dressed in rags, tired chickens and scrawny goats, sagging lines of faded laundry.

There were people everywhere, crammed into every available inch of living space. Each year more than one hundred thousand peasants migrated to Cairo from the surrounding countryside. The city gave birth to as many as a thousand children a day, and the fatality rate was now less than twenty per cent, and slowly dropping. Some districts had a population of more than four hundred thousand people per square mile, three times the density of the worst areas of Calcutta. For decades, successive governments had been building cheap concrete highrises on the constantly expanding edge of the city, but there would never be enough housing. An entire family, a dozen or more people spanning three generations, often lived in a single windowless room.

"Hey, check that," said Mungo as they drove past a theatre on the edge of a slum. There was a colour poster of Sylvester Stallone pasted to the wall next to the entrance, his features weirdly distorted, made to look vaguely Egyptian. The film was *Rocky III*, and there was a line-up.

A few minutes later the street suddenly widened, and the traffic tripled in volume. They drove over a bridge that spanned the Nile. In the distance, seen through a soft yellow haze, the three pyramids of Giza were faintly visible. They turned on to the Nile Corniche, the broad shoreline highway that parallels the river all the way to the Aswan High Dam, five hundred and ninety-six miles to the east.

For several miles they drove past rows of modern highrises, restaurants, nightclubs and various shops; the sort of urban mix that can be found in any of the world's major cities. Then, in the blink of an eye, the city had been left behind.

Off to the left, the river was about as wide as the Thames at Tower Bridge, and was buffered from the highway by a narrow strip of vegetation, plantations of date palms, the delicate green of tamarisk trees. To the right there were endless sand dunes punctuated by low outcroppings of limestone. The road was almost perfectly flat. Heatwaves shimmered in the distance, undulating seductively, reminding Charlie of the belly-dancers at the Snapper Club.

Mungo said, "Light me a smoke, Charlie."

The cigarettes were on the dashboard. Lucky Strikes. The matches were from the Hilton. "Mind if I have one?"

"Help yourself."

Charlie lit two cigarettes. "How's the arm?"

"Not too bad. Ever since the fifth grade, I've been a fast healer."

"The fifth grade?"

"That was the year a girl named Frances Bush broke my heart, taught me all I ever needed to know about women. Frances had the seat in front of me. Only girl in class who wore a bra. I spent the whole goddamned year trying to look down her blouse, drooling down the back of her neck. Finally, just before Easter break, I made a grab for her in the cloakroom. Know what she did?"

"Told the teacher."

"No way. Said I could squeeze 'em all I wanted, it'd cost me a quarter a time, same as the other guys."

Charlie flicked ash out the window. "And that was it, you never talked to her again?"

"Are you kidding? I ran straight home and took a ballpeen hammer to my piggy bank. Started mowing lawns, delivering papers. Anything to earn a quarter." Mungo exhaled; smoke dribbled out his nostrils. "She was the first mercenary I ever met. Turned my whole life around. Made me see the world in a completely different way."

Charlie lit another cigarette from the butt of the first. Except for the sparkling blue ribbon of the Nile, scattered date plantations and the odd limestone quarry marked by huge piles of white stone blocks, smoke and dust, the landscape was drab and monotonous – leached of all colour by the sun god, Ra. He finished the cigarette and flipped it out of the window, leaned back and closed his eyes. Within a few minutes he had dozed off, lulled to sleep by the steady hum of the engine, drone of tires, heat, and the mind-numbing sensation of movement without progress.

He woke about an hour later, alerted by a change in engine pitch. There had been an accident. A Mercedes lay belly-up on the side of the road. The car's front end was completely destroyed, the hood driven through the windshield. Rusty water dribbled from the punctured radiator. A wheel lay on the sand sixty feet from the body of the car.

Mungo stopped well behind Downey, leaving himself plenty of room to maneuver. A thin man wearing a white suit and sunglasses was standing with one foot on the running board, studying Sweets' International Driver's Licence. Three uniformed policemen peered through the Land-Rover's dusty windows, their faces pressed against the glass.

The man in the suit snapped his fingers and held out his hand, demanding further identification.

Charlie saw Downey lean across Sweets and hand over a sheet of paper. The man stiffened, quickly handed the paper back to Downey. The Land-Rover's tires chirped as Sweets accelerated down the highway. The man tossed off a hasty salute as Charlie and Mungo drove by.

In the shade of the stricken Mercedes, four corpses lay in a tidy row by the side of the road.

The terrain became semi-arid, the landscape empty except for the occasional stunted bush. They drove past the villages of El 'Aiyat and Barnasht and then the ruins of the pyramid of el-Lischt, reduced by vandals and the passage of time to a heap of rubble.

At the village of Gerza, a secondary road branched off to the right, heading south into the Fayyum, the largest oasis in Egypt. The Fayyum was watered by the Bahr Jusuf, Joseph's Canal, the land made temperate by Birhet Qarrum, a lake thirty miles long and six miles wide, but with an average depth of only thirteen feet. King Farouk and Winston Churchill had hunted the Fayyum, shot ducks and smoked cigars.

The narrow strip of green along the roadside had widened, and now there was vegetation everywhere, as far as the eye could see. Olives are grown in the Fayyum, and crops of rice and cotton, wheat and maize, bananas and a wide variety of citrus fruits. Charlie stared out at the soft greens of the fields, at a solemn young boy standing erect at the side of the road with a chicken perched on his head.

Mungo saw the boy too. Pointing, he thumped his fist on the wheel and laughed out loud. "What happens when that bird takes a shit?" he said. "Jesus, *what happens when he lays a fucking egg?*" The boy stood on the thin pedestal of his shadow. Mungo's laughter swirled around him, drifted across the fields.

They passed a small pond, home to a flock of ibises, large white birds with pipestem legs and thin, downcurved bills. As the Land-Rover shot past, the birds spread their wings and moved sideways in a peculiar, shuffling little dance.

They drove through the village of Medum, the turn-off to the enigmatic 'false pyramid' with its distinctive three-step design. The villages were spaced much closer together now, forcing Mungo to drive slowly to accommodate the local traffic – farm trucks loaded with produce bound for the markets, donkeys, the odd dromedary, many people on foot.

Charlie noticed that very few of the pedestrians were elderly. This was largely due to the snails that infest the rivers, canals, and drainage ditches of Egypt. The snails play unwitting host to microscopic larvae which, in the flatworm stage, enter the human body through the skin, then mate and discharge thousands of eggs. In time, the eggs break through the tissues of the bladder or bowel, causing internal bleeding. This cycle often continues for years. A cure is available, but it is only sixty per cent effective. Nearly all the treated peasants return to the fields. Reinfection is inevitable, and fatal.

Mungo trailed Downey's Land-Rover through the dusty villages of El-Maimum and Ishmant. Finally, they arrived at the Provincial Capital of Beni-Suef.

Beni-Suef is strategically located at the junction of the Corniche and Highway 22, which wends its way through the middle of the Fayyum and then back to Cairo by way of the desert. The town's population is about one hundred and fifty thousand. Beni-Suef was famous in the Middle Ages for the quality of its linen. Now it is widely known for its cotton processing factories.

Sweets made a left turn. Mungo followed him down a short, broad street. Sweets turned right. They crept past a huge wooden cart piled high with cabbages. On the narrow sidewalks, ageless women in black *meliyas* – bulky loose-fitting gowns – stood in the scant shade offering for sale small squares of mirror glass, boxes of flimsy wooden matches.

Downey made another left.

"Where the hell is he going?" grumbled Mungo. His arm ached. He didn't heal as quickly as he used to. Was he getting old? Something else he'd have to try not to think about, next time the shooting started.

Sweets' Land-Rover cut across to the far side of the street and stopped in front of a small café. Mungo parked behind him, under a wide awning made in the interests of economy from the remnants of many different bolts of brightly-coloured cloth. On the sidewalk stood a dozen mismatched chairs, several battered tables with tops of sheet tin.

It was apparently time for lunch.

Downey led Jennifer to a table near the café door, away from the dust and noise of the street. He pulled out a chair for her, sat down beside her with his back to the whitewashed wall. Sweets took the chair across from Jennifer. Charlie and Mungo sat at an adjoining table.

"I ate here once before," Downey said to the group at large. "About six months ago. The roast lamb was great, the beer cold enough to make your teeth ache."

The proprietor came through the doorway, the strands of glass beads rattling noisily. He was short and very fat, and he wore a grey turban and cotton galaba. The galaba was such a pure white that it had a luminescent quality. Charlie was reminded of the flock of ibises he'd seen earlier that day. The man was carrying a plastic box containing a dozen long-necked bottles of dark Aswan beer. He used his sandalled foot to drag a chair closer to the table, put the beer down with a thump.

"Naharak sa'id wemubarak!" he said. May your day be a happy one. This was the standard phrase with which Muslims greeted non-believers.

"Naharak laban," said Downey, replying in kind. May your day be white as milk.

Sweets had an opener. Froth ran over the necks of the bottles. Charlie could smell the hops. He was very thirsty. Even in the shade, the temperature was close to a hundred.

"Orid salata baeiaedi," said Downey. "Shawirmae. Roz." The salad would come with cucumbers, tomatoes, onions, parsley and watercress, green peppers and mint, and would be followed by the roast lamb and rice. He held up his left hand, fingers splayed to indicate five separate orders, and then, hoping to reduce the possibility of error further, pointed at his four companions and himself. "Orid waehid awhwae tork, shokran," he added. One Turkish coffee without sugar.

The man nodded, offered a shallow bow, and slipped back through the bead curtain into the depths of the café. A moment later a boy in a blue galaba with black stripes came towards them carrying five glasses of water, three in his right hand and two in his left, a dirty finger thrust deeply into each glass.

"Saves him cleaning his nails," said Sweets.

"Don't drink it," said Charlie.

"Think you had to tell me that?"

"I wouldn't risk the salad, either." Charlie told them about *Mansoni* and *Haematobium*, the two species of freshwater snails that acted as a kind of halfway house for *schistosomiasis* larvae. The only way to become infected by the parasitical worms was through exposure to tainted water, which was probably what the vegetables had been washed in. When he'd finished his lecture, there was a long, thoughtful silence.

Charlie drank some beer, played with the droplets of condensation on the side of the bottle. The label fell away in his hands. Poor quality glue.

The boy returned, carrying a tiny cup of thick black coffee. He put the cup down in front of Jennifer and gave her a huge, beaming smile, a smile so generous and unrestrained that it distorted his entire face, and made her laugh, and clap her hands in delight.

They were halfway through the lamb when a military jeep armed with a light machine-gun and festooned with several whip antennae rounded the corner and raced down the street towards them. A man leading a donkey down the middle of the road had to hit the creature with a stick to avoid being run over. As the jeep roared towards the café the driver altered course so that the vehicle straddled the curb, near wheels up on the sidewalk. The brakes shrieked and the jeep skidded to a stop in the shade of the multi-coloured awning.

There were two men in the jeep, both of them wearing the uniform of the Egyptian army. The driver was no more than seventeen years old. His passenger was a full colonel, a tall, hawknosed man in his thirties. The red tabs of a staff officer were fixed to his epaulets and three rows of gleaming service medals were pinned to his chest. He tapped his driver lightly on the shoulder with his cane. The boy stared unblinkingly down the street through the jeep's dusty windshield.

The colonel jumped lightly out of the jeep, pulled a chair up to Downey's table and sat down. He had bright blue eyes – a legacy of his Mameluke ancestors. He said, "May I see your papers, please." His English, Jennifer thought, was really very good.

Downey produced his passport and visa, green card and the mandatory insurance certificate.

The colonel flipped open the passport and turned it sideways to study Downey's picture. "Not a flattering portrait, is it?"

"A mark of its authenticity, colonel."

Chuckling, the colonel peeked inside the plump, pale grey envelope wedged between the second and third pages of the passport. He shuffled rapidly through the fat wad of crisp new hundred-dollar bills. "American money is so serious looking, don't you think."

"Eye of the beholder."

The colonel slipped the envelope inside his uniform blouse. He put Downey's passport and the other papers on the table next to Downey's plate. "What is it that I'm supposed to say to you now? Ah, yes. Everything seems to be in order!"

"Correct," said Downey. "And then you click your heels and do a quick fade."

"For now."

"That's right, I almost forgot. You get a couple more lines in the second reel."

"It's a small part, I agree. But crucial to the development of the plot, wouldn't you say?"

"Absolutely."

The colonel's bright blue eyes lingered on Jennifer for a moment, and then he stood up and pushed away from the table, climbed up on the hood of the jeep and stepped over the windshield and sat down, snapped his fingers at his driver. The jeep lurched forward and demolished a chair. Grinning, the colonel rolled his eyes in mock dismay. He slapped his driver on the back of the head, knocking his hat off. The jeep roared down the street, vanished in a cloud of dust.

"What the hell was that all about?" said Sweets.

"The colonel just agreed to sub-let his apartment." Downey showed them the heavy brass key the colonel had left beneath his passport. "He's also agreed to perform a few miscellaneous chores. A little bit of this and a little bit of that." Downey prodded at his lamb with his knife and fork, sliced off a chunk of fat and stuck it in his mouth. "Charlie, how do you say, 'How much do I owe you for the furniture?' in Arabic?"

"Bikaem," said Charlie.

They finished the meal. Downey produced a camera and made them say cheese. "For the golden years," he said as the shutter clicked. "When all I have left is a few fond memories."

Five miles past Beni-Suef they came to the village of Tizmat el-Zawaya, where a narrow bridge had been built across the river, and there was a *piste*, or track, that led almost one hundred miles through the Eastern Desert to Ras Zafarana, on the Red Sea coast.

Herodotus wrote that "Egypt is a gift of the river Nile", and there is a saying that although the country is seven hundred miles long, it is also, due to the great influence of the river, only about sixty feet wide. They drove over the hump of the bridge. Herodotus was right. A stone's throw from the river the land was barren, rock and dust.

The piste was fairly straight, in better condition than might have been expected. Mungo stayed about one hundred yards behind the lead Land-Rover, keeping to an average speed of about twenty miles per hour. The road climbed steadily.

Exactly five miles past the river, at a place where the road was relatively flat and there was a steep wadi off to the right, the two vehicles pulled over to the side and stopped.

Mungo turned off his engine. Downey and Sweets got out of their Land-Rover and walked towards him across the gravelly, hard-packed sand. Downey had a crowbar. Mungo got out of the Land-Rover and went around to the rear of the vehicle, swung open the tailgate. Charlie watched as Mungo and Sweets eased one of the wooden crates down on the sand. Downey handed Sweets the crowbar. Sweets popped the lid off the crate.

Downey had a gun, a .45 automatic. He squatted on his heels beside the crate, aimed carefully, and fired once. The gun kicked in his hand and the sound of the shot echoed across the landscape. Downey stood up. He gave the crate a violent kick.

Charlie caught a quick glimpse of a limp body and bloated, nightmare face. The corpse of Ahmed Mah tumbled over the lip of the wadi, and then there was nothing to be seen but a small cloud of dust that hung motionless in the hot, dry air.

Downey uncocked and holstered the .45. His eyes met Charlie's. He winked.

23

Richard Foster, CIA Chief-Of-Station Cairo, lay flat on his back in the middle of his bed, a lowball glass of Ballentine's balanced precariously on his naked chest and the new addition to the typing pool nestled in the crook of his arm. Sheila had boasted she could crank out more than a hundred and twenty words a minute on her IBM Selectric. He'd been sceptical at first, but now he was a believer. The young lady was extremely agile, with a pair of hands any wide receiver would be proud of.

Directly above Foster, the wicker blades of the ceiling fan rotated slowly, the soft hum of the electric motor lost in the more aggressive drone of the bedroom's air-conditioner. He sipped his Scotch, idly watched the blades chase each other in an endless circle. He was sexually exhausted, but wasn't feeling the least bit peaceful. He couldn't stop thinking about an unexpected telephone call he'd received that afternoon, from a Cairo police lieutenant named Omar Heikal.

Foster had spoken with Heikal twice before during the past few days. Both conversations had centred around Charlie McPhee.

Heikal was with the Cairo robbery squad. It was he who'd given Foster his background information on Aziz Mehanna, the safecracker who'd killed himself, a pair of French tourists and several camels on the night highway between Alexandria and Cairo.

Foster had taped the phone call and he had the tape with him now, in a portable cassette recorder. He drank the rest of the Scotch, put the empty glass on the floor beside the bed. Sheila muttered softly in her sleep. Sweet dreams, baby. He reached for the tape recorder, turned the volume down low and punched the PLAY button. The sprockets turned. There was a faint hissing sound. He activated the Dolby noise reduction system, adjusted the volume.

". . . may be of interest to you," said Heikal, and then sneezed three times in rapid succession, and apologized. Heikal sneezed a lot. His voice was hoarse, raspy, as if he had a permanent cold. But his problem, he'd explained at length, was that he had a deviated septum, and was prone to allergies.

"Tell me about it," said Foster on the tape. Sheila stirred in her sleep. She scratched her belly and her hand fell on Foster's thigh, red-lacquered nails resting a fraction of an inch from his penis. Foster turned to look at her, see if she was playing possum with him. Her eyes were closed. Her breathing was slow and steady. Her lips were slightly parted. For some inexplicable reason, Foster found the outward thrust of her prominent upper teeth extremely erotic. He felt a pleasant stirring in his groin.

"Do you remember the car accident?" said Heikal. "Do you remember the unfortunate thief Aziz Mehanna, whose tools were later found in the house on Gezira?"

"Yeah, sure. What about him?" Listening to himself, Foster had to grin. He sounded very tough, not at all the kind of guy who could be pushed around.

"One of the soldiers in the patrol that cleared away the wreckage has just been placed under arrest by his commanding officer. The fool was caught trying to sell some jewellery he'd somehow managed to steal from Aziz's wrecked Mercedes."

"Doesn't pay, does it?"

"What is that, my friend?"

"Crime," said Foster.

Heikal laughed appreciatively, as befits a poor man with a deviated septum who is deeply enamoured of expensive American hospitals and advanced American surgical techniques. It nagged at Heikal, the constant sneezing and dirty handkerchiefs, the snoring, fear of bad breath, unheard jokes and distant, whinnying laughter of his fellow policemen.

"A pair of diamond earrings were recovered, and a rather gaudy diamond-encrusted dinner ring. It took us quite a long time, but we've managed to trace the ring back to its rightful owner."

"Better late than never," offered Downey.

Lieutenant Heikal sneezed.

"Bless you," said Foster coldly.

"The jewellery belonged to the wife of a Libyan diplomat named Butros Murad, who is presently stationed in Istanbul. We are certain Murad is an officer of the Libyan Intelligence service."

"A colonel, by any chance?" Foster's voice was flat, incurious, betrayed no special interest.

"Yes, I believe so."

"How long has he been in Turkey?"

"Three months."

"And before that?"

"We cannot say."

"Do you by any chance have a photograph?"

"As it happens, I do."

"Wonderful." There was no point in asking Heikal where his information had come from, or even how he'd found out that Foster was interested in Murad. All he could do now was root out the leak, plug it solid. "I owe you one," he said to Heikal.

"Yes," Heikal agreed. He sneezed twice in rapid succession; nasty, viscous, burbling explosions, and then hung up.

Foster pushed the STOP and then the REWIND buttons on the tape recorder.

It was Sunday, 27th October. Despite Sheila's vigorous attempts to cheer him up, it had not been a very good day. Foster's people in London had spent a tall stack of Agency dollars following up Downey's visit to London. They had researched and discreetly interviewed every man, woman and child Downey had come in contact with – no matter how fleeting or casual the encounter may have been. Friday afternoon the results of this futile expenditure of cash and manpower had come thumping down on Foster's desk in the form of a file that was eight inches thick and weighed twelve pounds.

Foster had studied the photographs and reports until his eyes felt as if they were about to fall out of his head. It had taken him all of Friday night and most of Saturday morning. When he finally reached the last page, the only thing he'd learned for certain was that his agents seemed to be labouring under the misapprehension that they were being paid by the word.

The agent who had vanished near the Snowdon Aviary was still missing.

In his mind, Richard Foster slammed the cumbersome file shut and used it to pound some sense into the heads of his agents, then dropkicked them and the file out his window and into the Nile.

If there was anything of value in the file, it was the stuff on Jennifer Forsyth. Born 09 October 1954, she had been an only child. According to the public records, her mother had died of injuries suffered in a motorcycle accident in October 1961, one week to the day after Jennifer's seventh birthday. Jennifer's father, Edward, had been driving. The coroner's report had found him blameless. The other driver had been drinking, and was travelling at high speed on the wrong side of the road when the accident occurred.

Edward Forsyth had been an engineer, a builder of bridges. He'd been employed by a firm with offices in London, New York and Rio. During the last ten years of his life, he'd built bridges all over the world.

In Tripoli, Libya, in August of 1972, Edward Forsyth had vanished without a trace. At the time, he'd been in the country for several months. There was no mention in the police report of the project he had been working on when he'd disappeared. Were there any rivers in Libya? Foster wasn't sure, although he didn't think so. But there were canyons and valleys that had to be crossed by road and rail, innumerable large and small wadis that would have to be spanned in order to make them navigable during the rainy season.

Foster slipped out of bed, taking care not to disturb Sheila. He picked up his empty glass and padded silently out of the bedroom and down the hall to the kitchen.

His refrigerator was a deluxe model, equipped with all the extras, including an ice-maker. Foster pressed a red plastic button and cupped his hands at the bottom of the outlet chute to minimize the bang and clatter of the miniature avalanche of falling ice. He dropped two cubes into his glass and tossed the rest into the sink, poured himself a stiff shot of Scotch.

From his living room window he had an unobstructed view of the Nile. Despite its beauty, the river gave him no pleasure. During his stay in Egypt it had come to symbolize every last thing that was wrong about the country. The river was huge and sprawling, sluggish and utterly predictable, so heavily laden with silt that it was all but impossible to see beneath the surface. But most vexing of all – at least from the point of view of a bureaucrat like Foster, whose primary task was the rapid collection and analysis of information – was the fact that the river, like the city and twelve million souls who lived within it, moved at its own killingly slow pace, and there was nothing he or anyone else could ever hope to do about it.

He sipped his Ballentine's, rotated the glass in a tight little circle to make the ice tinkle. The brittle, cheerful sound did nothing to improve his mood. In his business the difference between spectacular success and crushing failure depended as often as not on an ability to separate half-truth from unadulterated fiction, lies from rumours, innuendo from fact. The rumour that vexed him in this particular case was that Forsyth had been a patriot as well as an engineer, and that during his travels across the globe he'd worked as a messenger boy and bit player for MI6, the British Secret Service.

As for the facts . . . Well, shit. The *fact* was that the Libyans had discovered Forsyth moonlighting on Her Majesty's behalf, and consequently tortured him to death at the military barracks at Sabha, about four hundred miles from Tripoli.

The fly in the ointment, however, was that the rock-solid, irrefutable *fact* of Forsyth's murder at the hands of Qadhafi's goons was based solely on the as-yet-unsubstantiated *rumour* that Forsyth was working for MI6.

Foster made a mental note to see what he could do about getting the Brits to dust off their files, poured himself another shot of Scotch and wandered back into the living room.

Dusk had fallen; the sky was the colour of rose petals and the lights of the city were spread out below him all the way to the horizon, as far as the eye could see. He filled his mouth with Scotch. There were a number of strong indications that Forsyth had been well-connected. For example, someone with a lot of juice had seen to it that the insurance settlement was made promptly, with none of the lengthy delays one would expect, given the circumstances of his disappearance.

Foster considered the information he had been given about Forsyth's daughter, Jennifer. As soon as news of his presumed death had reached her, she'd dropped out of art school and started spending the insurance money. Large sums had been wasted in a fruitless attempt to find out what had happened to her father. It was unclear as to whether she hoped to find that he was still alive, or merely wished to confirm his death.

By the summer of 1974, two years after Forsyth had vanished from the face of the earth, only a few thousand pounds remained of Jennifer's inheritance, and she had nothing to show for her efforts to discover her father's fate. She re-enrolled in art school, but left in the middle of the first term.

In the following year, she held a variety of jobs. Most were in retail sales. None lasted more than a month or two.

In January of 1976, at a party hosted by one of her art school friends, Jennifer met a man named William Scott, an antique dealer with a long-term lease on a small piece of strategically located King's Road frontage. Scott was 43 years old, almost twice Jennifer's age. Old enough to be her father, in fact, and perhaps that's what attracted her to him. Or it may simply have been that he happened to propose at the right moment, when she was in desperate need of the security, or happy illusion of security, that he was in a position to offer her.

In any case, Jennifer Sarah Forsyth and William Boswell Scott were married in a civil ceremony three weeks to the day after they first met, William acting more or less spontaneously for the first and probably the last time in his life.

There had been a small reception afterwards, in the shop. In retrospect, Jennifer had confided to one of her more talkative friends, the most powerful and abiding memory she had of her wedding day was the sticky-sweet odour of the waxes that had been liberally applied to the antique furniture and her new husband's moustache.

On 11th December 1976, ten months after they were married, Jennifer gave birth to their only child.

She named the girl Cynthia, after her mother.

William had inherited the antique business from a recently deceased older brother. Although he shared Jennifer's love of the exotic woods and craftsmanship of antique furniture, he hated the hours he was forced to spend in the shop, the casual loitering and polite dickering, the nasty business of closing the sale. He spent far too much of his time on buying trips, venturing as far afield as the north of Scotland. Often he was gone a week or more. It was not at all unusual for him to come back with nothing to show for his efforts but an empty checkbook and a few amusing anecdotes.

The business suffered, and so did the marriage. It was June of 1983 when William finally announced that he regretted to have to say he was not suited to the rigours of fatherhood, and that he wanted out.

It seemed he'd met another woman. Someone whose age and temperament and finances were more closely suited to his needs. In exchange for an uncontested divorce and promise of permanent relief from child support, he was willing to sign away the antique shop's stock, arrange a transfer of the lease.

It took Jennifer several long, hard years to turn William's bad habits into a thriving and profitable business. She'd barely turned the corner when Downey walked back into her life.

Standing at the window, staring blankly out at the purpling sky and maze of shadow and light that was Cairo, Foster sighed wearily and turned his mind to thoughts of Sheila. He'd hoped that an afternoon of sexual abandon with a social inferior who knew her place might clear his mind, but apparently it was not to be. His problems continued to crowd in on him. The abundance of sex had only managed to leave him feeling tired and dull, even a little bit old.

Charlie McPhee's wife's lawyers were nothing but a bunch of goddamn egg-sucking vipers, hissing at him over the telephone two and sometimes three times a day. The phone bills must be fucking enormous. It was getting so he dreaded fielding the calls. What could he tell them, that Charlie McPhee had taken a hike and that his prime suspect was his senior fucking field operative? *Shit!*

Foster massaged his forehead with the lowball glass full of melting ice. He'd specifically told Downey he wanted daily reports, but hadn't heard from the bastard in more than a week. Downey wasn't at his apartment and according to the super and other tenants, he hadn't been seen in the building for almost a month. Meanwhile, the Libyan, Colonel Butros Murad, was partying it up in Istanbul at the exact same time Downey was supposed to be putting together a team to smooth his defection from Libya. And to top it all off there was that single, infuriatingly enigmatic line that Downey had spoken to Jennifer as he stood beneath the downpour in that square off King's Road. *I have a short film I think you should see.*

And what was her response? Not what it should have been. Instead of demanding to know what the hell Downey was talking about, she had – acting completely out of character – submissively followed him through the rain and into the back of that goddamn taxi. Which, against all odds, happened to cruise past at precisely the right moment.

Chewing angrily on an ice-cube, Foster strode back to the kitchen counter, snatched up the bottle of Scotch and unscrewed the metal cap with a violent sideways flick of his thumb.

What film could Downey have shown Jennifer Forsyth that was capable of inducing her to turn her back on her daughter and business and fly to Cairo, if that's where she was?

Foster poured himself a healthy slug. Obviously the film was related in some way to the disappearance of her father. Was it possible Edward Forsyth was alive and that Colonel Butros Murad knew where he was and intended to retrieve him?

But why would Downey be interested in Edward Forsyth in the first place?

Because he was romantically involved with the guy's daughter?

Jesus Christ. Foster slowly screwed the cap back on the bottle. First thing in the morning he'd make a call to records, get them to pull Downey's file. Not the current stuff, but the one covering 1972, the year Edward Forsyth was supposed to have been tortured to death at Sabha.

Foster had no idea what Downey was up to, but he knew one thing for sure.

He was going to find out.

24

THE EGYPTIAN DESERT

There was a lot more room in the Land-Rover, now that the corpse of Ahmed Mah had been disposed of. Jennifer stretched out on the seat and concentrated on keeping her face averted from the open window, the hot, dry, vampire wind that seemed to drain the moisture from her skin.

In the front seat, Downey was sleeping quietly – an amazing feat, considering the jostling they were getting as they bounced along the piste, the narrow, bumpy track twisting and turning and rising and falling interminably through the hard, gritty landscape.

Jennifer had always thought of the desert as being romantic, but there was nothing romantic about endless expanses of sand punctuated infrequently by columns and outcroppings of wind-carved stone – the only movement in all that emptiness the distant flickering of heat-waves. She'd tried to engage Sweets in conversation several times since they'd crossed the Nile. Each time, he had brusquely rebuked her. Sweets was in an introspective mood. She shuddered, thinking of the long hours she'd spent with her head resting against the rough pillow of Ahmed Mah's coffin.

They were driving down a deep, narrow wadi. The bed of the wadi had been sand at first, then loose gravel. Now they were driving much too fast across a field of almost perfectly round stones the size of bowling balls. Sweets was hunched over the wheel, staring unblinkingly into the depths of shadow, as if in a trance.

"Shouldn't we slow down?" Jennifer's voice was low, hoarse.

Sweets, hunched over the wheel, gave no indication he'd heard her. She leaned towards him, and in the same instant the right front wheel glanced off a large rock, causing the jeep to swerve sharply to the left. Downey's head snapped sideways, bounced off the window frame. He swore. Sweets stabbed at the brake pedal and the jeep skidded across the stones.

Downey rubbed the side of his head. "Jesus, Hubie, the minute I nod off, you try to fucking kill me."

Sweets glared into the rearview mirror, as if the near-accident was somehow Jennifer's fault.

Downey leaned over to study the odometer. "How far have we come since we dumped the body?"

"Twenty miles, a little more."

"Pretty soon now, we should hit a fork going off to the left. Miss it, and we'll end up in the Gulf of Suez."

The wadi was opening out, widening. The banks on either side were much lower, offering less protection from the sun. Jennifer turned to peer behind her, into fading shadows. There was no sign of the Land-Rover carrying Mungo and Charlie. She tapped Downey on the shoulder. "We've lost the other jeep."

"What?" Downey twisted in his seat. He craned his neck to look past her, back down the wadi. "Stop over there, Hubie." He pointed towards a steeply rising ledge of rock a short distance up the wadi.

Sweets parked as close as possible to the wall of rock, hunting for shade.

"Turn the damn engine off," said Downey.

Sweets rotated the ignition key. The diesel engine clattered and died. It was late afternoon but the temperature was still rising. He was suddenly aware of the depth and intensity of the heat. He sipped from the water bag.

Downey climbed out of the jeep. Heat seeped up through the soles of his boots. Contracting metal ticked softly. "Hear anything, Hubie?"

"Nope." Sweets lit a cigarette. Flicked the match out the window. His mouth was as dry as a bale of hay, and despite his sunglasses, his eyes ached from constantly squinting into the glare. He sucked on the cigarette, drawing smoke deeply into his lungs.

Downey, his hands clasped behind his back, started walking down the wadi.

"Shouldn't we go back?" said Jennifer.

Sweets found her in the rearview mirror. Her hair was tied up high behind her neck. Her face was pale, her eyes dark. She looked pretty good. He shook his head. "No way of telling how far they've come. This kind of ground, you'd have to be driving a tank to leave any tracks." He filled his lungs with smoke, exhaled. "Best thing we can do is stay put and wait."

"Why aren't the Land-Rovers equipped with short-wave radios?"

"I'd say Jack fucked up. You could ask him."

Jennifer watched Downey pace back and forth across the field of stone bowling balls. She'd read somewhere that round stones were stones that had travelled. She tried to picture the wadi in the rainy season, a flash flood washing all those pieces of desert a little closer to the Nile. It was almost impossible to imagine it raining in a place like this, beneath such a faultless blue sky. Water falling into this kind of heat would evaporate a thousand feet up.

She remembered the King's Road, sitting under the plane trees with Downey while the rain made the leaves tremble high above them, the sound of water dripping down through the branches like a barrage of tiny, muted drumbeats.

Downey had worn a dark suit and lightweight poplin raincoat, wielded his expensive new umbrella as if it were a sword. Now he was dressed in a soldier's uniform of soft greys and yellows, the understated tones of the desert. On his right hip he sported a large black pistol in a canvas holster. As he marched aimlessly across the stones, he kept adjusting the weight of the gun.

The sound of the shot reverberated once again across the desert. Downey kicked out. Ahmed Mah's body vanished in a cloud of dust. Jennifer blinked; the horror faded.

She said, "How did you get involved in this kind of work?"

Sweets frowned. "By accident, I guess. The way most people fall into their lives. Circumstances and luck."

Downey was staring up at something in the sky.

Sweets leaned forward and peered out of the windshield. Thirty thousand feet up, there were the fleecy white lines of half a dozen vapour trails, sparkle of sun on metal. Fighters. He lost the airplanes in the glare of the sun. God, it was hot. He grabbed the water bottle, unscrewed the cap and offered the bottle to Jennifer.

"Thank you."

Sweets gave her a long, slow smile. "Hey, you're welcome."

The bag was heavier than it looked. Jennifer took the weight of it in her left hand, fingers splayed. The bag was limp, and had a tendency to roll sideways. A few drops of water spilled into her lap, and then she got the hang of it. She drank deeply. The liquid was warm and thick in her mouth, tasted strongly of chlorine. She handed the bag back to Sweets.

"Good, huh?"

"If it was any hotter, you could use it to brew tea."

"The canvas is supposed to breathe. Evaporation keeps the water cool. That's the theory, anyhow." He drank from the bag, screwed the cap on tight. "How are you and Charlie getting along?"

"Fine."

"Uhu. Well, if things don't work out, you just gimme a call, know what I mean?"

"No. I don't think I do."

He grinned. "Is that right? Really?"

Jennifer ignored him. Downey had wandered down to a bend in the wadi a hundred or more yards away. He was sitting on a boulder in a tiny patch of shade. He'd taken off his boots and socks. His feet were startlingly white.

Sweets cleared his throat. "I'm not the kind of guy usually who has to get pushy with women."

"Lucky you."

Downey had unholstered his big black gun. He pointed the weapon straight up and fired three times, spacing the shots. The spent cartridges tumbled through the air and were lost among the heatwaves and rocks.

"What's he doing?"

"Trying to signal Mungo and Charlie. Waste of ammo."

"Why?"

"Noise bounces off the rocks, echoes all over the damn place. A man standing a couple hundred yards away wouldn't have any idea where the sound was coming from."

"But he'd know we were somewhere nearby."

"Be able to tell anyway, he was that close. Could smell the Land-Rover. Oil. Rubber. Formaldehyde fumes leaking out of the upholstery. Hot paint. Perfume."

"I'm not wearing any perfume."

"No? Must be natural."

"Who was the dead man?" The question surprised her. She hadn't meant to ask it, not quite yet. It had just popped out.

"His name was Ahmed Mah," said Sweets. "He worked for Jack. Still does, in a way. Maybe."

Downey fired three more shots. Jennifer saw the muzzle flashes, pale orange in the slowly lengthening shadows. The last of the cartridges tinkled on the stones. Downey began to reload.

"What happened to him?"

"Charlie killed him." Sweets caught the look in her eyes. He said, "No kidding, cross my heart."

"Why?"

"Beats me, honey."

Sweets had been right about the sound of the shots not carrying. Mungo's Land-Rover came into view around a bend in the wadi a split second before Jennifer heard the laboured sound of its engine – a dull muttering that swelled in volume as the vehicle picked up speed and raced towards them.

Jennifer glanced at her watch. They'd been waiting almost two hours. Sweets had been dozing, but now he was wide awake, his eyes bright and wary. She heard the scrape of stone against stone, looked up and saw Downey striding towards them.

Mungo's Land-Rover skidded to a stop.

Downey leaned in the open window, forearms resting on the metal sill, the big .45 calibre automatic dangling negligently in his hand, muzzle an inch from Charlie's knee.

"Careful with that thing," said Mungo.

"You're the one who ought to be more careful. What happened?"

"We got lost."

"I figured as much." Downey yanked open the Land-Rover's door. He jerked his thumb down the wadi. "I fired eighteen rounds. I want the brass picked up. All of it."

"No way," said Mungo.

Downey blinked, but recovered fast. "Nobody asked you to do shit. I'm talking to Charlie."

Charlie said, "We've only got a few more hours of daylight left. Why don't we tidy up on our way back out of here."

Downey squinted up at the faultless blue sky. After a moment, he holstered his gun. "Okay, let's move out."

The two Land-Rovers bounced across the rocks like a pair of huge, mechanized puppies. Afternoon slowly gave way to dusk. The wadi had been an arena of stark contrasts, impenetrable black and blinding white; but as the sun dropped below the horizon, the desert was slowly enveloped in a soft, golden light.

The wadi widened and grew shallower as they continued across the desert. The ground was for the most part flat and hard, but the going became much slower as the light faded. Soon they were travelling in complete darkness, the wadi hardly more than a faint depression.

Mungo saw Sweets' brake lights flash crimson. Twin cones of light swept across the desert as Sweets swung the Land-Rover in a tight circle until it was broadside to the track. The headlights illuminated a wide gate set in a ten-foot-high chain link fence with a filigreed topping of razor wire. Fastened to the gate was a large sign – a skull and crossbones divided by a vertical black arrow with a red bar through it, both arrow and bar enclosed in a crimson circle. Below the arrow there were several lines of Arab script.

"It's a military zone," said Downey as Mungo parked alongside.

"Not Club Med? You sure?"

Downey tossed Sweets the heavy brass key the Egyptian colonel had traded for an envelope stuffed with American dollars at the sidewalk café in Beni-Suef.

"Open wide."

Sweets got out and sauntered down the road to the gate. He fumbled with the chain, inserted the key into a large padlock protected by a heavy steel sheath. On the far side of the fence a pair of bright green eyes glowed like drops of liquid neon, abruptly vanished.

"Desert fox," Downey said to Jennifer. "What they called Rommel. You hunt?"

"No."

"Me neither. Never could see the point of stumbling around in the bush trying to shoot some poor animal when it's so much easier to hit the local supermarket. Flirt with those pretty checkout girls."

Jennifer tried to imagine Downey flirting. It was like trying to imagine a dinosaur in flight.

The chain rattled harshly. Sweets pushed the gate open.

Downey slid across to the driver's seat. His belly pressed against the wheel. He put the Land-Rover in gear and drove slowly through the open gate, Mungo following close behind. Jennifer heard a clang as the gate swung shut. A few moments later, Sweets climbed back into the Land-Rover. Downey held out his hand, palm up. Sweets gave him the key.

Downey waved the key in Sweets' face. "Know what I paid for this?"

"Couple hundred bucks. But meals are included, and you can drink all the wine you want, for free."

"What?"

"Club Med, Jack."

"A hundred grand," said Downey. "But for that we get two thousand acres of land, a barracks, airplane hangar with half an acre of floor space, concrete parade ground, thousand-yard rifle range and a helicopter landing pad equipped with night lights and a real nice red-and-white striped wind sock."

"Flush toilets?"

"You're going to be too busy to take a piss, Hubie."

Sweets scratched his jaw. "Thirty days, Jack. Sure seems like a long time."

"We'll be here a couple of weeks at the most."

"Doin' what? Time we talked about that."

"This's boot camp for the recruits. I want you and Mungo to whip 'em into shape."

"For what?"

"Later, Hubie. Think you're man enough for the job?"

"I can fake it." Sweets lit a cigarette. In the flare of the match, his pupils were very large. "This's as far as me and Mungo go until you fill us in, okay? The hotel was a nice change of pace. This doesn't look as if it's gonna be any fun at all."

"Gotcha," said Downey. He spun the wheel sharply as the Land-Rover hit a rut. The road had apparently been used by a convoy of tracked vehicles; the surface was a mass of troughs and ridges that was a challenge even for the Land-Rover's suspension. Downey shifted into second gear. The headlights bounced across a drab moonscape of rock and sand.

"A hundred thousand dollars for a two-week holiday in the world's biggest gravel pit." Sweets' teeth flashed in the darkness. "Man, you a real sharpie, certainly do know how to strike a deal."

"This is the fucking Middle East. Life is cheap, but living costs a goddamn fortune."

A few minutes later the road levelled out, became much smoother. They accelerated past a concrete-block guardhouse and a raised zebra-striped gate studded with reflectors and warning lights.

Beyond the guardpost the road was paved; a narrow ribbon of asphalt with a solid white line painted down the middle. Downey straddled the line, shifted up into second and then third gear. They shot past a sign riddled with large-calibre bullet holes.

"What was that all about?" said Sweets.

Downey shrugged. "Some kind of religious revolt, flared up and got out of control. This was maybe six months ago. A couple of officers were shot. A field decision was made to bring in the Cobras. Place was a shambles, time they finished shooting. They executed the ringleaders, stripped the joint bare and locked up. Read the paper all day long, you'd never find a word about it."

Downey braked, turned left. The headlights picked out a low-slung brick structure with boarded-up windows and a flat roof. He stopped in front of the building, switched off the engine but not the lights. Mungo pulled up beside them.

There was a brief moment of silence. Something large and clumsy flew into the glare of the headlights. There was the chirp of an insect. A second insect joined in, and then a third. Within the space of a few seconds the night was filled with a shrill, metallic twittering.

"Sounds like we crashed a Tupperware party," Sweets said.

Downey flung open his door. The chirping stopped immediately, as if he'd flicked a switch. "All ashore that's going ashore."

There was a padlock securing the front door of the building, but Downey had a key. He told Charlie to fetch a Butagaz lantern.

Jennifer zipped up her jacket. It had been warm inside the cramped confines of the Land-Rover, but now, out in the open, she was beginning to feel the cold.

Charlie trudged towards them, a lantern in each hand. Sweets had matches. There was the malignant hiss of escaping gas, and then a burst of oppressive white light.

There were twelve rooms in the building, six to a side, divided by a central hallway that dead-ended at a communal washroom. Downey had it all figured out. Mungo got the first room on the left, Sweets bedded down directly across the hall. Downey took the room next to Sweets. He put Jennifer in the adjoining room. Charlie was quartered opposite Jennifer. Sweets rolled his eyes in mock dismay. "No playing musical chairs," Downey said, staring him down.

They unloaded the Land-Rovers, stored the equipment in an empty room. When they'd finished unpacking the supplies, Downey handed Sweets a loaded submachine-gun, binoculars and a flashlight, and sent him out into the darkness to stand the first watch.

Jennifer said a general good night to which only Charlie responded. She walked slowly down the hallway to her room, the moving lantern splashing light and shadow across the low ceiling and bullet-pocked walls.

Downey waited until he was sure Charlie and Jennifer were asleep, then called Mungo and Sweets into his room.

"I guess it's about time I told you guys what you're doing here."

"Past time," said Sweets.

"We're going into Libya, to wipe out Gadaffi."

"Just the five of us?"

"Four," said Downey. "I'm gonna stay home and wash the dishes."

Sweets lit a cigarette.

Downey said, "Jennifer's father was killed in Libya almost twenty years ago. As a public relations gesture, Gadaffi's going to let her have the body, take it back to England. Charlie's posing as her husband. You two are going in separately, disguised as Tunisian labourers. There'll be lots of pomp, lots of circumstance. One of those rare occasions when we'll know in advance where Gadaffi's going to be at a specific time. Charlie will be your contact man, keep you informed."

Mungo waited for a moment and then said, "That's it, that's the plan? Sounds a little vague to me, Jack."

Downey gave them all the details, answered all their questions. He waited until the very end before he hit them with the clincher: told them a dissident faction of the military were involved, that they were the hitmen for a CIA-sponsored coup.

Downey was very persuasive. By the time the meeting finally broke up, Mungo and Sweets were already counting their money.

Jennifer's room was about eighteen feet long by twelve feet wide. Three single beds took up most of the floor space. The only other furniture in the room was a grey metal footlocker and a portable wardrobe made of thick cardboard. The window was high up in the wall opposite the door. Jennifer climbed up on a bed to see if the window was locked, and found it had been painted shut.

She crouched to peer under the beds, held the hissing lantern well away from her as she peered inside the footlockers and wardrobe. In a corner behind the door she found a nest of cobwebs and a large scorpion. When she moved the light closer, the creature scuttled across the dusty floor towards her, its carapace gleaming oily yellow, tiny claws scratching on the concrete. She instinctively kicked out. There was a brittle sound, like shells breaking, and the creature was reduced to a dark wet smear, a shapeless stain.

She backed away from the corpse and sat down on the nearest bed. She sat motionless for several minutes, struggling to regain control, and then having thoroughly checked the bed lay down on it and wrapped herself in a coarse grey army blanket Downey had given her.

The blanket smelled of mothballs, and sweat.

Jennifer found herself staring blankly at the dark spot on the floor where the scorpion had died. She rolled over on her back. The ceiling was rough plaster painted a muddy green. There was a light fixture, but the tubes were missing and the wiring had been torn out.

She looked at her watch. It was fifteen minutes past midnight. The seconds ticked away, the hand shuddering around the dial. The lantern sighed endlessly. Off in the distance, a door slammed shut. Downey had told her to turn off the lantern as soon as she was settled in, because there wasn't much fuel and they had to make it last. Well, to hell with him. He probably didn't have an inexhaustible supply of bullets, either, but that hadn't stopped him from spending the afternoon shooting at vapour trails.

It had been a long and stressful day. The blanket warmed her, the hissing of the lantern had a hypnotic effect. Jennifer closed her eyes, and in a little while she dreamt that she was a child once again and that her father . . .

Her father was still very much alive.

25

In the morning Jennifer awoke to the tinny blare of a portable radio, the death rattle of a cheap speaker pushed beyond its limit. She rolled over on her back, stretched, blinked against the shaft of light streaming in through the window. Her body was stiff and sore – a legacy of the previous day's wild ride across the desert. She massaged the back of her neck. The sound of the radio was suddenly much louder.

Jennifer looked up. Sweets stood in the doorway. A portable radio dangled from his shoulder by a shiny black strap. "Is it true what they say about English women, that you always sleep with your clothes on?"

"Next time, knock first."

Sweets showed a few more teeth. "You don't loosen up a little, there might not be a next time."

"Perfect."

"Breakfast's on the table, honey. But you can have it in bed, that's what you want."

"What I want is some privacy. Shut the door on your way out."

Outside, in the shade of the building, empty crates served as a table and chairs. There was coffee warming over the thin blue flame of a camp stove, fried eggs in a pan, a bowl of tinned fruit and individual-size boxes of Kellogg's cereals.

"Mungo already grabbed the Bran Flakes," said Sweets. "I was too polite to ask why."

"Where is he, and where's Charlie?"

"Back in a minute."

"What about Jack?"

"Halfway to Cairo, by now." Sweets poured himself a cup of coffee. "Just the two of us left, it seems." He smiled, eyes glittering.

Jennifer used her thumbnail to slice open a box of cereal. The wax paper felt brittle beneath her fingers. There was an open can of cream on the table, but no milk. She began to eat the cereal dry, a few flakes at a time, picking at it not because she had an appetite, but to give herself something to do, keep herself occupied.

Sweets said, "Did I mention Jack left me in charge?"

"You get it in writing?"

Sweets kept talking, but she paid no attention to him, concentrating instead on the crisp, fragile sound of the cereal breaking under the pressure of her fingers. A few minutes later she heard the thud of boots on asphalt. She glanced up and saw Charlie and Mungo walking down the road towards her, both of them wearing wide-brimmed felt hats. Charlie had a bulky backpack slung across his shoulders. Mungo was carrying two packs. They were armed with automatic weapons and heavy black pistols identical to Downey's. Mungo handed one of the packs to Jennifer and dropped the second pack at Sweets' feet.

Sweets said, "Time to hit the road."

"Where are we going?"

Sweets shrugged elaborately, his dark green shirt tightening across his broad shoulders. "Ten miles out and ten miles back. Thought we'd start you off kind of slow, give you a chance to ease into it. Finish your breakfast, honey. Sooner we get started, the faster we'll get back."

"I'm not hungry."

Sweets shrugged into his pack. Mungo handed him one of the automatic weapons, a Steyr MPi submachine-gun, the Austrian Army's weapon of choice. Downey considered it more reliable than an Uzi, and he was right.

Jennifer, too, was given a pack and a Steyr, a pistol in a canvas holster. The pack was made of dun-coloured nylon. It had a tubular aluminium frame and padded shoulder straps, a cotton-mesh back-band designed to reduce heat build-up. The pack was heavier than it looked, but well-balanced.

Mungo tossed her a mud-coloured hat with a wide, floppy brim. The hat fit her perfectly. She wondered if there was anything about her that Downey didn't know.

Sweets said, "Okay, let's get at it."

Jennifer tilted the hat down low over her eyes and smiled at Charlie. "How do I look?"

"Terrific," said Sweets.

Jennifer ignored him. She kept her eyes steady on Charlie.

"Really terrific," Charlie said after a moment.

"You can steal my lines," said Sweets, "but don't even think about stealin' my girl".

Jennifer slung the Steyr over her shoulder. The front sight and cocking handle dug into her ribs. She adjusted the weapon so that it hung properly, and then swung the thick leather pistol belt around her waist. Several new holes had been punched in the leather. She fastened the big brass buckle and swung the holster around so the weight of the gun rested on her right hip. She wondered what was in the pack. Food, extra ammunition – maybe a couple of leftover cinderblocks? Sweets started down the road. Charlie fell in behind him. Jennifer hurried to catch up. She wondered what Downey had in mind, why he thought this kind of training was necessary. It was something she would have to ask him, next time they met.

They walked in single file down the narrow asphalt road, past an empty hangar. Heat radiated from the sheet metal. They passed a row of prefabricated metal quonset huts and an abandoned anti-aircraft gun emplacement; a ring of upthrusting metal bolts surrounded by a few leaky sandbags and low concrete walls bleached white by the sun. Jennifer turned and looked behind her. Mungo was standing by the hangar, watching.

She waved, but he didn't wave back.

Shafts of sunlight bounced off the corrugated metal roofs of the quonset huts where the camouflage paint had bubbled away. A gust of wind made an inverted cone of dust swirl across the road. They left the last of the huts behind.

For the first mile or so the ground was fairly flat, with a surface of coarse sand and stone, outwash material which had been eroded by the rains and winds of centuries from the low, distant plateaus that surrounded them. The predominant colour in this subdued and featureless landscape was pale grey. High above them, the sky was a thin, washed-out blue. Jennifer kept her eyes on the ground, following Charlie's footsteps, the marks his boots made in the sand.

Some time later, she became aware that Sweets was calling her name. She looked up, startled, and saw that she had fallen several hundred yards behind. She felt a flash of despair followed by a quick surge of anger, and picked up the pace. They crested a small hill. Sweets handed her a pair of Zeiss binoculars, waved at the area in front of them. "Take a look."

Jennifer used the binoculars to scan the floor of the desert. Her head swam with a thousand shades of grey, confusion of dense black shadows. Heatwaves made the ground shift and sway. In all of that vast emptiness, it was impossible for her to maintain any sense of scale. She handed the binoculars back to Sweets. "What's the point?"

"The point is, stay close. Don't lag behind, this's no place to get lost."

Charlie unclipped his canteen from the frame of his pack, unscrewed the top and drank deeply.

Sweets shook several oval brown tablets from a small tin box into the palm of his hand. He offered the pills to Charlie. "Eat up."

Charlie stared suspiciously at the pills, making no move to accept them.

"Salt tablets," said Sweets. "This kind of heat, you should take two or three every couple of hours."

Charlie screwed the cap back on his canteen. He made no move to take the tablets. Sweets tossed the tin to Jennifer. "Help yourself. Don't worry about how much water you drink, we got all we need."

Jennifer held up her canteen, shook it gently. "I hope you know something I don't, because I'm down to my last mouthful."

"Trust me. Okay, let's move out. Single file. Stay about twenty yards apart. If either of you thinks I'm going too fast, speak up. And keep drinking that water. This kind of heat, you need at least five quarts a day to stay healthy. Your canteen runs dry, give me a shout and we'll fill it up."

"With what?" said Jennifer.

"The water in your pack. What you think you had in there, honey, a change of cast-iron underwear?" Sweets started down the slope, across the jumble of stone and shadow, into the glare of morning sun.

The military base had slipped from view. All around them, as far as the eye could see, there was nothing but endless vistas of sand and rock, blurred, indistinct horizons, the faded blue of the empty sky.

About noon, Sweets led them into the scant shade of one of the thousands of dry streambeds which form the natural drainage system of the desert. The desert may remain dry for several years at a time. But when it does rain, two or more inches of water can fall on several thousand square miles of land within a period of an hour or less, and even the deepest of the wadis is filled to overflowing with an astonishing and sometimes fatal swiftness.

Jennifer slipped out of her pack and sat down, leaned back. Loose sand stuck to the sweaty skin at the back of her neck. She emptied her canteen for the third time that morning, watched Sweets over the canteen's metal rim as he yanked off his boots and thin woollen socks which he draped across a rock to dry. In the sunlight, loose strands of wool fibre glistened, seemed to dance in the heat. Sweets opened his pack, rummaged around inside and came up with a plastic Ziplock bag filled with a mix of nuts and grains, dried fruit. He shook some of the protein-rich food into the cupped palm of his hand, began to eat. To Charlie, he said, "Want some?"

"I'm not hungry."

"Don't matter. Gotta keep your strength up." He grinned at Jennifer. "Never know when you might need it." He tossed back another handful of nuts. His jaws moved energetically, and in the perfect silence of the desert, Jennifer clearly heard the sound of the nuts crumbling between his teeth. He drank some more water and put his canteen down carefully in the shade. "Ten minutes, then we move on." He tilted his hat down low over his head, closed his eyes.

Jennifer hunted through the outer pockets of her pack until she found a pouch of trail mix. She forced herself to eat a handful of nuts, then drank some water. Charlie sat cross-legged and listless, gazing sightlessly at the far side of the wadi. She said, "What are you thinking about?"

For a moment she thought he hadn't heard her, then he said, "Isthmus Cove," so quietly she almost missed the words.

"Where's that, Charlie?"

"Santa Catalina." Once a year, he had hired a float plane and he and two or three of his top executives had flown twenty-six miles out to the island to drink beer and scramble around on Orizaba Mountain, hunting the wild boar that flourished among the eucalyptus trees and dense scrub. He tried to conjure up a snapshot of himself down at the beach at the end of the day, digging into a cooler full of chunk ice and Dos Equis in long brown bottles.

The wadi grinned at him, radiating heat.

"Jack told me you're from Los Angeles."

Charlie nodded.

"Do you know anybody in the film business?"

"A few people."

"Actors?"

"Accountants," said Charlie, smiling.

Sweets woke up as effortlessly as he'd fallen asleep. He pulled on his socks and boots and started down the wadi. By the time Jennifer and Charlie were on their feet he was thirty yards away. He crouched, and quickly built a small cairn of stones.

He walked back towards them, gravel crunching under his boots. "We got about half the water we started out with. Should be able to squeeze it all into one pack." He jerked his thumb over his shoulder at the pyramid of stones – a makeshift target. "Low score carries the load. Any questions?"

"I've never done any shooting," said Jennifer. "I haven't the slightest idea what to do."

Sweets unslung his submachine-gun. "What we have here is a Steyr

MPi-69. Uzi clone, but an improvement on the original. This little thing on top of the barrel is the cocking handle. You pull it back – like this – when you intend to fire the weapon. Also you got to put the safety in the off position. That's this little button here, see how it goes in and out? The magazine holds thirty-two rounds. You can fire singles by using light pressure on the trigger. On full auto the rate of fire is five hundred and fifty rounds per minute, rips off a full mag in three seconds." He pointed at Jennifer. "Ladies first."

Jennifer cocked the gun and released the safety. She pressed the coathanger stock against her shoulder, aimed at the pile of stones and gently pressed the trigger. A fountain of dust and small pebbles erupted a foot to the left and several yards beyond the target. The shock of the recoil jerked the barrel upwards, wrenching her arm. Her finger convulsed on the trigger and the gun exploded again, burying several rounds in the heart of the sky.

"Not bad," said Sweets. "No, really."

For the next few minutes the wadi was filled with the crash and roar of gunfire. Jennifer's eyes stung from burnt cordite. Her ears hurt and her wrists and shoulder ached. Charlie had several near-misses, but she hadn't even come close to hitting the pile of stones. She pulled the trigger again. Her gun was empty.

"Lesson two," said Sweets, and showed them how to reload.

Jennifer aimed carefully, squeezed the trigger and emptied the magazine in a single, extended burst. The cairn vanished in a cloud of rock splinters and dust. Brass tinkled on the rocks. The last of the ricochets whined shrilly into the distance.

Sweets said, "Looks like you're our new water boy, Charlie."

With Sweets leading the way, they crossed a broad ridge of basalt columns; tightly-packed rods of shiny black stone that marched down the slope like a series of giant steps. Jennifer shifted her pack, easing the weight on her shoulders. During the course of the day they had walked almost fifteen miles. She could feel the distance in her thigh and calf muscles, across her shoulders where the straps of the pack had shifted minutely with each step she took, chafing her skin, gradually rubbing it raw.

The new boots had begun to bother her. Her feet felt warm, swollen. Her eyes were irritated by the extreme dryness of the air, dust, constant glare of the sun. She had a headache. She was bone tired.

She stumbled along, forcing herself to take it one step at a time, plodding along more by habit than conscious effort. The afternoon sun drifted slowly down through the blank, featureless sky. She broke stride to sip from her canteen. A distorted shadow danced across the floor of the desert, arms gyrating madly. Then, in an instant, the lunatic shadow crumpled and flew apart.

She was lying flat on her back. Her pack was gone. Her sunglasses had fallen off and the sun poured into her eyes, blinding her. Tears streamed down her cheeks, evaporation tightened her skin. She became aware of hands moving lightly across her face and shoulders. The hands pulled her into a sitting position. Charlie. She tried to smile up at him. Sweets stared down at her, his face huge, eyes full of darkness. Charlie's face and Sweets' face jostled for space. They shouted at each other. The words were slow and thick, distorted, as if she were deep under water.

Something pressed against her lips. Lukewarm water tumbled into her mouth, spilled down her throat. She swallowed, choking. More water splashed on her face. She closed her eyes, imagined she was lying in the surf at a place called Isthmus Cove.

"Is she going to be okay?" said Charlie.

"She'll live." Sweets picked Jennifer up in a fireman's lift. Her hat fell off, and her hair tumbled across her shoulders in a spill of molten copper. There was a faint, delicate tracery of mauve in her eyelids. Her cheeks were a translucent white, her lips slightly parted.

"Beautiful woman, isn't she?"

"I hadn't thought about it." Charlie picked up the hat.

Sweets laughed. A raucous, grating sound, like a crow high up in a tree. "You know something, Charlie? I almost believe you."

Still laughing, Sweets started towards an oasis of rock, a towering grey mass of stone perhaps a quarter of a mile away. He moved with surprising speed; Charlie had to work hard to avoid falling behind. By the time they arrived at the rocks he was soaked with sweat, trembling, exhausted. He sank to the ground. Chalky-white encrustations of salt stained his shirt. He watched blearily as Sweets poured water over a folded cloth and knelt beside Jennifer to sponge off her face.

"We're gonna have to wait here until the sun goes down," Sweets said. "Let the lady get some rest. Might as well make yourself comfortable, catch some sleep." He slipped his pack under Jennifer's head. She was lying on her side in the fetal position, hip outflung, her breasts rising and falling with her rapid, shallow breathing.

"Yeah, gorgeous," said Sweets. Lazily, he reached out and unfastened the top button of Jennifer's shirt.

"Hey," said Charlie.

"Good for her. Help her cool off." Sweets' fingers worked at another button.

Charlie pushed himself to his feet. He cocked his Steyr and pointed the stubby barrel at Sweets' belly.

Sweets hesitated. He was sure that Charlie wouldn't pull the trigger, shoot him in cold blood. But at the same time, he had a vivid memory of Charlie's face giving absolutely nothing away as he lifted his hands above his head in a gesture of surrender and then jumped on the gas pedal and slammed the big black Citroën into Ahmed Mah.

Sweets smiled, turned his back on Charlie and walked away.

With some people – the ones who were soft inside and always trying to do what was right – showing your back was the safest thing you could do. Sweets was just the opposite. He was all bone, no heart. When this little caper was over he was going to fix Charlie real good. Slice and dice. Get in close, cut the fucker up like a goddamn watermelon.

26

CAIRO

When Foster arrived at his office on Monday morning, he found Downey sitting at Dorothy's desk, his run-down shoes up on the dust cover of her IBM Selectric. It was ten past eight. Foster was early. His secretary wasn't due in for another twenty minutes.

Foster pointed at Downey's shoes. "She catches you like that, she'll break your legs."

"She could break my heart, too, the way she stares at me when she thinks I'm not looking."

Downey was eating a chocolate bar. A Baby Ruth, his favourite brand. He popped the last of the candy into his mouth, licked his fingers, tossed the wrapper into Dorothy's wastebasket and trailed Foster into his office.

Foster, backlit, stood by the greenish-tinged plate glass and stared out at the Nile. He'd obviously planned to arrive early; his pre-set Mr Coffee machine burbled like a lovesick pigeon on a marble-topped table by the window. Downey sat down. The coffee machine grumbled pompously. Or maybe it was Foster, passing gas. After a moment Foster turned away from the window and said, "Coffee, Jack?"

"Please."

Foster poured two cups. When he took the pot from the machine, dark-brown beads of coffee continued to pour from the dripper on to the warming plate. It sounded like somebody pissing on a camp fire, reminded Downey of Boy Scouts. He tried to recall the badges he'd won – there'd only been one or two . . . Knots. He remembered squatting in his tent with a length of quarter-inch rope, fingers moving as if they had a mind of their own. Yeah, knots. He'd been a whiz at knots. Still was.

Foster walked across the carpet like a man on a tightrope, handed Downey a full cup. Downey balanced the cup on his knee while he lit a filter-tip Marlboro.

Dorothy smoked Marlboros. Foster wondered if Downey had picked the lock on her desk. He went around behind his own desk and sat down, the chair creaking under his weight.

Downey's cheeks puffed and then deflated as he blew out the match. He dropped the match in his saucer and sipped his coffee, smacked his lips. "This is pretty good stuff, Richard. Real tasty. Maxwell House?"

Foster made no attempt to hide his displeasure. "My own special blend, a mix of French Roast and Colombian." He sipped. "My kid sister sends me a couple of pounds a week. It comes over in the diplomatic pouch. I've got my own grinder. A Braun." Sip, sip. "Where the hell have you been, Jack?"

"Here and there. I was up in Beni-Suef a couple of days ago. You know the oasis, the Fayyum?"

"I've been there."

"So has Charlie," said Downey, grinning.

Foster paused, the rim of his cup suspended an inch from his pendulant lower lip. "You've seen him? Know where he is?"

"Sort of."

Foster glared across his desk. "Don't fuck with me, Jack." His cup crashed into the saucer. "I might not be able to prove it, but I know damn well that you were the guide-dog who led him out of here."

Downey said, "Jesus, Richard. Gimme a fucking break. I had to do it. I needed him. The place on Gezira was a fucking Libyan safe-house. Charlie walked out of there with a fistful of cash and an envelope containing a list of the names of Libyan hit-men in the Middle East, Italy, France and West Germany. Plus he had the names of the so-called 'stray dogs' these guys were supposed to bump off."

"Where's the list now?"

"Ashes to ashes, Richard."

"How did he know what the names meant?"

"He didn't. I figured it out." Downey tapped his forehead. "Used my brain."

"I want the names, Jack. All of them."

"We're working on it."

"Work harder."

Downey said, "I have to tell you, from my point of view, the important thing is that the Libyans believe Charlie's got the list."

Foster nodded his understanding. "You need him for bait."

"What I need is a couple of Libyan agents. Seems to me, the easiest way to get them is put a tether on Charlie and sit back and listen to him bleat."

"So you snatched him."

Downey gave Foster a pained look. "You make it sound like I whacked him on the head with a ballpeen hammer and carried him out of here in a cardboard suitcase. Truth is, he was desperate to get the hell out of the embassy."

"Why?"

"You think he wanted to go back to Los Angeles? With his problems, would you?"

"He told me he was planning to go back. Working hard, saving his money."

"He lied."

Foster used the heels of both hands to push away from his desk. He stood up and went over to the Mr Coffee machine and poured himself a fresh cup, stirred in some cream. He neglected to ask Downey if he wanted a refill. Downey kept talking, careful not to show his gratitude.

"Charlie knows what's waiting for him in LA. His wife's lawyers, a pack of fucking barracudas, all primed to chew him up and spit him out in little pieces. Trust me, when I offered him the chance to jump, all he wanted to know was – where's the hoop?"

"You should have told me you were going to take him."

"You'd have said no."

Foster leaned back in his chair. He let his eyes drift out of focus but kept seeing a clear picture of his career going down the drain.

"Tell me something."

Downey cocked an eyebrow, waiting.

"Has Charlie got anything to do with this Libyan colonel you've been chasing?"

"Well, yeah. Maybe."

"What was his name again?"

"Murad. Colonel Butros Murad."

Foster watched Downey extinguish his cigarette in the dregs of his coffee. What a charmer.

Despite the excellent acoustic insulation provided by the triple-glazed bulletproof glass windows, Foster could faintly hear the laconic Memphis accent of the marine sergeant down in the courtyard as he shouted his way through a changing of the guard. The sergeant was a lifer. He'd done three tours in Vietnam and never been scratched, an accomplishment that, after a few drinks, left him feeling guilty and morose. Foster had shared a table on the Sheraton terrace with the sergeant, who'd plunked himself down with nary a word of encourage-ment, then spewed out a drunken three-minute history of his life and times; a garbled verbal slide show that Foster had found simultaneously terrifying and mundane.

The sergeant had run out of steam, more drinks had arrived. The two men sat in stony silence for half an hour or more, the sergeant sweating copiously in the sunlight while Foster watched him covertly from the shady side of the table. The sergeant was a big man, with a bony, insensitive face and the kind of belligerent and lifeless eyes that looked everywhere and saw nothing. His hair was cut so short his scalp looked shaved. He kept wiping his head with the calloused edge of his hand, sluicing the accumulated sweat across the bony planes and ridges of his skull. Sweat poured down the back of his thick red neck and soaked the starched collar of his shirt, staining the material black.

In the time he spent at Foster's table, the sergeant drank three bottles of Budweiser and exuded at least two of them through his pores. When he finally decided to leave, it was all Foster could do to stop himself from screaming his thanks. The sergeant, blessed with jungle cunning, must have sensed this. He'd left no money on the table.

Foster believed Downey and the sergeant were two of a kind. Downey would find the sergeant's scattered insights funny instead of shocking, respond by laughing out loud and slapping the man on the shoulder, jarring him out of his pathos. Maybe get drunk with him, chase some women. Both men radiated the same faint musk of barely restrained violence. Foster wondered how long Downey could sit motionless and silent and perfectly at his ease in the upholstered chair Foster had airfreighted all the way from Washington specifically because it was so fucking uncomfortable.

Foster leaned forward a few inches. The tips of his fingers pressed down on the polished surface of his desk. "Tell me more about Colonel Murad," he said. "What makes him worth the risk of involving a high-profile civilian like McPhee?"

"Murad made the first move," said Downey. "Mailed me a present."

"It arrived at the embassy?"

"My apartment."

"Wasn't that kind of risky?"

A condescending smile.

"What was it, what did he send you?"

"Information. Mostly on the 'Great Artificial River'." Downey meant the multimillion dollar underground pipeline Gadaffi was constructing to carry water from subterranean lakes in the desert to the barren coastal plains.

"Anything military?"

184

"Bits and pieces. He warned me about a six-pack of Mig 23s that were off-loaded at Tubruq three weeks ago. Planes came in on a freighter from Murmansk. Nobody else knew about them, I checked it out."

Foster picked up a pencil. He tested the point with the ball of his thumb, glanced out the window at the featureless sky. It was his way of indicating he was not particularly impressed.

"The information on the underground pipeline is worth a lot to us," said Downey. "If Gadaffi actually manages to suck water out of the desert, he'll be a hero. But if he fucks up, there could be a coup."

"And where, in your opinion, would that leave us?"

"Who can say? Maybe a little better off, maybe a little worse." Downey took a last drag on his Marlboro, and dropped it into his cup. There was a faint hissing noise. "You know as well as I do what the Middle East is like. Volatile. Completely unpredictable. No one, and I mean nobody, has the slightest fucking idea what's going to happen from one minute to the next. At this point, all Murad wants is to establish his credentials, convince me he's sincere."

"Has he succeeded?"

"Sure, why not?" Downey grinned. "Problem is, the suspicious bastard insists I put it in writing."

"What does he want?"

"Anonymity. Financial security. A nice house in a nice neighbourhood. Cablevision. Neighbours who are blonde and stacked and nymphomaniac. Eternal Youth. A shiny new car. The usual mix of hopes and dreams."

"Assuming we meet his conditions, what do we get in exchange? I mean, *exactly* what do we get. What's your wonderful colonel got that's worth letting him fuck the American taxpayer for the rest of his life?"

"Missile sites. Hardware. Anticipated scenarios and available responses. All the crunchy numbers on Soviet, Cuban and East German technicians and military personnel working in Libya." Downey lit another cigarette. "And he's got something else, an ace in the hole."

"What's that?"

"A younger sister named Tahia."

Foster blinked. He felt his face flush red, and found he didn't care. "*Gadaffi's wife?*"

"You got it."

Foster went over to the machine and warmed his cup, scratching a little extra time to collect his thoughts. Gadaffi's wife's brother. Jesus! The intelligence stuff was great, but the propaganda value was immense.

It'd be the snatch of the century, turn him into a fucking legend.

If it was true.

Foster went back to his desk, sat down. "Why wasn't any of the stuff the colonel gave you mentioned in your field reports?"

"It was a precondition." Downey spread his arms wide, in a gesture that was deliberately theatrical. A little coffee slopped over the rim of his cup and soaked into the carpet. He didn't seem to notice. "The colonel has no objections to a public wedding, but he wants the engagement kept secret."

"Fuck him. You should've kept me informed." Foster could emote too, if he was in the mood. He half-rose from his chair and thrust out his arm, stabbing at Downey with his index finger. "Remember this, Jack. We work for the United States Government. We're all family. No one walks alone."

"Right," said Downey. "Kate Smith's ghost gonna jump out of the closet, or do we go ahead and start the anthem without her?"

"When was the last time you talked to Murad?"

"Three days ago."

"This was actually a physical contact, *mano a mano*?"

"A blind date." Spookspeak. What Downey was saying was that he'd put himself at risk by meeting Murad at a location of Murad's choice. He'd used the arcane lingo of his trade because he knew that Foster, like most CIA bureaucrats, had a weakness for buzzwords.

"Describe him for me."

"Five ten, a hundred sixty pounds. Regular features. Curly black hair, brown eyes. Hawk nose."

"Scars?"

"None that I could see."

"What else?"

"His hair is a little on the longish side, parted on the left. He wears a platinum watch with a black face and Roman numerals, a diamond ring on the pinkie finger of his left hand. His ears are small and set close to his head, no lobes."

"Skin colour?"

"Fairly light. His eyes, as I said, are brown. He has heavy eyebrows. The nose is definitely his prominent feature, large and sharply hooked, flared nostrils. A symbol of his overall character."

"Which you consider . . ."

"Acquisitive. Predatory."

"How many times have you actually met him?"

"Once."

"That your idea, or his?"

"Mine." Downey was obviously mystified. "What're you getting at, Richard?"

"A very close and reliable contact recently told me there's a Libyan Intelligence Corps colonel named Butros Murad stationed at the Libyan embassy in Istanbul. He's been there six months. Hasn't left town since the day he arrived. And yet, you tell me you met him here in Cairo only three days ago."

"Turkey's just a quick hop across the Med. Cram enough horses under you, you're there in less than an hour."

Foster pulled a buff file marked TOP SECRET from the top drawer of his desk, flipped it open and turned it so Downey had a clear view of the glossy eight-by-ten colour photograph.

"Nice-looking guy. Who is he?"

"Guess."

The picture was a straight-on head and shoulders shot of Colonel Murad wearing his shiny-brimmed officer's hat and dun-coloured uniform jacket. The Intelligence Corps badge on the hat and two silver bars on his epaulets gleamed in the bright light of the photographer's flash. Murad was in his late fifties. He was bespectacled, fat, balding. He had a snub nose and Dumbo ears. There was a scar running from his left eye all the way down to the corner of his tight, disapproving mouth.

"It's Bob Hope, right?"

"You're a funny guy, Jack. But not quite funny enough."

Foster slipped the photograph back into the folder and locked it in his desk. "Looks to me as if somebody's been jerking you off."

"Maybe," said Downey grudgingly. "But on the other hand, it could be *your* zipper that's at half-mast." He exhaled a plume of smoke towards the air-conditioner. "I'll look into it, okay?"

"Good idea," said Foster dryly. He scratched his scalp, examined his fingernails. "I want Charlie McPhee standing in front of this desk by noon Friday."

"I'll do what I can."

"You damn well better."

Downey stood up. Cigarette ash spilled from his lap to the carpet. He started towards the door.

"Noon Friday!" Foster shouted. "He isn't here, it's all over. You're gone. History!" A pause. "In other words, you can kiss your pension goodbye!"

The ultimate threat. Downey shut the door behind him. The latch clicked softly.

Foster gave him time to clear the reception area, buzzed Dorothy on the intercom. He told her what he wanted and went into his private washroom and splashed cold water on his face, brushed his teeth, ran a comb through his thinning hair. He needed a drink.

Foster was the kind of man who craved routine, but that morning he spent an extra half hour at his table on the terrace of Shepheard's, knocking back Tom Collinses and watching the world drift by. When he finally returned to his office, a red-flagged file was waiting for him on his desk – a faxed photostat of the original, which was at Langley. The file was dated 1967, the year Downey was hired by the Company. Foster made himself comfortable and opened the folder.

It had been more than twenty years since Downey posed for the original photograph. Despite Foster's training, it was difficult to make the association between the Jack Downey he knew and the man who stared up at him now. It was the same face and yet at the same time it wasn't the same face at all. Or perhaps, Foster thought – a sudden, chilling insight – it was exactly the same face but the face belonged to a different man.

He skipped through the early stuff. The childhood in Boston. Mom and Dad. The talented younger brother who'd dreamed of playing left wing with the Bruins but had been cross-checked into a lifetime contract with a wheelchair.

College.

The girlfriend. Marriage. Pregnancy. Divorce. A couple of years at IBM. A problem with child support. Recruitment by the CIA.

Downey had spent the first two years of his career in Washington. A good place to be, you had an eye on the top rung of the ladder. In July of '69 he'd been posted to Libya. There was no mention in the file of why he had gone or who had sent him. But two months later, on 1st September, Gadaffi had staged the coup that had left King Idris al-Sanussi stranded on the Turkish coast, a deposed monarch with nothing to reign over but a castle of sand.

It wasn't common knowledge, but the coup had been partially funded by the Company. It was even possible that Downey had been directly involved.

The file was as thick as his wrist. Foster buzzed Dorothy and told her he was not to be disturbed for the remainder of the afternoon. At seven o'clock that night, bleary-eyed and exhausted, he stumbled across the file's solitary reference to Edward Forsyth, Jennifer's father.

During the years following the Libyan coup, Downey had bounced all over the world, starting fires and putting them out. In 1972, three years after the coup, he'd returned briefly to Libya. The reason for his visit was, at best, unclear.

According to Downey's notes, which were written in smudged green ink and a rollicking, wildly looping style that seemed more suited to a rollercoaster operator than a CIA agent, Edward Forsyth had been a British engineer who'd worked in Libya for eighteen months and then, three days after Downey's arrival, vanished without a trace in the desert near the town of Sabha. One hot summer night, apparently intending to walk off his dinner, Forsyth had strolled out into the desert and never come back. Search parties and helicopters had combed the area for a hundred-mile radius, but no trace of him had ever been found.

Until Jack Downey kindly rolled aside your stone and resurrected you, thought Foster. He wondered how in hell Downey intended to mesh his cast together: Charlie and the Englishwoman, Jennifer Forsyth, Colonel Butros Murad. The two mercenaries, Sweets and Martin.

And where, now that he'd come to think of it, did Cairo Chief-of-Station Richard Foster fit into the scheme of things?

Foster could feel a migraine gathering momentum. A great big bowling ball pounding down the alley towards his brain. He had a hunch the headache was going to be the least of his problems.

As it turned out, he was dead right.

27

THE EGYPTIAN DESERT

Sweets had shut the quonset hut door tight, bolted it. The windows had been covered with cardboard and the cracks had been stuffed with bits of rag.

The air was thick and warm as soup. The darkness was absolute.

"Ready?" Mungo's disembodied voice echoed off the steel walls and curved steel ceiling; jumped at Jennifer from a dozen different directions.

She nodded, and then realized that of course he couldn't see her. "Any time," she said.

"Charlie?"

"Yeah, sure." In the darkness, Jennifer could hear the change in Charlie's voice. There was strength there, confidence and vigour. This was their tenth day in the desert. The daily forced marches had hardened Charlie, made him stronger. His skin was deeply tanned. His eyes were clear, his gaze steady.

"Go!" cried Mungo.

Jennifer was sitting cross-legged on a threadbare army blanket that had been spread on the quonset hut's concrete floor. She leaned forward, her hands sweeping blindly across the coarse material, fingers splayed. The thumb of her left hand hit metal – the pressed-steel box magazine of her Steyr. She balanced the magazine across her blue-jeaned thigh. Off to her left she heard the soft click of metal on metal as Charlie reassembled his gun.

Sweets had disassembled the Steyrs and now Jennifer and Charlie had sixty seconds to put them back together and load the magazines. At the end of that time Mungo was going to flip a switch, illuminating a pair of combat targets at the far end of the building, sixty feet away.

The targets would be lit for exactly five seconds, and then Mungo would extinguish the lights. To make the exercise a little more interesting, he and Sweets had decided that low score would carry an extra twenty pounds during that afternoon's five-mile run through the desert.

A part of Jennifer's mind counted off the remaining seconds as she worked on her submachine-gun. It was hot and stuffy inside the metal hut, and her hands were slick with sweat. She wiped her palms on her thighs, guided the Steyr's bolt assembly into place and rotated the rear receiver cover into the locked position. The gun was now assembled and ready to fire. She groped for the box of 9mm bullets.

Twenty seconds.

Jennifer ripped the box open. The bullets were heavy and cold, waxy. She used the 'hand-finds-hand' method Mungo had taught her, and was still shoving bullets into the magazine when the shielded lights above the targets suddenly snapped on.

She slammed the partially loaded magazine home and drew back and released the cocking handle, at the same time bringing the weapon into the firing position. The coathanger stock slammed against her shoulder. She squeezed the trigger.

The Steyr erupted, the hot orange flare of the muzzle blast blinding her. She fought the recoil, struggled to keep the barrel down.

"Time!" shouted Mungo Martin.

The lights over the charging cardboard men suddenly went out. Jennifer kept shooting, ripping off another half-dozen rounds, emptying her weapon.

There was a brief pause, a moment's silence. She heard Charlie cursing softly, and realized he hadn't fired a shot.

"Safety on, weapons down," said Mungo.

There was a sharp click as Charlie pulled back and released the cocking handle on his weapon.

"*Down your weapon!*" yelled Mungo. The heat and boredom of the desert had taken its toll on all of them. Tempers were short. He didn't want any accidents.

With the Steyr on full automatic, it took less than three seconds to punch thirty-two perfectly round holes in the sheet-metal roof of the quonset hut. Standing erect with the empty gun cradled in his arms, Charlie was bathed in thirty-two tiny spotlights. It reminded him of the good old days back at the Snapper Club.

The air was thick with the acrid stench of cordite. Sweets hit the lights. The overhead fluorescents pinned them in a web of shadows. He opened a door.

Jennifer coughed. Overheated air escaping through the open doorway made the gunsmoke swirl around her. She looked up at the holes in the roof. It was a nice tight grouping.

"Sure am glad it ain't raining," said Mungo. "Don't believe we got anywhere near that many pots." He pointed at Jennifer and said, "Let's go see how many bad guys you wiped out."

They walked down the length of the hut towards the targets, which were standard Egyptian Army issue, similar to military targets all over the world. Made of thick grey cardboard, they depicted the head and torso of an androgynous soldier pointing an automatic weapon uprange, the soldier's body marked like a butcher's chart by concentric white lines that delineated fatal and merely disabling hits.

Jennifer squatted in front of her target. There were eight closely-spaced holes in the soldier's mid-section, each one a killer worth ten points. The rest of her hits veered in a diagonal line upwards from the stomach to the right side of the chest.

She started counting. There were fifteen holes in the target, eleven of them fatal.

"Full mag?" said Mungo.

Jennifer shook her head. "No, I don't think so. I was still loading when the lights came on."

"Count and load," said Mungo. "It's a rule, and you should never break it."

Jennifer nodded in agreement. They had been through it all before, far too many times. She was tired of fending off Sweets and she was tired of running around in the desert getting sunburnt. She'd had a lot of time to think about it, and had decided that Downey's primary intention was to force the four of them to get to know each other, come together as a team.

Mungo nudged Jennifer's shoulder, startling her. "A *piastre* for your thoughts."

"You wouldn't get your money's worth."

He smiled. "It's almost one o'clock. Why don't we knock off turning you into a finely-tuned instrument of death and destruction, grab some lunch."

They had gotten into the habit of eating their meals in the base's hangar – a cavernous, echoing structure half as large as a city block. Because of its size, the hangar was the coolest building on the base.

The supply of fresh food had been eaten during the first few days. For the past week there'd been nothing but dehydrated and tinned goods. Downey hadn't allowed any hard liquor, but Sweets had talked him into bringing along four dozen cans of Miller, to be rationed at the rate of one can per day per person. They were down to the last eight cans.

192

Sweets popped a tab. Foam spilled over the back of his hand, down his wrist, splattered on the oil-stained concrete. He offered the bubbling can to Jennifer, who declined with a wave of her hand.

"Don't like to mix with us black folks?"

"Why don't you try *drinking* it," Jennifer said. "Or is it more fun to pour it all over the floor?"

Charlie laughed.

"Think she's pretty funny, huh?" Sweets drained his beer. He threw the empty can at Charlie, hit him in the chest. The can rattled on the concrete floor. Sweets moved in on Charlie, fists raised, dancing lightly on the balls of his feet.

"Hey," said Mungo. "Knock it off."

"I'm gonna knock his head off, is what I'm gonna do."

Jennifer expected Mungo to step between the two men, but all he did was shrug, as if he believed a fight was inevitable and there was nothing he could do about it. "Stay away from his face. You mark him up, Jack'll kill you."

Grinning, Sweets turned to say something to Jennifer.

Charlie took full advantage of the moment, hit Sweets as hard as he could with an overhand right, catching him flush on the side of the head.

Sweets staggered backwards. His boot hit the empty beer can and sent it skittering noisily across the floor. He dropped to his knees.

"Now you done it," said Mungo.

Sweets had been cut. Blood welled up through his close-cropped hair, curled around his ear and splattered on the concrete. He stared down at the drops, shiny and red. He shook his head and more blood splashed on the floor.

He stood up.

Charlie backed warily away, towards the Land-Rover. Sweets went after him. Charlie stumbled. He lost his balance and nearly fell, arms windmilling. Sweets lunged forward. Charlie's left foot was extended, but Sweets fell for the left hook anyway, ducking sideways. Charlie hit him flush on the nose with a straight right, putting all his weight and power behind the blow. Sweets' head snapped back. His face was a smear of blood. He grunted in surprise and pain. Charlie swung wildly with another right, hoping to put him down for the count. Sweets saw the blow coming and jerked his head sideways. Charlie's knuckles grazed bone.

Sweets needed a breather. He back-pedalled, putting some distance between them. He wiped his mouth with the back of his hand, stared coldly at Charlie as he moved in on him, careful this time, not hurrying.

Charlie waited, gauging the distance. He cocked his right hand again and then went with the left. Sweets expected another feint and was caught by surprise when Charlie followed through, catching him in the ribs with enough power to make him wince.

Charlie shuffled backwards.

Twice stung, Sweets abandoned caution and went right after him. Charlie jabbed twice, hit him above the left eye and square on the jaw, the sound of the impact a dull thud.

Sweets was dazed but kept coming. Charlie hit him a third time, flush on his bloody mouth. Sweets grunted. He unleashed a looping right that hit Charlie high on the chest, directly over his heart. Charlie dropped his hands. Sweets lined him up and punched him again, hit him in exactly the same spot. Charlie's knees buckled. Sweets chopped at him as he fell, missed and hissed in frustration.

Charlie lay on his back on the oil-stained concrete. Sweets loomed over him. He grinned, teeth stained pink with blood.

"How you feel now, tough guy?"

Charlie didn't say anything, didn't move. When he'd taken the blow to the chest it felt as if his heart had lurched to a stop, arteries exploding in a wash of blood. He was breathless, dizzy. Numb all down the right side of his body.

But he wasn't finished.

He'd spent the past ten days marching across the desert with a forty-pound pack slung over his shoulders, sprinting ten minutes out of every hour, running a little harder each time out, until Sweets was hard pressed to stay ahead of him. He'd stopped smoking, drinking. He was tanned and lean and very fit, and he was a long way from finished. He lay on the concrete, waited for the strength to seep slowly back into his body.

Sweets turned away from Charlie. He gave Jennifer a proprietary look.

Charlie concentrated on the sound of his heartbeat, the slow, steady thumping. When he was ready, he stood up.

Sweets glared at him, looking more surprised than angry. He took three quick strides across the concrete, reached out to grab a handful of shirt, eager to see the fear in Charlie's eyes.

Timing it perfectly, Charlie lashed out with his booted foot, caught Sweets on the knee. Sweets' leg buckled. He toppled sideways, fighting to regain his balance. Charlie kicked him again. Sweets bellowed, a cry of frustration and pain. Charlie moved in on him, circled to attack his weak side.

Sweets tried to move with Charlie, but he was too slow, crippled by the sharp, stabbing pain in his knee.

Charlie telegraphed another kick. Sweets crouched. A fist slammed into his face. He covered up. Charlie played a tune on his ribcage. He tried to retreat, found he'd lost his mobility. Charlie hit him in the kidneys. He sighed noisily, all the wind going out of him.

"Had enough?"

Sweets shook his head, spraying Charlie with droplets of blood. He fell to his knees.

Charlie stepped forward, knelt to help him. Sweets clutched at Charlie's ankle and pulled hard. Charlie resisted and Sweets went with it, pushing the leg back and at the same time lifting the ankle high and rotating it, using the foot as a lever.

Charlie spun through the air, came down hard. The overhead fluorescents slid crazily across his field of vision, exploded in hot white flashes, violent bursts of incandescent brilliance. The back of his head bounced off the concrete. The world turned black.

Sweets leaned over him. Drops of blood fell into Charlie's open mouth. Sweets laughed harshly, turned and walked slowly away.

"Poor Charlie."

He opened his eyes. Jennifer's face swam in and out of focus. He squinted against the harsh glare of the lights, tried to stand up, staggered and fell to his knees.

"Let me help you."

"I don't need any help."

"Yes you bloody well do."

He ignored her, concentrated on the fat black flies that buzzed haphazardly around him, feasted on his blood. He listened to the soft buzz of flight, watched the wings glinting iridescent in the light.

Jennifer knelt beside him. She put her arms around him and helped him to his feet. Charlie felt the length of her body press against him. She moved away, took his arm, guided him towards a wide rectangle of light – the open doorway of the hangar.

Sweets and Mungo squatted in the shade, their backs to the corrugated tin wall. They watched Jennifer and Charlie step outside, walk slowly down the asphalt road towards the low brick building where they had their rooms.

"They holding hands?"

"Could be."

"Man owes me a big favour, he don't even know it."

"You'll tell him, Hubie, sooner or later."

"Damn right," said Sweets. His knee hurt like hell. It had already started to puff up, swell like a balloon. He needed an ice pack, but the closest ice was a hundred miles or more away. He watched Jennifer move down the road, admired the way she used her hips, those long, slim legs.

"What's on your mind, Hubie?"

"Same as you, I bet."

"I doubt it."

Sweets grunted, tenderly rubbed his knee. He took the wad of tissue away from his nose. The bleeding had stopped. Charlie had put up a pretty good fight. Sweets had underestimated him, paid the price. He flexed his knee. He was getting old, should have seen that kick coming before Charlie even realized he was going to try it.

He sucked blood from between his teeth, spat. It had been Downey's idea to try to bring Charlie and Jennifer together by thumping him around a little. He hadn't much liked the idea of playing Cupid, had gone along with the idea mostly so he could use Charlie for a punching bag. Funny how things turned out, sometimes. He shielded his eyes from the sun with the flat of his hand, peered down the road at Jennifer, took pleasure in the play of shadow and light that defined the shape of her body.

He gently probed the cut over his eye. He was gonna end up with a scar – a major handicap in his line of work, because it would make him easy to identify. He had a choice – plastic surgery, or early retirement.

Sweets had a healthy fear of hospitals, overworked anaesthetists, the surgeon's knife. He ran his finger along the line of distended, bloody flesh. Charlie owed him. And Charlie was going to pay.

28

CAIRO

Downey had driven from the base in the desert straight to Cairo, arriving late the following afternoon. He spent most of the following week tucked away in his apartment, a drab third-floor bachelor in an anonymous highrise in Dokki, a crowded middle-class residential district on the west side of the Nile. He whiled away the time drinking beer and listening to Charlie Parker records while he studied the district with his Zeiss binoculars. Much of his last day in the apartment was spent watching a young man at the far end of his block install a tape deck in his battered Peugeot. The man wore jeans and a frayed army shirt, sunglasses with mirror lenses. Whenever he moved, bright spears of light illuminated the Peugeot's interior, bounced off the windows of the surrounding buildings.

Downey snapped a roll of 400 ASA Fujichrome, using his Nikon and a 500 mm lens. He developed the negatives and blew up the photographs until he had half a dozen eight-by-ten headshots. The tip of the man's nose was missing. A wave of relief washed over him – he was sure he'd never seen him before in his life. An hour or so later, the man finished wiring the tape deck and drove noisily away.

Downey stuck a frozen pizza in the oven, ate several slices and drank some more beer, took a long shower and went to bed. The alarm woke him at three a.m. In darkness, he put on a pair of brown corduroy trousers, a pale-green shirt and grey Nikes with a silver swoosh. Except for the low and mournful tune played by the refrigerator, the apartment was silent. He went into the living room and peered furtively out the window. In the next apartment block, a woman was vacuuming her carpet. An early riser? He focused the binoculars, watched her move slowly and languidly across the room, plump hips swaying. Dancing, thought Downey. He smiled. It's three o'clock in the goddamn morning, and she's dancing in the dust. He put the binoculars on the windowsill and went back into the bedroom, yanked his windbreaker from the cupboard and made the coathangers rattle. He checked to make sure he had his wallet and keys and then left the apartment, pausing briefly to shoot the deadbolt and activate the electronic alarm system.

The musicians in the elevator always seemed to be playing the same tune: a tinny, persistent whine that sounded remarkably like a quartet of not very talented mosquitos banging miniature garbage can lids together.

The elevator descended fitfully towards the ground floor. He'd thought about using the stairs but decided against it. There was no point in wearing himself out. If Foster had him under surveillance it didn't really matter how he left the building – it was where he went and what he did afterwards that mattered.

The elevator jerked to a stop. The doors slid open. The lobby, a spartan affair of rough, unfinished concrete, was empty. Downey glanced at his watch as he walked purposefully towards the plate-glass doors. It was twenty-five minutes past three.

Outside, he paused and carefully scrutinized the street and dark, shadowy spaces between the featureless highrises that marched down both sides of the block like the pickets of a monstrous fence.

In the glare of the streetlights, the bats of Cairo chased nocturnal insects in quick, eccentric circles of death.

Downey put his hands in his pockets and strolled down to the far corner, turned left and trotted briskly across the street. Parked in the middle of the next block was a Volkswagen Beetle the colour of a bell pepper. He had discreetly checked the car out. The owner drove it to work first thing in the morning and was gone all day, home by five. The car's paint and chrome were flawless and gleaming. The engine sounded tight, strong. The rubber was better than average.

Even more important, the price was right.

Downey walked up to the car and delivered a short, sharp blow to the passenger's window with the side of his fist. The glass fractured into a web made by a psychotic spider, but refused to break. Downey hit it again, much harder this time. The window sagged and he cursed under his breath and stepped back and kicked hard. The glass exploded.

He unlocked and opened the door, brushed fragments of glass from the seat and climbed into the car.

It took him less than thirty seconds to hot-wire the engine. The radio shouted at him. He turned it off, hit the lights and pulled sharply away from the curb, powered forcefully through the gears, winding it out.

There was no activity in front of him or in his wing or rearview mirrors. He stopped two blocks from his apartment, killed the lights, lit a cigarette and pulled a tight U-turn, headed back the way he'd come.

No one was following him, not yet. He continued down the road, travelling south towards the Shari-el Giza and the long, fairly straight run along the Nile to El-Gama's bridge. In the small hours of the morning, traffic was as sparse as it ever got in this city of twelve million souls. If he kept to a route that ran primarily through the residential districts, he'd know soon enough if he was being tailed.

A dry, dusty wind rushed at him through the little hunchbacked car's shattered window. His mind turned of its own accord to his immediate problem.

When he'd waltzed out of the embassy with McPhee tucked under his arm, he'd known it wasn't something CIA Chief-of-Station Richard Foster would let slide. Foster *had* to react by jumping all over his bones. A mind-set, the poor jerk didn't have any choice. But Foster wasn't the only one wedged in a corner. Downey had constructed a house of cards so fragile that the slightest puff of wind would scatter it all across the face of Egypt. It was his bad luck that Charlie was the cornerstone of the whole damn edifice.

The problem was motivation. Unlike most of the men Downey knew, Charlie didn't salivate at the thought of what seemed like easy money. And he sure as hell hadn't fallen head over heels in love with Jennifer, either. Downey's threat to toss him to Cairo homicide had cooled him off, but how long would that hold up? All Downey had left were Charlie's wife and kid back in L.A. How would he react if Downey threatened to wipe them out? Downey had a hard time picturing himself chasing around southern California with a gun in his hand, like some kind of upscale Charlie Manson.

He should've taken a walk when Sweets and Martin showed up without Liam O'Brady. Liam had been his great white hope. Charlie was a damn poor substitute.

What he ought to do now was kick Charlie's ass back to the embassy, buy himself a one-way ticket to somewhere far, far away.

Downey took a corner on two wheels, drove half-way down the block and made a U-turn, parked close behind a towering heap of rubbish and turned off the lights. He slowly counted to a hundred, and then continued on his journey.

He had two problems. The first was Richard Foster, who wanted Charlie but could not under any circumstances be allowed to have him, and who'd looked at Colonel Butros Murad and smelled a rat.

His second problem was that he was quickly running out of time but was enmeshed in a goddamn situation where he couldn't allow himself to be rushed.

Halfway through an intersection, Downey realized he'd run a red light. There hadn't been any traffic – but that was just dumb luck. He pounded the steering wheel. Why kill himself, when so many people were waiting in line? His mind raced, weighing the options. Foster could do whatever the fuck he wanted, which, when you chewed right down to the cob, wasn't much. Leave terse messages on Downey's answering machine. Maybe authorize a covert entry to his drab little apartment. And what would Foster's team of spooks and goblins find when they wormed their way inside? A few empty beer cans, some leftover pizza and the keys to the blue Ford Downey had taken from the car pool.

Then what? *Think.*

They'd wait for him to show up. Drink his beer and piss in his toilet. Poke around in the cupboard and under the bed, try to put everything back where they found it and get most of it right. Eventually break down and ask the neighbours a few questions, make what they considered to be discreet enquiries.

Could he live with that? Yeah, sure.

He concentrated on his driving, guided the Volks through the city with a carefully plotted aimlessness, varying speed and direction according to whim and the dictates of the terrain, watched the road behind him as carefully as he watched the road ahead.

He reached the neighbourhood of Maadi at a few minutes past five o'clock in the morning, and parked the stolen car in a side street several blocks from the safe-house. Kneeling, he let the air out of the outside front tire. The flat would deflect idle curiosity, delay the police investigation, give him a tiny bit more slack.

In the false light of early dawn, accompanied by a growing chorus of unseen dogs that snapped and yowled all around him, he strolled down the empty streets until he reached the safe-house. He unlocked the gate, crunched wearily across the gravel forecourt. By the time he'd sorted out his keys, most of the dogs had fallen silent. He unlocked the door and entered the house.

He was tired, worn out, exhausted. What he needed was a long drink and a short nap. But he was a cautious and a careful man, a man of fixed, carefully cultivated habits. The first thing he had to do was make sure the house was secure. And so he padded from room to room, checked the windows to make sure the grillwork hadn't been tampered with, poked and prodded in the drawers and cupboards, lightly ran his fingers across the gathered drifts of dust, sniffed the air and took his measure of all the signs and portents, large and small.

In the room where Jennifer had slept he imagined a lingering trace of her perfume, the scent of her body on the sheets. Truth or self-deception, it was all the same. The distant memory of the smell and feel of her left him feeling listless and depressed. Confident that his security had not been breached, he went into the kitchen, unscrewed the cap from an unopened bottle of Dewar's and poured two thick fingers into a lowball glass.

He was about to yank open the door to get some ice for his drink when he noticed the chrome-wire shelf on the kitchen counter next to the sink. The shelf belonged *inside* the fridge. What was it doing on the counter?

Downey went for his gun – an automatic reaction. A man could hide inside a fridge, if he weighed less than a hundred pounds, had the flexibility of a gymnast and didn't object to death by suffocation. But what about a miniature breathing apparatus? One of those recycling devices used by frogmen? Ridiculous . . . He pulled his revolver from his jacket pocket. Death of a major household appliance. But if he shot up the fridge, how would he keep his beer cold – stick the bottles up Dick Foster's ass? He put the gun away and jerked open the door.

There was a cardboard box inside the fridge. The box was about eighteen inches square – too large to fit inside without removing the shelf. There had also been a need to rearrange Downey's supply of Fürstenburg. The bottles were lying on their side. He felt a raw surge of anger: taste was adversely affected when the beer was allowed to touch the metal caps.

He slid the box out of the fridge, was surprised by the weight of it. If there was a cake in there, it wasn't going to be a very good one.

He put the box on the kitchen counter. Snatched ice from the freezer and dropped a few cubes into his Dewar's. He stirred the drink with his finger, sipped nervously, lit a cigarette. The box squatted on the counter, waiting. The heavy, dark brown cardboard had a slick, waxy sheen, as if it had been waterproofed. He picked it up again, hefted it and guessed its weight at about ten or twelve pounds.

He put the box back down on the counter and carried his glass and the almost-full bottle of Dewar's through the dining room and out through the french doors leading to the enclosed courtyard. He turned on the fountain. The pool begin to fill. He walked around to the far end and sat down in the chair Jennifer had favoured, the one beneath the largest of the three palm trees.

The Dewar's bottle made a sharp clicking sound as he put it down on the tiles. He pulled on his cigarette, fancied he could feel the shape of

Jennifer's buttocks in the warp and weft of the wicker. He could see into the kitchen through the glass surround. He'd left the fridge door open. Shock. Someone had been in the house and he hadn't noticed.

He flicked the cigarette into the pool, watched the currents play with the butt. Life jackets should be made of cigarette filters – they never seemed to sink. He poured himself another Scotch. High above him, the early morning sky segued from lime green to cobalt blue, the pale, watery light shafting down through the spear-shaped leaves of the palm trees. Shadows began to collect on the tiled floor.

Downey fired up another smoke. He drained his glass, sighed wearily, screwed the cap on the Dewar's bottle and went back to the kitchen.

It could have been a hat box, because it was large enough to contain a hat. Something with a high crown, bouquet of bright silk flowers, a wide floppy brim. But he knew in his heart of hearts it wasn't a hat that was inside the box.

The Egyptian colonel they'd met at Beni-Suef had pointed out that he still had a walk-on part in Downey's little play, and he was right. The colonel had been paid a few extra bucks to act as a courier, make a delivery. What the box contained was what you usually found *under* a hat.

Downey took another drag on his cigarette, stalling. Then, with an abrupt, decisive gesture, he flipped open the lid and stared down at the bad penny that had been Ahmed Mah.

Ahmed grinned sightlessly up at him. His teeth were much more prominent now that most of the flesh was gone.

Downey's stomach did a slow roll. The Scotch and remains of his dinner clawed at his throat. The colonel had only partly come through. He was supposed to deliver a skull. No extras. No flesh, for example. Just the bones. God, but it was hard to get decent help. Downey crouched and pulled open a cabinet door, clattered among the pots and pans until he found a vessel large enough to accommodate Ahmed Mah's mortal remains. The pot was aluminum, battered with age. He couldn't, goddammit, seem to find a lid.

He filled the pot half full of water from the sink, carried it over to the stove and put it on the back burner, turned the gas up high.

He wandered restlessly around the house until the water was at a rolling boil, carefully tilted the grisly eyeless skull into the pot. The water quieted. A globule of yellow fat floated to the surface. The gas bubbled again; a weirdly cheerful, perky sound. Downey adjusted the flame. He backed slowly away from a drift of steam.

It was fifteen minutes past six. He had a hunch, deep in his roiling, fevered gut, that it was going to be a long, long day.

29

THE EGYPTIAN DESERT

She'd slept lightly, dreamt about her daughter, Cynthia. It had not been a good dream. Her ex-husband, William, had come to take possession, loudly demand his rights. They'd fought over the child. William had grabbed one hand and Cynthia had clutched at the other. They'd tugged at the girl from opposite directions, and in the dream the child's body had become horribly distorted and she'd screamed in pain. Jennifer, desperate, had held her tightly. There'd been a sound like cloth tearing. Her daughter had suddenly burst apart, flying into pieces like a cheap clockwork toy.

Jennifer sat up straight in bed, her body soaked in sweat, heart pounding. A dream. No, a nightmare. She saw that the door to her room was slowly swinging open, realized that it was the soft click of the latch that had rescued her from the horror.

Downey had twisted the doorknob all the way, then furtively swung the door open, used his grip on the knob to exert upward pressure and take the weight off the hinges. But they had creaked despite his efforts, made a high-pitched, mousy squeak.

He held the Butagaz lantern a little higher, stepped into the room.

Jennifer was sitting bolt upright, her back to the scaly wall. The barrel of her Steyr pointed straight at Downey's protuberant stomach. She must have been sleeping with the damn thing under her pillow. What the hell had been going on while he was in Cairo? Had Sweets pushed too hard, or was her quickness with the gun merely a consequence of intensive training? Her eyes were wild and her face was shiny with sweat. He took his eyes off the gun. "Jennifer, it's me, Jack."

"What do you want?"

"We're leaving." Downey lowered the hissing lantern to the floor. He turned his back on her, eased the door shut behind him.

Jennifer glanced at her watch. It was two o'clock in the morning.

Under Downey's orders, they packed their personal belongings but left everything else behind. The night air cold and still. There was no moon, and the sky from horizon to horizon was crammed with stars.

Jennifer heard it first, a low droning that seemed to come from the east. She cocked her head towards the star-filled sky. Downey looked at her.

"What?"

"I don't know . . . an airplane?"

Downey stood perfectly still, listening. After a moment he said, "Goddammit," very quietly. Sweets and Mungo came out the door of the barracks. Downey said, "Douse the lights, and get those vehicles away from the building. Don't start the engines. *Push* the fuckers."

"Right," said Mungo, thinking, did he say *vehicles*? How uptight can one man be?

Sweets crouched down, turned off the Butagaz lanterns. The hiss of escaping gas faded away, and in a moment the darkness was absolute.

They could all hear the plane now. It sounded as if it was two or maybe three miles away, closing fast.

Mungo said, "Charlie, gimme a hand." He tossed his Steyr in the back and reached in through the open window, put the Land-Rover in neutral and began to push. The tires crunched on the gravel. They bulled the Land-Rover thirty yards into the darkness and then jogged over and moved the other one.

Mungo knew what Downey had in mind. If there was going to be a firefight, Downey didn't want their wheels shot all to hell. It was a long hike back out of the desert.

Charlie was sweating. He heard a sharp click as someone cocked his submachine-gun. He said, "Where's Jennifer?" and was startled when she whispered, "Right here," and reached out and touched his arm.

Downey, speaking in a whisper that seemed loud as a shout, said, "Gotta be paratroopers. From the sound, I'd say it has to be a single-engine plane. Can't be very many of them, six or seven at most. Jennifer, you and Charlie get down behind one of the jeeps. Stay low. I can't afford to lose you. Hubie?"

"Right here, Jack."

"You and Mungo set up a crossfire by the door. Way I see it, we might as well let them come to us. They must figure we're asleep by now. Inside the building, chances are real good we wouldn't have heard them. Just stay cool and wait 'em out. Got it?"

"Stay cool," said Sweets. "Yeah, I think I can handle that."

"Been that way all our lives," said Mungo. "To the cooler born, you might say."

"Born with a popsicle in my mouth," said Sweets, and chuckled softly.

The plane was very close, almost right on top of them. Surprisingly, the sound of the engine wasn't as loud as it had been. A trick of the wind, maybe. Downey wondered if it had been fitted out with some kind of special muffler. He said, "Hey, knock off the adolescent locker-room bullshit. Charlie, remember what I said. Stay low. Okay, let's get set."

Charlie led Jennifer to one of the Land-Rovers, knelt at the rear of the jeep. He didn't mind taking cover, but he wasn't about to get down on his belly and crawl *under* the damn thing. He stared up at the night sky. A bright cluster of stars was blotted out, reappeared. He heard the wind soughing in the chutes, the first muffled thud of impact as one of the paratroopers touched down.

He crouched a little lower.

Mungo lay in the prone position twenty yards from the barracks doorway. He couldn't remember whether he'd shut the door or left it open. Too late now. His eyes had adjusted to the darkness, and he'd counted five of them, but there might easily have been more. They wore black and carried automatic weapons, and had obviously been thoroughly prepped, because they took up their positions without a sound.

Downey, crouched behind an empty oil drum, wondered how they'd handle it. He soon found out. Several men slipped into the building. Two more covered the door. Thirty seconds elapsed, and then there was the bright flash and heavy *thump* of exploding stun grenades, the deadly roar of weapons on full automatic.

Just wait, thought Downey.

Another grenade exploded. There were several more lengthy bursts of gunfire. One of the men stationed by the door stared straight at Downey and then looked away.

The stink of cordite drifted out of the building. Downey smelled smoke. The paratroopers began to come out. They didn't look nearly as disciplined as they had when they'd gone in. He knew exactly how they felt – that sour taste at the roof of your mouth when you were high on adrenalin, all dressed up with nobody to kill. Somebody barked an order in Arabic. The men rushed to form a half circle, facing outward. Downey hit the dirt. There was a tremendous, deafening thunder of gunfire, the muzzle blasts lighting up the night. Downey's oil drum vibrated under a dozen hits.

The firing stopped.

Now, thought Downey, *while they reload*. The words were still tumbling through his mind when the return fire started. He heard the thud of bullets striking flesh, saw men falling. The night was filled with shouts and screams.

Bullets shredded the air above Charlie's head. He ducked low. A round careened off the flank of the jeep. He caught a glimpse of a dark shape running towards him. He led the man by the thickness of his body and began to squeeze the trigger. Before he could shoot, Sweets fired a three-round burst that caught the man in mid-stride, spun him around and knocked him down.

Downey emptied his Steyr at the motionless forms on the ground by the lighted doorway. The last ricochet whined into the night sky. He listened for the sound of the airplane, heard only the harsh rasp of his own heavy breathing. It always happened that way. You waited and waited and then it was over, had happened so fast you'd never had time to think, only react. He slung the submachine-gun over his shoulder and drew and cocked his .45.

Mungo and Sweets knew how to set up a crossfire. The paratroopers had been cut to pieces in the first exchange of shots. Mungo counted them one by one. Four dead, two wounded.

Downey sent Mungo into the barracks building, to make sure there were no loiterers. He ordered Charlie and Jennifer out into the darkness to patrol the perimeter, where they were safe and out of the way. He and Sweets dragged the two surviving paratroopers over to the side of the building and hauled them into a sitting position so they were leaning against the wall.

Both men had taken multiple hits and were in pretty bad shape. Downey didn't have much time, so he asked each of them a single question, first in Arabic and then in English.

"Who hired you?"

No reply. Abdel al-Hony spat at Downey and missed. Downey stepped back out of range. Abdel'd had both his kneecaps blown off. He was in shock; his body was numb, without feeling. He stared down at his shattered legs. Soon, he knew, the pain would begin to flow. He stared up at the night sky. Omar Jalloud would be very angry when he found out the attack had failed. Abdel saw Jalloud's face turn purple. He saw him bare his teeth, foam gather in the corner of his mouth. What poor unfortunate soul would Jalloud vent his rage on this time, Abdel wondered.

"Who the hell are they?" said Sweets.

"Beats me."

"That don't cut the mustard, Jack."

Downey shrugged, hoping for the casual look. His mind raced . . . He said, "An operation this big, there's bound to be leaks."

"You been compromised, me'n Mungo are on our way home."

"Your next stop's Tunis. I'll look into this, find out what the hell happened. If we can't find the leak and plug it, we're all gonna pack our bags and walk."

"Bet your ass."

"Either way, your salary just doubled."

Downey crouched next to the other paratrooper and asked his simple question in Arabic and English. The man said nothing, but glanced quickly at his companion. Now Downey knew who was in charge. He turned to Abdel and repeated his question. Abdel tried to spit at him again, but his mouth was dry. Downey went back to the first man. He said, "Who are you working for?" and shot him between the eyes before he had time to answer. The second time around, he was slightly more patient with Abdel al-Hony. Not that it did much good. In the end, he had to shoot him, too.

The headlights of the Land-Rovers skittered across sand and stone. At Downey's insistence they were going back to Cairo in the same order that they'd arrived; he and Jennifer and Mungo in the lead vehicle, Sweets and Charlie bringing up the rear. Jennifer hadn't fired a shot, but she felt ill, in shock. She'd wanted to ride with Charlie, but Downey, for reasons of his own, had vetoed the idea. She wondered how Charlie was getting along with Sweets. They'd given each other a wide berth since the day of the fight. Mungo's gunshot wound had almost completely healed, and he had overseen the daily hikes through the desert, hand-to-hand combat training and firearms practice.

In the front seat, Downey and Mungo were talking quietly. It was difficult to catch their words over the sound of the high-revving engine, but she did manage to overhear Mungo ask Downey why they'd made no attempt to hide the bodies, and why they had abandoned the weapons and equipment at the military base. He sounded worried. Downey explained that the Egyptian Army colonel and his men had been well paid to clean up.

Jennifer shuddered. There was no doubt in her mind that the paratroopers had meant to kill them. Still, the carnage had disgusted and enraged her, filled her with guilt. She made herself as comfortable as possible and closed her eyes, but sleep eluded her.

A little more than three hours later, with dawn's light staining the sky pinkish-grey, they drove across the Nile and into Beni-Suef. Soon they had passed the town and were accelerating west on the main highway towards Cairo, speeding past lush green fields; the tiny, intensively-worked family farms of Egypt. Jennifer stared out of the dusty window.

In Cairo there was a white Hertz Fiat waiting for them in the shadow of the Citadel. Downey got behind the wheel. He patted the seat and Jennifer slid in beside him. Charlie sat alone in the back. The two Land-Rovers drove off, neither Sweets nor Mungo looking back.

"Where are they going?" said Charlie.

Downey started the Fiat. "Don't worry about it."

"I didn't say I was worried, I said, where are they going?"

"Tunisia." Downey glanced quickly over his shoulder, pulled into traffic.

They drove down the length of the Delta towards the Mediterranean, across land that was for the most part flat and featureless, endlessly green. Downey had packed a lunch, which they ate in the shade of an orange grove. He'd hardly opened the lid of his wicker basket when they were surrounded by a dozen or more beaming, giggling children. He tossed them a chocolate bar and shooed them away. The silence of the grove was broken only by the distant hiss of traffic and the sound of Downey licking sticky fragments of date from his fingers.

Late that afternoon, they reached the outskirts of Alexandria. Downey took great pleasure in pedantically informing them that the city had been founded by Alexander the Great in 331 B.C.

He'd reserved a suite for Jennifer and Charlie at the luxurious Palestine Hotel – a fantastic confection of white stone and pink brick that had once been a Royal summer residence. The palace stood at the far end of the Corniche, Alexandria's seafront promenade.

Downey had chosen the Palestine because he believed it was the most romantic spot in all of Egypt. Jennifer and Charlie's suite had two bedrooms, an unobstructed view of the water. Downey's rooms were considerably less opulent, but were strategically located directly across the hall.

Jennifer went out on the balcony, leaned against an immense stone pillar and looked across an immaculate expanse of jade-green lawn to the glittering aquamarine of the Mediterranean. A salt breeze ruffled her hair. Down on the beach a seagull stalked determinedly along the sand, shoulders hunched and head thrust forward. Behind her, she heard the muted rattle of ice in a glass. Anticipating Downey's plaintive cry, she turned and went inside.

The air-conditioned suite was full of oversized furniture made with dark, intricately carved woods and heavy, ornately patterned fabrics. Jennifer found the effect vaguely claustrophobic. She sat down on an overstuffed couch done in purple velour. Thin shadows flickered across her lap. She looked up. Directly above her, enormous polished mahogany blades slowly churned the air.

Downey was at the bar, fiddling with the gin. He was making a round of Tom Collinses, and, in his dishevelled and unconvincing voice, he kept telling her how good they were going to be, and that it was exactly what they all needed. He grinned his way across the carpet, handed out the drinks and raised his glass. "To success!" he crowed in a voice that was much too loud.

He drained half his glass and plunked himself down next to Jennifer, thumped his heels on a rosewood coffee table and snorted his contentment. Charlie had already finished his drink. He looked nervous, very tense.

Downey patted Jennifer on the knee, leapt to his feet and went over to the window. He drew the heavy curtains, plunging the room into a premature twilight – everything could be seen dimly but nothing could be seen well. He went back to the bar and switched on the projector.

"Everybody comfy?"

There was no reply. He picked up the wireless remote and pressed a button. The carousel jerked forward and the screen filled with colour.

"Recognize him, Charlie?"

"No."

"Jennifer?"

"It's Gadaffi." She spat out the name in the same tone of voice she might have used to describe a poisonous reptile.

"Colonel Mu'ammar al-Gadaffi," Downey corrected. "The big guy himself. Numero uno."

Gadaffi was sitting jauntily on a tractor in the middle of a field. The crop was long and yellow. Some kind of grain. The land was flat, endless. The picture might have been taken on the Canadian prairies, except for the fact that there were a number of heavily-armed Libyan soldiers loitering in the background. Gadaffi wore knee-length black leather boots, bulky grey trousers and what looked like a ski jacket. The jacket was dark grey with red trim, and had a stand-up collar and snap cuffs. Something that looked like a turban covered his head right down to his eyebrows. The loose end of the turban trailed around behind him and then came back to cover his chin and upper chest. He had both hands on the tractor's steering wheel, and – a nice touch – wore fluffy black wool gloves to protect him from the cold.

The carousel twitched. This time the picture was a closeup. Gadaffi's dark features filled the screen. Jennifer stared into his eyes, which were wide-spaced and very serious, such a dark brown that they were almost black. The nose was strong, with a straight bridge and wide-flared nostrils. His mouth was a study in contrast; the upper lip narrow and cruel, the lower wide and generous, with a hint of humour. His chin was nicely proportioned, broad and firm, uncompromising. Jennifer studied Gadaffi's eyes. To her, they seemed to be the eyes of a man who was capable of anything. And yet, viewed objectively, they were calm and depthless and gave absolutely nothing away.

The carousel clicked again, and the face was replaced by a picture-postcard shot of a small oasis. A pink tent was pitched in the shade of a palm tree.

"He was born in a goatskin tent a lot like the one you're looking at now," said Downey, invisible behind the brilliant shaft of light. "Gadaffi's parents were Bedouin. Gentle shepherd folk. He was one of seven children. They had to make a lot of sacrifices to send him to school. He's the only member of the family with a formal education."

Another head shot, right profile this time.

"As you probably know, Gadaffi is an army officer, a colonel. False modesty. He could be a fucking ten-star general if he wanted. He's been the big cheese in Libya since '69, when he and a bunch of buddies tossed King Idris out on his ass. It's no secret, by the way, that there was a fair chunk of Company money behind the coup." Downey smiled. In the light of the projector, a Cheshire grin. "Hey, we all make mistakes."

He switched the projector to automatic. Jennifer and Charlie were treated to a series of shots of Gadaffi admiring a camouflaged mobile missile launcher.

"Russian," said Downey. "The Kremlin sells him every damn thing he wants, from handguns to nuclear-capable Migs. He pays cash, petrodollars. What the damn Ruskies are really after is future shares in a Mediterranean beachhead."

Downey carried on. Like most people, he was a born lecturer.

"A lot of the small stuff Gadaffi buys isn't meant for domestic consumption. Over the years, he's provided cash and firearms to Black September, the Red Brigade, fucking Baader-Meinhof, the Japanese Red Army and Ilich Ramirez Sanchez, aka Carlos. That fucking butcher. Here in Egypt, he's supported Al Takfir Wal Higra. He's also supplied equipment and arms to the PLFP, PIRA, NAYLP and the PLO. The whole goddamn alphabet of international terrorism. And believe me, we aren't talking petty cash. Over the past few years he's paid Black September alone more than forty million dollars. That sum includes a ten-million payoff for the Munich massacre, if anybody can remember that far back. That's the other reason you've been invited to the party, Charlie. We've got plenty of inside help on this caper. But what our Libyan friends don't know is that we're gonna snatch every goddamn scrap of intelligence they've got on those murderous fucking terrorist bastards. Find out who the scumbugs are, and wipe them out. To pull it off, though, I need somebody who knows how to crack a safe."

A slide of Gadaffi in military whites filled the screen. He was wearing aviator sunglasses and a dark green tie. It was an oddly formal pose. He held an officer's cane in his left hand, and saluted the camera with his right. There was, Charlie thought, enough thick gold braid draped over his shoulders and the peak of his cap to get him a doorman's job at the Beverly Hills Hilton. Because of the tinted sunglasses, Gadaffi's dark, heavily lined face was dominated by his mouth. He looked, despite everything Downey had said about him, like a man who knew how to tell a joke.

"He's a ruthless bastard," said Downey, as if reading Charlie's mind. "A killer, and we're going to put him down."

"Not me," said Charlie.

"Don't think you could do it?" Downey snorted his amusement, in the same moment made a terse gesture of dismissal. "No problem. All you and Jennifer have to do is set him up. When you leave Libya, he'll be there for the closing ceremonies. Chance for him to get all dressed in one of his wonderful revolutionary ensembles. Guy's got more three-piece uniforms than Emelia Marcos had shoes. All you have to do is let Sweets know when and where. Like I told you, they'll pull the trigger."

Charlie shook his head. "I won't do it. Count me out."

Downey swung the projector around so the bright shaft of light pointed directly at Charlie, pinned him to his chair, blinded him. "You already forget about Ahmed Mah?" Downey screamed. His voice was shockingly loud, shrill as a child's. There was a silence broken only by the hum of the projector and the hiss of the ceiling fan's whirling blades. Then Downey said, "You want to spend the rest of your miserable life in a Cairo prison, it can be arranged."

Jennifer moved in front of the projector, blocking the light. "That's enough," she said. "Turn if off."

"Stay out of this," warned Downey.

Jennifer ignored him. She moved past him and bent to yank the electrical cord out of the wall.

Downey lurched towards her.

"Leave us alone," said Jennifer, standing her ground.

Downey pointed an accusing finger at Charlie. In a voice that was barely audible but quivered with tension, he said, "I saved your lily-white ass, pal. You owe me, and you better not forget it."

Jennifer said, "Would you mind leaving us alone for a little while? I think Charlie and I need to have a talk."

Downey hunched his shoulders, turned purposefully towards the door, yanked it open. A bright shaft of light sprang into the room. His silhouette filled the doorway, and for a moment his huge distorted shadow stained the carpet black. Then the door slammed shut behind him.

Jennifer went over to the window and pulled back the curtains. She was wearing a pale-blue cotton blouse, ankle-length white skirt. Her feet were bare, the nails unpolished. Despite her red hair, she tanned easily, and her skin was nut-brown. Outside, the sky was a flawless blue and the Mediterranean sparkled into the distance. A small sailing boat tacked into the wind.

"Tell me something," said Charlie. "What the hell are you doing here? Why are you working for Downey?"

"What's he got on me, you mean?" She smiled. "I think we could both use some fresh air. Let's take a walk, and I'll tell you all about it."

On the lawn in front of the hotel, a boy wearing a pair of Nike running shoes, faded Levis and an *I Love New York* T-shirt used a kitchen fork to pry up a weed shaped like a small green doily. He smiled at them as they walked past. Charlie found himself wondering if the kid was on Downey's payroll.

They walked slowly along the Corniche towards the heart of Alexandria. To their right the ocean heaved and glittered and then collapsed wearily upon the beach. In the distance Fort Qaitbay stood on the fat tongue of land that separated the city's Eastern and Western harbours. The fort dated from the fifteenth century. The remains of Cleopatra's palaces had recently been discovered beneath the silt at the bottom of the harbour, under less than thirty feet of water.

Jennifer glanced sideways at Charlie, and then moved closer to him and linked her arm through his. He looked surprised, but made no move to disengage. She felt his ribs beneath his white cotton shirt, layered muscle. The weeks spent in the desert had toughened and hardened him.

They continued to stroll along the Corniche, arm in arm. After a little while, Jennifer guided Charlie off the path and sat him down on a bench in the shade of a gnarled and stunted olive tree.

"How long is Downey going to keep us in Alexandria?" Charlie said.

"I have no idea, really."

"Did he tell you how we met?"

"At the embassy in Cairo, wasn't it? You were in some kind of trouble, and he helped you."

"For a price." Charlie smiled, but the smile had no warmth. "You told me once that you were in it for revenge."

"Jack didn't tell you about my father?" No, of course not. Downey was a pro. He knew the impact of the revelation, coming from her, would be much greater than anything he could hope to achieve.

A sudden gust of wind rattled the branches of the olive tree. Spear-shaped shadows danced across Charlie's face.

Jennifer said, "It was in September of '69 that Gadaffi and a handful of other Libyan Army officers staged their coup. King Idris was out of the country at the time. The coup was very well organized, more or less bloodless.

"My father was an engineer. He worked for a British firm based in London. He was sent to Libya in March of 1971, to work on a project in the desert outside Sabha."

The wind had knocked a windsurfer into the water. Charlie watched him crawl back on his board, struggle to right his mast.

"Eighteen months later, on 10th August 1972, he disappeared."

The windsurfer had managed to get his mast up, but the wind had died, and now he was becalmed.

"For years and years," Jennifer continued, "no one knew what had happened to my father. Then I was told there'd been an accident, a piece of heavy machinery had crushed him. They said he'd been drinking. They told me they'd buried him at the Christian cemetery on Al Jala road, in Tripoli."

"But it wasn't true?"

"It was the truth until a little over a year ago. I own an antique shop in King's Road. One day Jack Downey walked in the door. He introduced himself and said he knew what had really happened to my father. Jack told me he worked for the CIA, and that my father had worked for the CIA as well. He said they'd been friends. I was in shock. I didn't know what to think.

"He came back the next afternoon. We walked to a nearby restaurant, shared a pot of tea. It was all very casual, in a funny sort of way. Jack said my father had been arrested by Libyan Army officers, tortured to death. He was murdered, Jack said. And he had some photos, to prove he was telling the truth."

"And when you'd had a good look at them, he put them away in his pocket and wondered if you were interested in avenging your father's death."

"Simple, isn't it." A strand of hair fell across her face. She brushed it away.

"Then what?"

"He said he'd be in touch. But that was more than a year ago, and I didn't see him again until a few days before I came to Cairo. He must have been worried I'd change my mind. He had a film with him. It was only a few minutes long, but they were the last few minutes of my father's life."

Jennifer paused, stared blankly out to sea. "They had him strapped down on a metal table in a room with no windows, and they were burning him with electricity. I heard him screaming, Charlie. I heard him screaming and I saw him die."

The wind had picked up. The windsurfer adjusted the angle of his mast and sped away from them.

"Will you help me?" Jennifer said.

Charlie stood up. He said, "I will if I decide I believe you," and turned his back on her and started to walk down the Corniche towards the city.

The boy on the lawn was still picking at the weeds. He made a low clucking sound deep in his throat as she walked by, fluttered his eyelashes and waved at her with his fork.

She entered her suite half-expecting to find Downey sitting on the couch eating a candy bar. No luck. She prowled restlessly through the empty rooms, picking things up and putting them down. In the bedroom, she turned on the television and fell asleep watching a documentary on the construction of the Aswan dam. When she awoke, the room had darkened perceptibly, and the TV was ablaze with the bright, primary colours of a quiz show.

Jennifer glanced at her watch. It was almost nine. She decided to have something to eat. She wasn't hungry, but dinner would help to pass the time.

In the dining room, she ordered a rack of lamb and bottle of Veuve Clicquot. She picked at the food for a little while and then abandoned the meal and took the wine back to her room.

She stripped a blanket from the bed and carried the bottle outside, on to the balcony. The night air was cool and damp and smelled of salt. Off to her left, the string of lights along the Corniche curved gracefully towards the brighter lights of Alexandria. She curled up in a white-painted wicker loveseat, arranged the blanket around her shoulders. Out to sea, the tiny red and green running lights of fishing boats slipped through the darkness.

Time drifted past. The air grew chill. She sipped at the bottle until it was three-quarters gone, and the lights out on the water were blurred, indistinct. Was she drunk? She was still considering the possibility when she eased into a deep and dreamless sleep.

Charlie staggered in a little past four. He slammed the door, loudly apologized, banged his shin against a coffee table and hissed in dismay, managed to knock over a lamp. Muttering a string of oaths and apologies, he made his precarious way to the bathroom. A shaft of light was flung across the hall carpet, and then the door was shut with exaggerated care.

Jennifer was awakened by the thunder of the shower. She was still a little drunk, but not quite enough. She finished the wine and then started towards him, stripping off her clothes as she moved through the darkened rooms. In the bathroom, she slid back the frosted glass door and stepped naked into the hot rush of the shower. He stared at her, said nothing. She wrapped her arms around him, pressed against him, kissed him full on the mouth.

Charlie stood there, motionless, struck dumb. Then, with an awkward convulsive gesture, he took her in his arms and held her close.

Downey had placed more bugs in the suite than Harlem had cockroaches. He eavesdropped until he was absolutely sure his little lovebirds didn't have any problems they couldn't solve, then packed his bags and drove the Hertz Fiat out to the airport and chartered a plane to speed him back to Cairo.

While Jennifer and Charlie were taking in the sights along the Corniche, he'd taken a moment to phone Foster. Collect, of course. It was a lucky move. The skull had been delivered and somehow Foster had found out it wasn't Charlie's. All that slaving over a hot stove, and for what? Nothing.

He was finally in the home stretch. Foster was the last obstacle that had to be surmounted, and Downey was sure he was going to prove a real easy jump, no problem.

Pretty soon, he assured himself, all he'd have to worry about was how he was going to spend that great big pile of money.

30

CAIRO

Downey dialled Foster's private number from a public telephone on Shari Bab el-Wazir. Foster picked up on the third ring. The first thing he said was, "Where in goddamn hell have you been?"

A motor scooter racketed past, trailing a streamer of greasy blue smoke. Downey waited until the sound of the engine had faded down the street. He said, "Here and there. Around, you know?"

"Get your ass over to the embassy. I'll meet you there in half an hour."

"Can't do it. I'm booked solid until ten o'clock tonight. Is ten too late?"

The line tingled with repressed exasperation. Downey let the silence build. Finally Foster said, "Okay, ten it is. Be on time. Don't keep me waiting. Not a single goddamn minute."

Downey paused for the space of a heartbeat and then said, "Listen, do we have to do this at the office? I'd be a lot more relaxed if we could meet at Shepheard's, maybe lubricate the conversation with a Tom Collins or two."

Foster realized with a shock of anger that Downey, that sneaky little ball of suet, must have tailed him on at least one of his lunch-time excursions. *You bastard*, he thought, and slammed down the phone.

Downey, his back to the throb and hiss and gurgle of traffic, kept the receiver pressed against his ear long after Foster had disconnected. He heard nothing but Cairo static, decided that Dorothy hadn't been playing partyline, and hung up. It was a few minutes past two; he had a little less than eight hours until the meet. Not a whole lot of time to spare. His apartment had to be redecorated, and that would take a while. But first things first. He needed a woman. Those two lovebirds back at the Montazah Palace hotel had sparked his usually dormant appetite, filled him with a rare desire.

Where in this city of twelve million desperate souls could he find a whore who looked even a little bit like Jennifer?

Couldn't be done. Impossible.

He scratched his nose, smiled wistfully. Life was a series of second choices. He'd end up, as always, at Madame Tussad's. Tussad wasn't her real name, of course, but because of her fondness for makeup it was certainly richly deserved.

He had a favourite room at Tussad's. The room was furnished like a child's nursery. For him, sex was best taken in an adult-sized crib, on a soft and lumpy bed of stuffed toy animals, plush teddies, green-eyed lions and elephants with soft blunt tusks – all the beasts of the ark. There was a battered Fisher-Price record player that scratched its way through his favourite Dr Seuss album while his sweetheart of the moment twitched and squirmed beneath him and did her best to sing along. From previous experience, he knew it was wise to call ahead, make an appointment . . .

Downey left the whorehouse a little after six. He took a taxi to Dokki, disembarked as a routine precaution two blocks from his apartment. Standing at his door, he carefully studied his alarm system, locks. There were no signs of covert entry – but then, wasn't that what covert entry was all about? He licked his key with his tongue to lubricate the metal so it slid more easily into the lock, then drew and cocked his pistol, a fourteen-shot Browning 9mm automatic. Using his left hand, he turned the key with infinite care, then briskly kicked the door open.

It was so quiet inside the apartment that he could hear the carpet fading. He shut the door and locked it, prowled methodically through his rooms. When he was satisfied that the apartment was empty, he slipped on a pair of rubber gloves and went into the kitchen and helped himself to a can of Miller Lite from the fridge. There was no point at all in looking for bugs. He'd been gone almost a week, more than enough time for a CIA crew to tear out and rebuild entire walls, install a bunch of mini infrared cameras, fibre optics, electronic listening devices smaller than a gnat's ear – a ton of stuff it'd take him a year to uncover. But the thing was, he had a hunch Foster simply wouldn't bother.

If he was wrong, well . . .

He drank some beer and then opened the drawer where he kept his cutlery. He selected a knife and went into the living room and began systematically to shred the furniture. The impression he wanted to leave was that a madman had been at work; he plunged the knife into the sofa over and over again, hacked and slashed, thrust his rubber-gloved hands into gaping wounds, yanked out fistfuls of stuffing. It was tough sledding. He had to pause every few minutes to catch his breath, ease the pounding of his heart. By the time he hit the bedroom he was down to his shirtsleeves, most of the way through his third can of beer. He shredded the Sealy Posturepedic and left his knife sticking out of the bed's oak-veneer headboard, then turned his attention to the bureau, flung clothes and emptied drawers blindly to the floor.

When the room had been reduced to a shambles he sat down on the ruined bed and looked at his watch. It was ten minutes past nine. He made his way into the kitchen and ate some leftover pizza, guzzled another beer.

Refreshed, he went back into the living room and attached an Israeli-designed noise suppressor to the Browning.

There was a large plate-glass mirror hanging over the mock fireplace. He snapped off three shots. Shards of silvered glass crashed down on the fireplace mantel and tile surround.

Downey tossed the Browning on a chair and took out a hypodermic kit. He rolled up his shirtsleeve, flexed his biceps. The hypo was in a cellophane package. He ripped it free, depressed the plunger, took a deep breath and jabbed himself in the crook of the arm. The point of the needle hit a tendon, veered into muscle. The pain was intense. No wonder nurses were always so cheerful.

He bit his lip and tried again, stabbed himself with a frantic, controlled viciousness.

Blood splashed up into the glass vial. He gripped the hypo with his right hand and took the plunger between his teeth, drew his head slowly back and drained himself of 150 ccs of B negative.

It was a convenience, having an uncommon blood type.

He eased the primed needle out of his arm, the flesh puckering like a tiny volcano as the point slid out. A thin stream of blood trickled down the inside of his forearm to his wrist, splattered on the carpet. He made no attempt to staunch the flow.

Feeling a little lightheaded, he aimed the needle straight up and violently depressed the plunger.

Blood sprayed wildly across the room's white-painted ceiling. A last few drops fell on his shoes. He sat on an arm of the gutted sofa, succeeded in once again piercing the vein.

He refilled the vial and sat there for a moment with the loaded hypo in his lap. His hands were shaking. He felt giddy and sick.

He took a few deep breaths, clearing his head, and then stood up and walked carefully towards the fireplace. This time he shot the blood in a looping arc that curled from the height of his throat down towards the floor, across the shattered mirror. He rested for a few moments and then, his stomach churning, filled and emptied the vial a third time.

Enough was enough. The apartment looked like an abattoir. Christ, it was like spilling coffee. There was always so much more on the floor than had ever been in the cup.

He went into the bathroom, ran cold water over his wounds, dried himself with a towel, rolled down his shirtsleeves and fussily buttoned the cuffs. He used the towel to wipe blood off the counter, threw the towel in the shower stall.

He went back into the living room, ejected the slide and reloaded the Browning, left the apartment.

The hallway was empty, deserted. The deadbolt shot home with a satisfying thud, a punctuation mark that nicely brought the episode to a close.

There was a marine corporal with a face straight out of an Uncle Sam poster sitting at Dorothy's desk. He was reading an old copy of *Sports Illustrated*, and he glanced up as Downey stepped out of the elevator. Downey ignored him, went over to Foster's big oak door and rattled the knob. The marine put down the magazine. Downey checked his watch. There was a dark smear of dried blood on the crystal. He licked the ball of his thumb and wiped the crystal clean.

"Can I help you, sir?"

"Did he call in?"

"Sir?"

Downey pointed at Dorothy's telephone. "In the past hour or so, did that shiny black thing make a sound like somebody punched you in the head?"

"There haven't been any calls, sir."

Foster, peering myopically at his gold Marlin pocket watch, stepped out of the elevator at half-past ten. His idea of an apology was to complain loudly about the conduct of the people who'd kept him up late having a good time. Downey stayed in his chair while Foster fumbled with his BMW key ring. Was Foster drunk? Maybe not, but he'd certainly had a few. Downey winked at the marine, who diplomatically looked away. Foster finally managed to unlock his office door. Downey heaved himself to his feet and followed him inside.

Foster scuttled around behind his desk, switched on a brass reading lamp with a green glass shade. Downey shut the door and walked across the room towards him, his heels making little dents in the freshly-vacuumed carpet. He sat down in the Queen Anne reserved for visitors. A leg squeaked. It wasn't a question of craftsmanship. With the passage of time, wood shrank and glue failed, dowels loosened. Every goddamned thing in the world eventually wore out, that was a given. The tricky part was correctly anticipating when the breakdown was going to occur. Downey crossed his legs, settling himself. He lit a cigarette. The sex had been a mistake. He was tired. He shifted his weight and the Browning's butt dug into his ribs.

Foster was wearing a black tuxedo cut from a bolt of cloth so dull the material seemed to suck the light out of the room. The tux combined with his solemn mien and the unnatural quiet of the empty building lent him an air that was almost judicial.

Downey felt the first vague stirrings of suspicion that something might have gone terribly wrong. Maybe the marine's job wasn't to keep him from prematurely entering Foster's office, but, *au contraire*, to stop him from leaving.

Now that he'd had time to think about it, he wasn't so sure Foster was drunk, either. The man seemed nervous rather than intoxicated. He wondered why.

Foster didn't keep him waiting. "Some time ago," he said, "you came to me with a story about a Libyan Intelligence Corps Colonel named Butros Murad. You told me Butros was hot to defect, asked for authorization to put together a team."

"Authorization and funding."

"Right. Sweets and Martin, where are they?"

"Sidi Mahares."

Foster gave him a blank look.

"It's a beach resort on the island of Djerba, off the Tunisian coast."

"What the hell are they doing there?"

"Scuba diving. Boozing. Screwing the local talent." Downey paused. "Oh yeah, and waiting for Colonel Butros to show up."

"Then what?"

"A flight back to the mainland and an Air France 747 to Istanbul, via Rome, where the colonel is skedded to prematurely disembark. And announce that he's defected."

"Where does Jennifer Forsyth fit in?"

"Who?" said Downey stupidly. He fumbled in his pocket and pulled out a Snack Bar, tore off the wrapper and bit down hard. Fragments of chocolate and roasted peanut fell into his lap. He chewed vigorously, bit off another enormous mouthful.

"You talked to her in London," said Foster. "No doubt you discussed the death of her father."

"Have you been *spying* on me?" said Downey, amazed.

"Where is she now?"

"In Djerba, with Hubie and Mungo."

"Doing what?"

"Biding her time. She's uh . . . a *distraction*, in the event we happen to need one."

"How did she become involved in the first place?"

"It was her idea. She wanted a piece of the action. I happened to owe her a big one."

Foster cocked an interrogative eyebrow.

"It's personal," said Downey, and stuffed the rest of the chocolate bar into his mouth.

Foster surprised him by letting it go. "You were in Libya when her father disappeared. That was back in '72, right?"

"God, was it that long ago?"

"What were you doing there, Jack?"

"Intelligence analysis. Paperwork. I was stationed at Wheeler, hardly ever got off the base. It was nothing heavy, believe me. If I hadn't been able to type thirty words a minute, they'd probably have sent me home."

"You're denying you were involved with Forsyth's disappearance?"

Downey was genuinely shocked – no need to fake it. "I didn't have anything to do with it, Richard. Not a single damned thing. Jennifer was a sweet kid. I was touched. Maybe it was a mistake, but I promised that if I ever found out what happened to her dad, I'd let her know."

"Which you did, last month in London."

"Right."

"And since the colonel had something to do with her father's death, she's going to help you bag him."

"Not really, no. I mean, of course not. But that's what she'll end up thinking, so she'll go away happy."

"If you say so, Jack."

Foster twisted to reach behind him. He picked up the skull Downey had sent him, stuck his fingers in the eye sockets as if the skull was a bowling ball. He placed the skull in the middle of his desk and made it spin. Dark hollows and white bone flashed in the light cast by the desk lamp. He said, "Ever hear of Amm Khalil?"

Downey shook his head, no.

"He's a forensic odontologist. Told me among other things that odontological evidence helped identify Nero's wife's body, 'way back in AD 66."

"Amazing."

"Not compared to what they can do nowadays. Khalil compared the postmortem dental record obtained from this skull with the ante-mortem dental record Charlie's Los Angeles dentist faxed to this office. Khalil was very impressed. Said the gold work was top-notch. Occlusal wear of the mandibles, by way of an example, was exactly identical." Foster stared at Downey with the eyes of a sparrow, small and bright. "You only made one mistake, Jack."

Downey smiled politely, leaned forward a little in his chair.

"Racial characteristics," said Foster.

"I'm not sure I follow you."

"The most distinctive racial characteristic in a human skull is a tooth – the shovel-shaped incisor. It occurs in ninety-five per cent of American Indians, more than ninety per cent of Chinese, and approximately half the Palestinian Arab population."

Foster turned the skull so the sightless eyes were staring directly at Downey.

"Charlie wasn't an American Indian, or Chinese, and he sure as hell wasn't a fucking Palestinian. So why does his skull have shovel-shaped incisors? C'mon, Jack. Confess. He's alive, isn't he? Romping on the beach at Djerba along with the rest of your crew."

"As a matter of fact, he's here in Cairo."

Foster thumped his desk in triumph. "I knew it! All that bullshit about Butros . . . He never had any intention to defect. You're planning to snatch him."

Downey was stunned. He managed to arrange his face in a display of reluctant admiration. "Mossad wants him real bad. We were going to do a swap."

"With the Israelis? Why? What the hell do they want him for?"

"The Syrians have a nuclear capability, and Butros knows all the details."

"*What?*"

"It's ultra hush-hush, but they managed to get their hands on an Israeli self-propelled gun and several rounds of nuclear ammo."

"Jesus Christ!" Foster frowned, chewed at his lower lip. "Where does Charlie fit in?"

"Want to talk to him?"

Foster hesitated, hauled out his Marlin, pondered for what seemed an eternity, or maybe even a little longer.

They left Foster's BMW in the embassy garage. Downey had no trouble convincing him it made a hell of a lot more sense, security-wise, to use one of the cars from the embassy pool. He'd lined up a dark-green Ford Tempo. Like most of the embassy vehicles, the car had reinforced body panels and bulletproof glass.

Downey stopped just outside the gate to check the two-way radio. The girl on duty at the switchboard sounded as if she had a mouth full of oatmeal, but was quick to respond to his call. Downey told her that musty old joke about the camel herder who was always getting humped but never getting laid, turned the speaker up so the raucous sound of her laughter filled the car.

Foster, slouched down in his seat, grinned sloppily. Downey smelled whisky on his breath. The dumb bastard was half-drunk, bless his soul.

He drove at maximum legal speed upriver past the island of Roda and the brightly-lit Manyal Palace. At the southern tip of the island there were the bright floodlights of the Manisterli Palace and then Cairo's famous Nilometer, useless now except as a curiosity to sun-glazed, uncomprehending tourists.

Downey reflected that if the Nile ever flooded again, it would be because the Israelis or Libyans had nuked the Aswan dam.

In half an hour, they had left the luxury hotels far behind and were speeding through an area of warehouses and light industry. The streets were narrow and ill-lit, choked on both sides by huge semi-trailers destined to be loaded or off-loaded in the early hours of the following morning. Downey noticed that Foster was sitting a little straighter in his seat. Starting to sober up, maybe.

Foster said, "The radio gonna work this far from the embassy, if we need to get in touch?"

"No problem," said Downey. "Don't worry about it." He followed the roadmap of his mind for another quarter of an hour, weaving in and out of a dozen narrow streets and alleys before suddenly and without warning arriving back at the river. They drove across a space of waste ground, past a rusty steel barge festooned with strings of naked bulbs.

Foster shifted restlessly in his seat.

"Real close now." Downey drove down a narrow unpaved alley between two brick buildings, parked beneath the yellowish glare of a security light fixed to the top of a tall wooden pole. He turned off the engine and got out of the car.

Foster followed him out of the pool of yellow light, down a slippery dirt path towards the dark, shifting waters of the Nile. The air was cool and damp and stank of mud, fetid and decaying. Mist curled lazily around their legs. The path steepened and the light faded. Foster slipped, fell to one knee, cursed noisily. A long, dark shape loomed up in front of him; the ghostly profile of one of the massive, open-hulled steel scows that hauled limestone from the quarries downriver to the city.

Downey continued along the path towards the bow of the vessel. The river was a solid black mass that slid with deceptive smoothness towards Cairo and the Delta, into the Med. Near the bow of the ship a narrow gangway about thirty feet long climbed steeply from shore to rail.

There was a locked wire-mesh gate topped with barbed wire. Downey had a key. He opened the gate and motioned Foster past him, then shut the gate and reached awkwardly through the mesh to lock it.

"What's Charlie doing *here*?" Foster demanded.

"Reading. Sleeping. Hiding out from you and me." Downey started up the gangway. He waved his hand at the scow. "She's been tied up in court for the past six months. An ownership squabble."

Foster gingerly tried the gangway. It seemed solid enough. Somewhere out on the black water an unseen bird croaked eerily, and for a moment he thought he heard the spooky sound of disembodied voices, soft and indistinct, that seemed to come from very far away.

Downey reached the end of the gangway. His heels thumped reassuringly on the solid steel plate of the deck. He turned and offered his hand as Foster reached the end of the gangplank.

Foster instinctively reached out. Much too late, he saw the cold gleam in Downey's eyes. The tips of their fingers touched briefly. Foster snatched back his hand. He went for his revolver.

Downey yanked at Foster's jacket, pulled him off balance, kicked him in the knee. The back of Foster's head hit the deck. He aimed the gun at Downey's fat stomach. Downey kicked him in the face. Foster dropped the gun, and was kicked again. He retched noisily. His nose had been broken. A mist of blood sprayed across the starched front of his shirt.

Downey tied Foster's ankles and wrists with loops of yellow nylon rope. The gun, a snubnose .38 Colt revolver, lay on the deck a few inches from his bloody nose. He found spare ammo in Foster's pocket.

Downey said, "Some asshole blew up my hotel room in London. Used a Claymore. Was that your idea?"

Foster muttered something incomprehensible.

Downey kicked him in the head. "Louder, please."

224

Foster spat a mouthful of blood on the deck. "Jack, this is news to me!"

"A squad of paratroopers attacked my base camp in the desert. What do you know about *that?*"

"What base camp? Nothing!"

"Not good enough, Dick."

"It's the truth!"

Downey said, "That's what I was afraid of," and grabbed Foster by the collar and dragged him into a sitting position, got his hands under Foster's armpits and hauled him to the rail. Foster struggled weakly, like a newborn kitten dangled over a bucket of water. Downey crouched, levered him up and over the rail and let him drop.

The echo of the splash was swallowed by the dense fog that lay upon the river. Downey glanced over the rail. Foster lay on his back, arms and legs thrashing the water into a white foam as he fought to stay afloat. Downey crossed to the far side of the scow. One end of the long length of rope tied to Foster's ankles was secured to the rail with a clove hitch. He gathered in the slack. It was a little like fishing – that same tremulous sensation of struggle and torment telegraphed through the line. He braced himself, began to pull the rope in hand over hand.

Foster, frantically writhing and twisting on the cold black surface of the water, suddenly felt something tug sharply at his legs, yank him down. He screamed. The rusty, pitted hull loomed over him. The rope tied to his wrists lay in slack coils on the surface of the water, led up the side of the scow and vanished over the rail. He grabbed at the rope, managed to lift himself out of the water until his head and shoulders were clear.

Downey was taken by surprise by this unexpected show of resistance. He banged his knuckles against the steel railing as he lost ground, swore like a sailor and then yanked savagely, lengths of quarter-inch nylon falling at his feet in stiff, dripping coils.

Foster gulped foggy air, managed to fill his lungs one last time. He burned the skin off the palms of his hands as he was pulled beneath the surface, into the sightless depths. His body scraped against the hull of the scow, bumping and twisting as he was hauled down through the Nile until his shoes struck the keel.

Downey secured the rope to the rail with a round turn and two half hitches, went over to the landward side and did the same thing with the rope tied to Foster's hands. He policed the deck. Foster's treasured Marlin pocket watch lay only a few feet away from the Colt. He flipped open the Colt's cylinder. The revolver was fully loaded. What a suspicious guy! He shoved the gun in his pocket and made his way back across the gangplank, up the dirt path to the waiting Ford.

Sheila, the typing-pool recruit with the magic fingers, had sublet a leased apartment in the district of Giza, within walking distance of Cairo University. Downey had made enquiries and learned that she lived alone.

And so, as he slipped the lock and strolled into her apartment, the deep-throated sound of male laughter caught him completely by surprise.

He eased the door shut. There was another burst of raucous laughter. He dropped the Marlin on the carpet and stamped on it with the heel of his shoe, stopping the watch at one forty-two. He pulled on a pair of rubber gloves, drew Foster's Colt and crept soundlessly down a narrow hallway. The bedroom door was wide open. He risked a quick peek. Sheila was squatting on top of a black marine sergeant from the embassy. Downey knew his name but, in the heat of the moment, couldn't think of it. She moved her hips. The sergeant made an animal noise, reached up to fondle her breasts.

Downey, slouched in the doorway with the Colt in a two-handed grip, grinned broadly. Drowned and cuckolded within the space of an hour. Foster was having a rough night.

Time to put an end to it.

He aimed at the base of the girl's spine and squeezed the trigger twice. Gouts of blood sprayed across the paisley-patterned sheets and pillows, the headboard and built-in bookcase, digital clock, the bedroom wall and the sergeant's broad, hairless body. Sheila collapsed across her lover, saddling him with a hundred and fifteen pound handicap.

Downey squeezed off two more rounds, drilled her through her cheatin' heart, blew away a pillow. The air was filled with goose feathers and lots more blood.

The sergeant flung the corpse aside, rolled off the bed, vanished. My, but he was quick. Downey fired into the mattress at an acute angle. The sergeant screamed in pain. Downey jumped up on the bed, hoping for a better view. The sheets were silk, and very slippery. He lost his balance, fell flat on his back. The sergeant came at him with a knife the size of a machete. Downey shot him in the chest at point-blank range, scooted over to the far side of the bed. The sergeant stood there, naked and bloody, the knife held low in front of him. Downey aimed carefully, intending to shoot him between the eyes.

He pulled the trigger. The hammer clicked on a spent casing.

The sergeant grimaced, flashed teeth stained red with blood.

Downey dropped Foster's Colt and yanked out his big fourteen-shot Browning automatic. The sergeant was no dummy. He turned and ran.

Downey went after him, going slow because of the knife, his memory of how Liam O'Brady had died.

The sergeant made it as far as the living room and then fell headlong across a coffee table made out of a big sheet of kidney-shaped glass. The table shattered and he ended up on the floor, chest wound pumping blood.

Downey moved cautiously in on him, and then backed away. The sergeant's breathing was fast and shallow. His mouth was wide open, slack. He had that special look in his big brown eyes: detached, faraway. Downey stuck the Browning in his waistband and went back into the bedroom and scooped up Foster's Colt, reloaded. He was gone less than a minute, but by the time he got back the sergeant had vanished.

Downey found him in the bathroom, stuffing a wad of toilet paper into his wound. The man glared at him, whimpered in distress. Then ripped a chrome-plated towel rack out of the wall and hit Downey on the collarbone, bringing him to his knees. Downey scuttled out of the bathroom.

The sergeant lurched after him, chased him in slo-mo down the hall past the bedroom and into the living room. His eyes were red and murderous, the pupils tiny black pinpoints of malice. Downey picked up the pace a little, shuffling backwards. Grunting and bleeding, the sergeant shambled after him. Downey went around behind the sofa. The sergeant swiped at him. The knife hissed through the air.

Dancing backwards, Downey led the sergeant into the kitchen, waltzed him through the dining nook, past the congealing remains of the sergeant's last supper. Jeez, the son of a bitch was relentless. Downey cruised back along the hallway towards the bedroom, but this time the sergeant didn't follow him. He'd broken off the pursuit, headed for the phone.

Downey moved in on him. The sergeant slashed at him with the knife, picked up the telephone. He'd begun to shake uncontrollably. Each breath he took sounded as if someone was letting the air out of an over-inflated balloon. He dialled two numbers, then slid down the wall to a sitting position, trailing a smear of blood like a giant exclamation mark.

Downey circled, inched closer. The sergeant dialled a third number. The receiver fell out of his hand. He stared blankly at the instrument as if he'd forgotten what it was for. Downey feinted. The sergeant dropped the knife and rolled over on his side. The nap of the carpet filled his eyes. He didn't blink.

On his way out of the apartment, Downey paused to take a quick look in the bedroom, trying to view the scene through neutral eyes. What he saw was Richard Foster's honey-pie in bed with a black noncom, breaking ranks in a way that simply couldn't be countenanced. The investigating team would picture Foster arriving on the spur of the moment, unannounced. See him turn red as a beet, blow a fuse, pull his Colt and shoot a bunch of .38 calibre holes in his nightmare.

Downey thought about what would happen next. The Cairo homicide cops would go hunting for Foster, and so would the embassy. They'd try to contact Downey, among others. The first place they'd look was his apartment.

All they'd find was a truckload of ruined furniture, more bullet holes and gore.

It wasn't the perfect crime, but it would do.

31

TUNIS

At Tunis airport a short, fat man who looked remarkably like Peter Lorre guided Mungo and Sweets past customs and then drove them to a crumbling whitewashed building on the fringe of the warehouse district. The building was three storeys high. Their room was on the top floor, and was furnished with a cold-water sink and two beds. A naked light bulb hung from the ceiling by a frayed wire. The window had been nailed shut. Mungo scrubbed grime from the glass with the palm of his hand.

Sweets lit a cigarette. The air, despite the closed window, was heavy with the smell of blood. He said, "What the fuck we doin' here, pal?"

"There has been a delay. Wait here, please." Eyes bulging, Peter Lorre eased shut the door.

Sweets tilted his head and sniffed the air. "What's that smell?"

"Lemme put it this way, we get hungry, we're real close to a nice fresh chop."

Sweets joined Mungo at the window. On the far side of the street, foreshortened men in turbans and bloody plastic aprons were shovelling the guts of slaughtered sheep out of wooden wheelbarrows into fifty-gallon steel drums. As they watched, one of the men picked up a drum lid and a rubber mallet. He placed the lid carefully on top of a drum filled to the brim with entrails, blood, and chunks of glistening white fat, and then pounded the lid tight with the mallet. One of his companions said something to him in Arabic and he laughed and began to play a cheerful tune, slapping the side of the drum with his free hand as he hit the top with the hammer.

Mungo glanced up and down the narrow, busy street. He moved away from the window, sat down on the nearest bed. It was a bitch, being in a strange city. Trying to keep pumped right up but at the same time maintain your cool, keep your eyes off the clock.

Mungo studied the back of his hand. The skin was slick with sweat.

They'd been up all night, and he was bone-weary, but couldn't keep still. He and Sweets had talked for hours about the paratrooper attack in the desert. Downey had said he'd look into it, cancel the operation if necessary. He'd even thought his Cairo chief-of-station might've been involved. Some asshole named Foster. Downey had always been a stand-up guy. Mungo trusted him. But he was worried, on edge, ready to bail out.

Restless, he went back to the window and stared down through the glass. A man in a lime-green suit was striding down the middle of the street. The guy looked as if he was thinking about buying the whole goddamned world, and had the cash right there in his pocket. Never had Mungo seen anybody who looked so goddamn cocky, full of himself, out of place. "Remember Bogota?" he said to Sweets.

"Never forget it." An image of Lolita stepping daintily out of the tub came to him. He'd spent a long time in the desert, and now this. He needed a woman real bad. It was like one of them dumb country-and-western tunes. He ached inside.

"Jesus, we thought Colombia was hot and dusty," Mungo said. "What did we know about heat? Nothing. What did we know about dust? Not a goddamn thing."

Half and hour later, there was a soft, somehow comically furtive knock on the door.

It was, no surprise, the man in the lime-green suit.

"Mr Sweets and Mr Martin?"

The man's voice was soft as a chamois. He gave Mungo a welcome-wagon smile. Sweets slipped up behind him and grabbed him by his fried-egg tie, yanked his colour-blind ass into the room and spun him around and shoved his face against the door hard enough to slam it shut.

"What's your name, handsome?"

"André."

"French people always dress so nice," said Sweets.

Mungo kicked André on the inside of the ankle. André spread his legs – an automatic reation. Mungo expertly patted him down.

"May I turn around now, please?"

"Yeah, sure."

"I have been employed by Mr Downey. He told me . . ."

"Who?" interrupted Sweets.

"Downey," said André, placing the accent on the last syllable this time. "I am to drive you to Zuwarah, on the Libyan side of the border. I am to deliver you to a green Citroen van parked in front of a silversmith's shop on the main road, then return to Tunis."

230

"We know all that," said Sweets. "The thing is, where in hell have you been?"

André shaped an hourglass with his hands. "I was, how shall I put it, unavoidably delayed." He gave Sweets a conspiratorial smile, reached inside his gaudy jacket and produced a pair of battered Tunisian passports.

"These are for you."

Sweets snatched at the passports, flipped them open. He didn't recognize the name, but it was his picture, all right. He tossed Mungo his passport. Mungo studied the photograph, stamp, watermarks and binding. He rolled the passport into a tight cylinder and gave André – or whatever his real name was – a sharp jab in the ribs.

"Let's hit the road, chum."

They hurried down the stairs to street level, into the heat and noise and rich stink of blood, motes of dust that wandered sluggishly through thick yellow light.

The slaughterhouse doors were wide open. In the dimly lit interior of the building Mungo saw beads of light glisten on the oiled links of overhead chains and pulleys, shine dully on the fat white bellies of sheep waiting to be slaughtered.

The animals hung head-down from steel hooks. Short lengths of sisal bound their rear legs together. There was the sound of an electric motor. The chain staggered forward, tossing sparks of light. The sheep squealed in panic, plump bodies jerking and swaying.

A man in plastic safety goggles and a full-length rubber apron stepped into view, grasped a sheep by its offside ear and twisted its head up and away from him. The sheep bleated in fear and then the gleaming blade sliced deeply into its throat, nearly decapitating it.

Blood sprayed across the goggles and apron. The sheep's eyes widened as if for one last quick look at the world. Then the chain jerked forward and the man wiped himself clean and prepared for the next stroke.

Mungo was standing there in the middle of the street like a damn fool tourist. He felt sick, weightless and giddy. He forced himself to resume walking. Never in his life had he allowed himself the luxury of worrying about the future, but suddenly he had a premonition that it was all about to go terribly wrong and he couldn't do a single damn thing about it.

André's car was a battered Mercedes 180, its black paintwork sun-bleached and streaked with dust. The floorboards were awash with old newspapers and plastic water bottles, assorted trash. The leather seats were stained with impacted dirt and oil. Sweets climbed into the front next to André. Mungo got in the back.

André started the car and gingerly revved the engine. The exhaust vented a cloud of pale-blue smoke. He jammed the car into gear and hit the gas.

Mungo rolled down his window, leaned back and watched the scenery glide by. The whitewashed buildings on the outskirts of the city were squat and geometric, with few of the architectural flourishes found in Egypt. They drove past the shop of a carpet-maker, hanks of brightly coloured wool framing the narrow doorway.

Within minutes they'd left Tunis behind and were speeding under the heat of the sun along the coastal road leading to the border of what was officially known as the Socialist People's Libyan Arab Jamahiriya.

They cut across Cape Bon and passed through the tourist towns of Nabeul and Hammamet – chains of hotels and fast-food stalls and white sandy beaches covered with forests of brightly-coloured umbrellas. Inland, there were salt flats. The miles slipped past. To the north of Nabeul there was rich farmland and the towns were smaller and farther apart. From Sousse to Sfax the coast was full of long, sandy, shallow bays and neatly-tended olive groves, the trees twisted by the offshore winds. They passed a man stalking sparrows with an air-rifle. André tooted the horn, and the man waved at the car, the barrel of his rifle gleaming in the sun.

They drove all through the afternoon and into the night, finally stopping at Gabes, a resort town famous for its huge oasis and forest of three hundred thousand palms. Downey had reserved rooms in a cheap hotel on the beach. Mungo, following instructions, paid cash and asked for a receipt.

By the time the sun came up they were already back on the road. The rising heat of the day combined with the motion of the car soon lulled Mungo to sleep. Sweets shook him awake a few miles from the Libyan border, at a town called Ras Jdayr.

At the border, André did the talking. The guards were armed with automatic weapons, but they were bored and the sun had drained them of energy. André risked a joke and the youngest of the guards laughed uproariously, tightly gripped his weapon so the canvas strap wouldn't slide off his shoulder. Their Tunisian passports were perfunctorily stamped, and they were waved through the barricade. Mungo sank a little lower in his seat. André caught the significance of the movement. He smiled into the rearview mirror.

"Eighty thousand Tunisians work in Libya. They are always passing through the border, coming or going. As long as Gadaffi needs skilled labour, they will continue to be welcome."

The highway ran parallel to the Mediterranean. Mungo stared out at the ocean, greenish-blue near the beach and shading into a clearer, paler blue on the horizon, where it merged with the cloudless blue of the sky.

"What're you thinking?" said Sweets. It wasn't the sort of question he usually asked. He'd twisted in his seat and was looking straight into Mungo's eyes.

"Wishing I could swim."

"All the way to Italy?" Sweets rubbed the cut over his eye. "Yeah, I think I know what you mean."

They reached the town of Zuwarah a little more than two hours after they'd crossed the border. The Citroën van was parked directly in front of a silversmith's, just as Downey had promised it would be.

"Keep driving," said Sweets. "Go around the block. Don't slow down."

André smiled. "Relax, my friend. If they wanted to pick you up, they'd have done it at the border."

"Don't argue. Do what you're told."

Zuwarah was situated about thirty miles from Tripoli, at the junction of two major highways. As they circled the block, they drove through patches of shadow and light, a hundred different sights and sounds and smells. A hundred yards from the Citroën, Sweets tapped André on the shoulder. "Stop here."

A hubcap grated against the curb. André made a small sound of dismay.

Sweets opened his door. "I'll drive."

"Where you want to meet?" said Mungo.

"Let's say two blocks down and one to the left. In ten minutes, okay?"

Mungo nodded carefully, glanced at his watch.

"Don't get lost." Sweets slammed shut his door and started down the crumbling sidewalk towards the Citroën. The Mercedes accelerated away from the curb, but Sweets didn't look up as it went past – he was too busy checking out the street. He was nervous, tense. Times like this, any little thing could set him off.

He approached the Citroën from the rear, drew level with the bumper and stooped to take a quick peek up the tailpipe. Nothing there but soot. The driver's side door wasn't locked. He climbed into the

233

vehicle. No one seemed to be paying any attention to him. The glove box was locked, but there was a rusty screwdriver lying on top of the dashboard. Sweets used it to pop the box open.

The ignition key was inside a small white envelope, together with a crude map of Tripoli's inner core and an address on Sidi Issa Street.

Sweets folded the envelope in half and stuffed it in his shirt pocket. He tried the key. It fit. The engine caught immediately. He checked his watch. Four minutes down and six to go. He put the transmission in gear and checked the side mirror, waited for a bright-green taxi to drive past. He let the clutch out slowly, not wanting to stall the damn thing. The engine growled and the truck shuddered and then lurched away from the curb, out into the middle of the road. Sweets overcorrected and then got the hang of it. At the first intersection, he turned left.

The way André saw it, he'd done what he had been paid to do, and so there was clearly no longer any reason for him to hang around. Problem was, Mungo refused to spring him loose until Sweets showed up. André sat behind the wheel of the Mercedes, looking hurt. He pulled a plastic bottle of mineral water from under the front seat, drank deeply and reluctantly offered the bottle to Mungo.

Mungo drained the bottle. The water was warm and flat and tasted faintly of oranges. The Citroën rounded the corner. There was nothing about the pedestrian or motor traffic to arouse his suspicions. He heard the sound of the diesel engine as Sweets downshifted into a lower gear. He opened his door and climbed out of the Mercedes. André smiled up at him. The guy was probably already thinking about how to spend his money.

Sweets stopped the truck close beside the Mercedes, casting it in shadow.

Mungo got in. He said, "Back to the highway, right?"

Sweets nodded.

Mungo glanced behind him. The rear of the truck was full of wooden packing crates marked with Arabic in heavy black letters. "Take a look?" he asked Sweets.

"No time."

The Mercedes started off. Sweets gave André thirty yards and then pulled in behind him, maintaining the distance. An old man standing in a puddle yelled at them and held up a string of fish. The dark skin of his arms and face were sprinkled with fish scales, festive and silvery in the insect-riddled light. They turned on to the town's main street and then down a curving access road towards the highway. The road was under construction, lots of heavy machinery parked on the verge. Hand and power tools lay here and there in the dirt as if the men wielding them had suddenly gone on strike, dropped their shovels and picks and simply walked away.

"Must be prayer time," said Sweets uneasily.

A huge mound of earth had been pushed across the roadway, narrowing it to one lane. The Mercedes slipped past a bulldozer. Sweets saw the brake lights flash as the car vanished around a sharp bend. The van was wider than the Mercedes. There was barely enough room to crawl past.

Sweets was concentrating on his side mirrors as he eased past the bulldozer, so it was Mungo who saw the roadblock first. There were dozens of heavily-armed soldiers, a jeep with a light machine-gun and a Russian T-52 tank. The Mercedes, braking hard, had slewed sideways across the road.

Mungo heard the low drone of hydraulics. The T-52's cannon swivelled towards them. "Move it!" he yelled.

Behind them, a gout of black smoke erupted from the bulldozer's exhaust. The huge machine lurched across the road, treads creaking. Sweets slammed into reverse. The rear end of the van smashed into the bulldozer. He shifted into first, but there was nowhere to go – they were trapped between the bulldozer and the Mercedes.

The drone of the tank's hydraulics stopped, and then the cannon boomed and the Mercedes leapt into the air and exploded, the hood cartwheeling across the dirt, ripping into the ranks of soldiers. The car landed on the road belly-up, spewing dirty orange flames and corkscrew funnels of dense black smoke.

"Jesus Christ," whispered Sweets. The windshield of the Mercedes was starred and cracked, smeared with blood and unidentifiable bits and pieces of flesh.

There was the sound of hydraulics again. The muzzle of the cannon swung towards them.

32

ALEXANDRIA

The alarm on the battery-powered Braun portable went off at six o'clock sharp. The phone rang a few moments later. It was a backup call from the hotel switchboard. As always, Downey had thought of everything.

Charlie and Jennifer had breakfast in the hotel restaurant – a tourist's meal of scrambled eggs and fried tomatoes, hash browns and wholewheat toast.

They were on their second cup of coffee when a tall, thin Arab wearing leather sandals, wrinkled khaki pants and a gaily-coloured Hawaiian surfer shirt limped over to their table. He ignored Charlie, smiled at Jennifer with the kind of teeth that only money can buy and said that he was their driver and they would have to leave immediately, please.

Charlie gripped his arm. "What's your name, pal?"

The man shrugged. "You can call me Amir, if you like. Hurry, please. We must not be late."

There was a twin-engine Beechcraft waiting at the airport. Amir hunched into the cockpit and started the engines. There was a crackle of static from the radio, followed by a short burst of Arabic. Amir spoke a few words in response. He adjusted the throttle. The plane spun around in a tight circle and then taxied slowly out to a secondary runway. The propellers whined and the Beechcraft shuddered and then shot down the narrow strip of asphalt, accelerating fast. Amir pulled back on the joystick; the nose tilted sharply up and then the earth fell steeply away.

Charlie peered out the Perspex window, through a dense cobweb of tiny scratches and down at the shallow waters of Lake Maryut, the dwindling city of Alexandria. Light flashed off the windshields of the cars on the Corniche. A clot of freighters squatted in the outer harbour. He tried to find the Montazah Palace Hotel but the wing obscured his view.

They turned south, towards the Egyptian-Libyan border.

The Beechcraft climbed to a ceiling of 8,000 feet as they flew over the Gulf Arabs on a course parallel to the coastline. Seen from so far up, the ocean was flat and calm, an endless expanse of blue, the coastline marked by a thin froth of white. The distance between Alexandria and their destination, the border crossing at Amsaad, was a little more than three hundred miles. The plane's airspeed was a hundred and twenty knots and Amir had told them he expected to arrive at approximately ten o'clock.

Jennifer squeezed Charlie's hand. "What are you thinking about?"

"Nothing much." He could see her reflection in the glass. She was watching him carefully.

"Wishing you'd never become involved, that you were back in Cairo?"

Charlie thought about his squalid little room, the bars of red and blue and green light that crawled slowly across the wall, the desolation, loneliness. "I wish we were somewhere else, that's all. Both of us."

She leaned towards him, kissed him on the mouth. "I love you, Charlie."

"Do you?"

"Yes. Very much."

It was a few minutes past ten when the pitch of the engines deepened, and they began to lose altitude. The landscape, an abstract of yellows and blues, gradually acquired form and substance, definition.

Jennifer pointed out the window. "There's a town down there."

Amsaad.

They continued to lose altitude. Charlie pointed out the border crossing, customs post and zebra-painted barriers, the Land-Rovers in the parking lot. A man walked out of the guard post, stretched his arms wide and then shaded his face with his hand as he looked up at the airplane. They swung wide. The ground rushed towards them.

Charlie heard a thin, piercing sound – Amir whistling tunelessly through his teeth. The airport was small; a dirt track and a few metal quonset huts. They touched down hard. The hydraulics took most of the shock but the impact was severe enough to make him glad he'd fastened his seatbelt. Amir cursed fluently in Arabic. The engines roared as he used the air brakes. Dust billowed around them and was instantly swept away by the wash of the propellers.

Amir removed his headset and unbuckled his safety belt. He brushed past them and unlocked the door, swung it open and gave the folding steps a kick.

"Out, please." He grasped Charlie's arm and Charlie shook him off. Amir grinned like an idiot, nervous as hell. Jennifer stood up and moved towards the open door, sunlight and swirling dust. Amir muttered something in Charlie's ear but, with the cabin door open, the sound of the idling engines was enormous and it was impossible to catch what he had said.

Charlie followed Jennifer down the aluminum steps. The backwash from the props tore at his clothes. He glanced behind him. Amir stood in the open door. Their eyes met. Charlie caught a glimpse of compassion, even pity. And then Amir's dark eyes glittered like a wolf's, the cabin door thudded shut, and he was gone.

What in hell had the man been thinking, to look at him like that? Charlie stared at the cockpit, but the sun reflecting off the glass made it impossible to see inside. The throb of the engines deepened as the plane turned into the wind. It hurtled down the runway, hit a crosswind and suddenly veered sideways. Wings flashed in the sunlight. Climbing steeply, the plane shrank to a tiny dot, vanished.

Jennifer took Charlie's hand and they began to walk towards the nearest of the quonset huts. Despite their proximity to the coast, the temperature was in the high nineties. They stood in the shade of the building, the metal radiating heat.

"I thought Jack told us there'd be a car," Jennifer said.

"He did."

"Well, where the hell is it?"

"Relax, it'll be here sooner or later."

Jennifer nodded. She was very tense. London seemed as far away as the moon. She couldn't stop thinking about her father. She had watched him die, vividly and in colour. But then the steady drone of the projector's fan had filled that small, dark room in Chalk Farm, and a part of her mind had focused on the sound, kept her safe, reassured her that what she'd seen was only a film, just another film.

But now, as she was about to enter the country where her father had died, the terrible, crushing reality of the situation began to press in on her. He was dead, and she had come to collect his remains.

The car was a glossy black stretch Audi. It crawled slowly towards them, a dense shadow that glided silently across the ground. The tinted windows were rolled up but they could hear the soft, tinny sound of Arabic music. The limo cruised slowly past them and disappeared behind the quonset huts, only to reappear a few moments later. The radio had been turned off. The only sound that came from the car was the hushed whisper of the tires on the hard-packed ground.

"Think he can see us through that glass?" Jennifer said.

"Let's hope so."

The Audi swerved suddenly towards them, as if on cue. It skidded to a stop beside them in a roiling cloud of dust. The rear door swung open.

Charlie had a vision of Jennifer climbing into the car and the door slamming shut as the car sped off, leaving him stranded, alone. "I'll get in first," he said quietly.

The driver was wearing a peaked cap and dove-grey uniform, no insignia. He could have been a chauffeur or an army officer. The Audi glided away from the huts.

"Where are we going?" said Charlie. The man frowned and shrugged elaborately, puffing out his cheeks.

"Do you speak English?" said Jennifer.

Another shrug. The driver fiddled with the car's tape deck. Music flowed from hidden speakers, and the voice of the popular Egyptian singer Oum Kalthoum filled the car. Charlie knew the woman by reputation – she was a vociferous supporter of the Palestinian cause.

The Audi picked up speed as it swept past the last of the quonset huts. Charlie peered out the rear window. Seen through the tinted glass, the landscape was lifeless and grey, desolate.

They drove through the border without slowing down. The red, white, and black-barred flag of Libya fluttered in a breeze made by a large electric fan mounted on the roof of the guard's quarters. Even through the closed window of the car, Charlie could hear the drone of the motor and rattle of the blades.

They continued along the highway for several miles, then turned cn to a paved secondary road which wound sharply down towards the sea, through a stand of acacia trees with mottled green and brown camouflage netting suspended from the branches.

Less than a mile down the road, the car burst out of the thin, dappled shade of the woods and into bright sunlight, an open patch of ground dominated by the squat, menacing bulk of a helicopter.

The helicopter was an Italian-made Agusta A-109 Hirundo. The turboprop engine whined shrilly. The main rotors slowly began to turn. Their driver climbed out of the Audi, opened the back door and offered Jennifer his hand.

The helicopter took them eight nautical miles to the desert town of Abdun Nasser, where they boarded a sleek Russian-made SU 20/22 *Fitter* E/F/J Fighter-Bomber. The fighter's interior was cramped, stuffed with electronic gear. Charlie and Jennifer sat in a pair of folding seats directly behind the cockpit. A man who introduced himself as

Halim sat down opposite them. He was short and stocky, bald. He had no trace of a beard and his arms and the backs of his hands were hairless. Halim fastened his seatbelt as the jet's powerful engines rose to a shriek. The fighter shuddered, and then the pilot released the brakes and they shot down the runway.

TRIPOLI

A little more than an hour later, they touched down at Tarabulus International Airport. A green Mercedes drove Charlie and Jennifer and Halim across the tarmac to the main building. Inside, they were met by a tall, thin man with swept-back hair and pockmarked skin, heavily-lidded eyes. He introduced himself as Mustafa, and offered Charlie his hand. His skin was hot and moist, soft as a baby's. He led them down a series of wide, brightly-lit hallways and through an open doorway, into a huge conference room.

There was the mutter of voices, the babble of a dozen different tongues. As Charlie and Jennifer entered the room there was a moment of silence and then a flurry of shouted questions, the soft metallic shuffling of power winders.

"What the hell's all this?" said Charlie.

"A press conference, of course." Smiling, Mustafa patted him on the shoulder, as if he were a small boy in need of reassurance.

"I thought we'd meet the press *after* we talked with Colonel Gadaffi."

"The Leader is unavailable at this time. We have been forced to reschedule events. Please be patient."

More questions were shouted from the floor as Halim led them up a short flight of stairs to a small stage and stood them behind a plexiglass podium spiked with microphones. There was a television camera off to one side, another at the rear of the hall. In rapid bursts of Arabic, French, English, German and Italian, Halim introduced them to the throng of journalists and then pointed at a dark, swarthy man standing at the front of the crowd.

The man cleared his throat. "Ibn Saad, *Al-Siyasah*. Mrs McPhee, is it true that you are in Libya at the express invitation of Colonel Gadaffi?"

"It is indeed true," said Halim promptly. "Mr and Mrs McPhee are the honoured guests of the Libyan people."

"How long will you be staying in Libya?" came a voice from the floor.

Jennifer hesitated, turned to Charlie. Halim stepped forward, spoke into the bank of microphones.

"Mrs McPhee and her husband are welcome to stay in the Socialist People's Libyan Arab Jamahiriya as long as they wish," he said. "The people of Libya welcome them with open arms and warm hearts." In a theatrical gesture of goodwill, he put his arms around Jennifer and Charlie. "While they are in Libya," he continued, "they are free to come and go as they please, although of course we have provided them with a guide in order that they might properly view the many cultural pleasures of the great city of Tarabulus." He smiled. "Or Tripoli, as the city is known in the west."

As the conference continued, Charlie realized it was a set-up; a carefully-orchestrated series of questions and answers designed to enhance Libya's image in the eyes of the world. *Jesus, why hadn't Downey thought of this?* Charlie brushed past Halim. "My wife and I have had a long and difficult journey. We're exhausted, and we need to rest. Naturally we'll be happy to answer more of your questions at another time."

Halim frowned, but quickly recovered. "Our guests will be staying at the Bab Al Madinah," he said into the microphones. "It is a deluxe hotel. No less than five stars."

Charlie took Jennifer's hand and led her away from the podium. He had no idea where he was going, all he knew was that he had to get out of there. How in hell could Downey have overlooked the certainty of just such a press conference, packed with pre-fab questions and tame journalists? It was a public relations man's dream. And there was something else that nagged at him. Why hadn't there been any questions about Jennifer's father?

Halim guided Charlie and Jennifer through the noisy crush of reporters and photographers, the blinding wash of television lights. He was clearly upset that Charlie had cut the conference short. In a terse voice he said, "You have a little over two hours until your meeting with Our Leader. Time enough for a short nap and chance to freshen up, wouldn't you say?"

Their suite at the Bab Al Madinah was on the hotel's top floor. Charlie stood by the window, his shoulders hunched, staring out at the ocean. First he had tired of the desert and now he was tired of the sea.

Jennifer went over to him, put her arms around him and kissed him on the lips. Charlie just stood there, responsive as a block of wood.

She said, "What is it, what's the matter?"

"The press conference. The timing was all wrong. And there was no mention of your father, not a single goddamn question."

"Yes, I know."

"Christ, aren't you worried about it?"

Jennifer pressed up against him, held him close. "I need you to be strong, Charlie."

She took his head in her hands and kissed him again and again, lightly as leaves falling from a tree.

"Halim said we've got an hour and a half. It isn't very much time. When this is finally over, won't it be nice to remember how we spent it?"

They had made love once and were beginning to explore new possibilities when the bedside telephone rang. It was Halim, calling from the lobby to inform them that a car was waiting to take them to see Gadaffi.

"We'll be down in a few minutes," said Charlie, as Jennifer nibbled his shoulder.

"Colonel Gadaffi does not like to be kept waiting," said Halim.

"Is there a colonel anywhere who does?"

The car was the same glossy Mercedes that had picked them up at the airport. The door was held open for them by a fat man in a rumpled white linen suit. He had a large, droopy moustache and sad, disinterested eyes, nails that were bitten to the quick. Charlie and Jennifer got into the back seat. To his surprise, the man climbed in with them.

"This is Adem Jedalla," said Omar Halim from the front of the car. "He is a Bedouin. Like all members of his tribe, he is very jealous of his possessions." Halim chuckled noisily, as if he had made a joke. As they drove away from the hotel, Jedalla twisted in his seat and Charlie saw that the bulky cut of his suit concealed a large revolver fitted in a shoulder holster.

They drove a short distance along the Al Kurnish road, turned past the Islamic Call Society building and around a ring road and down Al Fat'h street, the inner harbour, busy carpenters' market and the Old Castle built in the shape of a ship at the junction of Umar Al Mukhtar street. The architecture in this part of the city was new, and the streets thick with automobiles; Italian Fiats and Russian Zils. Almost all of the cars had the windows rolled up. In Tripoli, air-conditioning was apparently considered a necessity rather than a luxury.

The Mercedes continued down Al Fat'h street until they reached Ash Sharif, the main boulevard that passed through the embassy district. The driver turned right and then right again, on to Sidi Issa street. They parked in front of a tall, narrow building made of grey brick.

"The Criminal Investigation Department," said Halim, smiling.

The building in which the CID was housed had been constructed after the coup of 1969, and it had been built like a fortress. In a cramped office off the lobby, an official with the demeanour of a small-town barber took Polaroid shots of Jennifer and Charlie, laminated the pictures on to diagonally striped green-and-yellow day passes, deftly attached the passes to their clothing with plastic alligator clips.

"This way," said Halim, leading them towards a bank of elevators.

"Is this where we're going to meet Colonel Gadaffi?" Jennifer asked.

"Don't be ridiculous."

"What do you mean?" said Charlie.

Halim smiled. "Be patient, my friend."

The elevator stopped and the doors slid open on a narrow hallway with a black tiled floor and dull grey walls and ceiling. The hallway was deserted. Jedalla herded them out of the elevator and down the hall.

There was a green-painted door about every twenty feet, alternating on both sides of the corridor. Halim stopped at the second door on the left, swung the door open. He gestured to Charlie and said, "Step inside, please."

Charlie looked at Jennifer.

"She and Jedalla will have a room all to themselves. Divide and conquer, eh?"

"I want to see the British Consul," said Jennifer.

Jedalla put his hand on her shoulder and pushed her down the hall.

Charlie lunged towards him. Jedalla sidestepped and pulled his gun. He pointed the weapon at Charlie's face and then at his heart, groin, knee, back to his face again. Charlie slowly backed away.

Halim laughed. "That's right, be sensible. You'll live a little longer, perhaps."

The interrogation room was small, about twelve feet long and eight feet wide. There were no windows but one of the walls, from floor to ceiling, was mirrored glass. There were two men in the room, both of them stocky and muscular.

"If you cooperate," said Halim, "you have no reason to fear them."

The room was lit by spotlights sunk into the ceiling, and was furnished with a small metal table and four metal chairs.

"Sit," said Halim, as if he were speaking to a dog.

Charlie sat in the nearest of the three chairs.

"Not that one. That one is mine."

Charlie moved over to the next chair, but Halim waved him out of that one, as well.

"It is better that we should be at opposite ends of the table. I want to be able to look directly into your eyes. Do you understand?"

Halim fumbled in his shirt pocket, produced a packet of breath mints. He pinched one of the mints between his index finger and thumb, offered it to Charlie.

"No thanks."

"From my point of view, you should take one."

"Why?"

"It will help form a small bond between us." Halim tapped his temple with his index finger. "Psychology. A very useful science for someone in my line of work."

Charlie stared at him. The Libyan's odd, clockwork style of speech kept him off-balance. He said, "Where's Jennifer? Why have you separated us?"

Halim popped the mint into his mouth. He chewed reflectively. "These rooms are used only when we are forced to deal with serious criminals – murderers or political extremists like you."

"I don't know what the hell you're talking about!"

"Shut your stupid mouth!"

In the quiet that followed this outburst, Charlie heard a tiny crackling sound – in his excitement Halim was strangling the cellophane packet of mints.

"Have you noticed how *clean* this room is, even though the building is almost twenty years old? Can you guess the reason for this? It is because almost every time the room is put to use, we are required afterwards to scrub down the walls, even the ceiling . . ."

A piece of mint had become stuck in the gap between his front teeth. He sucked at it for a moment, and then carried on with his lecture.

"When the room is needed, it's usually to question someone like yourself, a foreigner. As often as not a worker from the oil rigs. The Americans have a drinking problem, the Italians are hot-headed . . . But the work is most rewarding when we capture a terrorist: some poor, misguided, dangerous soul."

"I am *not* a terrorist."

"You are an employee of the CIA who has been sent here to murder our Leader. You are a failed assassin. We know every detail of your despicable plan. All that remains is for you to dictate and sign your confession."

"There's been a . . . mistake."

Halim roared with laughter. He slapped the table with the flat of his hand, startling the mints and making them jump. The two observers grinned cheerfully.

"Let me tell you how it will be. First we talk with you, try to reason with you. Then, if that doesn't work, we become violent." Frowning, he indicated the two men behind him. "What they do is very unpleasant. I'm not a sadist, and I don't pretend to approve of their methods. But I must warn you, their tactics are effective."

"I'm not a terrorist," said Charlie. "And neither is my wife."

"Who?" said Halim, grinning.

"Jennifer. If you'd only . . ."

"You need time to calm down, think rationally. I'll give you twenty minutes. In the meantime these two will keep you company." Halim paused at the door. "I don't know anything about you, Charlie. Perhaps you anticipate the pain, even look forward to it. But one thing I must say to you. If you care at all for Jennifer Forsyth, you will cooperate without further delay."

Halim opened the door.

"Wait," said Charlie. He stood up and a fist hit him in the back of the neck, smashed him face-down into the metal table.

Halim shut the door.

Charlie sat there, slumped in the chair. He knew Halim was right about Adem Jedalla, and in Libya there were none of the western biases that would normally serve to protect a woman in Jennifer's position. He thought about the way Jedalla had looked at Jennifer. As if she was something to be played with, an insect to be crudely dissected by a vicious child.

Half an hour later, when Halim reentered the room, he immediately saw that Charlie's resolve had already crumbled, and that the interrogation would now proceed smoothly. He was more than a little disappointed. He'd never had an opportunity to work with an American spy, and had eagerly anticipated the chance to practise his techniques, the various skills he and all members of the élite Bureau of External Security were taught by their Czechoslovakian tutors.

Charlie McPhee was a big man, but he was not strong inside, where it counted. Halim could see the weakness in his eyes. A pity, because he'd eagerly anticipated the clash of wills and slow, inexorable crushing of all hope.

Still, there was a bright side. During the period he had left Charlie alone to soften up, he'd strolled down the corridor to the second interrogation room and watched through the one-way glass while Jedalla expertly questioned the woman. Jedalla was being gentle with her, a technique designed to emphasize the cruelty that would soon follow. He would break her, but he would do it at his leisure. And this was his weakness – that he enjoyed his work too much. Jedalla would still be toying with Jennifer while Gadaffi studied Halim's report, learning everything he needed to know about Jennifer Forsyth and the coward Charlie McPhee.

"Strip."

Charlie looked up, blinking in dismay.

"Take your clothes off," said Halim. He spoke very slowly, with exaggerated care, as if Charlie was a dull and uncomprehending child.

Charlie stood up. He began to unbutton his shirt. A part of his mind wondered if the same routine was being carried out with Jennifer. Feeling helpless and enraged, he balled up the shirt and threw it angrily down on the floor.

"A man with spirit," said Halim mildly. "Who could ask for more?" He patted Charlie gently on the shoulder. Halim was an ambitious man, but the truth was in his heart and it lay there like a lump.

He was full of envy, acidic and bitter. He'd much rather have interrogated the woman.

33

ZUWARAH

Mungo watched the Libyans set up the camera, a 35mm Panaflex mounted on a big wooden tripod. The equipment wasn't exactly state-of-the-art, but on the other hand, this was obviously no low-budget production. There was a cast of hundreds, uniforms running around all over the place. People shouting and being shouted at. There was also the platoon of bright-eyed kids armed with automatic weapons who were guarding them. The soldiers were nervous and jittery even though he and Sweets wore leg-shackles and were securely handcuffed to the flank of forty-one tons of T-72 tank.

Mungo watched them fiddle with the camera, adjusting the focus or whatever. How did the song go . . . *I wanna be in pictures, I wanna be a star* . . .

"I remember when I was a little kid and my mom tried to toilet-train me," Mungo said. A soldier poked him in the ribs with the barrel of his Kalishnikov rifle, grinding the blade front sight across the bones. Mungo gave him a long, cold look. The boy slowly backed away. Mungo said, "She used to sing to me, you know?"

"Miss her, do you?"

"Let's see if I can remember how it went." Mungo lifted his voice to an off-key falsetto.

"*If you were a star, little man, you'd twinkle. But since you ain't, could you please tinkle* . . ."

"A voice like that," said Sweets, "it'd *scare* the piss outta me."

The Libyans shot film for another half hour, taking footage from all angles of the troops and armoured cars, the T-72 and smouldering Mercedes, moving in for tight shots of the senior officers. When they were finished, they removed the shackles and herded the two men back into the Citroën van.

"What the fuck they up to now?" said Sweets as he settled behind the wheel.

"Maybe they realized they made a mistake, decided to let us go."

"Yeah, right." Sweets peered through the dusty, blood-streaked windshield. A soldier scrambled up on the hood of the truck and began to scrub at the glass with a rag.

Sweets noted the new location of the camera, and the milling troops that surrounded them. "We're gonna do it over again," he said.

"Do what?"

"Drive around the corner and spot the tank. Try to scoot and then give up and sit there looking dumb. Only this time they'll be ready, get the whole thing down on film."

"What about André, they gonna blow him up all over again?"

"I got five bucks says yes."

"You ain't got nothin', Hubie, and neither do I. We might as well both get used to it."

The filming took all the rest of that afternoon. For the final shot, Mungo and Sweets were forced to stand beside the smouldering wreckage of the truck and wave tiny American flags.

"Know what I wish," said Mungo.

"No, what?"

"Somebody'd lend me a copy of the script, so I knew what the fuck was going on."

"In the last scene, they tie you to a post and give you a last cigarette. The firing squad marches up. They offer you a blindfold, but you refuse. Then *you* offer *them* blindfolds, and they accept . . ."

Sweets paused.

"What?" said Mungo. And then he heard it, a heavy, percussive thudding. He craned his neck to look behind him and saw the helicopter coming in fast and low, as if for a strafing run. It was a Bell-121, made in the good old USA.

"Think we're being rescued?"

"They're dumb enough to use an American chopper, I doubt they'd be smart enough to put Libyan decals on it."

"Makes sense, I guess." Mungo twirled his paper flag around its tiny toothpick mast, put the flag in his shirt pocket and buttoned the flap.

"What the hell you gonna do with that?"

"Treasure it always, I guess."

The helicopter sped them across four hundred miles of desert to the military barracks at Sabha. By the time they arrived it was full dark. Mungo had slept fitfully throughout the duration of the flight, but when they touched down he awoke instantly. He glanced at his watch and saw that it was gone. He rubbed his wrist and then turned and stared suspiciously at Sweets.

"Don't look at me, man. I didn't take it."

"Who did?"

Sweets pointed at one of the green-clad soldiers, a lieutenant.

"Hey," said Mungo. "Gimme back my watch."

The officer frowned at him. Mungo stood up. "That's a goddamn Seiko, pal. Made in Japan. Cost me a hundred and fifty bucks."

"He took my Rolex, too," said Sweets.

"Bullshit."

"Okay, Timex. I still want it back."

Mungo shot his cuff, tapped his wrist.

The officer reached into his pocket and came up with Mungo's watch. Smiling, he stepped forward and dangled the watch in front of Mungo's face.

"Careful, I think he wants to hypnotize you. Never know what he's got in mind."

The lieutenant shouted an order. Sweets and Mungo were dragged out of the Bell, across the compound and into a matt-black Brazilian EE-9 Urutu armoured patrol car. The hatch slammed shut.

In the bucket seats across from them sat a quartet of armed men in full battledress.

Mungo's head banged against the steel wall as the troop carrier accelerated across the tarmac, the throb of the diesel engine reverberating through the hull. The men sitting opposite him were older and tougher than the troops who'd ridden shotgun on the helicopter ride in from the coast. He flexed his leg muscles, doing some isometrics. The Urutu made a sharp left turn and jerked to a stop, brakes squealing harshly. They were waved out of the armoured car and found themselves in a brightly lit walled compound.

One of the soldiers bent to remove their shackles. A short, thin man wearing a baggy brown suit walked up to them, nodded tersely. The lieutenant avoided his eye. Mungo and Sweets were marched briskly across the compound towards a long, low building. The door was a solid block of steel. The building's concrete walls were at least eighteen inches thick.

"When they said your place or mine," said Sweets, "we made a real bad choice."

The man in the baggy suit chuckled softly.

"You speak English?" said Mungo.

"Yes, of course." He smiled. "I am Dr Abdel Hamid Asfar. It is a name you will remember the rest of your lives. No matter how short a time that may be."

Sweets rolled his eyes in mock dismay.

An elevator carried them two floors below ground level. They marched down a wide corridor with ceiling and walls of smoothly-finished concrete, unpainted except for three narrow parallel lines of red, green and yellow that ran into the distance. An unseen motor hummed faintly. Fluorescents crackled overhead.

Dr Asfar stopped in front of two wide metal doors. He snapped his fingers and one of the soldiers stepped forward, breaking an electronic beam. The doors opened on a large, brightly-lit room. An operating theatre; a surgery.

Dr Asfar waved them inside.

The floor and walls to shoulder height were finished with square white tiles. The lighting was cold and hard and very bright. There were six operating tables, each neatly fitted with crisp white sheets. A wisp of steam drifted from a stainless steel sterilizing cabinet at the foot of the closest table.

Dr Asfar crossed briskly to the cabinet and slid open the top drawer. A variety of scalpels and other cutting instruments glittered under the lights. He picked up a scalpel, held it delicately between his thumb and index finger. "Our hospital is small, but modern," he said. "It was built primarily for times of conflict, although of course now and then a staff member or soldier attached to the barracks falls ill or is injured during the normal course of duty, and requires treatment." His smile was without warmth. "For the time being, however, this area is for our exclusive use. While we are here, we will not be disturbed."

"Excuse me," said Sweets, "but I think there's been a mistake. See, there's nothing *wrong* with us."

"Not yet, perhaps." The muzzle of a rifle dug into Sweets' spine. Asfar said, "Don't move, or you will be shot." He dragged the gleaming blade of the scalpel lightly across the surface of Sweets' eyelid, and then stepped back.

The pain of the knife cutting him had been bad enough, but he'd been terrified by the threat of sudden blindness. The release of tension made Sweets tremble violently. Blood clogged his eyelashes, dripped down his cheek.

"We require a complete confession," said Asfar. "And that is exactly what you will give us."

"What're we supposed to confess to?" Mungo said.

"You are both agents of the CIA, operating under the direct control of your Cairo chief-of-station Richard Foster. Your mission was to assassinate Our Leader."

"Okay, fine. Then what?"

"You will be executed."

"That ain't much of an incentive, doc."

"It soon will be, I assure you."

They were led out of the operating theatre and back to the elevator, up one level and along another hallway to a steel-bar door that opened on a row of cells.

Sweets was thrown into the nearest cell. The door slammed shut with a solid *thunk* that reminded him of his daddy's old DeSoto.

The cell was about eight feet deep and six feet wide. The ceiling was so low that there wasn't quite enough room for him to stand upright. There were no windows or furnishings of any kind. The light came from a bulb in a glassed-in recess in the wall above the door. Sweets hit the glass with the heel of his hand. It felt like it was about a foot thick. He inched his way slowly around the room, examined every millimetre of floor and wall and ceiling. The concrete was smooth and seamless, the door and frame made of thick steel plate.

Sweets gingerly lowered himself to the cement floor. They had taken his jacket, and he was cold. The bleeding had stopped but his eyelid stung whenever he blinked – a constant, painful reminder of what Asfar had in store for him.

Several hours crawled past and then the door opened and the doctor and three soldiers crowded into the room.

"Your friend has agreed to sign a confession."

"Lemme tell you something, the room service here is fucking awful. Where in hell is my complimentary crust of bread and glass of water?"

"Why don't you confess too, Hubie?"

"Who's your interior decorator, Idi Amin?"

The door slammed shut. Sweets wondered how a pro like Downey could have screwed up so badly. There had to be a way out but, for the life of him, he couldn't think of what is was.

TRIPOLI

Mustafa broke off the interrogation, walked down the hall to his office and dialled Dr Asfar's private number at the Sabha military barracks. It took him only a moment to verify that the prisoners were in custody and that Asfar felt confident he could deal with them. Mustafa gave the doctor the green light, hung up, and hurried back to the clean white room on the fifth floor of the Criminal Investigation Department building.

"I'm sorry to have kept you waiting, Jennifer. Are you all right?"

A whispered response.

"What did you say?" Sharply. "Speak up, please. I cannot hear you."

"I said, I'm fine."

"Are you sure?"

Jennifer nodded weakly.

Mustafa placed his hands on her shoulders, let her feel his weight, power. The coarse, bristly hairs of his moustache pressed against her cheek. "Is there anything else, anything at all, that you wish to tell me about Charlie McPhee?"

Jennifer shook her head.

"Open your eyes!"

Jennifer blinked up at him, yawned. Mustafa smiled. "You are repeating yourself. A waste of time." His lips brushed her earlobe. He inhaled deeply, taking the sweet scent of her exhaustion and fear deep into his lungs.

Jennifer had not been allowed to sleep. She had been given a carefully measured allotment of water, but no food. Her cramped, brightly-lit cell had been kept at a constant temperature of fifty degrees. She had been watched at all times. When she needed to relieve herself they gave her a tin pot, but no privacy.

She had repeatedly demanded to see an official from one of the several embassies in Tripoli that maintained diplomatic relations with either Britain or the United States. Mustafa had shrugged and said it was impossible. When she'd asked to see Charlie he roared with laughter, making a joke of her request, resting his sweaty palm on her forehead as if he thought she must be feverish.

"He's my husband. I insist that you let me see him!"

"He is not your husband. And you are most certainly not his wife."

"Where is he?"

"Jack Downey told you he found Charlie in a Cairo gutter. Jack tells wonderful lies. The truth, Jennifer, is that Charlie is a CIA agent. Just like Mungo Martin and Hubie Sweets."

"I don't believe you."

"Yes, you do. Of course you do. Charlie's worked for the CIA all his life. He was recruited out of UCLA. Jack thought he was exactly what you needed. A lover, some handsome fellow to hold your hand."

"You're lying."

"Am I?" Mustafa began gently to massage Jennifer's shoulders.

"Leave me alone."

"You don't find this relaxing?"

"Stop it, just stop it."

When she leaned forward, trying to get away from him, he could see the white strap of her bra, her smooth and flawless skin. The heavy mass of her hair flowed across his hands, the individual strands catching the light, shining copper and gold. That afternoon, he'd made a special trip to the Palace Hotel on Khalid Ibn Al Walid street. The hotel catered to the international tourist trade, and from the chemists' shop in the foyer he had been able to buy an expensive bottle of perfumed Italian shampoo and a bar of delicately scented soap shaped like a seashell. He'd given the soap and shampoo to her and then cleared all staff from the observation room and watched her on the bank of colour television screens as she'd filled the tub and languidly removed her clothes. The way she stripped, so slowly and casually, made him wonder if she knew she was being watched. He'd stared at her multiple images on the screens, his eyes jumping from one shot to another as she stepped into the tub and lowered herself cautiously into the steaming water. When she worked up a lather and began to wash her breasts, he had thought he would faint with pleasure.

Now, as his fingers rubbed the base of her neck, he inhaled deeply, relishing the smell of her and vividly remembering how she'd looked in the tub, sleek and wet, deeply tanned by the Egyptian sun.

He went to the window. It was a little past three o'clock in the morning. The lights of the city drowned the stars, but the sky was clear, and there would be a full moon hovering above the eastern horizon. He turned from the window and snapped his fingers.

"Come with me."

"Where?"

"Wherever I like. Haven't you learned at least that much by now?"

A car and driver were waiting for them at the curb outside the building. Mustafa opened the rear door and waved her inside. Instead of getting in beside her, he shut the door and walked around to the far side of the car and got in next to the driver. They sped down Sidi Issa Street past the Palace Hotel, made a left and drove two blocks and turned right, on to Al Fat'h Street, a main thoroughfare that ran parallel to the city's inner harbour and dock area. Five minutes later they abruptly pulled over to the side of the road. The driver switched off the headlights. Mustafa said something to him in Arabic, and a black-tinted window slid smoothly down.

Mustafa waved towards a span of open ground that lay between the road and the ocean. "The American cemetery. It is where your father is buried."

"Where you buried him after you tortured him to death."

"His death was an accident. He lost his balance and fell off a steel I-beam, and broke his neck. The film Downey showed you. It was a fake."

Jennifer tried to open her door, but it was locked. Mustafa tapped the driver on the shoulder and the car accelerated away from the graveyard, back towards Sidi Issa Street, the Criminal Investigation Building.

"For Christ's sake, why couldn't you at least let me see his grave!"

"It is unmarked. Anonymous. Impossible to find. I know, because I tried." He offered her a monogrammed handkerchief. "I was trying to do you a kindness. If I've made a mistake, well then, I'm sorry."

"Like hell you are, you bastard!"

He slapped her hard, his open hand catching her high on the cheek. She scrubbed at her face with her fists, desperately trying to hold back the flood of tears.

Her father hadn't broken, and neither would she.

Late the next day, Mustafa came unannounced to her cell and showed her the pictures of Cynthia.

In most of the shots the girl was accompanied by a tall, slim, well-dressed young man who seemed, unlike her, to be always aware of the camera. In shot after shot, he grinned wolfishly into the lens as if sharing a secret joke. The last few pictures were of Cynthia in a hotel room, lying in various poses on an unmade bed. She was naked. Her eyes were unfocused. She looked as if she had been drugged.

Mustafa lightly stroked Jennifer's arm. He held her hand in his, fingers intertwined, bent to kiss her wrist.

"If you don't give us what we want, that handsome young man will kill her."

Jennifer pushed the photographs away. "That won't be necessary."

"You'll cooperate?" Mustafa sounded surprised, as if he somehow hadn't expected that the threat to murder her daughter would be of any consequence.

"Yes, I'll confess."

"But to what?" he said, playing with her.

"Anything you like."

254

"You admit you are an agent of the CIA? And that you have been authorized by CIA chief-of-station Cairo Richard Foster to assassinate Colonel Gadaffi?"

"I told you, anything you want."

"You admit it, then?"

"Yes, certainly. I'm an assassin."

Mustafa smiled. He leaned over and kissed Jennifer lightly on the mouth. "I'm so happy. Do you know why?"

She shook her head, no.

"Because now we will not need the electricity. Or have to smash your bones or inject particles of asbestos fibre into your lungs." Mustafa's laughter was light, musical. He held Jennifer's head in his hands and stared into her eyes. "On the other hand, you realize that the moment you sign your confession, Charlie will die."

"What does *my* confession have to do with him?"

"You will implicate him, of course. And Hubie Sweets and Mungo Martin as well. Consider how the world will react to the news that the CIA has trained and sent a team of terrorists into the Middle East to assassinate a head of state. What a tremendous blow we will have dealt to CIA Director William Webster and his crew of killers, to America and her rabid, militaristic president."

There was a pitcher of ice-water on the table between them. Mustafa poured himself a glass, drank deeply. He wiped his mouth with the back of his hand.

"Imagine the repercussions in England, the immense loss of prestige the British and Americans will suffer throughout the Middle East and Europe."

He poured more water into his glass. "Your trial will make headlines throughout the world. Mr Downey has provided us with more than enough physical evidence to prove conclusively that you are CIA operatives. We have originals of all the documents and vouchers you and the others signed, photographs of you and Downey in London and at the Cairo Hilton. We have your meeting at Sabha with the Egyptian Army officer, pictures of the four of you training in the desert, honing your killer's skills."

Mustafa gave Jennifer a sad, wistful smile. "I fear I must also tell you we possess film of you and Charlie making love in the Montazah Palace Hotel."

He drank some more water, licked his lips. "We are concerned that the news of your arrest may cause the United States to react irrationally. So, shortly before we sentence your terrorist friends to death, we will announce that you were an unwitting pawn, a victim. This will appease the British and confuse the Americans. And then, because we are a kind and generous people, we will send you home.

"But first, Jennifer, you must confess your sins."

Mustafa threw a pen and a pad of paper on the cell's cot. He went over to the door, paused, stared at her for a long moment and then said, "Let me remind you that your daughter's life is in your hands." He smiled. "Take off your clothes, please."

"What did you say?"

"I think you heard me."

Jennifer began to unbutton her blouse.

Mustafa stared at her, his eyes missing nothing. He had been ordered to take Jennifer and Charlie to Sabha. Her fate had been placed in the bloody hands of Dr Asfar. He waited until she was naked and then said, "You think I desire you. Nothing could be further from the truth." Then he turned his back on her, to hide what was in his eyes, and strode briskly out of the cell. The steel door slammed shut behind him.

The pen was metal, a brushed aluminum cylinder about five inches long. The point was hard and sharp, lethal as a stiletto. Her hand went to her throat, searched for her pulse. If she killed herself, Mustafa would take revenge by murdering Cynthia.

But if she wrote a confession, she would be sending Charlie to his death.

34

SABHA MILITARY BARRACKS

Mustafa had a fear of heights. The helicopter ride in from Tripoli had, as always, been a very unpleasant experience. He was in a foul mood as he slid back the steel-plate disc and stared into the cell through the spyhole of shatterproof glass. He was not a tall man, and he had to get up on his toes to view the tiny cell in its entirety. The white-painted room was brightly lit, but because Charlie was wearing a white shirt and pants, Mustafa didn't immediately see him. For the space of a panicked heartbeat he thought Charlie'd somehow managed to escape.

But no, there he was, crouched absolutely motionless in the far corner, eyes squeezed shut.

Mustafa turned to the heavily-armed guard. "Has he asked for anything?"

"No, nothing."

"Has he said anything at all?"

"Not a word."

"What activity have you observed?"

"None. He's been like that all night long." The man adjusted the shoulder strap of his automatic weapon. "He might as well already be dead, for all the life he's living."

Mustafa grinned. The guard was from Al Khalij, a rugged, mountainous area near the Egyptian border. The men of the region were noted for their philosophical bent, as well as their eagerness to do battle.

"How much sleep has he had?"

"Very little. He is under constant observation. I check him every fifteen minutes. The moment I open the door, he is watching me."

"But he says nothing, asks for nothing?"

"He wants to die, perhaps."

"Open the door."

The guard from Al Khalij punched his identification number, and then the day's six-digit alphanumeric code into the membrane keyboard set into the wall to the left of the door. A buzzer sounded. There was a double click as the carbon-steel bolts withdrew into their housings. He swung the door open. Charlie didn't look up.

"Lock it and watch carefully," said Mustafa.

The guard nodded, although he believed Mustafa was being unnecessarily cautious, acting like an old woman rather than an agent of the Mukhabarat, Libya's élite Secret Police. But he was no fool, and his eyes gave away nothing.

Mustafa entered the cell. Charlie didn't move, but his bright-blue eyes peered unblinking at Mustafa from behind the sleeve of his shirt. Now that he was closer Mustafa saw that the shirt wasn't as white as it had appeared to be. There were flecks of dried blood across the chest and around the collar, and the cuffs and area around the armpits were stained dark grey with dirt and sweat. Mustafa took a single step towards Charlie – a step that carried him halfway across the tiny cell. The door swung shut and the bolts thudded home. He knelt at Charlie's side. Ignoring the sour unwashed smell of him, he hunched closer.

"How are you feeling?" he whispered. No reaction. "Would you like something to eat?"

The guard was right: Charlie might as well have been dead. Mustafa bared his teeth and bit him on the earlobe, clamping down hard enough to draw blood.

Charlie cried out. He tried to wriggle away, but he was wedged into the corner and there was nowhere for him to go. Mustafa kept up the pressure, grinding his teeth. Blood trickled down Charlie's neck. The heels of his bare feet pounded on the concrete floor. Mustafa licked his lips, tasted blood, warm and salty.

"Do I have your attention now, Charlie?"

Charlie nodded, trembling.

"Speak up!"

"Yes, yes!" The words a schoolgirl croak, verging on hysteria.

"Would you like to have a little talk with your two friends, Mungo Martin and Hubie Sweets?"

Mustafa patted Charlie on the back.

"These past three days have not been easy for them. They've handled the pain much better than we expected, but now we feel it's time to bring your little adventure to a conclusion."

Charlie crouched, tense and waiting.

Mustafa rested his arm on Charlie's shoulder. "Tell me about Jennifer. Do you love her? If you do, you must talk to her. *Explain* the situation. She knows that as soon as she confesses, you and your friends will be shot. But what she refuses to believe, no matter how many times we tell her, is that you are all going to die in any event. That it is simply a question of minimizing the amount of pain you will suffer in the meantime.

"So what you must do, Charlie, is convince her to let you and your friends die without further punishment. I have planned a press conference, to take place in three days' time. It will be your last opportunity to confess. I have something to show you. Afterwards, perhaps you will be more inclined to see things my way." He smiled sympathetically. "How are your legs, by the way? I understand they've been beating you. Can you walk?"

"I don't know."

Mustafa went over to the door, which immediately swung open. He said, "Bring the wheelchair."

Whistling cheerfully, Mustafa rolled Charlie along the corridor and into a waiting elevator, up one floor to the hospital wing. One of the hubs needed lubricating, and the wheelchair squeaked shrilly whenever they rounded a corner.

Charlie kept his eyes on the floor, but glanced up as a pair of wide double doors swung open with a sharp hiss of compressed air. Mustafa pushed the wheelchair into the operating theatre. The bearing squeaked as he swung the wheelchair sharply towards the far side of the room.

Two of the operating tables had been pushed against each other, side by side. Sweets was strapped down on the nearest table. Mungo lay beside him, almost close enough to touch. Dr Asfar stood beside Sweets with his back to Charlie.

"Starting with the left wrist," said Mustafa, "Dr Asfar will remove all the major arteries from his body. I do not mean to say he will actually sever and detach them. The intention is merely to excavate them, bring them into the light of day and lay them on the surface of the skin."

Charlie watched the blade of the scalpel drift slowly up Sweets' arm.

"A local anaesthetic is used," said Mustafa. "I am told that once it wears off, the pain is unbearable. The surgery will not be complicated at first, because the veins lie so close to the surface. But once we move up past his throat, into the area of his chest . . ."

Asfar leaned over Sweets and made an incision in his right arm, from the crook of the elbow all the way down to the back of his hand. He slipped an instrument like a crochet hook into the wound, probed carefully and then applied upward pressure. The artery from elbow to wrist suddenly wriggled free, like a worm rising out of the earth. The blood vessel was a gelatinous purple colour, thick as butcher's twine, greasy, dully gleaming.

Asfar sponged away the blood and began to suture the wound. The artery pulsed, measuring the rapid beating of Sweets' heart.

"Tomorrow the other one will go under the knife," Mustafa said. "How long, do you think, will it take to completely eviscerate them?" He smiled. "It is something to think about, yes?"

Charlie was sent back to his cell, where he found Jennifer waiting for him. She was wearing a white blouse and long white summer skirt, perfume that smelled faintly of roses. Her eyes widened when she saw the wheelchair.

"Five minutes," said Mustafa. He shut the door but left it slightly ajar.

Jennifer knelt beside Charlie and put her arms around him. "Oh Charlie, what have they done to you!"

"It isn't as bad as it looks," said Charlie hoarsely. He pulled Jennifer close and whispered, "The Libyans are planning another press conference. Hubie and Mungo have got to convince Mustafa that they'll cooperate. It's the only chance we'll have to be together."

"I'll try to convince Mustafa to let me see them," Jennifer said quietly.

Screaming incomprehensibly, Charlie grasped her by the shoulders, his cracked and dirty fingernails digging into her flesh.

The door crashed open and Mustafa hurried into the cell.

Two days later, Mustafa and a quartet of soldiers came without warning and took Charlie from his cell, marched him into the bright, slanting sunlight of late afternoon. He was bundled across a short span of open ground to a low, grassy knoll where he was seated in a plain wooden chair. A uniformed barber cropped his hair and then shaved him with a straight razor. When the barber had finished with him he was taken to a nearby barracks building and a communal shower room where he was handed a bar of soap and nailbrush and two thin towels.

Mustafa gave him five minutes, and then turned off the water. He playfully slapped Charlie on the rump with a towel. "You're clean enough. Dry yourself off and get dressed."

His dirty clothes had been exchanged for a starched white shirt, heavy black brogues and a black suit with narrow lapels. Was this, he wondered, the preferred style of terrorists and assassins? The jacket was tight around the shoulders. The waistband of the pants was several sizes too large, but there was a narrow belt of translucent green plastic.

Mustafa walked slowly around Charlie, critically examining him from every angle, then stopped and made a production of straightening the collar of his shirt. He pinched Charlie's sallow cheek. "Look me in the eye."

Charlie glanced at Mustafa and then flinched and looked away.

"Wonderful! If you can manage that same furtive look for the cameras, everything will be perfect!"

Back in his cell, Charlie was given his first meal in days, a small plate of rice and cooked vegetables. He ate as slowly as he could, knowing that if he wolfed the food, he wouldn't be able to keep it down.

At a few minutes past midnight, Charlie was taken to a makeshift conference room in the basement of the building. There was a raised platform at the far end of the room, and on it four folding metal chairs arranged behind a plain wooden table weighted down with several water jugs and several microphones. Behind the table was a huge colour photograph of the stern face of Colonel Mu'ammar al-Gadaffi, the pores of his flesh large as dimes. Charlie was led up on the dais and told to sit in the second chair from the left.

There were a dozen armed soldiers in the room, and several technicians at work behind a bank of television cameras. Orderly rows of folding metal chairs provided seating for about a hundred.

Charlie could feel Gadaffi's eyes on his back, dark and accusing.

A door at the back of the conference room swung open and Mustafa walked in, followed by Sweets and Mungo. A soldier armed with a submachine-gun brought up the rear. The prisoners were wearing camouflage outfits of mottled brown and green. Sweets carried his left arm at an odd angle. The sleeve of his shirt had been rolled down to hide his wounds.

The men made their way up the wooden steps to the dais. Mustafa sat next to Charlie. He waved Sweets and Mungo into their chairs, glanced at the soldier with the submachine-gun and made a flapping gesture with his hand. The man shuffled out of camera range.

"Where's Jennifer?"

Mustafa hesitated, but Charlie's tone, shrill and defensive, put him at his ease. "She will make her appearance at the end of the press conference, after you have been returned to your cell."

"Why?" Charlie glared and blinked and flinched away. In his baggy black suit he looked vaguely Chaplinesque, a harmless figure of fun.

Mustafa smiled. "Security, my friend. We thought it best to keep you apart."

A bank of overhead lights came on. The technicians were busy with the cameras, making adjustments to their equipment. High-ranking Libyan army officers filed into the room in twos and threes, eased stiffly into the front row of seats. Charlie didn't know when the press were due. He had no intention of letting the Libyans get anything down on film. He leaned across Mustafa towards Mungo. Speaking in a casual tone of voice he said. "You take the guy with the machine-gun."

"Yeah, okay. When you want it done?"

"*Now!*"

Mungo pushed back his chair. He stood up and started towards the soldier. Mustafa stared at Charlie in shock and disbelief. Charlie waited until Mustafa went for his pistol and then chopped at the back of his neck with the calloused edge of his hand.

Mustafa grunted and slumped forward. Charlie grabbed the pistol. Behind him, he heard a shout of surprise and then a dull, meaty thud. The table went over on its side and Sweets jumped off the dais, heading for the front rank of officers.

Mustafa's gun was an automatic. Charlie pulled back the slide.

Down on the floor, Sweets kicked a five-star general in the groin and deftly relieved him of his pistol, fired a warning shot into the ceiling. The room stood silent and immobile, frozen in shock. The moment wouldn't last. Mustafa groaned. Charlie hauled him to his feet. A television camera swung towards them. Mungo fired a short burst. The lens of the camera shattered and the cameraman fell face down on the floor, headphones still clamped firmly over his ears. A soldier near the back of the room unslung his rifle. Sweets shoved the barrel of his pistol into the general's gaping mouth, screamed a warning. The soldier dropped his weapon.

"Take the general!" Charlie yelled at Sweets. He grabbed a handful of hair, dragged Mustafa to his feet. "You're coming with us."

"No, I refuse."

"Then we'll kill the brass. Tell them that, if you like. But be quick."

Mustafa turned to the assembled officers and spoke rapidly in Arabic, his voice high-pitched, barely under control.

"Let's go," said Charlie.

They hurried to the far end of the room and Charlie yanked open the door. A soldier ran down the hallway towards them. Mungo fired a burst. The man's legs went out from under him.

Charlie pointed his gun at Mustafa. "Where is she?"

Mustafa shrugged, looked away.

Charlie shot him in the wrist. Mustafa screamed, clutched at the gaping wound.

Charlie shoved the muzzle of the gun up against his chest. "Where is she?"

"In the hospital. Asfar is sedating her."

A soldier poked his head around the corner at the far end of the corridor. Sweets took a snap shot at him and the man ducked out of sight.

"The stairs," said Charlie.

"They'll be waiting for us." Mungo plucked at the gold braid on the epaulets of the captured general's uniform. "No problem, right?"

Sweets shook his head in disagreement. "If the guy had more stars than Hollywood Boulevard, they still wouldn't let us go."

"We're wasting time." Charlie pushed Mustafa down the hallway. He scooped up the dead soldier's rifle. Mungo grabbed the general by the arm. They hurried down the stairs, boots clattering on the concrete. There was a glass door at the bottom of the stairs, and on the other side of it, two Libyan soldiers. In the confined space of the stairwell, the roar of Mungo's submachine-gun was deafening. The door collapsed in a welter of glass and blood.

They ran down the corridor towards the surgery, into a hail of bullets that struck chips from the white-tiled walls, ricocheted down the length of the corridor. Mungo wheeled and fired, shooting from the hip. The general screamed in Arabic, and the Libyans fell back.

There was a hiss of compressed air as the automatic doors of the surgery swung open. Asfar stood on the far side of the room, near an open doorway with his back to the wall. He held Jennifer tightly against him. A hypodermic needle dimpled her throat.

Charlie moved slowly towards them, his pistol at his side.

"Stay back!" Asfar jabbed the point of the needle into Jennifer's flesh.

Charlie moved a little closer.

Asfar's thumb trembled on the plunger. A yellowish fluid coursed inside the barrel.

Charlie slowly raised the pistol, aimed at a point midway between the doctor's dilated pupils.

"Do it," said Sweets.

Asfar's nerve broke. The hypo smashed on the tiles.

Jennifer gave a little cry and ran into Charlie's arms. He held her tightly, marvelling in the warmth and softness of her.

Out in the corridor, there was a sustained burst of fire.

"What're they shootin' at?" said Sweets.

Mungo grinned. "Each other, probably."

"Is there another way out of here?" Charlie said to Mustafa. The Libyan didn't answer. He was pale and sweating, in shock. Charlie went over to the open doorway. It led to a supply room. His eyes lingered on two steel canisters of gas. The canisters were about four feet long and eighteen inches in diameter, and were strapped to a sturdy four-wheeled dolly. He rolled the dolly out of the supply room into the operating theatre.

"Good idea," said Mungo. "But I got an even better one." He forced Asfar to wrap his arms around the canisters and then used a roll of surgical tape to bind him in place.

"Nasty," said Sweets.

"Stay tuned, you ain't seen nothin' yet." Mungo wheeled the dolly towards the double doors.

"Move!" Sweets prodded Mustafa and the general with the barrel of his pistol.

"Give yourselves up, before it's too late!" hissed Asfar.

"It's already too late," said Sweets. He winked at Jennifer. "See, the thing is, we come from a different time zone."

The doors hissed open. Mungo took a quick look down the hallway. A bullet whined past his head. He ducked back.

"Now what?" said Jennifer.

"We shoot out the lights. The elevator's about thirty feet away, on the left. We tuck Dr Caligari and the canisters inside, hit the button for the main floor. By now, whoever's up there should be pretty goddamn trigger-happy."

"A diversion," said Sweets. He smiled coldly at Asfar. "I like it. I like it a lot."

"Where do we go?" said Jennifer.

"Up the stairs to the main floor," Charlie said. "We stay down here long enough for them to close off the exits, we're trapped."

Sweets aimed carefully, squeezed the trigger and shot out a fluorescent ceiling light. There was a volley of Libyan fire. The air was thick with dust, jagged splinters of concrete and tile.

"Sounds like they set up a light machine-gun," said Mungo. He recoiled as a hand grenade skittered past, bouncing and clattering on the floor. There was a deafening explosion, bright flash of light. Shrapnel ricocheted off the tiles. The corridor darkened as a row of lights went out.

"Too much weight," said Sweets.

"Give 'em time. Sooner or later, they'll get it right."

Another grenade skipped towards them. Sweets stuck out his foot and stopped it and scooped it up and threw it back all in one fluid motion. The grenade exploded and the hallway went black. The machine-gun fell silent. Someone cried out; a thin moan of pain.

Charlie pointed his rifle and fired blindly into the darkness. There was a ragged burst of automatic weapons fire. An officer shouted hysterically. The shooting stopped.

"Let's go!"

Charlie kept his weapon trained on to Mustafa and the general. Mungo rolled the dolly with its cargo of gas cylinders towards the elevator. Jennifer stayed next to Charlie and Sweets brought up the rear. The cries of wounded Libyans echoed down the hall. There was just enough light to see the elevator, the door panels scarred by shrapnel. Mungo pressed the UP button. The doors slid open, and the elevator's interior light dimly lit up the corridor.

There was a shout of dismay and a flurry of shots. Charlie and Sweets returned the fire as they ran towards the stairway. Mungo wheeled the dolly into the elevator. He pressed the button for the main floor, used the butt of his gun to smash the overhead light.

The doors started to slide shut. Asfar screamed in fear, his mouth open, eyes bulging.

They were climbing the second flight of stairs when the elevator reached the main floor. A short burst of small-arms fire was swallowed by a deafening thunderclap of sound and then a dirty orange ball of flame lit up the stairwell and was gone, leaving behind the stench of scorched paint and charred flesh, the sharp hiss and crackle of flames.

They kept moving up the stairs. At the main floor level there were bodies everywhere, the corpses jerking and twitching spasmodically in the flickering light of the fire.

"Keep moving," said Charlie.

They continued up the stairs. Charlie expected to run into a squad of Libyans with every step they took, but the huge building was empty, deserted. They reached the second floor. The wide central hallway was brightly lit but the offices to either side were dark, silent.

"Where the fuck is everybody?" said Sweets.

"Outside," said Charlie.

Mungo nodded his agreement. The Libyans, reasoning that they wouldn't get that far, had neglected to secure the upper floors of the building.

265

"The roof?" suggested Mungo.

"Where would we go from there?" Charlie trotted to the end of the hallway and risked a quick glance out the window. A mix of troop carriers, jeeps, light trucks and armoured cars encircled the building. The darkness and glare of headlights made it impossible to see how many men had been deployed. He eased away from the window.

Jennifer and Sweets came out of one of the darkened offices.

Sweets said, "They've got a tank down there, parked right up against the side of the building."

"Let's go take a look."

The tank was directly below the office window. The hatch was open. The machine-gunner, in headphones and flak jacket, was perched on the edge of the hatch, half in and half out of the tank.

A bank of windows ran the length of the room. Each window was about eight feet high by four feet wide, and was designed to open outward and up, pivoting on steel pins set into the jamb.

Mungo slipped the latch and pushed open the window directly above the tank. A hinge squeaked. He climbed out on the window ledge, crouched low. The gunner looked up. Charlie shot him. Mungo dropped on to the tank, fired blindly down into the hatch.

"Jump!" Jennifer went first, then Sweets. Charlie waved his pistol at Mustafa and the general, keeping them at a distance. He jumped. Mungo rolled the gunner's corpse out of the way and opened up with the tank's .50 calibre machine-gun.

"Everybody inside!" yelled Charlie above the chatter of the machine-gun.

An armoured car raced towards them. Mungo fired a long burst at it but it kept coming. Jennifer dropped down inside the hatch. Sweets yelled something at Charlie. A stream of tracers arced towards them from a machine-gun position in a stand of palm trees. They scrambled down inside the tank. Bullets struck sparks off the armour plate. Charlie reached up to secure and lock the hatch.

There were two uniformed soldiers inside the tank, both of them dead.

Mungo sat hunched in a bucket seat, experimenting with the tank's controls, peering out the narrow slit of the observation window. He grasped what looked like a joystick, pushed it away from him. The tank jerked forward.

"What about the troop carrier?" yelled Sweets.

"Shoot it."

Sweets squinted into the gunner's telescope. The fire-control system incorporated a computer and a laser rangefinder. The control was a curved steel lever with a ball on the end. A video game. He pushed the stick to the left. There was a low-pitched drone. The sighting mechanism was equipped with an infra-red sensor. The profile of the troop carrier glowed bright green in the cross-hairs. Sweets pushed the stick a bit more to the left.

In a recess on top of the control, a plastic button flashed red.

He hit the button with his thumb. A long tongue of orange flame spewed from the muzzle of the 125mm cannon. The troop carrier exploded in a huge, roiling ball of fire.

Small-arms fire thundered like heavy rain on the tank's four-inch thick steel plate. Jennifer clung to Charlie, holding him close.

"Can you find the airport?" Charlie yelled at Mungo.

"Might as well give it a try."

The Libyans had set up a roadblock where the access road to the barracks intersected the main highway leading to the airport. Mungo turned off the road and churned through a field of barley. A self-propelled gun fired repeatedly at them as they raced through the field, the shells spewing huge gouts of earth into the air.

The tank lurched as they crossed a drainage ditch on the outskirts of the airport. They ripped through a chain-link fence, turned on to a runway. Mungo hit the accelerator and the T-72 quickly reached its maximum speed of thirty-seven miles per hour.

Not far ahead of them, the lights of the passenger terminal shone brightly.

"Charlie," said Mungo, "get the hatch open and work the machine-gun." He glanced at Sweets, the fresh blood that soaked his shirt-sleeve. "You okay, Hubie?"

"Perfect," said Sweets. "And I always have been."

"What can I do?" said Jennifer.

"Stay low."

Mungo tossed Charlie a pair of goggles. "You spot the service area, gimme a shout. Look for catering and cargo trucks, planes being fuelled."

Charlie unlocked the hatch, braced himself and pushed upwards with both hands. The wind tore at him. He swivelled the machine-gun around. Off to his left a big passenger jet raced up a parallel runway, lights blazing. They were less than half a mile from the terminal now, racing out of the darkness towards the lights. There were at least a dozen big jets parked on the apron around the semi-circle of the building. He aimed and fired a long burst, squinting against the flare of the muzzle blast. The tank swerved sharply to the right, throwing him against the steel rim of the hatch. He fired again and a jet exploded, tossing a massive sheet of flame a hundred feet or more into the night sky. The near wing of a 747 parked next to the stricken jet caught on fire.

The shrill scream of sirens pierced the night.

Searchlights tracked across the runways, seeking them out. They were drawing considerable fire from airport security. Bullets zipped through the air all around them, ricocheted off the concrete.

Charlie elevated the muzzle to bear on the control tower. He squeezed off a dozen rounds with no visible effect, gave the gun a little more elevation and fired again, ran through several feet of belt. A cluster of people standing at the glass scattered and he knew he'd scored a hit.

They were less than a hundred yards from the terminal now, racing on a course parallel to the building. Mungo turned the tank sharply towards a helicopter parked on a pad near the building. The chopper was painted in yellow and black stripes, like a huge malevolent wasp. Its navigation lights sparkled, and the rotor blades turned lazily. Charlie could see the shape of the pilot's body through the Plexiglass bubble.

Mungo braked hard. The tank's metal treads scarred the concrete.

Charlie knew what Mungo had in mind. He waited until they'd jerked to a stop, aimed carefully and fired. The pilot baled out. Charlie tracked him as he ran towards the passenger terminal, but didn't shoot.

Down at the far end of the building there was another tremendous explosion as a second jumbo blew up.

Charlie crouched as a flurry of bullets struck the hull of the tank. The blades of the helicopter whispered overhead. Jennifer scrambled out of the hatch, closely followed by Sweets and Mungo. Sweets held his arm close to his body. His sleeve was soaked in blood from elbow to wrist. Bullets thudded into the chopper's fuselage. Mungo climbed into the pilot's seat. The steady whine of the engine mounted to a deafening roar.

Charlie pushed Jennifer and Sweets inside and then climbed in himself. There was another burst of fire from the terminal. The helicopter rose several feet into the air and abruptly dropped back, hitting the ground hard. A bullet punched a jagged hole in the Plexiglass. Mungo swore furiously, red-lined the engine and yanked back on the joystick. The machine clawed its way up into the air and then heeled over. Charlie watched the ground come up to meet them. A stream of hot pink tracers flashed past the windshield.

"Goddamn!" Mungo shouted.

The helicopter levelled out and they screamed across the airfield at a speed of a hundred and fifty knots and an altitude too low for the instruments to measure. A red warning light flashed and a buzzer shrilled. Mungo took them up to fifty feet and turned the machine in a wide curve. There was only one direction they could take – south, towards the Egyptian border.

"You wanna go back and strafe the fuckers?" Mungo shouted at Sweets.

Sweets, slumped in the co-pilot's seat, wearily shook his head.

Mungo twisted in his seat to see how Jennifer and Charlie were doing.

The way they were holding each other, it looked like they were doing just fine.

Now all they had to do was figure out how to cover a little more than seven hundred miles of hostile desert in a bullet-riddled aircraft with a maximum range of approximately one-third that distance.

35

THE LIBYAN DESERT

Mungo had the Hirundo up to its maximum cruising speed of a hundred and forty-two knots. They were flying by the light of the stars at an altitude of about one hundred feet, the moonlit desert landscape a blurred patchwork of shadow that made accurate depth perception impossible.

"Figure out where we are yet?" Mungo shouted above the roar of the engine.

Sweets was in the co-pilot's seat, clutching his wounded arm. Charlie and Jennifer crouched behind him, studying a small-scale map of Libya. The map was colour-coded. In the greenish light of the chopper's instrument panel it was almost impossible to differentiate shading. Charlie pointed. "To your right, on the horizon. See the red lights?"

Mungo nodded.

"That's the new highway Gadaffi's building to link Sabha with the Tazirbu oasis. There's a water wells field . . ."

Mungo eased the joystick back. "Anything on our ass yet, Charlie?"

"All clear." Charlie pushed forward, squeezing into the narrow gap between the two seats. "The road from Sabha to Tazirbu drops down towards the bottom of the map and then jogs back up again. If we cut straight across, how far could we get?"

Mungo jabbed at the map. "Somewhere around there, about two hundred and fifty miles from Sabha."

Charlie peered at the dent Mungo's fingernail had made in the map. Fifty miles past the oasis and water wells at Tazirbu there was a paved road that ran more or less parallel to the border. Beyond the road nothing but a blank expanse of pale yellow: hundreds of square miles of empty desert.

The map also showed a strip of Egyptian border territory twenty-five or thirty miles wide. There were no towns or villages on the Egyptian side either, just an elevation marker and more empty desert.

"If they're building a major highway," Charlie said, "they'll have all kinds of heavy equipment. Fuel. Maybe even another chopper."

"Yeah, right. Let's do it."

Charlie put his arm around Jennifer and hugged her tightly.

They had been flying for nearly two hours when he saw the lights of the two pursuing gunships.

Mungo swore and thumped the fuel gauge. The needle jumped off empty and then settled back.

"What now?" said Jennifer. The gunships were three or four miles behind them, gaining slowly.

Charlie said, "If they're smart, they'll sit back and wait for us to run out of gas. That's maybe what they've been doin' only we didn't catch 'em at it till now."

Sweets lifted his head. "Put it down." His voice was low, weak, and his eyes were far too bright.

"What've you got in mind, Hubie?"

Sweets moved his arms a few inches away from his body. The front of his shirt was in tatters. His lap was full of blood. There was more blood all down his legs, a widening pool of blood between his feet.

Charlie remembered the way Sweets had grunted and suddenly clutched his stomach just as they'd lifted off from the airport.

And Mungo, staring at Sweets, suddenly remembered the wounded man they'd finished off in the Colombian coca field. Hubie had that exact same look in his eyes. Sad and desperate. Pleading, resigned. Mungo tightened his grip on the controls. For a crazy moment, the screaming of jungle parrots drowned the thunder of the Hirundo's engine.

"Jesus, Hubie . . ."

"Hey, don't get all emotional on me."

The ground came up faster than Mungo expected, and the Hirundo hit hard. Mungo gave Sweets an apologetic look. "Sorry, man."

Sweets grinned. "Don't worry about it; it ain't *my* fuckin' chopper."

Jennifer stayed with Sweets while Charlie and Mungo hunted through the rear cabin for emergency supplies and weapons, anything that might help them survive the Libyan desert.

"We could've made beautiful music together," Sweets whispered.

"You mean Muzak," said Jennifer.

Sweets tried to laugh, spilled a little more blood. Jennifer kissed him lightly on the lips. Mungo tugged at her arm. The roar of approaching engines filled the night; she could hear the heavy beating of rotor blades, shrill whine of turbochargers.

Charlie jumped out of the helicopter first, and then Jennifer. Mungo crouched beside Sweets. Tears streamed down his cheeks and he simply couldn't believe it. He hadn't cried since he was a baby.

"Want me to say hello to Liam O'Brady?" Sweets said.

"No way. Snub the bastard."

"Yeah. Good idea. But you be sure and give Jack a big kiss for me, okay?"

"The big kiss-off, Hubie. He's dead meat. Count on it." Mungo squeezed Sweets' shoulder, jumped clear.

Sweets hauled back on the joystick. The roar of the engine deepened.

The downdraft from the rotor blades filled the air with sand. Mungo crouched, shielding his eyes. Sweets switched on his riding lights and turned back towards Sabha. The Libyan gunships were less than a mile away, closing fast. The pilots, snatching at the bait, sped towards Sweets.

Mungo stood and watched, knowing exactly what was going to happen, waiting helplessly. Sweets cut to his right. The Libyan gunships moved to intercept. Sweets throttled down, lost altitude. One of the Libyans got in tight behind him. The second chopper attacked from the left flank. Sweets accelerated, turned right into him. The main rotor blades of the two machines clanged like huge swords. A split second later a massive ball of flame engulfed both machines and sent them crashing to the desert floor.

The ammunition started to go off, rockets booming heavily, machine-gun belts snapping like firecrackers, tracers shooting streaks of light high into the clear night air.

"Dig in!" yelled Charlie, and used his cupped hands to scoop a shallow trench in the sand. Jennifer stared at him, unmoving. She was in shock. He took her legs out from under her, laid her on the ground. "Close your eyes and cover your face with your hands! Don't move!"

Charlie and Mungo buried Jennifer under a thin scrim of sand and rock, then worked feverishly to dig their own temporary graves. The surviving chopper circled the burning wreckage. Charlie threw a few handfuls of sand over the pair of emergency survival packs and Kalashnikov AK-47 assault rifle they'd taken from the helicopter. He wondered if the Libyan machine was equipped with infrared sensors.

The Libyan's searchlights swept back and forth across the desert floor. There was a burst of machine-gun fire. Charlie knew they were shooting blind, hoping to make the survivors, if any, bolt and run.

The helicopter moved lazily towards him. The earth trembled with the engine's thunder and the rotor blades whipped the sand into a frenzy. The dazzling glare of its lights blinded him. Charlie willed himself not to move. The machine-guns fired, a deafening blast of sound.

The helicopter accelerated towards the east, moving in ever-widening circles. He sat up, blinking sand from his eyes, spitting sand out of his mouth. He helped Jennifer to her feet. Mungo picked up the survival packs and the rifle, stared at the fiercely burning wreckage of the Hirundo – Sweets' funeral pyre.

"Let's move," said Charlie.

They went due north, using the stars to guide them. For the first hour or so the ground climbed steadily, but then it levelled out and in the distance they could see the string of lights that marked the new road Gadaffi was building from Sabha to the water wells at Tazirbu.

"How far away is it?" said Jennifer.

"Hard to tell," said Charlie. "The air's so clear it makes distances tricky. Somewhere between eight and ten miles."

They were about a mile from the highway when the sky to the east began to pale, a thin slice of the horizon fading imperceptibly from dark blue to a sickly, greenish yellow. They'd been following a wadi. Ahead of them in the darkness they had occasionally heard the shrill cry of small animals, hunter and hunted. But now, as the light brightened and the stars in their thousands faded from the sky, the desert grew quiet and still.

Not long afterwards, they heard the clatter of a diesel engine. The Libyans would start work early, rest through the heat of midday and then continue working until the sun went down.

"We stay out in the open," said Mungo, "we're gonna fry."

"The road," said Charlie.

Mungo nodded in agreement. If they could find an unused toolshed or some other building . . .

Just as the sun came up, they stumbled upon the dusty corpse of an articulated dumptruck. The huge vehicle's windshield was smashed. There was a pool of thick black oil beneath the rear axle. The hood had been removed and the engine ripped out.

Charlie glanced up and down the highway. The surface of the road had been prepared for the paving crews, and then the workers and machinery had moved on. The deep shadow beneath the belly of the truck would protect them from the sun. If someone did happen by, it was unlikely they'd be spotted. In any case, there was nowhere else to hide.

The fat red ball of the rising sun glided so rapidly above the horizon that it might have been filled with helium. The hot, dry air smelled of oil, diesel fumes. Heat waves flickered on the sand. A million small stones squatted on their shadows.

Charlie, crouched on the sand beneath the belly of the truck, thought about all the pictures Downey'd taken at the abandoned military base in the Eastern Desert. He remembered Downey's insistence that they sign a chit for every dime spent and bullet fired. Now it made sense. Downey had been gathering evidence, setting them up for the Libyans. A failed attempt on Gadaffi's life would have an enormous negative impact on American influence throughout the entire Middle East. Charlie wondered how much Gadaffi had paid Downey to put together a sacrificial hit team of CIA agents.

Mungo, sitting in the shade with his back against a huge tire, was also thinking about Downey, trying to figure out where he was, right that minute. Not in Libya. If there was one thing a guy like Jack knew, it was that no matter how carefully you set something up there was always an outside chance it'd go wrong.

Well, things had certainly gone wrong. And Sweets had paid the price but Downey hadn't. Yet.

Jennifer said, "You thinking about Hubie?"

Mungo scratched his arm. His fingernails left pale marks that quickly faded. He scooped up some sand and let it run between his fingers.

"Jack. Where he's likely to be and how I'm going to kill him when I find him." He stared at the stones, the small shadows they made on the surface of the road. Time was crawling by, the sun easing slowly up into the sky.

"You think he approached the Libyans, or it was the other way around?"

"Could've gone either way. But Jack always did like to take the initiative."

In the distance, Mungo could hear the roar of heavy machinery. The road crew would have all the water they needed. He licked his lips, tried not to think about how thirsty he was, how little water they had, and how hot it was going to get during the long, slow day that lay ahead.

Charlie wondered what had awakened him, realized it was the perfect silence, total lack of sound. The sun was at its zenith and the Libyans had downed their tools, taken a break. The heat pressed down on him, the air was heavy and still, so dry it seemed to clog his throat. He was sweating, his body striving to keep his temperature down. Jennifer looked flushed, feverish. He opened his pack and dug out a plastic two-litre bottle, woke Mungo and then gently shook Jennifer awake. Her eyes were bright, unfocused.

"Time for a drink."

Mungo squinted up at the sun, nodded his agreement.

They each took one mouthful. The water was warm and brackish, tasted faintly of chlorine.

Jennifer said, "They threatened Cynthia. They told me they'd kill her."

"She's safe enough." Charlie stroked her hair and hoped it was true. "They were using her as a lever. Now that we've escaped, she's useless to them." She took his hand, seeking reassurance. He leaned towards her and kissed her on the mouth, then moved away and looked into her eyes and moved back and kissed her again. They held each other close, and after a little while Jennifer fell asleep again, dozed lightly in the heat.

After an interval of several hours, the roadwork started again. Charlie listened with half an ear to the heavy, low-pitched throbbing of unseen machinery. At the edge of his vision the floor of the desert twitched and jumped, pebbles and stones dancing in the light as if they were alive.

He blinked, wiped his eyes. He recalled the hashish parlours of Cairo, waiting anxiously for the pipe to come around, sucking the acrid smoke deeply into his lungs. In Cairo he'd gone hunting for hallucinations. Now they were chasing him.

He dozed off again, drifted into a light, dreamless sleep. When he awoke, the road was in shadow and the sky was a soft, burnished gold. He crawled out from under the truck. The sun was perched on the curved rim of the horizon, so close that it seemed he could almost reach out and touch it. In minutes, the pale-blue sky was streaked through with purple, and the stars in their thousands were bursting free.

He shook Jennifer and Mungo awake. They drank the last of the water, crawled out from beneath the truck and began to walk down the road.

Twenty minutes later, they rounded a bend in the road and suddenly the lights of the construction site were very close – no more than two or three miles away. As they drew nearer, a long, low building material-ized in the darkness, and then a fenced compound containing a dozen or more dump trucks, graders and other pieces of heavy equipment. A hundred yards down the road stood a row of brightly lit mobile homes. In the darkness they could hear muttered conversations, laughter, the blare of a television. Mungo had to think hard, but he finally recognized the programme's theme music. The Libyans were watching *The Brady Bunch*.

There was another sound as well, the drone of an approaching engine. They ran off the road and into the darkness, dropped to the ground. A few moments later a jeep cruised slowly past. There were two men in the vehicle, and it was equipped with a light machine-gun. A rifle lay across the back seat. Charlie heard a burst of Arabic from the short-wave radio.

Mungo stared at the jeep as it continued down the dirt road, headlights stabbing into the darkness.

"How far to the Egyptian border, Charlie?"

"Four hundred and fifty miles, more or less."

"We've got about six hours till sunrise. With any luck, by the time they missed that jeep we'll be a hundred and fifty miles away. A real small pin in a real big haystack."

"We'll need enough water for at least three days," said Charlie. "Food and gas, weapons . . ."

Charlie stood guard while Mungo and Jennifer raided one of the mobile homes, helped themselves to plastic containers of distilled water, all the tinned goods they could carry. Jennifer carried the food and water outside while Mungo searched quickly through the other rooms. He found two sleeping bags in a storage closet, tucked them under his arm.

It took them fifteen tension-packed minutes to gather the food and water. The gasoline was easy – there was a row of hundred gallon drums and a handpump where the dump trucks were parked, a stockpile of ten-gallon cans in a nearby shed. They filled six of the cans and would have taken more, but Charlie didn't think the jeep could take the weight.

It took them half an hour to move the supplies far enough up the road to escape the glare of the compound's lights. The jeep had driven along the road twice since they'd first seen it – Charlie estimated it took about twenty minutes for the vehicle to make a complete circuit of the camp.

They crouched in darkness at the side of the road, waiting.

Jennifer saw the headlights first. She lay down by the side of the road, her arms spread wide and one leg twisted at an awkward angle.

The jeep drove towards them and then the driver saw her and shouted and stabbed at the brakes.

Charlie got a foot up on the rear bumper just as the jeep came to a full stop. The vehicle rocked on its springs and the driver turned to peer behind him, an expression of alarm on his face. Charlie rabbit-punched him on the side of the neck, just below the ear. The man's head sagged at an odd angle. Mungo used the butt of his AK-47 on the other soldier. Jennifer was already hurrying down the road towards their cache of supplies. Charlie climbed behind the wheel. He switched off the headlights.

They loaded the gasoline first, and then the water and food, a canvas tarp Mungo had found in the cab of a dumptruck. Charlie hit the gas and they bounced across the road and up a slight incline, into the desert.

Jennifer popped open the glove compartment. It contained a flare gun and three rounds of ammunition, a box of wooden matches, two pairs of clear plastic goggles with wraparound lenses and a battered paperback copy of *The Koran*.

Above them and all around them the sky was crammed with stars – tiny specks of brittle white light that shimmered and sparkled in the clear air like the diamond Aziz Mehanna had held in his doomed hands on the road to Cairo.

Ten miles from the construction site, they buried the dead soldiers in a shallow grave.

Six hours later, they had put almost one hundred and fifty miles on the clock, and in the east the sky was lightening. All around them, as far as the eye could see, there was nothing but sand and stones and empty sky.

During the long night's drive they'd debated whether to keep moving through the day or stop and wait for the cover of darkness. Jennifer wanted to keep going. Mungo pointed out that their passage across the desert would raise a column of dust that could easily be seen from the air. And so they'd decided to travel only at night.

They drove a few more miles and then stopped in the lee of a small hill. Charlie and Mungo spread the tarp over the jeep. The canvas was pale yellow. It would reflect much of the sun's heat, as well as make it almost impossible to spot them from above.

"I'll take the first watch," Mungo said. He slung his rifle over his shoulder and trudged up the slope of the hill.

Jennifer put her arms around Charlie and kissed him on the mouth, took him by the hand and led him under the tarp.

They unzipped a sleeping bag and spread it out on the sand on the shady side of the jeep. Jennifer kissed Charlie's unshaven cheeks, his mouth. He lay down beside her, fumbled with her clothes.

Mungo, lying prone on the crest of the hill, heard the distant cry of a bird, but saw no birds. He glanced down at the jeep, smiled and turned away.

It was mid-morning when Charlie jogged up the hill to relieve Mungo. The desert shimmered in the pale thin light, waves of heat rippling into the distance like liquefied sand. Mungo pointed east, towards the horizon. "See anything?"

Charlie squinted into the haze. He shook his head, no.

"Now take a look over there." Mungo waved towards the south.

Despite the heatwaves and the haze, the eastern horizon was clearly defined. But towards the south, the horizon was vague and indistinct, and it was impossible to see the demarcation point between land and sky.

"What is it?"

"Sandstorm."

"How far away would you say it is?"

"Fifteen, maybe twenty miles." Mungo studied the horizon. "Keep an eye on it. The damn thing gets any closer, wake me up." He handed Charlie the AK-47 and started down the slope towards the jeep.

Charlie squatted on his heels. Every fifteen minutes he drank a mouthful of water and stood up and looked all around him. Nothing moved. The desert was a still life painted in a hundred subtle shades of beige.

By the time Jennifer relieved Charlie, there was a ring around the sun, and the first traces of cloud were streaking the sky. But it was the southern horizon that held Charlie's eye. It seemed closer now than when he'd relieved Mungo. Maybe his eyes were playing tricks on him, but he thought he could detect movement within the mass, a slow, roiling action, a kind of churning.

Jennifer put her arms around him and kissed him, then reluctantly moved away. "Go get some rest, Charlie."

"If you need me, give me a shout."

"I will."

In the shade of the tarp, Mungo was sound asleep, snoring loudly. Charlie helped himself to an open tin of sardines and a loaf of heavy brown bread. When he'd finished eating he emptied one of the ten-gallon gasoline tins into the jeep's tank. The fuel gauge registered three-quarters full. He poured most of a second tin into the tank, topping it up. The jeep had four-wheel drive and most of the night they had ground along in first or second gear. He doubted if they were getting more than ten miles to the gallon, but even so, he was sure they'd have enough fuel to penetrate well beyond the Egyptian border.

He dug a shallow hole and buried the empty gas can, checked the radiator and topped up the water. The oil level was low, but there was nothing he could do about that. He used a piece of rag to wipe a thick coating of dust from the windshield and headlights. The work had made him thirsty. He sat down with his back against the rear wheel of the jeep and drank a mouthful of water.

The light under the tarpaulin was thick and yellow, liquid honey poured through a shaft of sunlight. Charlie was reminded of how the light had looked as it passed through the stained-glass panels of the mashrabiyah in his room in the Old City. He closed his eyes and conjured up his sagging iron bed and rusty sink, the ticking of his cheap tin clock. Somehow, despite the clarity of memory, the room no longer seemed real to him. It was as if that part of his life had been nothing but a dream.

His eyes snapped open. Mungo was shouting his name. He jumped to his feet.

"There's a convoy headed right at us!"

"Where?"

"Off to the south. Could be a routine patrol, trying to outrun the storm. They see us, first thing they'll do is call in air support. Help Jennifer roll up the tarp, we got to get the hell out of here!"

The sky had darkened, and the sun was a pale ball of silvery light. Charlie turned towards the south. The horizon was much closer than it should have been. A sudden gust of wind made the sand dance. Whirlpools of dust rose swiftly into the air and were torn to shreds. He helped Jennifer with the tarp. Wind-blown sand and small pebbles rattled against the side of the jeep.

Mungo climbed into the back of the jeep, cursed as he ripped a fingernail unfastening the grommets on the dust cover of the machine-gun. Jennifer buckled herself into the passenger seat. Charlie climbed behind the wheel and started the engine.

"Over there!" said Mungo.

Charlie twisted in his seat to look behind him. The Libyan convoy was a mile or so away, racing directly towards them, closing fast. He let out the clutch and they churned up the flank of a dune. As they neared the crest, the wind became much fiercer, snatching at the sand and throwing it into the air, whipping it in all directions. There was a rapid popping sound from behind them. Mungo fed the ammo belt into the machine-gun, yanked on the cocking handle. The direction of the wind changed, and the sound of the shots suddenly grew louder.

Jennifer took a pair of goggles from the jeep's glove compartment. Charlie tried to put them on but the jeep was bucking and lurching so badly he needed both hands on the wheel. He leaned towards Jennifer and she slipped the elasticized band over his head.

The sky suddenly grew darker. A frenzy of thick black cloud raced and swirled above them. Visibility was no more than half a mile. Charlie glanced at Jennifer. She'd given Mungo the other pair of goggles and then wrapped herself in the protective cocoon of a sleeping bag.

Mungo fired the machine-gun – a long, ear-splitting burst. Charlie risked a quick look over his shoulder and caught a glimpse of a small camouflage-painted tracked vehicle speeding towards them. Bullets tore through the air over his head. He yanked at the wheel. They raced over the lip of a wadi, plummeted six feet down an almost vertical slope and crashed into the opposite bank.

The engine died.

Charlie frantically turned the key. The starter turned over with desperate slowness. He counted to five and then tried again. The engine caught with a roar. He shifted into reverse. The tires spun uselessly and then dug in. The jeep shot backwards. The wadi was just wide enough to get straightened out. He shifted into first gear and hit the gas. They were climbing now, following the course of the wadi up the side of a rocky hill. He took a quick look behind him. The Libyans had vanished. They'd lost them or, just as likely, the convoy had decided to take refuge against the oncoming storm.

Mungo knelt behind the machine-gun, grinning, teeth gleaming white against his dust-streaked face. "Nice driving, Charlie."

"The L.A. freeways, there's no better place to hone your skills."

They continued on for another hour. Visibility was less than a quarter-mile. The sun had vanished, and the wind was less erratic but more violent, blowing steadily from the south.

Charlie crouched low behind the windshield. His hands ached and his face felt hot and raw. There was a faint hissing sound, and then, high above him, a burst of light and crackling explosion.

"What the hell was that!" Mungo shouted.

There was another explosion. Sheet lightning raced across the sky, lighting up the desert and then plunging it into darkness.

Charlie drove down an incline and stopped on the lee side of the next dune. The lightning was an incandescent pink, bright neon sheets exploding all across the black, lowering face of the sky. Ear-splitting thunder crashed around them. The air smelled scorched and burnt. Wind ripped at them. The floor of the desert shifted crazily in the fractured light.

Charlie turned the jeep away from the wind, hit the brakes. He stayed behind the wheel while Jennifer and Mungo laid the tarp on the ground, then drove forward and secured one end with the front wheels. They pulled the canvas over the length of the jeep and held it firm while he backed up enough to hold the other end in place. When the tarp was secure, pinned down by all four wheels, he switched off the engine. Jennifer and Mungo crawled under the canvas and into the jeep.

The windshield at the front and machine-gun at the rear supported the tarp and gave them a little headroom. In the swiftly-gathering darkness, they ate a supper of stale bread and tinned corn. Charlie calculated that there was enough water for two days. On the other side of the tarp, lightning shredded the sky and the wind tore at the sand, hurled it against the canvas.

Charlie wondered how long the storm would last. The jeep was already buried to the axles. He remembered reading something about traditional Muslim funerals, that desert tribes simply allowed the shifting sands to bury their dead.

If they died here, the heat would suck every last drop of moisture out of them.

Mummify them.

He listened to the snap and rumble of thunder, the hissing of the wind and the scratch of sand clawing at the tarp; all the terrifying sounds of a desert on the march.

He took Jennifer in his arms and held her close, shielding her with his love.

Epilogue

ARMACAO DE BUZIOS, BRAZIL

The fishing village of Buzios is located on the peninsula of Cabo Frio, seventy miles north of Rio. Downey had planned to idle away his golden years at the end of a narrow dirt track about twenty miles past town – well beyond the range of all but the most determined tourist.

The house was low and massive, constructed of huge sheets of green-tinted glass sandwiched between slabs of rough grey concrete, the whole thing cantilevered out over the steep slope of the hill to give Downey a few more degrees of view, so he could relax on the patio beside his heated pool and admire the islands or watch the sun drop into the Atlantic.

Mungo sat on the edge of the flat tar-and-gravel roof, his long legs dangling over the side. The house was set back just far enough from the beach to protect it from erosion during the winter storms. He listened to the cheerful slap and splash of waves on fine white sand, the murmur of the early-morning breeze playing with the leaves of the fig trees.

It was six forty-five a.m. The sun had been up for almost two hours. In the background, beneath the rustling of fig leaves, he could hear soft music and heavy breathing. In the living room, almost directly below him, Jack Downey was sitting on his ass on the wall-to-wall with his toes tucked under the edge of a grey leather sofa, drooling over the latest Jane Fonda videocassette and grunting his way through a set of situps.

Mungo scooped a handful of loose pea gravel off the roof, discarded the smaller pebbles and kept the rest.

Despite the babble of the television, it was kind of nice, being up on the roof. It was mid-February, summer in Brazil, and the temperature was in the high seventies. But the surrounding fig and palm trees protected him from the direct rays of the sun, and the offshore breeze kept the insects away. Mungo studied the fig trees. He liked them, the way they looked. The trees were big, maybe eighty or ninety feet high, their trunks and branches heavily veined with the roots of strangler vines. He knew what the vines were called because he'd asked one of Downey's muscle boys about them, just before he'd taped the guy's mouth shut and tucked him away where he could do no harm.

He glanced at his watch. In a few more minutes the tape would end and Downey, creature of habit that he was, would hit the rewind button and saunter out to the pool with a pile of fluffy purple towels under his arm, a brandy snifter of fresh-squeezed orange juice in his hand and a big cigar in his big fat mouth. What he'd do, his morning routine, was to drop everything on the patio table, struggle out of his designer sweats and ease into the pool, shuffle through twenty-five slow and ponderous laps.

Usually one of the maids or an import from Rio swam naked with him, keeping him company and giggling at his jokes.

But this morning, as it happened, Downey was all alone.

Mungo counted the pebbles in his hand. Idly passing the time, giving himself something to do. He lifted his head and stared out at the ocean, the sweet, gentle curve of the earth. It occurred to him, not for the first time in his life, that it was a hell of a beautiful world, for those who could afford it.

Below him, the glass doors slid open. Downey's sandals slapped on the patio tiles. Mungo held out his hand and spread his fingers wide. This day had been a long time coming. He was a little nervous – could feel the sweat drying on his palm.

Downey passed beneath him, the top of his balding head brown as a nut, gleaming in the sunlight. He walked across the tiles towards a fancy wrought-iron table with a plate-glass top. He'd put on a lot of pounds since Cairo. His shadow was bulky, cumbersome, an anchor that seemed to weigh him down and slow his progress. Mungo watched him put his juice and the towels on the table, drop the cigar and a gold Ronson butane lighter into a heavy crystal ashtray and then stroll over to the patio railing.

Downey admired the view for a few minutes and then went back to the table and shuffled out of his sandals, stripped off the sweatsuit. Underneath the sweats he was wearing boxer shorts, white with little red hearts. He took off the shorts and scratched his groin and peered into the house, probably wondering where everybody was. Mungo watched him waddle over to the deep end of the pool and, without hesitating or even breaking stride, dive clumsily in.

Water splashed over the lip of the pool and stained the tiles dark red. Downey came up snorting, churned his way to the far end and did a slow roll and started back.

Mungo checked his watch. It had taken Downey two minutes and fifteen seconds to swim the sixty-foot length of the pool. If he thrashed his way through his usual twenty-five laps, the silly bastard would be at it for at least an hour.

More time than Mungo was willing to give him.

He waited until Downey had floundered back to the near end of the pool, and then started tossing pebbles at him. The height and his target's turtle pace made working out the trajectory a piece of cake. He scored a hit right away, bounced several pebbles off Downey's back and then popped him right on top of his shiny bald head.

Downey stopped swimming. He rolled awkwardly over on his stomach and got himself into a position to tread water. He was smiling expectantly in the direction of the house, but his smile faltered when he saw that nobody was home.

"Up here, Jack."

Downey's head snapped back. Mungo tossed the rest of the pebbles into his face, levered himself off the roof. It was a twelve-foot drop to the tiles. He landed lightly as a cat, knees flexed and arms spread wide for balance. Downey stared bug-eyed at him. Water swirled and foamed around him as he struggled to stay afloat.

"Since I happened to be in the neighbourhood," Mungo said, "I thought I might as well drop in and say hello."

"Just don't try to sell me any Tupperware." Downey grinned, showing all his teeth. "How in hell did you find me?"

"Got downwind, followed my nose." Mungo was wearing a tan three-piece and a soft white shirt, no tie, a pair of snakeskin cowboy boots he'd bought in Rio. He said, "It's been a long and expensive trip. A guy named Jalloud helped with the finances."

"The Libyan secret service dummy, didn't know what the hell was going on?"

"That's the dude. A real badass. Sore loser. Man, was he pissed that you didn't give him all those receipts you saved, pictures you took. Without your evidence, he had no real proof that there ever was a plot to murder Gadaffi."

Downey said, "I figured, what the hell. The way it turned out, they couldn't be too happy. In for a penny . . ."

"Jalloud called me about six months ago. Dropped a dime in a payphone outside a McDonald's that's a couple blocks from my place. I met him there, bought him a chocolate shake and some McNuggets. Told him the joke about the hooker and the rooster. You heard it?"

"No," said Downey, shaking his head.

"It's a real gut-buster, but Jalloud gimme this look. Pure death. No sense of humour, never cracked a smile. It was him had your hotel room in London bombed all to hell."

"Killed those poor innocent folk from Miami."

"Yeah. And organized the team of paratroopers. Snatched Jennifer's kid, Cynthia. See, he found out you were planning to hit Gadaffi. No one told him the whole thing was a set-up. What is it they say, a little bit of knowledge . . ."

"Was it you told him about our training base in the desert?"

"No way, Jack. Remember the Egyptian Army colonel we met in Beni-Suef? Turned out to be one of those fellas like to fill both sides of his wallet. How Jalloud made contact with him, I don't know. Probably he had feelers out all over the damn place, got lucky."

"How'd Jalloud find you?"

"A man's got the motivation, he can do just about anything he wants, in America. You executed his best buddy, out there in the desert."

"Sure, but I can't help wondering how he found out about it."

"*I* told him," said Mungo. "We had a talk, decided we loathed you more'n we hated each other. The deal is, I take care of you, and he forgets about me and Jennifer and Charlie, Cynthia."

"*Take care of me*," said Downey. "I like the way that sounds."

"You got a bad ear for dialogue, Jack."

Mungo lifted his jacket so Downey could see he was armed. "Jalloud even agreed to send Jennifer's father's body back to England, if I found you. One corpse for another. A straight exchange." Mungo smiled grimly. "Best drag yo' ass out of the water."

Mungo backed away from the pool as Downey found his feet and strode powerfully through the shallows. The man was old and fat, but he was tricky as hell and if he did twenty-five laps a day he still had a little wind left in him.

Downey hauled himself out of the water and headed towards the patio table, his splay feet leaving shapeless splotches on the tiles.

"The way you came off that roof," Downey said, "it reminded me of those guys in the desert, came floating down out of the sky. It was driving me crazy. Who *were* those fuckers, that wanted my ass so bad? Jalloud didn't know about the thing I had going with Gadaffi. That it was a setup, the man was in no danger. How the bastards found out about me in the first place, I still don't know."

Downey reached for his sweats. Mungo told him to use a towel or stay naked.

Downey was amused. "You think I carry a gun around the fucking house?"

"If you don't, I bet you wish you did."

Downey wrapped a purple towel around his belly. It was a big towel but there wasn't a great deal of material to spare. He said, "What'd you do with the hired help?"

"You really care?"

"Just curious."

"Locked 'em up in the garage. Put 'em in the trunk of your Mercedes."

Mungo sat down at the table, keeping his back to the beach. He waved Downey into the chair nearest the house.

Downey gave him a slow smile. "You won't believe it, but you know something? I'm glad you got away."

"You're right. I don't believe it." Mungo drank some orange juice and then picked up the cigar and bit the end off it and lit it with the gold lighter.

Downey frowned, but didn't say anything.

"Why'd you pick Brazil, Jack?"

"Columbus missed it – I thought you might, too."

Downey toyed with the gold *figa* – an amulet in the shape of a clenched fist, but with the thumb protruding between the first and second fingers – that hung from his neck by a chain. The figa is very popular in Brazil. It's believed to ward off evil spirits, but is only effective if it's received as a gift. Downey, not knowing this, had bought his own. He shrugged. "I liked the climate. Rio's a great little town, you know your way around. Good supply of cheap domestic help." He grinned. "But most of all, I love to do the bossa nova."

Mungo waved his left arm, taking in the pool and the patio, the house. "What'd it all cost, Jack?"

"I don't *own* it. Is that what you think? Jesus, nobody's got that much money. It's a lease."

"Bullshit. You're too fucking insecure to rent." Mungo spat a shred of tobacco. "How much did Gadaffi pay you to set us up?"

"I never got a cent." Downey tilted his head, poked a finger in his ear. A few drops of water dribbled out. He wiped his finger on the purple towel and rolled his head sideways and drained the other ear. "What happened to Hubie and Jennifer and our good friend Charlie?"

Mungo reached into his shirt pocket and withdrew a Polaroid photograph, a colour shot of Jennifer and Charlie and Cynthia and an infant child sitting on a wooden bench in the square off the King's

Road. The sky was blue. The plane trees were in leaf. Everybody was smiling. Happy days.

Downey cleared his nose, one nostril at a time. He said, "Cynthia's okay, huh. Good, terrific."

"It was part of the deal I made with Jalloud." Mungo helped himself to a little more orange juice. The juice was fresh-squeezed, nice and cold.

"What about Hubie?" said Downey.

Mungo smiled.

Downey was used to the heat, but suddenly he was sweating. "I've got three million bucks tucked away in a numbered account in Zurich," he said. "All you have to tell me is how much you want."

"Every franc," said Mungo. "Every last centime." He reached under his jacket.

The gun was a Colt automatic, a chrome-plated .45. The world was full of them, but as far as Downey knew, only Sweets' had a ruby mounted on the front sight. His shoulders slumped. All the force and cunning drained out of his eyes.

Mungo said, "Hubie almost made it, but not quite. Rode a chopper into the desert. All those hi-tech metals, magnesium and shit, burn real hot. By the time the fire died down, all that was left of him was a handful of warm ashes."

Downey made a weary gesture with his hands. "The cash is in Switzerland, the Banque Centrale de Zurich."

"I thought Panama or the Bahamas was where you hot-money types liked to stash your loot."

"I don't trust those coloured guys," deadpanned Downey.

Mungo grinned. "You know what really pissed me off? That room in Tunis, right across the street from the fucking slaughterhouse. Man, that was a shitty thing to do."

"There's nobody in the whole world can't be bought," said Downey, speaking the truth as he knew it. "At least I didn't go cheap."

"The account. Gimme the password. Gimme the magic numbers."

"Yeah, sure. Okay. But . . ."

Mungo shook his head, cutting him off. "Today's the last day of the rest of your life, Jack. All you have to think about is who you want to give the money to, me and Jennifer and Charlie, or some asshole banker?"

Mungo pushed the rest of the orange juice across the table, dropped the burning cigar in the ashtray.

Downey sipped at the juice, puffed thoughtfully at the secondhand cigar. He watched the play of sunlight on the ocean, followed the unspeakably graceful flight of a seabird across the blue bowl of the sky. The last day of the rest of his life, and he felt as if he'd just been born. Jesus, he'd never known how alive he could feel. All seven senses jostling for attention. How he wanted a woman! Touch him, he'd explode.

Mungo cocked the .45. He was too close to aim, so he merely pointed. Downey stared at the unwinking red eye of the ruby. He rested his elbows on the arms of the chair and pressed the palms of his hands together. Mungo said, "Jennifer. Cynthia. Charlie. Any outstanding contracts I should know about?"

Downey shook his head. "They're in the clear. Hey, it was nothing personal."

"Wish I could say the same, Jack."

Downey, taking his time, smoked the cigar all the way down to his fingers. He squashed the butt in the ashtray and gave Mungo the codeword and numbers. Then he grabbed the edge of the table and flipped it on its side, ducked down behind it, snatched up the gold Ronson.

Mungo took a shot at him. The bullet hit the glass tabletop and didn't even make a dent. Downey pinched his nostrils shut, turned the Ronson in his hand so it was pointing at Mungo's face.

Mungo realized he was about to be killed by a goddam poison-gas cigarette lighter. What a stupid gimmick. He thought, *No, please, don't let it happen.*

Charlie, standing in the shade of the fig trees down at the far end of the pool, squeezed the trigger of the Remington pump they'd bought at a pawn shop in Rio. The gun was on full choke. The load of buckshot caught Downey in the right leg, blew most of his knee away. Downey screamed, more in anger than pain. Mungo banked a shot off the tiles, hit him in the wrist. Streamers of blood jetted into the air. The lighter hit the deck. Mungo kicked it into the pool and it sank without a trace.

"Wanna pray?"

Downey opened his mouth to speak. What his answer might have been it is impossible to say, because before he could utter a single word, Mungo thrust the Colt at him and shot him in the heart. Downey spread his arms wide. The purple towel came loose. His fat, deeply tanned body spilled across the tiles. Mungo stepped back and emptied the clip into him, burning all seven rounds, for luck. The copper-jacketed bullets ripped through Downey's corpse and ricocheted off the tiles, smacked into the picture windows and concrete walls of the house. Downey twitched once, and lay still.

The echo of the gunfire faded. Soon Mungo could once again hear the whisper of the wind in the fig trees, gentle splashing of waves on the beach. Charlie walked down the length of the pool, the shotgun cradled in his arms.

Mungo said, "Nice shot. The way you came over the rail, I hardly even knew you were there."

Charlie was pale, trembling. He said, "He was going to kill you, wasn't he? I aimed at his chest, but . . ."

"Don't put yourself down. You ever want to get into the business, you'll do just fine."

Charlie swung the Remington by the muzzle, tossed it down the cliff and into the ocean. He said, "No, I don't think so."

Mungo used a Polaroid camera to take a dozen candids of Downey lying beside the pool, circling around the body to photograph the carnage from all angles. He'd airmail separate sets of pictures to Langley and Tripoli, get the CIA spooks and Gadaffi's goons off his back.

He wiped his fingerprints from the empty Colt with a corner of the bloody purple towel, wedged the gun in Downey's hand.

Maybe, just to clear the file, the local cops would call it suicide.

Stranger things had happened, hadn't they?